PRAISE FOR THE PETER SAVAGE NOVELS

"I would follow Peter Savage into any firefight."
–James Rollins, *New York Times* bestseller of *The Demon Crown*

"Edlund is **right at home with his bestselling brethren**, Brad Thor and Brad Taylor."
–Jon Land, *USA Today* bestselling author of the *Caitlin Strong* series

"This **compulsively readable** thriller boasts a whiplash pace, a topical plot, and **nonstop action**. Edlund fans won't be disappointed."
–*Publisher's Weekly*
Praise for *Lethal Savage*

"a near-perfect international thriller"
–*Foreword Reviews*
Praise for *Guarding Savage*

"With **a hero full of grit and determination**, this action-packed, timely tale is **required reading** for any thriller aficionado."
–Steve Berry, *New York Times* bestselling author,
Praise for *Hunting Savage*

"**Crackling action**, brisk pace, timely topic…"
–*Kirkus Reviews*
Praise for *Deadly Savage*

LETHAL SAVAGE

A PETER SAVAGE NOVEL

LETHAL SAVAGE

A PETER SAVAGE NOVEL

DAVE EDLUND

 Light Messages

Durham, NC

To Eileen.
Without you, life isn't worth living.

ACKNOWLEDGMENTS

WHO WOULD HAVE THOUGHT that an action/political-thriller series based on a character who lives in a small city in central Oregon, far away from the international centers of political intrigue, a character who is more MacGyver than he is Jason Bourne, would be so popular? My hand is raised, because many years ago this was only a dream. You know, the type of goal you secretly aspire to, but have no idea how to achieve it, or reasonable expectation you could ever achieve it.

That was me. I still recall sitting on a deck, overlooking East Sound on Orcas Island, with my bride-to-be. With an unlimited future in front of me (because that's how I thought when I was twenty-something and thirty-something), and a Blaine MacCracken novel by Jon Land open on my lap, I arrogantly began to daydream about how much fun it would be to create thrillers to be published and shared with a large audience.

Fast forward a number of years (I'd rather not recount how many), and here I am today, with the sixth Peter Savage novel soon to be released, and more on the way.

I refer to my dream as arrogant—whereas other times I describe it as crazy—because I had no clue about how much work, and from so many different people with special skills, it takes to complete and publish a novel. One thing I am certain of is that without the support and contributions from my publisher, Light Messages, none of my dream would have been realized. It would have remained a pipe dream. Thank you to everyone at Light Messages, especially Betty and Wally, for believing in me, and for your support. These words, simple as they are, cannot truly convey my feelings of appreciation, but I try.

As any author will admit, editors possess mystical ability to take a manuscript—no matter how well written it may be—and make it so much better. Editors challenge the writer for clarity, continuity, logical flow, thoughtful and reasonable expression, and good entertainment value. They also catch those pesky typos, improper grammar, and incorrect punctuation that authors are always placing, sometimes haphazardly, into their manuscript as if a challenge to the editor. I have been blessed with a truly marvelous editor, Elizabeth. And so again, I offer my humble appreciation for her work that makes my work much better than when it left my desk. Thank you, Elizabeth, for your insightful help, for always challenging me to do better, and for believing in me. And I also want to acknowledge and thank Meghan Bowker for her proof editing. She has an eye for detail and uncanny ability to sort out all the typos that I (with the help of auto correct) manage to sprinkle through the manuscript. Finally, I want to thank my two good friends, Gary Stout and Bill Shank, for stimulating discussion of the final draft and for finding more of those aforementioned typos.

My publicist, Rebecca, has been super. From eye-catching graphics to reaching out to media (social and traditional), bookstores, and prominent people in the community, I am so grateful for all the help she has generously given. Thank you Becca.

The thriller-author community has been utterly fabulous in their collective support for fellow authors, and for welcoming new authors. Specifically, I want to express my sincere gratitude to the International Thriller Writers (ITW) for welcoming me into your company. The many ways that ITW promotes its members is truly appreciated. Thank you.

A special shout out is due to Steve Barry, Jon Land, and James Rollins for their generous praise for the Peter Savage novels. These extraordinarily accomplished authors give back so much to the thriller community, be it teaching and mentoring or endorsements for fellow authors. The positive impact of these contributions is impossible to quantify. Gentlemen, thank you very much.

I also want to acknowledge and thank another giant in the field, the man to whom is attributed the creation of the modern thriller. Yes, I am referring to David Morrell, author of *Rambo* and many other exquisite novels. Thank you, Mr. Morrell, for your patient advice and tips (especially for recommending *Dreyer's English*).

As essential as all of the above contributions may be—and yes, essential is the correct word—still none of my dream would be possible without fans who read the latest adventures of Peter Savage and friends. Thank you so much!! (I know, it is poor form to use double exclamation marks, but in this case, it is warranted.) Without an audience to read these novels, there would be no reason to write them. Please continue to share your comments and post reviews on Amazon, Apple Books, Barnes and Noble, Kobo, Goodreads, and other social media sites. And if you want to reach me directly, I'd love to hear from you:

PeterSavageNovels.com
dedlund@LightMessages.com

AUTHOR'S NOTES

OVER THE PAST THREE DECADES, concern over global climate change—often labeled global warming—has grown to the point that today, this issue plays a significant role in international politics. It's already clear that climate change will be fundamental to the primaries leading up to the 2020 U.S. presidential election. The unifying factor driving the political and social debate is that climate change is believed to be a direct result of man-made emissions of carbon dioxide (a potent greenhouse gas). Without question, the atmospheric concentration of carbon dioxide has increased dramatically since the advent of the industrial age, and with it a rapid increase in the combustion of first coal and later oil.

Science is all about drawing conclusions from data, and although the daily media and political rancor is dominated by the conclusion that climate change is real and it's happening now, I'm still eager to see the underlying data (my education and professional experience are in chemistry and chemical engineering).

Two important questions demand solid answers—is the climate changing in an abnormal fashion, and if so, is the change induced by human activities (anthropomorphic climate change)? Answering these questions is immensely difficult. For example, over the geologic record, we know with certainty that the Earth's climate has changed multiple times. So, changing climate could be a natural artifact, or it could be an unnatural event tied to industrialization.

However, some experiments are simply too risky to undertake, and if there is reasonable probability that carbon dioxide emissions cause global warming and rising ocean levels, then it's likely a good idea to reduce carbon emissions.

But the foregoing discussion on anthropomorphic climate change misses the big picture. What if climate change is merely a symptom of a more invasive problem? I'm referring to the general impact of human activity on our ecosystem, planet Earth. The oceans are filling with plastics; deforestation has transformed large areas that used to be jungle into farmland; rivers and groundwater are polluted with pesticides, herbicides, and antibiotics; and black soot from flaring gas (associated with oil production) is blanketing the Arctic ice, causing it to melt faster.

Over the last 2,000 years, global population has risen from about 250 million to about seven billion. Just over the last 200 years, the population has exponentially increased from 1 billion at the beginning of the 19th century. That's an increase of six billion people inhabiting the planet in only 200 years!

What are the impacts of these seven billion people on our ecosystem? If human activity is causing damage to the environment (such as global warming), is the root cause really the number of people? If so, what can be done to reduce the population to a sustainable level? This last question is especially troublesome and has deep implications. It is a weighty topic that deserves thought and consideration, but I wouldn't suggest using this as a conversation starter at your next cocktail party (unless you don't care about getting invited back).

This question of human-caused environmental damage is at the core of *Lethal Savage*. In addition to being entertaining, I hope that the story is also thought-provoking, even just a little. And who knows, if you find yourself at that cocktail party, wanting to start a stimulating discussion on anthropomorphic climate change, you can always use Peter Savage as a segue!

DE

CHAPTER 1

DARNELL PRICE FELT LIKE HE WAS LIVING TWO LIVES—
one as a successful businessman and the other as an evangelist
for the environment. His true passion was reducing the
impact of humankind on the Earth. In his mind, the logic was
irrefutable—planet Earth had finite resources and, therefore,
a finite carrying capacity for the population of all species. If
humankind was to continue to grow in number exponentially,
we would eventually reach a point where a catastrophic
correction was inevitable.

Perhaps we already had.

He hadn't always subscribed to this idea. His education in
science and business had instilled mainstream knowledge and
reasoning—more a belief, really—that modern technology
would solve any and all problems encountered by society and
shape the world accordingly for the better. But following a
series of tragic, personal losses, his beliefs began to change.

Science taught that species evolved to adapt or perish;

was mankind any different? Evolutionary adaptation was an extremely slow process of biological trial and error, requiring time—thousands of millennia.

The historical record demonstrated that time and again, species had successfully adapted to radical alterations of the environment. Far from stagnant, the Earth was subject to constant change, although those changes had occurred over eons. But Darnell was convinced this was no longer reality. The global population of humans had increased at an exponential pace over the previous centuries—a mere blink of the eye in geological perspective. And with that explosion of numbers came an unprecedented pace of change in the global environment.

Governments acted as if they could engineer solutions to disease, climate change, drought and famine. But they ignored the most fundamental reason for human-caused stresses to the environment: the sheer number of people inhabiting the planet.

Were people living in a state of denial? Was the human race doomed to suffer global disasters? Or would people wake up one morning suddenly realizing that the species had to adapt to a world of limited resources—that all individuals needed to self-regulate their numbers?

He concluded it was far better to gradually reduce the human population through voluntary measures rather than suffer a sudden correction, whether it be through disease, famine, warfare, or other means. He'd felt the pain of suddenly losing loved ones; vibrant, youthful lives cut short prematurely. He didn't wish that on anyone.

He completed typing yet another article and posted it to several social media accounts. In his mid-fifties, he had a stocky build, not overweight but not lean either. He sported a short, graying beard that matched his hair color. His face was round, and he bore a striking resemblance to the actor Lawrence

Fishburne.

Having completed his post, Darnell should have felt good, that he'd accomplished one more, albeit small, step toward changing the course of humanity. But he didn't.

Instead, he felt disillusioned. He'd lost count of the number of articles and commentaries he'd posted, always accompanied by a chorus of support from the usual sympathetic minds. But substantial changes never followed. Governments refused to implement serious policies to curb the number of children families could have. Even China had reversed its one-child policy.

Anthropogenic climate change, encroachment of human development upon unspoiled habitat, endangered species, over-fishing, deforestation—these topics were still the subject of the domestic and global dialog, but the talk always ended without productive action.

It seemed that nearly everyone agreed we needed to change habits, to consume less, to act more responsibly. But the consensus was that someone else should do so first. The mentality was that there was still time to take corrective actions later. Eventually time would run out.

How can people be so stupid? he thought with a sigh. His phone rang. The display indicated an unknown number.

"This is Darnell," he greeted.

"Mr. Price. My name is Simon Ming. I run Utopian-Bio. Maybe you're familiar with us? We're also located in Eugene, so I guess we're neighbors. Anyway, we haven't met, but I'm a big fan of your blog."

Being a member of the entrepreneurial community in Eugene, Darnell was vaguely familiar with Utopian-Bio. He knew it was a startup company with fewer than one hundred employees. The company mostly conducted research in molecular biology and genetic engineering. Rumor had it that funding came from private sources, and many speculated that the founder, a wealthy and mysterious molecular biologist by the name of Simon Ming, was the sole source of capital. It was further said that Ming was a genius, specializing in genetic engineering using the CRISPR-Cas9 gene editing process. Exactly what goal Utopian-Bio was working toward was the subject of yet more speculation. The entire corporate operations were heavily veiled in secrecy: a perk of being privately held.

Darnell was surprised. "You've read my postings on population control?"

"Yes, I find your arguments compelling."

"Well, unless enough people begin to pay attention and take action, it really doesn't matter what I write."

"Perhaps," Ming said, his tone suggesting he was holding something back.

"I keep trying to catalyze action, but no one really seems to care. The politicians say the right things but do nothing."

"What you are advocating makes sense. It's only logical."

"To you and me, but those who are actually in a position to make a difference don't act as if they really understand. You see, whether we are concerned about plastic nanoparticles polluting the oceans, or greenhouse gases altering weather patterns, or antibiotics polluting our water supplies—all are tied to a common root cause."

"You're referring to human population."

"Of course," Darnell said with exasperation. "I mean, sure, we need to recycle and conserve resources, especially when it comes to using energy. But that's only a Band-Aid. These efforts don't address the fundamental cause. It should be obvious even to a politician that if they want to reduce the impact of human-caused climate change, the most direct route is to limit the number of people."

"I agree," Ming replied, his voice even.

Darnell snorted a humorless chuckle. "Environmentalists love me, and pretty much everyone else thinks I'm certifiable. I've even been accused of being a Nazi extremist advocating for global genocide."

"I don't think that, not at all. We have a lot in common. I'd like to meet you, if that's convenient, of course."

Not expecting such a direct reply, Darnell stammered. "Uh, yeah, sure. My schedule is open the rest of the week. Do you want to meet for coffee or lunch?"

"Actually, I think a more private setting is appropriate. I have a proposal I think you'll be interested in."

"Proposal? What do you have in mind?"

"Let's just say that I share your vision and would like to offer a pathway to achieving meaningful change. Would you be willing to meet me at my office, tomorrow at four p.m.? It's near the University of Oregon campus."

Intrigued, Darnell readily agreed. After the details were exchanged and confirmed, the call ended. For the remainder of the day, he was consumed with speculation about what, exactly, Simon Ming had in mind.

The next day, promptly at four p.m., Darnell entered the facilities leased by Utopian-Bio. It was a modern structure, built as part of a state-subsidized university-industry collaboration. Such collaborations were a popular mechanism for the state government to show that investment in higher education paid dividends, and it was highly regarded by faculty since it provided avenues to export their research into the private sector.

After signing in at the reception counter, he was led by a security guard to a large office on the top floor of the five-story building. The door was open, and the guard announced Darnell's presence.

"Please, come in Mr. Price," said the man rising from behind his desk. He was slim and not especially tall, with jet black hair cut very short on the sides and allowed to grow much longer on top. It was combed back without a part and held in place with gel. His chin sported a neatly-trimmed goatee, but otherwise his face was clean-shaven. He wore a dark gray suit and white shirt, unbuttoned at the collar, conveying a casual business attire more to be expected in a Silicon Valley boardroom than a small Oregon start-up. As he approached, he extended his hand. "Nice to meet you. I'm Simon Ming."

The guard closed the door and Simon motioned to a conference table at one end of the office. "Please, have a seat. Would you like coffee or tea?"

"No, thank you," replied Darnell. Although he was a poor judge of age, he surmised that Simon Ming was rather young to be leading a biotech company, even a small start-up company. His smooth facial features and tight skin suggested a man who was no more than thirty-five years of age.

"Thank you for taking time to meet me."

Darnell smiled. "I must confess, I know only a little about your company, and that's only what I've heard from other tech-business owners. But I gather Utopian-Bio is doing well?"

"Yes." Ming smiled. He was pleased that his guest had invested time and energy in conducting background research. It meant he was taking the meeting seriously. "We have made some remarkable advances in genetic engineering. Perhaps I can offer you a tour. I think you'll appreciate our achievements. From *my* research I know you have an education in medical engineering plus an MBA. But now you own and are the CEO of Cascade Aqua, a water bottling company. I'd imagine you receive a lot of criticism for using plastic bottles. That hardly fits with your pro-environment stance."

"I'm very proud of the fact that we use 100 per cent recycled

PET. My competitors use less than ten percent recycled plastic in their bottles. Sure, I pay more for my bottles, but it's the right thing to do."

"Plus, I'd imagine, it's a good marketing strategy. Still, switching from medical engineering to water bottling is a major transition. Some might even think it's a step backwards."

Darnell shrugged. "Medical devices can be a very lucrative business. I did well when I cashed out and decided to follow a different lifestyle. One that provided time for my environmental evangelism."

"I suspect there is more to your decision than wanting to pursue a different lifestyle. Perhaps family matters?"

Darnell stared back, his face expressionless.

Ming continued. "As I said, I did some research on you. It is only natural that I'd want to know something of your history before asking for this meeting."

"I have to say your approach certainly is unusually direct… and intriguing. Had me thinking all night just what you wanted to talk about."

"Right to the point, I like that." Simon leaned back in his chair and crossed his legs. "I've read all of your posts, and I see a central theme. You believe the human population is too large, and still growing at an alarming rate."

"Yes, the facts are undeniable. But even worse is that the global population is completely unregulated. I mean, take for example wildlife populations such as deer, wolves, coyotes, cougars—all species native to Oregon and the Northwest. Historically, as people moved outward from cities, expanding development—roads, houses, businesses—pushed away the native species. So we find ourselves with overlapping habitats. In some rare cases, such as deer and cougar, the animals adapt fairly well. But there is still conflict between people and animals, and the result is that our State Department of Fish and Game regulates the deer and cougar population through controlled hunts."

"That's a good analogy," Simon said, rubbing his goatee. "But surely you are not advocating for the government to take a similar approach to reducing human population."

"Of course not. It is unconscionable to think that killing people is the solution to human overpopulation."

"I agree."

Darnell leaned forward. "But my point is more than academic. As populations of any species exceed the carrying capacity of the ecosystem, the population must be managed, or it will face catastrophic corrections."

"And by 'catastrophic correction' you mean what?"

"I mean mass die-outs."

"Like famine and disease?"

"Exactly," Darnell replied. "Pandemics are not relegated to the history of the Dark Ages. HIV has claimed thirty-nine million lives; the Spanish influenza of 1918 killed twenty million. And more recently, the Asian flu of 1957 to '58 took two million lives. The Hong Kong flu of 1968 to '69 killed over a million.

"As sobering as those totals are, they pale in comparison to modern conflict. Warfare in the twentieth century has resulted in four to five times as many deaths, with estimates ranging as high as 230 million people. Famine and natural disasters account for many tens of millions of additional fatalities."

"It would seem Nature has a way of dealing with overpopulation."

"It sounds like you know something of the natural order?"

Simon nodded. "But I confess, until I began to follow your blog, I was comparatively ignorant of the topic."

"The problem is that science is making advances in quality of life at an ever-quickening pace. Modern medicine, especially with the power of genetic modification, makes it very unlikely that large numbers will ever again be killed by disease. And the probability of mass famine has been significantly reduced— thanks to advances in farming machinery and pest control. Warfare is still a threat, but even large-scale conflict, something engulfing a continent or a world war, appears to be relegated to a footnote in history rather than a real risk."

"I understand your point. Humankind has advanced its knowledge of science and technology to counteract the opposing natural forces that would normally be a check on population growth. But there is still a limit to the number of people we can feed, right? I mean, there still are natural checks and balances."

"Of course," Darnell said. "But as the global population continues to increase, we are pushing closer and closer to that hard limit. Where it is, and when do we reach it, I can't say. But think of the problem this way: imagine the human population is exactly at the carrying capacity of our ecosystem—the Earth— such that only a hundred thousand more people pushes us over the edge. What is the result?"

Simon clasped his hands, pausing in thought. "Well, conceptually, I think it means that everyone has to consume less of what is required to survive. But if we are already at the limit of what people must have to survive—food, air, water— then I guess the added stress with having less will result in some people dying."

Darnell leaned forward, pleased that his host had thought through the hypothetical exercise. "Many will die. And that will be the beginning of a cascade. Because when an organism, any organism, is stressed it is less able to ward off disease. When people are competing for resources, conflict ensues. So the inevitable result will be pandemics and global, catastrophic, war."

"You think it could lead to the extinction of humans?"

"No, but it would be a major population correction. Billions would die. It would represent pain and suffering of Biblical proportions."

"An interesting metaphor, since we are discussing science and not theology."

Darnell held Simon's gaze. "The outcome is inevitable. It is only a question of when."

"Unless we make a change—put mankind on the path to *regulated* population growth."

"Which probably means a negative global growth rate for several generations."

"Population reduction."

Darnell nodded. "Yes—in certain parts of the world, those areas where populations are growing much faster than elsewhere."

"I agree with your assessment." Simon paused, making certain he had Darnell's undivided attention. "And that leads me to my proposal. What would you say if I told you I know how we can effect change, real change?"

Darnell's eyes widened. This was exactly what he'd been working to achieve. Yet, Simon Ming was not a politician, nor did he possess any known connections with the power to influence national policy. "Okay. I guess this is where I ask what you have in mind?"

"A gentle correction where, as you said so elegantly, population growth is rampant."

"What type of correction?"

Simon shrugged. "If people will not voluntarily rein in procreation, then we have no choice but to implement a biological limit."

"Birth control has been tried in Africa and Southeast Asia. And it has failed."

"Yes, I know. Homo sapiens are like any other creature. We are hard-wired to reproduce. The drive to have sex is undeniable and virtually irresistible. If we are to succeed, we must take a different path. One where individual choice is eliminated. A path where the consequences of giving in to passion are not so severe."

"But, you can't," Darnell objected. Others had proposed birth control hormones be added to food staples and distributed in poor regions where families tended to be very large in number. Even chemical sterilization had been put forward for consideration. But the vociferous objection that such measures were racist, aimed at persons of color in poor and underdeveloped countries while citizens of wealthy nations—mostly caucasian—continued to exercise free choice, always won the debate. "That would be unethical."

"Perhaps. But to do nothing is equally immoral. Maybe even worse." Simon leaned forward, his eyes ablaze. "People are unwilling to see beyond their own self interests. You've said as much yourself, on your blog. We cannot allow the ignorance and self-centered actions of a segment of the population to drive humankind to the brink of extinction. Imagine the suffering that billions will be subjected to simply because those who can least afford to have offspring are unwilling to rein in their lust. To allow that to happen is nothing short of the worst crime against humanity the world will have ever witnessed."

Darnell rose from his chair and nervously paced the executive office. For several uncomfortable minutes, he considered Simon's argument. Logically, he could not find fault with it. What did that say? Did it mean he was cold and callous? Or logical and courageous enough to do what he knew had to be done?

Finally, he spoke. "And if I agree?"

"Then I would have something to show you. A

breakthrough of biochemical engineering made possible by genetic modification. Only a few short years ago, what we've achieved here would have been dubbed science fiction. Now, it is science fact."

"I don't know," Darnell frowned. "There has to be another way. This just doesn't seem right."

"What else would you propose? Please, share your ideas. If you can tell me how to solve this problem, then I'll give you my undivided support."

Darnell stared back in silence.

"You don't have any better ideas," Ming said. "No one does. This is all that is left. You know, as I do, that we must act. You know we must do this—for the greater good. Historians will write about this day, the day that two heroes saved mankind from self-destruction."

With trepidation, Darnell agreed. "For the greater good."

CHAPTER 2

BEND, OREGON
PRESENT DAY, MARCH 3

"A TALL LATTE, FOR HERE." He paid the cashier, placing the change in the tip cup.

"Robert, right?" she asked with pen poised to write on the paper cup.

"You remembered," he said. Every morning for two weeks, Robert had been hanging out in the coffee shop. Arriving promptly at seven thirty a.m. and savoring his large latte, sometimes drinking two.

The coffee shop was a popular location in the Old Mill District—a posh shopping and dining area on the west side of Bend along the banks of the Deschutes River. The shop was frequented by local professionals as well as tourists, all aiming to satisfy their morning caffeine fix.

He sat at a table facing the doorway, pretending to be engrossed in email or something on his phone. In fact, he'd been doing research. Over the past two weeks he'd established that his mark would arrive about eight a.m. and order a cappuccino to go.

Today was the day. Robert—which was a convenient alias—was ready. From across the street he saw the man approach. He stood about 6 feet tall and wore his brown hair in a conservative cut. He was of medium build and average weight. By all measures, rather plain and unremarkable. Except, that is, for his eyes. They were steel gray and conveyed determination and confidence.

Robert had no idea why this man was his assignment. His name—Peter Savage—meant nothing. He wasn't a politician, and as far as Robert knew, he wasn't a professional criminal either. Not that it mattered. The contract was too enticing to pass up. Once he fulfilled the terms of the agreement, the payout would be extremely good—the kind of payday that could set someone up for life.

The bells hanging on the door chimed and the man walked up to the order counter. "Good morning," Peter said.

"Cappuccino to go?" the cashier asked.

"Ah. You know me too well."

"No lid, right?" she added while writing his name on the carboard cup.

"No, I don't need it. Only means more trash."

After paying, Peter shuffled to the end of the counter. Like almost everyone else in the coffee shop, he scrolled through messages on his phone. His inbox was already filled with a couple dozen emails, mostly offers for loans and executive recruiting that he wasn't interested in. He ran his company—EJ Enterprises—with a minimum of staff. Marketing wasn't really a challenge. His company designed and manufactured high-tech small arms, called magnetic impulse weapons. It was a breakthrough technology—the product of brilliant science and engineering. His only customer was the U.S. government. Even sales to Uncle Sam's closest allies were forbidden. But the revenue was steady, and the margins attractive, though growth was limited.

Robert moved behind the man, standing close to the counter. He didn't have to wait long. The server pushed forward a cup with the name Peter written on the side. Robert cradled his hands around the cup just as Peter turned.

"Oh, my apologies. I thought this was my order," Robert lied.

Peter smiled and lifted the cup to his mouth. But before it reached his lips, the barista grabbed his arm forcefully. The cappuccino sloshed in the cup and spilled onto the counter, nearly scalding his hand.

"I wouldn't drink that," she said. "I saw him put something in it." She motioned with her head toward Robert, who was turning to leave.

Peter glanced at the foamy top of his drink and saw a sprinkling of tiny white crystals that should not have been there. He handed the cup to the barista and then followed Robert out onto the sidewalk. "Hey!" Peter called, jogging to catch up.

Robert looked back over his shoulder and then took off in a sprint. He was fast, and already a full block ahead of Peter. He turned the corner, Peter still in pursuit, dodging other pedestrians on the sidewalk.

By the time Peter made it to the corner, the man was nowhere in sight. He thought about calling the police, maybe filing a report, but what would he say? He couldn't offer a good description. He'd only briefly noticed the man's face and all he really recalled was that he was bald. And why would someone put a drug—or something—in his beverage?

Weird, Peter thought as he walked back to the coffee shop. "Do you still have my coffee?" he said to the barista.

She shook her head. "No, I poured it out."

"But you're certain you saw that man put something in the

cup?"

"Absolutely certain. He tried to hide it, but I keep an eye out for that type of thing. I tended bar for a while before this job. You'd be surprised at how often some creep tries to drop Klonopin or Xanax in a woman's drink. Anyway, I wouldn't expect someone to try to drug a guy, usually it's the single females who have to be careful."

"Huh," Peter grunted, still trying to make sense of it all.

"I can tell he's not your type." The barista smiled. "Can I make another cappuccino for you?"

CHAPTER 3

IT WAS COLD, BITTERLY COLD. Frigid air from Canada had dipped south and settled over central Oregon, dropping temperatures fifteen degrees below normal. Wrapped in a down-filled jacket and flannel-lined cargo pants—both black as night—she felt comfortable in her concealed position except where the icy air assaulted the exposed flesh on her face, as if someone was pricking her skin with needles. She rose to her feet; it would feel good to move again.

Avoiding the moonlit clearings—preferring to hide in the shadows cast by mature pine trees—she could easily hear the cheers emanating from the barn standing about a hundred yards to the front of her position. Through binoculars, she'd watched about eighty people, mostly men, enter the barn more than two hours ago. Given the early morning hour—approaching two o'clock—this fact confirmed her suspicions. The raucous cheering started soon afterwards. It was punctuated by periods of relative quiet, during which two men would exit the barn and retrieve one or two dogs from the kennels. Three times she watched motionless animals being dragged from the barn and roughly dropped in a separate caged pen.

The kennels were clustered at the far side of the barn from the main entrance. It wouldn't be good for business to have the spectators pass too close to the combatants. The dogs' snarls and aggressive lunging in the cages could be most frightening. And the owner of the operation certainly didn't want his guests to linger over the mortally and hideously wounded losers.

During the moments of silence, if she listened carefully, the soft whimpering of the injured canines carried across the still night air. She'd occasionally heard about dog fighting rings—how they mostly used pit bulls and trained them to be monstrously aggressive and vicious. But not all dogs responded to the training the same way. Some dogs, the ones naturally timid, or those smallish in stature, became bait for the more combative and larger males to hone their fighting skills.

She wondered if that's what had been going on. Bait dogs being sacrificed to the fighters? Spilling blood to amp up their trained aggression? A grotesque warm-up; a prelude to the main event? She shivered, but not from the cold, and lowered her hand to the SIG Sauer P226 holstered on her thigh. Slung across her back was an FN Mark 1 tactical shotgun, modified with a folding stock. With the muzzle pointed down alongside her thigh, the weapon could be swiveled up in a fraction of a second and fired. Completing her armaments was her vade mecum—a combat tomahawk sheathed to her belt at the middle of her back. A nearly indestructible and wicked weapon with the head forged onto a high-strength steel handle, the tomahawk had a razor-sharp blade on one side that tapered to a hardened steel spike on the other side.

By placing discrete inquiries that circulated through the petty criminal element populating the many small cities in this part of Oregon, she'd learned about the opportunity to wager on dog fights. In hushed voices, she was told that this was the place—a remote, isolated barn on one thousand forested acres of private land north of La Pine.

Danya Biton had been living a shadowy existence off the grid. No bank account, no tax returns, no official employment, no permanent address. She used an evolving list of aliases and lived in a travel trailer, never staying in one place for long. Spurning credit, she conducted all transactions using cash.

Which is what brought her to this barn.

Having grown very proficient at liberating illegal gains from various drug cartels within Mexico, she needed to change her modus operandi. She was becoming too well-known south of the border. Word of her raids on the Sinaloa Cartel, the Juarez Cartel, and Los Zetas was fast becoming the stuff of legends. And with that notoriety came a huge bounty on her head— preferably alive, but dead would suffice.

Danya advanced to a cluster of young trees and slid her body between the flexible branches. Nestled within the copse of trees, she felt secure. The branches broke up her silhouette and blocked out the moonlight, creating dark shadows that swallowed her form. The door from the barn to the kennels opened again. Through the binoculars she watched as a lone man looped a line attached to the end of a catch pole around the neck of a dog. The canine had retreated from the man to a far corner of the kennel, and now was being dragged back to the arena inside the barn. Cheers erupted from the spectators in anticipation of another round of the blood sport.

Danya silently moved from her position of concealment. She needed to complete her reconnaissance of the building. With large sums of money being wagered, there would be guards outside as well as inside. Earlier, she spotted two men at the main door that provided access for the onlookers. She watched as each person was searched with a metal detector before entering the arena.

Reason dictated that there would also be at least two roving sentries, and farther from the barn, where the private gravel drive split off from a public forest road, there would be one or two men. All would have hand-held radios to report any suspicious activity, as well as give warning of an imminent bust.

Holding the barrel of the FN tight against her side to avoid any rattle that might alert others to her movements, she crept forward in total silence. This is what she had been trained for, and she was very skilled at her tradecraft, honed to near perfection on clandestine battlefields around the globe. But that was another time, another life, when she'd been one of the best killing machines of her former government.

It was when that realization had dawned on her, like an epiphany, one day during an operation not far from her current position in the Cascade Mountains of Oregon—that she was nothing more than a machine, lacking any moral checks and balances—that she quit. But in her profession, no one was allowed to resign.

You served, until you died.

As she neared the kennels, the whimpering of injured dogs became louder. In a crouch, she edged closer, using the available foliage, which included bitterbrush and rabbit brush in addition to the evergreen trees, for concealment. Glassing the kennels, she saw three badly injured canines, barely moving. The shiny, black wetness on their fur suggested they were all bloodied. The head and neck of one of the dogs had severe lacerations, and blood was freely dripping from the horrendous wounds.

The crunch of dead pine needles and twigs drew her attention. Someone was nearby.

She lowered the binoculars and concentrated on listening. There it was again, but the sound indicated the person was moving at a normal walking pace, and not trying to be stealthy. Danya surmised that the sentries were likely amateurs, and that this dog-fighting ring was a second-tier criminal outfit—unlike the drug cartels.

The footsteps grew nearer, and then she heard the sound of a zipper. Seconds later, the tinkle of water. It was close, maybe only ten to twenty feet away. Wishing she had night-vision goggles, she reached for the tomahawk and grasped it firmly by the leather-wrapped grip. She launched forward before the man finished draining his bladder. On the third stride, she saw the shadowy figure in front of a large tree.

Two more strides and she rammed her shoulder into his back. The guard had turned his head a fraction of a second before the collision, so the side of his face slammed into the rough pine bark. He let out a grunt and reached for his holstered weapon. Before he could draw, Danya swung the tomahawk, planting the spike into the center of his back. The steel pierced through muscle and lodged in his heart. She raised the handle, causing the spike to further rip the heart tissue, which was now contracted tightly in a death spasm. Without uttering another sound, he sank to his knees and then fell to the side, dead.

Danya placed her boot on his torso and yanked out the edged weapon. She wiped the blood and gore off onto the man's jacket, then returned the weapon to its sheath. She removed his Glock pistol and stuffed it into her waistband. Lastly, she grabbed the radio he'd stashed in a jacket pocket. It was on, and she turned the volume down.

Circling around the kennels to the far side of the barn, she came across a large tree stump conveniently nestled in deep shadows. It was about three feet in diameter with an uneven cut at a height of about four feet—most likely an old-growth tree logged a hundred years earlier. The center of the stump had rotted away decades ago. She squeezed into the opening, knowing the stump would break up her outline from any viewing direction.

Resting her elbows on the stump, she resumed glassing the barn and the surrounding forest. The roving guards would be out there, not too far from the building but far enough to offer warning should law enforcement or a rival gang attempt to approach from the woods.

So far, Danya had been lucky. The sentry she'd just dispatched was careless. But she didn't count on luck. It was planning, the element of surprise, and, above all, ruthless skill that allowed her to prevail time and time again in life-and-death contests that had played out around the globe.

Another roar of cheers and whistles erupted from within the barn. The obvious joy that so many found in such a cruel event—she didn't accept dog fighting as a sport—sickened her. She reflected on how she could easily kill another person and yet be repulsed by this barbaric cruelty to the animals she viewed as innocent. Often, when she lay awake at night, she would see the faces of those she'd killed, eventually arriving at justification. They had it coming. Guilty of murder, rape, torture—all at the behest of the cartel. Or they were enemies of the State; responsible—directly or indirectly—for the slaughter of civilians by the hundreds.

Danya had encountered scores of truly evil people, and she had no qualms about eliminating them. It's not that she enjoyed it, but she viewed it as necessary. She thought of herself as a warrior protecting the innocent, those who could not protect themselves. And on rare occasions, she prayed that the good in her deeds outweighed the bad.

Although she came tonight to steal money from illegal betting, she now found herself wanting to end the lives of these men. Seeing the mauled dogs in the kennel and hearing the screams of agony as flesh was ripped from bone, the pitiful whimpers as the survivors clung to life by the thinnest of threads, these men had it coming.

The binoculars amplified the ambient light somewhat, and with a full moon, she easily spotted another roving guard about fifty yards away. He was bundled against the cold and walked with hunched shoulders. He seemed to be moving along a path that was easy to traverse, rather than trying to remain concealed in the shadows.

She continued to watch, and before long, the sentry turned and began ambling toward Danya's location. He held a short, pistol-grip shotgun in one hand. In the darkness, with only her shoulders and head rising above the stump, she was confident he would not recognize the threat he was approaching.

After several minutes, the guard walked through a break in the thick forest. In the moonlight, Danya could make out his facial features. He was looking mostly straight ahead, failing to show much interest or concern in what might be secluded amongst the trees.

Definitely second tier. These jokers are amateurs, not the professional mercenaries the drug lords hired. Still, she knew better then to relax her discipline.

He steadily approached, passing behind a dense grouping of young pine and fir trees. Danya took advantage of the cover to tuck away the binoculars inside her jacket. She didn't want to chance that he might notice her movement. Then she grasped the tomahawk and crouched.

Another minute ticked away, and then two. Danya was beginning to fear she had miscalculated, when the guard emerged from the far side of the young evergreens. He hadn't seen the assassin, clad in black and concealed within the hollow stump, and now he was walking directly toward her. He approached at a constant pace—just a bit faster than an amble, but still lacking any evidence of being alert. Whatever was going through his mind, she doubted he had any thought about his job.

From within the barn the cheering from the crowd reached a crescendo. Although Danya had no way of knowing, the final battle was nearing an end. This was the main event that drew the heaviest wagering, and the spectators were alternating cheers and boos.

Danya steadied her breathing, taking deep but slow breaths, exhaling fully but being careful not to make a sound. And then, only ten feet away, he stopped. His head twisted from side to side. Something had spooked him.

She watched as his grip tightened on the shotgun. Then he looked straight at the stump where she was hiding.

For several agonizing seconds, he just stared in Danya's direction as if he had some visual acuity that allowed him to see her in the blackness of the shadows.

Suddenly, his arm jerked the shotgun upwards. At the same instant Danya propelled herself from the stump. She collided with the guard before he could fully bring his weapon to bear. The impact of her slim but muscular frame knocked him backwards. He stumbled but remained on his feet.

Danya felt the impact too. This guy was solid muscle. She recovered her balance and swung the tomahawk blade in a vicious slice across his chest. The razor-sharp blade lacerated deeply, but with the addition of several layers of thick winter clothing, it was only a superficial wound. Painful, but not lethal.

He pumped the shotgun to chamber a shell. Before he could aim the muzzle, the edged weapon came down again in a powerful swing. The blade clanged on the barrel and knocked the gun from the guard's grip.

He reached through the slice in his jacket, trying to remove his sidearm from a shoulder holster. At the same time, he took several steps backwards to increase the distance from his attacker. Danya pressed forward, closing the gap. She swung again, and he immediately twisted defensively. The blade buried deep in his left shoulder. He gasped. Had it not been for the thick muscle, the blow would have broken his humerus bone.

His torso dipped to the left, a reflexive response to the wicked wound. Blood was already flowing freely down his useless arm. He fumbled with his right hand, still trying to remove the holstered pistol.

Without hesitation or remorse, Danya swung the tomahawk again. The blade sliced horizontally, cleanly severing both carotid arteries. Gurgling, the guard placed his hand against his throat in a vain attempt to stem the flow of blood. He fell first to his knees, then forward onto his face as the life-force drained from his body.

Danya hoped the metallic clangs and the other sounds of conflict had not been noticed by any other guards. The cheering from the spectators had just reached its peak, and now settled to a disorganized rumble.

She picked up the pistol-grip shotgun and jammed it into the hollow tree stump. Then she ripped open the jacket on the corpse, found his radio, and turned it off. She removed his pistol, another Glock. The grip was covered in blood. She ejected the magazine, which she pocketed, and placed the pistol within the tree stump. If she hadn't been concerned about making more noise, she'd have heaved both the pistol and the shotgun into the forest.

In the distance, Danya saw people filing out of the barn. Some were slapping others on the shoulder, likely congratulating one another on their winnings. Others wore scowls, shaking their heads in disappointment at the outcome.

The door adjoining the barn to the kennels opened. A man led a large dog to an empty pen using a catch pole, the cable loop firmly cinched around the neck of the creature. The dog appeared to move freely but was bloodied on the neck and had drool coming from its mouth. It's snarls and growls were easily heard by Danya. After loosening the cable and releasing the animal in the kennel, it spun around and snapped aggressively at the catchpole.

She held her position, carefully scrutinizing the activity, wary of other guards that may have heard the commotion and might be seeking out their compatriot to ensure everything was good. One minute passed... and then two.

After what she judged to be about ten minutes, the last pickup drove away from the barn.

As the forest returned to silence, save for the moans and occasional yelps from one or two dogs, Danya knew it was time.

Cautiously, she advanced on the kennels using the shadows for concealment of her approach. No guards were visible, but that didn't mean no one was looking. With practiced skill, she gently placed each boot on the forest floor, feeling for resistance that might indicate a twig or loose stone before transferring all her weight to that foot. It helped that it was early spring and the duff covering the ground was still limber from its moisture content.

Soon, she was at the kennels. In total there were six, all fenced to a height of eight feet using chain link and steel poles. Three kennels were on either side of a wide, muddy path that led to the back of the barn. Corrugated metal sheets covered most of the kennels offering meager protection from rain and snow. Inside each pen was a rickety plywood box, closed on three sides and the top, some weathered straw thrown inside on the dirt for bedding. Plywood covered the bottom four feet of each shared fence to provide a visual barrier and deter combative behavior of neighboring dogs.

A sliver of light escaped around a door in the weathered wood wall of the barn. In the moonlight, she saw three motionless carcasses in one kennel, and wounded dogs in three other enclosures. They cowered away from her approach, their bodies trembling in pain and fear. The sight sickened her. The putrid odor of feces and urine was rank, even in the frigid temperature, and only added to her revulsion.

The large dog that had been led out only minutes earlier was growling and pacing at the far side of one of the kennels closest to the wall of the barn, fearful of Danya. She had no doubt that the dog, obviously trained to fight, would be equally aggressive toward people.

She removed her gloves to improve dexterity and reached for the door latch. Suddenly, the door opened, nearly striking her. Instinctively, she stepped away and to the side, holding her breath and melting into the black shadows. A man dragged a bloodied dog behind him, the steel cable loop of the catch pole dug deeply into the folds of flesh on the animal's neck. He exited the barn with the carcass in tow. The door slowly closed behind him. Silently, Danya watched as he opened one of the kennels and kicked the motionless body inside. He removed the catch pole from the dog, hung it on the chain fence next to a slip leash, and closed and latched the gate. He took three steps toward the doorway into the barn when he nearly walked into Danya's SIG Sauer pistol, only inches away from his nose.

"Don't utter a sound, or I'll blow your goddamn head off," she said, her voice low, her tone menacing. "Clasp your hands on your head."

He complied, his eyes wide in fear. Danya stepped behind him, never lowering the pistol even for a second. With the muzzle pressed against the back of his head, she used her free hand to search for a weapon, which she found in a hip holster. She tossed it aside. "How many inside?" She pushed the steel muzzle hard into his flesh. "And keep your voice down when you answer."

"You're dead, lady. Billy and Mitch probably already have their guns aimed at your back."

"Those the two idiots wandering around out there?"

No reply, which was a clear answer to Danya.

"Well, your buddies should have had more job training. But it doesn't matter now. Their training days are over."

"Did… did you kill them?" he asked, his voice trembling.

"What do you think? I'm not out here looking for a date. Now answer me, how many are inside?"

"Just… just my boss." His voice was steady this time.

"Really. Your boss runs a dog fighting ring in the middle of nowhere, and he only has three morons for protection?" Danya spun the man around and pushed his back against the chain link fence. With one hand clenched around his throat, she lowered the gun and pushed the barrel against his groin, causing him to wince. "I hear on a good night your boss will pull in twenty, maybe twenty-five grand. Now, if I were the boss, I'd have some hired guns inside, near the cash. So, last time, how many men inside? And before you answer, I want you to close your eyes and think hard about what will happen to your family jewels if I pull this trigger and send a 115-grain hollow point into your manhood." To emphasize the point, she pressed the gun harder. The man stifled a cry as he tried to shrink away through the wire fence and into the kennel.

"Okay. Okay," he answered in short breaths. "Two. There's two. My boss and Kenny."

Danya studied his face and after a few seconds concluded he was speaking truthfully. "Your boss got a name?"

"Reggie."

"That's it, just Reggie?"

"Reggie White."

"Good boy. Now, tell me what your boss and Kenny are doing."

"They'll be gathering the receipts—the money—and packaging it up for storage in the safe."

"Where is the safe?"

"It's… it's in the barn."

She rammed the gun into his groin again. "*Where* in the barn?"

"I don't—"

"I'm growing impatient."

"By the front entrance." He was gasping for air. "Underneath… underneath some straw… in the horse stall."

Danya relaxed the pressure. "Good. Now, on the dirt. Face down."

He dropped gingerly to his knees, and then lay prostrate, hands out to the side. Danya grabbed the slip leash hanging on the fence and looped it around his ankles. She cinched it tight, bending his legs back so his ankles were nearly touching his buttocks, and then dropped her knee into the small of his back. A muffled grunt escaped his lips.

Still pointing the gun at him, she pulled first one hand and then the second behind his back. Only then did she holster the pistol and tie his hands securely. Hog-tied, he wasn't going anywhere. She stood and glanced around the kennels, eyeing a dirty cloth that appeared to have been used to wipe blood off an injured dog. She snatched it and not too gently stuffed it into his mouth until no more would go in.

"If you have any brains at all, you'll just relax and lay still. And pray that it's the sheriff who comes for you and not me. Trust me, you don't want to see me again. *Ever.*"

She stood and was at the door in four strides, her shotgun in her grip. Slowly, she inched the door open just enough to peek inside. Warm air flowed across her face from the heated barn. At first, she didn't see anyone, but she could hear voices. "Looks like it was a good night, eh boss?"

"Yeah Kenny, we did alright. That's for sure."

"That big 'ol gray bastard sure is a fighter. Tore up those other dogs like they were nothin'. Did you see him chewing on the leg of that smaller dog?"

Both men laughed, but Reggie never took his eyes off the bills passing through his fingers. "I tell ya, those dogs are wild beasts. Once they get the scent of blood, something in them just goes berserk. And when they get the taste of hot blood on their tongue, there ain't no stopping 'em. That gray bastard? He'd just a'soon eat you as not when he goes crazy like that."

"Well, his shoulder was chewed on pretty good. Might get infected if we don't get it looked at by the vet. Maybe some stitches and antibiotics. I could take him in to the emergency clinic, if you want me to."

"Shit, Kenny. That dog ain't worth a couple hundred in vet bills. Man, there's a hundred more, just like him, waitin' their turn to be the top dog."

Kenny nodded. "What do you want me to do with the dead dogs?"

"Leave 'em in the kennel tonight. It's late. But first thing in the morning take the backhoe and bury them. And dig it deeper this time. I don't want the bears digging up the half-rotted carcasses again."

"Should I put out some food and water for the others?"

"Nah. Let's finish up. It's been a busy night, and I've got a bottle of whiskey waitin' for me."

Through the opening, Danya saw a chain link cage. Wire fencing lined the path from the doorway where she stood to the cage, creating a slot that the dogs would be brought through. There was a gate at the end of the slot and another at the opposite side of the cage—both were open. On either side of the cage were tiered benches, like the bleachers one would see at high school sporting events. And just beyond the cage was a table where a man with black hair and beard sat counting money. A lanky fellow was standing at his side.

Danya drew a deep breath and slowly exhaled. She placed the toe of her boot just inside the door and firmly grasped the tactical shotgun with both hands.

A round was already in the chamber.

Show time.

CHAPTER 4

REGGIE WHITE WAS A BIG MAN. Dressed in dark indigo blue jeans, snake-skin boots, and sporting a leather flying jacket, he was an imposing figure, even if he did show a bit of a belly bulge. His black hair was tied tightly back in a ponytail that terminated at his shoulders, and his full beard was braided into a single strand that covered his Adam's apple.

He obviously liked to flaunt his money. From the large gold rings on every finger of both hands, to the gold Rolex wristwatch and thick gold chain around his neck, he stood out from the folks who worked hard to scrape out a living in La Pine. Although he frequented the local diner and dated most of the eligible women, he otherwise kept to himself. With a reputation for a hot temper, the local sheriff knew Reggie well. He'd had several run-ins with the law, but nothing ever stuck.

Looking like he was only a couple years out of high school, Kenny was easily fifteen years younger than his boss. He was about six feet tall, but thin and wiry. His red hair and freckled face conveyed an appearance of innocence that was very much out of place.

Danya kicked the door open and stepped inside. At the same time, she raised the shotgun to her shoulder and sighted on the two men. "What the…" Kenny started to say, but stopped when he recognized he was looking into the business end of a 12 gauge shotgun.

Danya advanced in purpose-filled strides, both eyes wide open to maximize her visual awareness. Kenny slowly edged to the side. Reggie stopped counting and looked up. "You've made a big mistake, lady."

"I don't think so," Danya answered.

"My men will—"

"Your men," she said, her voice raised in anger, "are accounted for. All are either dead or incapacitated." She was at the end of the slot where it joined up on the cage.

"What do you want?" Reggie asked.

"You must be the boss of this operation."

He nodded his head. "That's right."

"And that would make Kenny your hired gun, right?"

"Yeah, so what? Who are you, anyway?"

Kenny continued edging to the side.

"Who I am is not important. I'll take that cash, along with everything you've got in the safe."

"Safe? You see any safe around here? What makes you think you can come in here, on my property, and rob me?"

Kenny's fingertips were brushing against the holster on his hip. Riding high and designed for comfort and concealment under a waistcoat, it was not a fast draw configuration. Danya read the look in his eyes. "Don't do it Kenny."

His fingers wrapped around the grip and he jerked the pistol up and out of the holster.

Danya fired. *BOOM!* The load of nine 00 buckshot pellets

was still in a tight cluster when it blew apart Kenny's chest, sending him sprawling backwards as his arms were flung out to the side.

The auto-loading FN shotgun smoothly chambered another round and Danya swung the muzzle, pointing it at Reggie. "Do we have an understanding now?" she asked.

Reggie nodded his head at the same time he raised his hands. "Sure thing, lady. You can have the cash."

"And the contents of the safe." Danya was standing directly in front of Reggie.

"My men will have heard that blast. They'll be here real soon. That was careless of you."

"You mean it was careless of Kenny. He's the one lying on his back in a pool of his own blood. As for your men? All you have left are the two checking the cars about a half mile from here where your private driveway joins the Forest Service road. The way I figure it, you've got about fifty vehicles leaving. And your guys will stop each and every one of them to make sure the same people who came in that vehicle are in it when it leaves." Danya smiled. "Don't imagine you want any guests lingering around to rob you after you've gone to sleep. With that many engines running, they never heard the shotgun report."

Reggie's lips were drawn tight, his eyes narrowed. "You're going to regret this. I will find you and kill you."

"Yeah, yeah. If I had a dollar for every time I heard that, I wouldn't have to rob you. Stand up. And keep your hands on your head."

Holding the shotgun aimed at Reggie with her right hand, finger on the trigger, she quickly patted along both sides of his chest and his waistband. She removed the pistol holstered at the center of his back and a folding knife from a belt sheath, tossing the gun to the side while pocketing the knife.

Then, she reached into her cargo pocket and retrieved a

compressed nylon duffle bag. She dropped it on the table and took a step back. "Put the money inside."

Reluctantly, Reggie flapped the nylon sack open and swept the bills off the table into the bag while Danya stood in front of him where she could see every move. He slid it across the table toward her. "There. That's all of it. You have what you came for, now leave."

"Now the safe."

"There is no safe!" Reggie exclaimed, his voice raised.

Danya motioned with her chin. "By the front entrance, underneath the straw in the horse stable."

For a moment Reggie's eyes opened wide, then he suppressed his surprise.

"Move!" Danya ordered.

Gripping the bag in one hand, Reggie moved toward the front of the barn. She pushed the muzzle of the shotgun into his back as encouragement.

"I keep telling you, there ain't no—"

Danya suddenly swung the butt of the gun into his right kidney. Reggie grunted and staggered to the side. Before he recovered, she held the spike tip of her tomahawk against his neck, pressing the point into his flesh and drawing a drop of blood.

"Do you really want to play this game?" she asked.

He hesitated for a moment before answering. "Okay, okay."

They moved forward toward the main entrance to the barn, passing a garbage can. Danya glanced inside—lots of crumpled paper napkins, disposable cups, soiled paper plates, and even scraps of hot dog buns and what looked like half-eaten bratwurst. "You running a snack concession too?" she asked, somewhat incredulous.

"Of course. People come here to be entertained. They want something to eat, maybe a drink—it helps them to enjoy the sport."

Reggie's nonchalant, matter-of-fact explanation pushed her over the brink. She rammed the buttstock into his kidney again. This time, he fell to his knees, favoring his right side as he worked to catch his breath.

"Goddamn lady! What the hell is wrong with you! You asked a question and I gave you an honest answer."

"You son-of-a-bitch. You think this is all just innocent entertainment? People pay you to come here and place some bets, maybe win some money, laugh a little, have a good time. Everyone goes home at night to a warm bed. Right?"

"Yeah. So what?"

Danya lifted the shotgun like she was going to strike Reggie again. He raised his arm to block the blow that never came. "Those dogs, that's what! You've sentenced them to a living hell. All they know from day to day is pain, fear, hunger, thirst. Their entire life, that's all they know! You think it's all fun and games to them?"

Reggie shrugged. "They're just animals—wild animals at that. Jeez! You a card-carrying member of the SPCA or something?"

Danya locked Reggie's eyes with a malevolent glare. After several moments she said, "Get up."

He rose to his feet, and she stabbed the muzzle of the shotgun into his back to prod him forward. They stopped at the front entrance. The doors were closed to keep the cold out. To the right was what looked to be a horse stall. Straw was haphazardly spread across the dirt within the stall, suggesting that it might be a comfortable place for a farm animal to bed down in.

"Move the straw aside and open the safe."

Reggie opened his mouth to speak but thought better and began scraping the straw away with the side of his boot. Danya took two steps back to allow him room to do his work while keeping the scatter gun outside his immediate reach. After half a minute, the edge of a concrete slab was revealed. He continued removing the straw and soon a steel safe door appeared. It was recessed into the concrete slab and about two feet square.

"I thought you said there wasn't a safe?"

Reggie shrugged. "It's not something I advertise. Bad for business."

"Open it."

He sighed and then kneeled and began to spin the tumbler. It was a four-number lock, and soon Reggie cranked the lever, freeing the locking bolts. He grasped the lever with both hands and muscled the door open. Danya glimpsed stacks of bills still wearing the bank wrappers.

No sooner had Reggie released his grasp of the lever when he thrust a hand into the safe.

"Don't!" Danya ordered.

But Reggie's hand came up with a snub-nose revolver. Before he could bring it to bear on Danya, she pulled the trigger and a load of buckshot ricocheted off the safe door, some of the pellets striking Reggie in his hand and arm closest to the steel door. He yelped and dropped the gun. Red lacerations marked the backside of his hand where lead pellets had ripped the flesh. "Damn, lady!"

"You'll live. Fill the bag."

Wincing, he reached into the safe and removed a dozen bundles of hundred-dollar notes. It was a good score, but Danya wasn't done yet.

"Your jewelry, in the bag."

"What?"

"Did I stutter? I said, take your jewelry off and place it in the bag. I want it all—rings, chain, Rolex."

Reggie rolled his eyes. "Shit," he muttered and removed

the items as instructed. "You want my boots, too?" he added, sarcastically.

Danya thought for a moment. "Yeah, why not."

"Are you serious?"

"Take 'em off! Socks too."

Again, Reggie complied, firmly convinced that this woman would just as soon shoot him as not.

"Now, stand up and place your hands on your head." She saw a coil of sturdy rope hanging from a nail beside the door and grabbed it. Stabbing Reggie in the back with the barrel, she said, "Move!"

He walked back toward the fighting cage, but Danya stopped him at the garbage can.

"Pick up that sausage."

"Come on," he objected. "I've done everything you asked."

"And you'll keep doing what I ask, or that nice jacket of yours will have a big hole in it."

He reached into the garbage can and picked up the bratwurst between a finger and thumb, as if it was the dirtiest thing he'd ever touched.

"Now keep walking," she ordered. When they reached the cage, Danya said, "That's far enough." She took two steps back. "Take your jacket off."

Reggie dropped the half-eaten bratwurst and slipped off his leather jacket. "Throw it over there, against the fence."

Aware of the minutes passing by and the need to wrap up her mission, she ordered Reggie to lie on his belly, hands out to the side. She removed a heavy-duty metal cable tie from a cargo pocket and dropped a knee hard into the small of his back. Although not as common as the plastic zip ties, she preferred the stainless-steel version for its superior durability. Even the strongest man was not going to break the fastener once it was locked tight around the wrists or ankles.

"Umpf," he grunted as the air was forced from his chest.

"Left hand first. Behind your back. Then the right hand." As Reggie complied, Danya placed his hands palm to palm, and then slipped over the steel cable tie, pulling it tight.

"Ow!" he complained. Next, Danya slipped the shotgun over her shoulder and then tied his bare ankles together with the rope. The rough cord bit into his flesh. She dragged him the three feet to the chain link fence, raking his face through the dirt.

"Damn! Take it easy," he said.

"Sure. Like you took it easy on those dogs."

Danya raised his bound feet, bending his legs at the knees. She then looped the rope through the fence and tied it securely. Lying on his stomach, hands bound behind his back, legs bent, and feet tied to the fence, Reggie wasn't going anywhere. Danya retrieved the piece of bratwurst and rubbed it over the exposed side of Reggie's face, rubbing it over his ear and through his scalp. Then she stuffed the greasy meat in between the palms of his hands. As a last measure, she flipped open Reggie's knife and slashed the fleshy heal of each hand and the bottom of both feet.

"Ahh! What's that for?" he asked, the pitch of his voice higher than normal, suggesting a sliver of fear taking root in his mind.

"What was it you said to Kenny? Oh, yeah. Something about when the gray bastard gets the taste of blood, nothing will stop him."

"Look bitch, I've done everything you wanted. What the hell is your problem? Let me go!"

"You're my problem Reggie, but I'm about to take care of that." She walked around, standing near his head, and squatted down in front of his face. "Oh, and for the record, my name is not *bitch*—it's *karma*."

She stood and walked out of the cage, headed for the kennels.

"Hey! Don't leave me here!"

"Goodbye, Reggie."

"Where are you going?"

"To get a friend of yours."

"No! Please! Don't leave me!"

Back in the cold night air, Danya dragged the gagged and trussed guard farther away from the barn and out of the way of the kennel gates. The large gray male that had been the final victor of the evening was wary of her approach, emitting a guttural growl, a warning to stay away. She unlatched the gate and then opened it, taking care to stay behind the steel mesh as it swung open. The opened gate blocked the path between the two rows of kennels, so the only way the gray canine could go was back into the barn, a path it had probably taken many times and seemed to recognize.

With its blocky head in line with its muscular shoulders, the tormented creature entered the barn. There it stopped and raised its head, nostrils flaring. It detected an enticing mix of aromas—greasy pork and blood.

At a faster pace, it closed the distance to the fighting cage. It paused, wary of this place that had always brought pain and fear. Sniffing the air, the gray male locked on to the source of the odors.

Reggie saw the dog coming, and in the distance, at the door to the kennels, he saw Danya. She was clutching the bulging duffel bag and he could have sworn she mouthed the words *karma's a bitch.*

Reggie struggled frantically against his bonds. "No! No! Please! Don't leave me!"

She closed the door just as the first screams came from Reggie.

CHAPTER 5

La Pine, Oregon
March 3

WITH THE AID OF HER HANDHELD GPS UNIT, Danya covered the roughly two-mile distance to her truck in about twenty minutes. Stealth was not a significant issue anymore, and she maintained a steady speed, weaving between the trees and dense patches of immature evergreens, preferring the moonlit openings whenever possible.

The forest service road she had parked alongside was little more than a rutted dirt path that at one time had served as a road for log trucks to haul their valuable cargo out of the forest. The road had not been maintained in decades, but fortunately it was still passable with a rig that had high ground clearance and four-wheel drive.

The rough condition of the road was a plus, as it meant she was very unlikely to encounter any traffic—not like the maintained gravel lane that directed visitors to Reggie's barn every few weeks. She placed her tomahawk and weapons on the passenger seat and then climbed into the Ford pickup. After starting the engine, she dialed 9-1-1.

"What is the nature of your emergency?" the voice said.

"There's some men running a dogfighting ring. Tell the sheriff he'll find them at a barn on private land just north of La Pine." Danya read the coordinates for the barn from her GPS. There was a pause, and she imagined the operator was making a notation on paper. She didn't repeat the coordinates since she knew the call was recorded and available for reference.

"Are you there now?" the operator asked.

"Where I am doesn't matter. The men are armed and dangerous. They tried to kill me."

"Are you okay ma'am? What's your name?"

"I'm a concerned citizen—you don't need to know my name. Oh, and you'd better send animal control and a veterinary doctor if you can get one out of bed. Those dogs that are still alive are badly hurt."

"Is anyone injured? Do we need an EMT?"

Danya paused before answering. She turned the wheel and slowly nudged her truck forward on the rutted dirt road.

"Yeah, the lucky ones. You might need a couple EMTs."

"Ma'am. Where are—"

Danya disconnected the call and threw the cheap burner phone out the window. She'd pay cash for another phone tomorrow. With both hands firmly gripping the steering wheel, she accelerated the Ford, slowing just enough when a rut or hole was encountered to maintain control. Soon, she came to the junction of Highway 97 and turned left, heading north for Bend.

It was still dark when she arrived at the RV park between Bend and Redmond. She turned off the headlights and navigated by the dim amber glow of the parking lights. She parked next to a modest travel trailer, turned the engine off, and quietly closed the door, not wanting to attract any attention.

Inside the trailer, Danya placed a pot of water on the gas stove. She was still running on adrenalin and a cup of herbal tea would help her to relax.

She glanced at her watch. "Might as well do something useful," she murmured to herself as she powered up her laptop. Only a few emails had been received since the last time she'd checked her mailbox several days ago, and all were junk—except for one. It had been received less than two hours ago. The sender's address simply read 'info@information.com', and he called himself Carlos, although she doubted that was his real name.

Danya had found Carlos through the dark web, and both parties had insisted on anonymity. In fact, Danya knew almost nothing about Carlos. She didn't even know his gender, but she assumed he was male based on his phrasing of messages and his chosen name.

"New job you might be interested in," he wrote. "A contract on an American. Reply for details."

She started typing, hoping that Carlos was still at his computer. "Like I've told you before, I don't do that type of work anymore."

The water began to boil and Danya filled a cup and added a tea bag. As she sat down, a reply came in from Carlos. "I know. But like I said, you might be interested in this one."

She pinched her eyebrows. "Why?"

"The mark—I believe you may know him. His name is Peter Savage."

She stared at the monitor for a full minute, her mind filled with swirling thoughts. "How do you know that?"

"The police report about that incident in the Cascade Mountains. The media called it the Battle at Broken Top."

"You hacked the Bend police report?"

"Of course. Mr. Savage seems to be the main character, although I think you're named in it, too. Nadya Wheeler is one of your aliases, right?"

"Not anymore."

"My instinct tells me that you know a lot about what happened out there, maybe even why the police were so convinced he was a murderer, but then cleared his name almost immediately after he surrendered. Curious that you went missing. Seems the authorities would still like to talk to you."

"The feeling is not mutual." Danya continued typing. "And before you get any stupid ideas about turning me in, forget it. You've got nothing on me other than an IP address which can't be linked to a physical address."

"Relax. I don't snitch—bad for business. Just letting you know, that's all."

"Why are you telling me this? I don't do murder for hire."

"Like I said, just thought you might want to know. Besides, that information you shared with me about the Sinaloa cartel proved to be quite valuable to the right people. Consider this a return favor, payback. Anyway, this guy—Peter Savage—the contract is large. It's already drawing attention."

"From whom?" Danya asked.

"Can't say. All I can see is that several persons have replied. From their questions, some are pros, others may be amateurs trying to look like professionals. But even an amateur can get lucky."

Danya's mind was racing. She'd had zero contact with Peter following the gunfight on the slopes of Broken Top about a year and a half ago. She'd left Mossad right after that and had been on the run ever since. "Who put out the contract?"

"Someone with a hell of a lot of money. And they don't want him alive, proof of death is all that is required for payment. You're a smart lady, so you tell me who would be motivated to pay five million for this guy's head?"

44

CHAPTER 6

ROGER CORBETT WASN'T THE TYPICAL corporate tour guide. He didn't work in the marketing department, nor research and development. As the head of security, he managed a small army of well-trained guards. He had been in Simon Ming's employ since the founding of Utopian-Bio. The pay was good, generous in fact, and he was smart enough to understand that that meant the science being done under Ming's direction wasn't exactly the type of work that would receive widespread approval.

Presently, he was standing outside one of Utopian-Bio's clean rooms, looking in through a wall of safety glass. Each room was constructed to biosafety level 4 standards. The specialized lab was maintained at negative pressure so that any airborne pathogens would be forced through the sterilizing, high-efficiency filtration systems. Scientists clad in level A hazmat suits, complete with a full-facepiece and self-contained breathing apparatus, were busy tending to experiments in

45

specially-designed hoods. Several benches ran perpendicular to the windows lining the hallway. The tops of the benches held a range of laboratory equipment, only some of which were recognized by Corbett—centrifuges, digital balances, automatic pipetting machines, incubators, and a bank of DNA sequencing machines lined up along the far wall.

Despite the safety protocols and equipment, Corbett preferred to be outside looking in through the windows which afforded visibility of everything going on in the room. With the approval of Simon Ming, he was taking Darnell Price on a confidential tour of the research labs. They were accompanied by a senior scientist and trusted member of Ming's team.

"You believe you've manufactured the correct agent?" Darnell asked the scientist who was describing the work currently being undertaken. The scientist pointed to a figure inside the clean room who was holding a large culture flask with both hands for Darnell to examine. It contained an amber-colored fluid.

"We do," the scientist explained. "Genetically engineered to be stable in water for a month, the virus is close to perfection in design. We drew on the genetic code—nothing more than a large collection of base pairs—from hepatitis C and mumps. This allowed our scientists to modify both the protein shell and membrane envelope surrounding the virus. Once ingested or inhaled, infection is guaranteed."

"Sounds complicated. How confident are you in the effectiveness of this engineered virus?"

"We've tested the ability of the virus to infect human tissue cultures in limited trials in the lab," the scientist explained. "In fact, that's how we reproduce the virus—using human tissue medium." He continued to explain that the virus was grown in a fluid suspension, and once mature, the pathogen was extracted and dried onto a water-soluble substrate.

Inside the clean room, the flask was returned to an incubation chamber, one of a dozen placed around the room. The scientist, with Corbett in tow, moved along the windows and directed Darnell's attention to another section of the clean room where a machine was slowly removing liquid from a spinning suspension. "This is the drying operation," he explained. "We have ten more batches after this one, and then we are done with production here."

"Will the manufacturing process be carried out elsewhere?" Darnell asked.

"This is a pilot facility. Once any new process is validated, we always export volume manufacturing to other sites. That's easily accomplished with the dry agent. We have a small supply in the refrigerator," he motioned, Darnell's gaze following.

In a corner of the clean room near the window was a large double-door refrigerator. The doors were glazed, and inside Darnell saw dozens of square, wide-mouth jars. The lids appeared to be sealed in place with a tamper resistant ring. "The dried agent is stored here until it is needed for testing or to seed off-site manufacturing operations. Refrigerated and dried, the virus agent can be stored for years and still remain viable. All of the containers you see here will be delivered to more than a dozen manufacturers around the country to begin their own cultures."

"Why not simply produce the virus here?" Darnell asked.

"Given time, we could. And that would be easier," the scientist replied. "But it might attract attention. Utopian-Bio is an R and D company, and if we started producing quantities of the virus, other employees might take notice. Only a handful of us are involved in this project—we compartmentalize the information and share only on a need-to-know basis."

"That makes sense."

"Do you have any other questions?" the scientist asked.

Darnell shook his head. "No, thank you. This is very impressive, and I commend you and your team. Brilliant work."

The scientist thanked Darnell and excused himself.

"Very impressive," Darnell repeated to Roger Corbett.

"Dr. Ming has impressed upon me how important it is that you have confidence in our operation."

"Then I trust you are making arrangements for the volume manufacturing? I mean, other than preparing the virus as a dried powder, there are many details that will require attention in order to set up proper facilities. If our experiment goes well, we should begin production soon, I think."

Corbett nodded. "Dr. Ming approved your suggestion to use an *unregistered* lab for the production."

Darnell smiled at Corbett's choice of wording. He knew from his career in the medical equipment business that illicit drug laboratories were typically provisioned with high-tech laboratory equipment stolen from chemistry labs and medical centers.

"Just to be clear," Darnell said, "I have a lot of exposure here. This needs to be a clean operation. Nothing can be traced back to me. If anything goes wrong, I'm not taking the fall for anyone."

Corbett narrowed his eyes. "Just to be clear, is that a threat?"

"No. It's a fact."

Darnell Price ran his fingers along the stainless-steel pipe, imagining the flow of water the pipe would carry during the bottling process.

"Working late again, Mr. Price?"

He turned, startled by the voice. It was the shift manager.

"Oh, yeah, I suppose so. This new filtration system cost a small fortune," he said, indicating the array of cylindrical filter housings, pressure gauges, valves, and piping. Cascade Aqua normally only ran two shifts a day. But the bottling line had been down to complete the upgrades, so Darnell had temporarily implemented a third shift to catch up on production.

"The technicians just completed the installation an hour ago," the manager explained. "We'll be bringing it online real soon, following the shift change. The manufacturer says these filters will remove any single-cell bugs that might be in the water."

Darnell nodded. "That's the idea. The EPA and the Oregon Department of Environmental Quality are pushing out new regulations. After cryptosporidium and giardia were detected in the Bull Run watershed outside of Portland, I think it spooked the regulators. Everyone thought Bull Run had some of the cleanest water in the country."

"I thought the new regulations won't take effect until next year?" the manager asked.

"True, but just imagine the customer backlash if someone gets sick from my bottled water. The brand—the value of the product name Cascade Aqua Natural—is what sustains this business. Anyone can bottle water."

"Pretty smart, Mr. Price. Staying ahead of the curve."

He nodded again. "And, the marketing department is ready to roll out a series of ads touting our new, state-of-the-art filtration process to assure the health of our customers. It'll send our competitors scrambling to catch up. I expect to erode at least five percent of their customer base."

"Brilliant, Mr. Price. Well, I have to oversee to the shift change. Have a good evening, sir."

Darnell watched as the manager walked away and rounded the corner. Then he donned latex gloves and popped open the clamp holding a flanged steel cap on the last filter housing in the array. Reaching into his pocket, he removed a sealed plastic bag holding less than an ounce of off-white granules. Using a ballpoint pen, he punched a hole through both sides of the bag, careful not to spill the contents. He removed the steel cap and dropped the bag into the filter housing, then replaced the cap and secured the clamp. The entire process took less than thirty seconds.

Ben Jarvis knocked on the door and then entered. "You wanted to see me, Mr. Price?"

Darnell looked up from the stack of checks he was signing. Even though he was already extremely successful and wealthy, he still maintained daily involvement in the management and operations of the company.

"Good morning, Ben. I understand the new filtration line worked well last night?"

"Yes. According to Operations, the graveyard shift had no issues at all with it. As you directed, they ran the line at a little more than half the normal production rate and everything was fine. No problems with the new filters. Pressure drop was within specifications. We should be fine to ramp up production."

"Better to start slow and make sure there are no issues."

"I completely agree, Mr. Price. Anyway, it's all wrapped and on pallets, ready to ship."

"Good," Darnell said, his eyes again on the checks he continued to sign. "I want you to truck all of last night's production to the Warm Springs reservation. The tribal council is expecting the donation."

Ben's eyes widened. "Excuse me, sir? But that's more than seven thousand bottles. That's a lot of product."

"I can afford it, and it's for a good cause."

"But we've already donated more than a hundred cases to the tribal council."

"Well, with about a third of the population living below the poverty line, I figure they could benefit from a little help.

Besides, I won't hold it against your sales targets." Darnell knew what motivated his VP of sales. "Oh," he added as an afterthought, "the entire output of the day shift is to be palletized for shipment to Nigeria."

"Excuse me?" Ben said, certain he did not clearly hear this last directive.

"Nigeria. Africa. There's a cholera outbreak there. It's a small donation, but everything helps."

"Okay, Mr. Price. You're the boss." Ben's tone indicated it wasn't okay, but he knew better than to press the issue. He closed the door on his way out. The operation was small by any standard, and that meant margins were always tight. The brand was gaining market share, but the competition was stiff.

Ben returned to his office and composed an email to the day-shift operations manager, but he couldn't let go of the thought. He just didn't understand why his boss was giving away bottled water—first to the Warm Springs tribes and now Africa. He'd never donated product before, instead staying focused on sales and margins. *What could possibly be the reason for giving away so many cases of water? The company should be investing in the brand, not giving away the profits, slim as they were.*

Darnell signed the last check, meticulously stacked the papers, and closed the folder. He delivered the folder to the accounting department before moving on to the Operations Manager. The door was open, and he saw the day-shift manager at the desk.

"Wendy, at the conclusion of your shift I want you to sterilize the new ultrafiltration line."

She looked at Darnell with a confused expression. "But it just went into service last night. Those filters aren't scheduled for cleaning for another four weeks."

"I understand, but I'm not taking any chances that the

technicians who did the installation did their job correctly. I've seen it before—the guys doing the work have their mind elsewhere and details get overlooked. At the end of the day, it's my reputation and the reputation of this company that are on the line."

"But—"

"Wendy, just humor me, okay? Shut the line down at the end of the shift and sterilize all the filter housings with bleach, along with the connecting pipes and valves. Then install new filters and flush the line thoroughly. I know it's extra work, but I want to be certain the quality of our product is not sacrificed."

Wendy rolled her eyes. "Okay, Mr. Price. If you say so. But the line will be shut down for at least four hours until the bleach is completely flushed."

CHAPTER 7

DESCHUTES COUNTY DISTRICT ATTORNEY Neal Lynch anxiously read the report from the Oregon State Police Crime Lab. It concerned fingerprints lifted at the forested crime scene just north of La Pine, apparently the site of a dog fighting ring. The case was being investigated as a triple homicide, spiced up with two assault victims. Since murder was a rarity in Deschutes Country, this case was his department's top priority.

One of the victims, a low-life thug named Reggie White, had been tied up and severely mauled by a dog. He was hospitalized in serious condition. An ear was missing, and the side of his face was lacerated. One hand had been amputated, and several toes on both feet had also been surgically removed. The surgeons reconstructed as best as possible the vascular network in his feet, hoping to save them. Time would tell.

The DA had no pity for Mr. White. Their investigation had quickly revealed that White owned the property where the crimes had occurred, and that he orchestrated dog fighting to gain from money bet on the contests. *Serves the asshole right*. Lynch had two dogs of his own—well-trained and well-pampered. Animal abuse was on his top-five list of despicable crimes, and training dogs to fight to the death certainly fit the category of abusive treatment.

As a professional in the criminal justice system, he also knew that persons who abused animals were more likely to move on to violent, even homicidal, behavior toward people. Still, despite the fact that he did not have an ounce of sympathy for the victims, his duty was to investigate the case with the goal of convicting the perpetrator. That assumed law enforcement was able to find and arrest the suspect. Which was why the crime lab report he was now reading was significant.

The other survivor, an employee of Reggie White, was found by the sheriff deputies hog-tied next to the kennels. Not far away, the deputies recovered a pistol, presumed to be carried by the hog-tied victim based on fingerprints found on the weapon. But there was a second set of prints. Those prints were matched to a thumb and index finger in the database.

"Now that's interesting," he spoke to himself as he continued to read the report. Following a routine search of the fingerprint database, the technicians determined that the second set of prints matched prints recovered from weapons used in a brazen assault of military precision that had transpired in the Cascade Mountains not far from Bend eighteen months ago.

Lynch lower the report to his desk and stared at the far wall of his office. *What are the odds of that?* He read further, expecting the prints to be confirmed as from one of the captured or killed assailants from that assault. "No way," he muttered. "How is that possible?"

Lynch picked up his desk phone and dialed a number from memory.

"State Police Crime Lab," the voice said.

"Yeah, hi. This is DA Lynch from Bend. I'd like to speak to…" he glanced at the author of the report. "Marissa Mendoza."

"Just a moment while I transfer your call. Her extension is 334, if we get disconnected."

After a short wait, a pleasant feminine voice answered. "Mendoza speaking."

"Ms. Mendoza, this is DA Lynch, Deschutes County. I just read your report on the print analysis from the triple homicide outside La Pine five days ago."

"Oh, yeah. Just wrapped that up last night."

"I'm interested in the thumb and index fingerprints lifted from a pistol, a Taurus Model 92—"

"What page are you referring to?" she interrupted.

"Uh, bottom of page two. You said the prints are not from the hog-tied victim and presumed carrier of the gun. Furthermore, you reported that the prints turned up in the database. They are associated with one or more persons connected to that gun battle in the Cascade Mountains."

"Yes, that's correct."

"But the prints are not from any of the captured or deceased assailants from that incident. Did I read that right?"

"Yes, Mr. Lynch, you did."

"So, who are the prints associated with?"

"Beats me. Could be almost anyone. All I can say with certainty is who the prints are not associated with."

Lynch was silent, contemplating the statement.

"Mr. Lynch? You still there?"

"Oh, sorry. Yes, thank you. Just thinking. So, these prints belong to someone who was at the scene of that attack in the Cascades, but not among those captured or killed."

"No, that's not what I'm saying. Look, *when* the fingerprint was placed on the weapon is indeterminable. But, off the record, fingerprints on something that is handled and manipulated aggressively, like a firearm, don't last long. We got a bunch of clean, crisp prints from an unknown person from one of the weapons recovered at the Cascade Mountain crime scene eighteen months ago. My hunch is that person escaped the scene and has not resurfaced."

"Until now," Lynch muttered.

"Sorry?"

"Uh, nothing. Thank you, Ms. Mendoza."

Lynch carried the folder with the crime lab report and drove the short distance to the Bend Police Station. He showed his ID at the window and asked to speak with Detective Ruth Colson. He was buzzed through the security door and a uniformed officer led him to a conference room where he was joined by the detective. He quickly brought her up to speed, pointing out the key portions of the report regarding the fingerprint evidence.

"I understand you were the lead investigator for the Bend PD on that case, the gunfight near Broken Top."

"Yeah," she said with a frown. "That was the oddest case of my career. The newspaper ran a headline calling it "The Battle at Broken Top." The name seems to have stuck. I was involved only because the case began and ended here in Bend, but the dramatic shootout that you're referring to in the Cascade Mountains is obviously outside of Bend jurisdiction. The state police and the Deschutes county sheriff ran that part of the operation."

"That makes sense," Lynch said. "I'll reach out to those agencies, but I wanted to speak with you first. Do you have a few minutes?"

"Yeah, sure."

"I did a little research on the case before I came over. You know it happened before I was elected DA." Lynch had been in office for only a few months.

Colson nodded.

"It seems a Bend resident was at the center of the entire affair."

"That's right," she said. "Peter Savage. He got wrapped up in some sort of security issue with the Feds. At one point, he handed me a memory stick that he claimed had important information relative to the case, but before I could look at it, the Feds—"

"FBI, right?"

"That's right, FBI. They demanded that I turn it over to them."

"And you did?"

"I didn't want to, but I had no choice. Anyway, a week or two later, a local reporter for the Bend Bulletin published an exposé about the real events involving an attack on the *USS Liberty* by Israeli military in 1967. Citing unnamed sources, the reporter presented evidence that the government had been covering up an act of treason by then-President Johnson and his Secretary of Defense, Robert McNamara. She won a Pulitzer for her reporting. I've always suspected Peter Savage was her source."

"But if that information was on the memory stick that Mr. Savage gave to you, how did the reporter get it?"

"Heck if I know," Colson replied with a shrug. "Maybe he had a copy."

Lynch nodded. "Before the ordeal was over, Savage and a woman were kidnapped and later rescued from a location in eastern Oregon, correct?"

"Yes," Colson said. "I was there when they were rescued, although they'd done a damned good job of defending themselves. If you ask me, they didn't need our help."

"And the woman?" Lynch pressed. "Nadya Wheeler?"

"Yeah, that sounds right. I can check my notes and official

report if you like."

He shook his head. "That's not necessary. Just want to make sure I'm tracking with you."

"Anyway, Ms. Wheeler and Mr. Savage were brought back to Bend along with the man behind the crime spree, a Mr. Claude Duss. We were to meet right here in this conference room the next day, only Ms. Wheeler never showed. The FBI issued a warrant for her arrest, but to my knowledge she has never been apprehended. Duss pled out of federal charges in exchange for information. We pressed charges and, as you know, your predecessor successfully prosecuted Duss on several felonies. He'll be in prison for a long time."

"Thank you," Lynch said. "That's consistent with what I gleaned from the report before coming over here. But I'm interested in the woman, Nadya Wheeler. In particular, I want to know why her fingerprints showed up on a pistol recovered from a crime scene outside La Pine five days ago."

Colson shrugged. "Can't help you with that one. As I said, she never showed for our meeting. You might want to ask the Feds. If anyone knows where she is, it would be them."

"Don't suppose you'd have a photo?"

"No reason to. Like I said, she was a victim when we first came in contact, not a suspect."

"Okay. Well, I guess that does it. Thanks for your help. This is one strange case."

Colson chuckled. "Get used to it. There is nothing ordinary when it comes to events involving Peter Savage and his associates."

CHAPTER 8

PETER WAS SITTING BEHIND the wheel of the Rolls Royce Wraith, a beautiful and sleek two-door sedan—a gift from the Sultan of Brunei as a token of his appreciation for Peter's efforts to protect the life of his niece not long ago. Although at first Peter had refused the automobile, the sultan was most persistent.

As the two-lane highway dropped from the high desert plateau down toward the Deschutes River, Mount Jefferson, still capped in snow, loomed ahead. The perfectly symmetrical volcanic peak dominated the skyline. Cliffs of igneous rock, the color of dark chocolate, loomed two hundred feet above the fast-flowing water. Above the cliffs, steep, grass-covered slopes were just beginning to green. Juniper trees dotted the sparse landscape.

The hour-long drive from Bend to the Warm Springs Reservation had passed quickly; Peter's thoughts were preoccupied with why a tribal council member had contacted him and insisted on a face-to-face meeting.

He glanced at the GPS map shown on the in-dash display and signaled to turn right at the approaching intersection. A quarter mile ahead was his destination. He slowed the car to a stop in front of an old ranch-style house.

Paint was peeling from the trim, and the weathered and worn asphalt shingles cladding the roof were definitely at the end of their useful life. Around the spacious yard were rusted cars and pickups, all in various stages of disassembly. There was no landscaping to speak of, just a natural scattering of native rabbit brush and sage.

There was nothing exceptional about the house. The city of Warm Springs did not boast any high-end neighborhoods. There were no mini-mansions set back on well-manicured yards. If anything was remarkable about the community, it was the high unemployment rate and low standard of living, two facts which made Peter self-conscious of driving his luxury automobile to his appointment. He knew the Wraith cost more than most families in Warm Springs would earn in a decade, maybe two.

As he got out, he was greeted by a large man with raven-black hair braided in a ponytail that extended to the middle of his back. He was wearing worn blue jeans and a long-sleeve, salmon-colored western-style shirt beneath a leather vest. Around his neck was a black braided-leather bolo tie, adorned with a brown-and-black obsidian arrowhead. His tanned and weathered face hinted at his years.

The man said, "Nice car. Don't think I've ever seen a Rolls Royce on the reservation before."

Peter extended his hand. "Hi, I'm Peter Savage."

"Lee Moses. I'm the Paiute chief and member of the tribal council."

They walked inside and sat at the wooden kitchen table. It

was also old and worn, in keeping with the house. "Thank you for agreeing to meet with me," Lee said.

"I have to admit, you have piqued my curiosity. Your request sounded important."

Lee nodded. "Coffee?"

Peter shook his head. "I'm fine, thank you."

"Well, Mr. Savage—"

"Please. Call me Peter."

"Okay, Peter. I'll get right to the point, the reason I contacted you. I know you've volunteered your time teaching our school children about science, and your donations have been used to purchase computers for the high school. Our teachers are so used to making do with worn textbooks and a lack of supplies, that many thought I was joking when I announced your gift. You're a hero to them."

"I'm happy to help."

"You wouldn't do that if you didn't care about our young people." Lee shifted in his chair. "I've also read about you in the newspaper. Seems you have a habit of getting into trouble."

Peter smiled at the understatement. Truth be told, his life seemed to be marked by one harrowing adventure after another. He didn't seek out trouble, but invariably trouble found him. "I suppose I'd have to agree with you," he said.

"And yet you always seem to be on the side of truth and honor."

"I hope so. Those aren't just words. They're ideals that are very important to me. Call it my code of conduct, my moral compass."

"I know," Lee replied. "You know, we Indians have learned not to trust the white man. It's not just a cliché. Of course, there are exceptions. But the history of relations is marked by lies, deceit, even murder. In the beginning, my ancestors signed treaties with the settlers, gave up our land in exchange for promises of peace. It was never long before the treaties were broken because the settlers wanted more land. The United States Army, in an act of biological warfare, even gave blankets infected with smallpox to Native Americans. The suffering was indescribable. Many died—mostly women, children, and our elders.

"Eventually, my people were pushed onto reservations— those that weren't slaughtered by the army. On the reservation, the Bureau of Indian Affairs was supposed to look after our natural resources. But being as the BIA is part of the United States federal government, they did not care about being fair to my people, and we were cheated out of hundreds of millions of dollars in timber and mineral wealth."

"I regret the way the indigenous tribes have been treated," Peter said. "It was wrong, a tremendous injustice that Washington has not adequately acknowledged, or apologized for."

"Believe me when I say that an apology is not what my people want. But I want you to understand why trust in the government is still lacking."

"Certainly. And I do understand. But what does this have to do with me?"

"Exactly what I said. I think you are a man of truth and honor. A man who can be trusted. And my people need your help."

"Help? With what?"

"I've read about you. Asked around to people who know you," Lee explained. "You are an engineer, a scientist. You are very good at solving problems to get to the truth."

Peter looked into Lee's eyes. He didn't see anything other than trust and humility. "What do you need my help with?"

Lee leaned forward, resting his arms on the table. "The Tribal Committee on Health and Welfare keeps accurate records of illnesses contracted by residents of the reservation. For the most part, the types of illnesses and frequency of occurrence are statistically no different from other areas in Oregon and the Northwest. However, there is one alarming exception."

"I don't have a degree in medicine or molecular biology," Peter said.

"I know. You have a degree in chemistry from the University of Oregon. And you own and operate EJ Enterprises, a small business in Bend that designs and manufactures special pistols for the military. I've read your biography."

"Okay."

"Over the last four days, the health clinic has reported a high number of cases of orchitis. Do you know what that is?"

Peter shook his head.

"It's an inflammation of the testes. It's a rather rare illness, which is why the anomaly was spotted so quickly. Ordinarily, it might take a few weeks to observe a statistical deviation for rates of infection from more common diseases such as the flu."

"I assume you've already reported this to the Oregon Health Authority?"

"Yes. But they dismissed my concern and said I should wait two weeks, that it might be a short-term spike that goes away. They told me that the few cases we have seen are not statistically significant." Lee paused while Peter ruminated over the choice of words. To say that disease on the reservation was not significant was a slap in the face, demonstrating ignorance or insensitivity—or both—to the history of relations between native Americans and the encroaching white settlers.

Lee continued. "Besides, they said they have no jurisdiction on the reservation, and told me I should call the Centers for Disease Control in Atlanta."

"Did you?"

Lee nodded. "They were not helpful. They told me that if

we still see a higher-than-normal number of cases after two to three weeks, then they will consider opening an investigation."

"I'm assuming an infection of the testicles can be painful."

"Very. I've learned that it's an occasional complication of the mumps in post-pubescent males that may result in sterility. But with vaccinations against the mumps quite common and widespread, there hasn't been a case reported on the reservation in more than six years. So, I am left to wonder, why a sudden spike in reported cases of orchitis? I'm asking for your help. I need you to use your knowledge of science to help us solve this problem. We can't wait for the CDC to decide that we have an outbreak, and then who knows how long for them to do anything meaningful."

"Well, I can't fault your mistrust of the government. But why not just wait a couple weeks? I don't understand the urgency."

"Native Americans have always felt a spiritual relationship with Nature," Lee said with a twinkle in his eye. "Maybe not so much anymore, but the elders still feel a connection to the natural order. Something is wrong—the balance in Nature is disturbed. I don't know by what, but I fear that if we wait, the consequences will be severe."

"And how many cases have been reported so far?"

"Fifteen. But I suspect the actual number is greater. It is difficult for young men to seek medical help for a disease that afflicts their genitals. Young men are very prideful."

Peter leaned forward, resting his elbows on the table. "Maybe I'll have that coffee now."

Lee rose from the table and poured two mugs of steaming brew. "Sugar or cream?" he asked.

Peter declined both.

"So you'll help me?" Lee asked.

He sipped from the mug before replying. "Yes. I'll take a couple days off and do what I can. But understand that investigating the cause of an outbreak is something I haven't done before. I can't promise anything more than I will do all I can to help you."

"How do we start?"

"The first step is always to examine the data for each person who has contracted the infection. I need everything you have. Name. Age. Where they live. What they ate and drank. Where they work. Everything. No detail is too small or insignificant."

"I have asked the staff at the clinic to put everything we know into a spreadsheet."

"Then that's where we begin. Do you have a copy here?" Peter asked.

Lee shook his head. "It is only on the server at the clinic. We can go there. If you need a copy, I'll make sure one is provided to you. We will have to remove the names of the patients, of course."

"Well, let's go. The sooner we start the better."

"Okay. Just one more favor to ask."

Peter raised his eyebrows.

"Can I ride with you in that fancy car of yours?"

Peter reached into his pocket for the keys. "Catch," he said as he tossed the keys across the table. "Since you know where we're going, I guess you might as well drive."

Lee's face split into a big grin.

CHAPTER 9

WARM SPRINGS, OREGON
MARCH 14

LEE DIDN'T STOP GRINNING during the entire ten-minute drive to the tribal health clinic. He parked in a handicap spot in front of the entrance and turned off the engine. As Peter reached for the door handle, Lee offered his cell phone. "Would you mind taking a picture of me behind the wheel? I could never afford a car this expensive. At my age, figure it's my first and last time to drive a luxury automobile like this."

Peter snapped a half dozen photos before they both exited, and Lee returned the keys.

Inside, Lee greeted the receptionist. "Hi Lucy. This is Peter Savage. He'll be helping us investigate the cases of orchitis."

They walked past the counter into a back office. Against a wall were two utilitarian metal office desks, pushed end to end to create a long work surface. At each desk was a rolling office chair. The austere furniture was functional though dented and scratched. On each desk sat a keyboard, monitor, and mouse. The walls were painted mint-green and decorated with faded posters of different cities from around the world.

Lee eased himself into a chair and opened a spreadsheet. Peter looked over his shoulder as he resized the array of rows and columns to fit the display.

"These are the fifteen reported cases," Lee explained. The first column contained a unique number, rather than a name, to identify each patient. He pointed to the second column. "Their ages are entered here. The youngest is fourteen and the oldest is thirty-four. They live all over the reservation."

Peter pointed to the column giving their addresses. "We need to get these residences plotted on a map. Do you have someone who can do that?"

"Lucy is pretty good with computers." He leaned back and called out. "Lucy!"

"Yes, Mr. Moses?" she said as she entered the office. Her hair was raven black and straight, pulled back behind her ears and just reaching her shoulders. Like many of the people living on the reservation, she was Native American. Peter estimated her age to be about thirty, less than half the years he figured Lee had racked up. She wore a white medical coat over jeans and white turtleneck sweater.

"Peter would like to have these addresses put onto a map."

"Sure," she said. "That's easy. I'll pull up a digital map of this area and plot each residence."

"Would you also put a marker where each of the patients works or goes to school?" Peter asked. "If we're lucky, there's a pattern—something they all have in common. And that could be the source of the illness."

Lucy went to work on the other desk computer while Peter and Lee continued to review the data tabulated in the spreadsheet. "The two youngest patients are still in school," Peter observed. "And four of the adults are unemployed? I don't see a work address for them."

"Yes," the tribal elder replied. "Unemployment is high on the reservation. When the casino opened several years ago, that created many good jobs. But there still are not enough jobs for everyone."

Pointing to empty cells, Peter said, "There are some big gaps here."

"I know. I have three staff from the clinic out conducting interviews to get as much information as possible about what each patient ate. We are trying to go back two weeks, but I don't know how complete or reliable the information will be. It's easy to remember what you ate and drank for the past two or three days, but longer than that and memories become incomplete and unreliable."

"Has the cause of the inflammation been determined yet?"

Lee shook his head. "Nothing definitive. Blood samples were collected from every patient, but so far, the doctors can't say if it's a virus or bacterial infection. They're simply treating the symptoms, which also include mild aches and a low-grade fever, and trying to make the patients as comfortable as possible."

"At least it doesn't sound life-threatening. That's good."

Lee nodded. "I agree. The symptoms most closely resemble the mumps, or the flu."

"Are they quarantined?"

"Yes, but it's voluntary. They have all agreed to stay home until they recover."

"And family members sharing the households?"

"Yes, they have agreed to stay inside and not go out. Relatives and neighbors are providing meals. This is working, for now. But if the outbreak spreads…"

"I understand." Peter drew in a deep breath and exhaled. He quickly ran the math through his head. The number of infected and exposed people would grow exponentially if they were dealing with a contagion. "Well, the information in this spreadsheet is a start. Let me spend some time studying this. It will help if I can have a copy."

"I'm just about done with the map," Lucy said. "Five more addresses."

"Promise me," Lee said, casting a stern look to Peter, "that you will not share the addresses with anyone. Even though the names have been removed from the spreadsheet, I shouldn't provide you with their home addresses. I'm bending the rules a lot because I trust you, and we need your help."

"You have my word." Peter gave a business card to Lee. "If you don't mind, just email the file and map to me. I'll start looking for correlations today, as soon as I receive the data summary."

"It will be in your inbox by the time you get back to Bend." Lee extended his hand to Peter. "Thank you again for your help."

Peter was deep in thought as he steered the Wraith south on Highway 26. Leaving Warm Springs behind, he crossed the Deschutes River, not paying attention to the black pickup stopped on a gravel turnout next to the river. It was a popular spot for anglers to leave their vehicles while they fished the river for several hundred yards in each direction. As the Wraith passed by, Peter glimpsed the man sitting behind the wheel, shaved head, sunglasses on. That brief glimpse reminded Peter of another face he'd seen, the man at the coffee shop a week and a half ago. Or was it simply a figment of his imagination?

It was a nice day for a drive—a beautiful spring day, rather cool but sunny and dry, not even a wisp of wind. He replayed the conversation in his mind. Dozens of questions demanding answers. *Is this how an epidemic starts?* He wondered.

As soon as he was back in his office, he planned to do some research on orchitis, focusing on known causes. Lee Moses had referred to the ailment as an inflammation, an infection, similar to the mumps and the flu. He knew that both those diseases were viral infections. Could that be what had stricken so many in Warm Springs? Or maybe the illness was caused by exposure to certain chemicals. Perhaps a reaction like an autoimmune disorder? After gaining a rudimentary knowledge, he would visit St. Charles Hospital tomorrow and try to speak with a physician to learn more. If he could identify likely causes, that would help with the data review and search for a pattern.

After clearing Redmond, the highway became two lanes in each direction. He was driving in the right lane staying at the posted speed limit. A few cars passed on the left.

Glancing at the rear-view mirror, Peter noticed a black pickup approaching quickly. But rather than moving to the left to go around the Wraith, it closed on his bumper. *Come on, buddy, the lane is open. Just go around like everyone else who thinks the speed limit is not fast enough.*

Peter maintained his speed, and after a minute the pickup darted into the left lane and accelerated. It pulled up abreast of the Rolls Royce and then slowed again, matching Peter's speed. There was no traffic within a mile in either direction.

Peter glanced to the side and saw the passenger window was down. The driver was bald and wearing dark glasses. For several seconds, the truck kept perfect pace with the Wraith. Peter turned his head again, waving the driver on. Then he saw the man raise a gun—a sawed-off shotgun. He held it one-handed, by the pistol grip, and swung the muzzle toward the open window. For an instant, Peter's mind registered the smile on the driver's face.

Instinct took over as Peter slammed on the brakes. The car rapidly decelerated and the pickup rocketed by as the driver fired. The shot missed the Wraith by inches, and Peter swerved to the gravel shoulder, sliding to a complete stop. The cloud of dust behind the car slowly dissipated. His heart was pounding, and he gripped the wheel so hard his knuckles popped. The pickup sped away too fast to make out the license plate.

Peter leaned back in the seat. Sweat dappled his forehead. He rolled the windows down, deeply breathing in the fresh air. Other cars zipped by as if nothing was out of the ordinary. He doubted there were any witnesses given that no other cars were close at the time.

He picked up his phone and dialed. "9-1-1. What is the nature of your emergency?" the feminine voice said.

"Someone just tried to kill me."

CHAPTER 10

BEND, OREGON
MARCH 14

THE 9-1-1 OPERATOR INSTRUCTED Peter to remain in his car on the shoulder of the road while she dispatched a sheriff patrol car. About ten minutes later, with blue and red lights flashing, the deputy pulled up and stopped behind Peter.

The uniformed sheriff's deputy introduced himself and took notes while Peter retold the attempted murder. Another fifteen minutes was consumed by the deputy taking photos and completing a cursory examination of the Rolls Royce. "I don't see any indication that your car was struck by a bullet or shot," he said.

"When I slammed on the brakes, he was taken by surprise. If he'd pull the trigger a second sooner, you'd be scraping my brains off the upholstery."

"You're pretty sure he fired a shotgun?"

"No doubt at all. Double barrel. Side by side. The barrels were short, and he held it one handed by a pistol grip."

"That's a lot of detail to capture."

"When you have a sawed-off shotgun pointed at your face from only a few feet away, you tend to take notice."

Skeptical, the deputy pressed. "You're sure it was a shotgun and not a pistol?"

Peter stared back in silence, irritation beginning to take hold.

"You know something about firearms?" the deputy asked.

Peter nodded.

"So you can tell me what I have holstered?"

Peter glanced to the deputies sidearm. "Glock," he said matter-of-factly. "Probably 9mm or .40 caliber."

The deputy raised his eyebrows; he'd thought he had him. "Yes, .40 caliber. Okay, so you know what you saw, I believe you. Can you give me anything on the driver?"

"No, just what I already told you. It happened so fast."

"Nothing on the truck?"

Peter shook his head. "Just that it was a black, full-size pickup. I'm sorry."

The deputy closed his notepad and returned his pen to a breast pocket. "Well, I'll be honest with you. There isn't much to go on. I'll write up the report and forward it to the DA, but it's unlikely an arrest will be made. Maybe if we get lucky and the guy is arrested for another crime, and says something during questioning, we might be able to tie him to you. But it's a long shot. This might have just been an extreme case of road rage."

"There was no one else on the road. He had the left lane all to himself. It's not like I was holding him up."

The deputy shrugged. "You'd be surprised at how the smallest thing can set off some guys. It's really hard to say."

"Can I go now?"

"Sure. Thank you for your statement. We know where to reach you if anything comes up, but I wouldn't expect much."

⊕

At least the questioning by the sheriff's deputy helped Peter to calm down. He drove the dozen miles to his condominium in the Old Mill District without any other incidents. He thought pretty hard about having a shot or two of Scotch, but then remembered the data that Lee Moses and Lucy had promised to email. Instead, he opted for a mug of strong coffee. A poor substitute, but the better choice under the circumstances. He needed to keep a rational mind.

He turned on his computer, and there it was, an email from the Warm Springs health clinic. It had the spreadsheet as an attached file. Lucy had also attached a digital map of Warm Springs that used two different colored icons to denote the locations where the patients lived and worked or attended school.

As he sipped the brew, he studied the map. There was nothing obvious, no patterns were unveiled to his eyes. The homes and apartments where the patients lived were scattered randomly across the city of Warm Springs, and several were in rural areas outside the city limits. The same was true for the work locations.

Peter opened a new window in his browser and pulled up a description of the city water system, such as it was. City water was limited to a small portion of central Warm Springs. Most residences and business operated on independent wells.

Striking out with the map, he turned to the spreadsheet. As before, he initially scanned the entries, looking for obvious commonality. There wasn't any. But then again, many of the cells were empty, especially regarding what the patients had consumed—food and drink—over the days prior to becoming ill. Five had consumed salmon, but did they all? Hopefully the answers would come from further questioning. And there was no data regarding the use of tobacco products, alcohol, or illegal drugs. *Could meth or some other drug be contaminated, and that's the cause?* As quickly as the thought came to mind, Peter began to discount it since two of the patients were school-aged boys. Although it was possible they were drug users, their young age made it less plausible.

One potentially important factor missing from the spreadsheet was who each patient had been in contact with. *Maybe they all contracted the illness from a common carrier?* Peter made a note to raise that question with Lee Moses and ask that this be included with the questions asked of the patients and their immediate family and close friends.

Peter's education in science had taught him that coincidence was rare, being simply a product of statistical probability. Almost always an event predictably followed a cause. In this case, he just needed to identify what the cause was. The medical treatment and cure—if a cure was known—would come from the medical community.

After a frustrating hour of pouring over the spreadsheet and digital map, Peter concluded he had gleaned all he could from the meager data. Shifting gears, he opened his browser and started searching orchitis, focusing on the symptoms and cause. As he researched, he took notes—painful inflammation of the testes… usually caused by a viral infection… although rare, most commonly occurs in post-pubescent males who have contracted mumps… not life-threatening… no cure… patients typically recover in one to two weeks.

Peter rubbed his temples. "I feel like a pre-med student cramming for a final," he mumbled. He decided that a walk and fresh air might help clear his thoughts. Pushing away from his desk, he called his canine companion. "Diesel." Startled from his slumber, the red pit bull rose to his feet and trotted to Peter's side. One ear was torn from a fight with another dog some time ago. It had healed well, but with half the ear missing it gave the pit bull a very distinctive appearance, not comical but certainly unusual. Years earlier, Peter had adopted the eight-month-old dog from the Central Oregon Humane Society. The puppy had been confiscated from a dog fighting ring. As Peter nursed the dog back to health, a deep trust and bond had developed between the two, to the point where they had become inseparable companions.

Since Peter's children were both grown and following their own lives, Diesel was a welcome companion. He passed a photo hanging on the wall in the entry. The image was of a young woman, her smile radiant. It was Maggie, his wife and mother of their children. When she died in a car accident years earlier, Peter felt his heart had died, too. Only recently had he been ready to date another woman. There was still distance between Peter and Kate, and she seemed to understand that his wounds had to heal before their relationship could have a chance to grow. At least for the moment, she was content with that.

"Let's get you leashed up," he said. Minutes later they were enjoying the pine-scented air as they walked along the sidewalk in the Old Mill District. They strolled past store windows displaying a range of upscale merchandise from apparel to lingerie to fine art. Amongst the retailers were many popular restaurants, including Anthony's, a favorite of Peter's.

Diesel kept his nose low to the ground for the most part, drawing in an unimaginable range of scents. Occasionally, he'd greet a passerby, wagging his tail in a steady beat as the visitor petted his blocky head.

After they'd completed the circuit around the shops, Peter led the way back to his condo. The sun was low, nearly touching the snow-crested Cascade Mountains to the west. And as the sun settled lower, so did the air temperature. In tandem, man and dog climbed the steps to the massive, solid-wood front door.

Across the street, wearing a black windbreaker and sunglasses, a stocky man with shaved head watched patiently.

CHAPTER 11

HE WAS STILL ANGRY over missing the opportunity on the highway. The shot was easy—a textbook example of a quick and certain kill. Even if by some miracle the buckshot didn't do the job, the resulting high-speed crash would have finished him.

He ran a hand across his smooth pate, the cool air becoming noticeable. He'd missed twice now. First, it was the poison. If the server at the coffee shop had been minding her own business, she would not have warned Peter Savage that his cappuccino was laced with something. He'd taken his time to study the mark and formulate a plan, considering the variables and refining his strategy to ensure success. It should have been a success, only it wasn't.

The shooting on the highway should have worked, too. All the conditions were right. If it wasn't for the sudden reaction of the mark, the shot would not have been blown. That was twice he'd failed—he wouldn't fail again. This was highly uncharacteristic. He was good at his profession.

At one time, he'd been a soldier in the U.S. Army. He'd completed two tours in Iraq and had grown tired of killing for a meager monthly salary. Recognizing he had a skill—one somewhat rare in the civilian sector—he left the military with an honorable discharge. After working in a paramilitary private security firm, and then for a year as a bodyguard, he stumbled upon an Internet chatroom that introduced the profession of hired killer. *Sounds exactly like what I was doing for the army,* he thought. After months of digging deeper and making anonymous connections through the dark web, he decided to apply his skills in the public sector.

The mark, or target, was most often a gang banger or small-time thug. When someone in a competing gang had reached the decision that the mark had to go, a contract was issued. The reason why was never disclosed, nor did it matter. What did matter was the payment. Ten thousand dollars seemed to be the going rate for the average murder-for-hire. Naturally, payment was always in cash. And with no taxes being withheld, and no taxable income reported, completing a few contracts a year was sufficient to pay for a rather comfortable lifestyle.

So when this contract popped up—five million dollars for proof of death—it immediately caught his attention. It was the kind of job he'd dreamed about, a payday big enough he could retire to somewhere with warm, sandy beaches, cold beer, and no extradition treaty with the U.S.

There was still time to salvage the operation and collect on the contract. But he had to act before someone else did. With the bounty so high, there would surely be others trying to beat him to the prize and collect the reward. And as he watched Peter Savage return to his home, a new plan was taking form.

The dog, that was the key. A quick surveillance of the condo showed it had no yard, which meant that Savage must walk his dog several times daily. It was still early evening, so he'd certainly take the dog out again before retiring for the night. That's when he'd strike—under cover of darkness and with the element of surprise. Death would come swiftly.

He was already imagining the possibilities he could realize with five million in cold, hard cash. He could buy a small, beach-front shack and fall into anonymity. Or maybe he'd buy a sailboat. That would offer greater freedom, and without a permanent address, and the ability to move easily from one tiny island to another, it would be impossible for anyone to track him down. That's assuming the authorities could successfully identify him as the killer. Unlikely, given that he had no connection to the mark, and would leave almost no evidence at the scene.

He'd killed before and was confident he would continue to escape scrutiny. The key was the lack of any connection to the mark. Law enforcement always looked first to friends, family, and acquaintances of the murder victim. This is where they usually found the killer. Without that connection, and with a dearth of physical evidence, the police just didn't have anything to work with. He'd murdered eleven people in different cities over two years, a respectable tally, and not even once had he been questioned by police.

With urgency in his step, he returned to his pickup parked nearby with a hundred other cars. He placed a brimmed black-felt hat on his head and then retrieved a semi-auto pistol from under the seat. With practiced moves, he threaded a suppressor onto the barrel. It would not truly silence a shot, but it attenuated the sound greatly. Most people would not recognize the report as a gunshot when he fired the weapon.

He also slipped on a knee-length duster, meticulously fabricated in waxed canvas and dyed black. The loose fit of the duster easily concealed the pistol stuck in his waistband at the center of his back. Properly equipped, he returned to the shadows between stores, but always maintained a clear view of the condominium.

The hours passed slowly, and he meandered from one vantage point to the next, never staying in one location long enough to attract attention. The sun had long set, revealing a beautiful, clear sky dotted with countless stars. The foot traffic thinned as the retail stores closed, leaving only a few restaurants open. Before long they would close too. He glanced at his watch—almost ten p.m. *Come on. You've gotta take the pooch out one more time before going to bed.* No sooner had he completed the thought when a crack of light shone around the front door.

Peter descended the steps to the sidewalk with Diesel by his side. In a matter of minutes, the contract would be fulfilled.

He watched as the two walked casually down the sidewalk on the far side of the street. He silently stepped from the shadows, matching Peter's pace but keeping a discrete distance. Now was not the time to become impatient. He reached to his back and clasped the pistol, stuffing it into a generous pocket in the duster.

They were alone. Far behind he heard the distant voices of people punctuated by laughter, probably a small group having enjoyed a fine dinner and plenty to drink. He picked up his pace.

Diesel was intently sniffing a particular spot on a small patch of grass. Beyond the grass was a parking lot, and off to the left more grass and then a belt of thick bushes that lined the edge of the Deschutes River. He walked closer, able to see the outline of Peter Savage, but the details of his face were obscured in the darkness. The conditions were perfect.

Peter was peering off in the distance, looking away from the approaching man. He was within ten yards when Diesel suddenly raised his head. "What is it boy?" Peter asked, his voice barely more than a whisper. Peter turned his head, attempting to see whatever had distracted his dog.

The bald man continued to advance, his pace perfectly normal, faster than a meandering gait but not at all rushed or threatening—just another person returning to the parking lot to drive home after an evening of shopping and dining.

At five yards, he removed the pistol, clutching it tight against his side. Although Peter saw the movement, he could not distinguish what the man was holding.

A deep, menacing growl rumbled from Diesel, whose eyes were locked on the approaching stranger. "Easy boy," Peter said, glancing first toward the pit bull and then at the man.

Suddenly, the figure stumbled and lurched forward. He seemed to be struggling to stay on his feet, when his torso contorted spasmodically as if he'd been slugged by a steel bar. He fell face-first to the concrete, the pistol pitching from his hand.

It all happened within two seconds, and it took Peter that long to realize the object that spilled from the man's grip was likely a gun. Still firmly holding Diesel's leash, Peter rushed to the fallen man. Even in the dim light he could see two glistening patches on his back, and a growing pool of black liquid spreading on the sidewalk from beneath his chest. He pressed a finger against the man's neck but could not find a pulse.

Diesel was growing increasingly distraught, whining and growling. Up close it was clear that a pistol with a silencer was resting next to the body. Peter knew well enough not to touch anything, and for the second time that day, he called 9-1-1.

It was only 110 yards from the edge of the river to the dead body of the would-be assassin—an easy shot for a trained marksman using a scoped rifle. The sniper was diligent and retrieved both cartridge cases so there would be no physical evidence for the police. Wearing a black neoprene dry suit to protect from the cold, snow-fed waters of the Deschutes River, the shooter quickly disassembled the rifle and packed the pieces into a case. She waded through the flowing water in a crouch to reduce her profile to nothing taller than the surrounding bushes and reeds, moving slowly to avoid splashing sounds. The sound of flowing water further helped to obscure her movements. After covering a little more than two hundred yards, she exited the water and returned to her pickup truck.

CHAPTER 12

PETER WAS CLEANING THE DISHES after cooking a hearty breakfast of sausage patties, country skillet potatoes, and scrambled eggs, when there was a knock at the door. He opened the door and was greeted by a middle-aged woman dressed in jeans, knit sweater, and neon green Oregon Duck sneakers. Her gray hair was cut short, exposing both ears. She was about four inches shy of Peter's height.

"Mr. Savage," she said. "Detective Ruth Colson. We've met before."

Peter rolled his eyes. "How could I forget?"

"May I come in? I have a few questions for you."

"Look, Detective. I told everything I know to another detective last night. A guy named…"

"MacRostie. You spoke with Detective MacRostie. He's a good cop, but he's never handled a murder investigation."

Peter opened the door and motioned with his hand for her to enter.

From the great room, the pit bull raised his head and issued a guttural growl at Colson. "Diesel, enough," Peter said, and his companion lowered his head again but kept his eyes locked on the suspicious visitor.

"Your dog still doesn't like me."

"Well, what can I say? He's a pretty good judge of character."

Colson faced Peter. "That investigation was eighteen months ago. I was only doing my job, following the trail of evidence wherever it led. I'm sorry for the trouble the department put you through."

"You mean for the trouble *you* put me through."

"Like I said, I was only doing my job. Besides, it all worked out. And in the end, you were exonerated."

"Yeah." Peter entered the kitchen and Colson followed. He poured a cup of coffee and offered one to the detective, which she declined. "So, what do you want to know that wasn't already covered late last night?"

"I understand you had an encounter with a crazy guy on the highway yesterday. The report filed by the sheriff department called it road rage. You think that driver could also be the one who was murdered last night?"

"Maybe. I only got a brief glimpse of the guy driving the black pickup. But he was bald, like the dead guy. Still, there are a lot of men with shaved heads."

"We impounded a black Dodge Ram pickup from the parking lot not far from the crime scene. Pulled a bunch of good prints from the truck, and we're running them now but expect a match with the victim. The vehicle is registered to a Darren Block. That name mean anything to you?"

Peter shook his head. "Never heard of him."

"Well, we also found a sawed-off shotgun under the seat."

"So, it is the same guy."

"Any idea why he was trying to kill you?"

"No. None at all. I don't know anyone named Darren Block. But…" Peter hesitated.

"Don't hold back on me. Any information could be of importance, no matter how insignificant it may seem."

"Okay. You'll probably think I'm paranoid, but someone apparently put some powdery substance in my cappuccino a little over a week ago. The barista called my attention to it, and I didn't drink it. The guy dashed out of the coffee shop, and I didn't really notice his face. But he was bald and about the same height as this guy, Darren Block."

"We won't get any evidence now. You should have reported it at the time."

"Wouldn't have mattered. The drink was poured out."

"Well, assuming that it was Block who laced your drink, and assuming it was meant to kill you, any idea why he had it in for you?"

Peter shook his head.

Colson moved on. "Right. For now, we'll shelve that. Has anyone new entered your life in the past six months or so? Girlfriend, business associates, long lost high school or college buddies?"

"No. I'm still seeing Kate. My kids are both adults and living their own lives. Nothing significant on the business front. Still working with the same people in the defense department."

"So your personal life is just chugging along on autopilot."

"You make it sound so banal."

"I'm not judging." Colson folded her arms and sighed. "The Oregon State Police will examine the 9mm pistol Block was carrying. But I doubt they'll find any records of value. If you ask me, he was about to put some hollow points in you when he was shot dead."

Peter sipped his coffee. "This whole thing just doesn't make any sense."

"I agree. I'm struggling with it, too. That's why I wanted to talk with you myself."

"I've told you all I know."

"I probably shouldn't share this information with you," Colson said. She looked at Peter, considering her options. "Oh, what the hell. Keep this confidential. Block was killed from two gunshot wounds. Looks like a small caliber round, and probably high velocity. The exit wounds were massive. Once the autopsy is completed and the crime lab techs have finished their analysis, we'll be certain. But assuming he was shot by a rifle—it must have been suppressed."

"I didn't hear anything that sounded like a normal rifle report," Peter said.

"MacRostie said you thought you heard what could be a muffled shot."

"That's true, but I can't swear to it. Diesel was growling at the guy and I was focused on getting him to calm down. Then it looked like he pulled something from a pocket in his overcoat. To tell you the truth, I'm really not certain what was going on other than those facts. When Diesel gets worked up like that, he always has a good reason."

"Trouble seems to follow you, Mr. Savage. Any idea why someone would want you dead?"

"Presently? No."

"Presently? What the hell does that mean?"

"It means now."

"Don't get smart with me, mister." Colson was pointing her finger at Peter.

"I simply answered your question. There isn't a lot more I can tell you. But as you know, eighteen months ago some really bad people wanted to kill me."

"And do you have any reason to believe that interest may have been rekindled?"

Peter shook his head.

"So, if no one wants to kill you, why was Block trying so hard to do just that?"

"Good question, Detective. I'm sure you'll figure it out. That's why you get paid the big bucks."

Colson looked at Peter for an uncomfortable moment. "You have an interesting history, Mr. Savage. A history that is still classified and even I can't get a complete explanation about what happened in the Cascade Mountains a year and a half ago."

Peter's eyes narrowed, but he didn't comment.

"But I have to wonder," she continued, "if that Israeli woman you were involved with… what was her name?"

"Nadya Wheeler. And I wasn't *involved* with her."

"That's right. Ms. Wheeler. I have to wonder if Ms. Wheeler is somehow connected to this murder and the attempt on your life yesterday. After all, she was trying to kill you back then, right?"

"You know how that came out—and I'm still alive."

"Right. But she disappeared. Any idea where she might be?"

"No idea at all. We didn't exactly stay in touch."

"Not even a Christmas card?"

"Not even," Peter replied with an icy glare.

"Did you read about that triple homicide near La Pine close to two weeks ago?"

Peter nodded.

"On one of the weapons recovered from the crime scene we found two *very* interesting prints. Index finger and thumb print—a perfect match to Nadya Wheeler. So, you're sure you haven't had any contact with her?"

Peter was dumbfounded. He seldom thought of the Israeli-trained assassin, but when he did, he'd imagined she was living in self-imposed exile in some third-world country. If Detective Colson was right, she was in central Oregon, and not far away at all. "Doesn't matter how many times you ask me, my reply won't change."

"I see. Just to be clear, let me recap for you—you know, in case you missed some of the key points. We have a corpse—believed to be Darren Block—who, based on your account, attempted to kill you at least once, and very likely twice. In the same day, no less. And if Block also doctored your coffee with poison a week ago, then we're up to three attempts. That's a lot, so I'd say he was motivated. And if that's not unusual enough, the deceased became that way because an unknown assailant shot him, probably from a distance, just before he would have successfully completed attempt number three on your life." She paused long enough to be sure the facts had registered with Peter before continuing. "So, what is my working hypothesis?"

"What do you mean?"

"Come on. You're a very intelligent man. You tell me."

With all that had transpired over the last twenty-four hours, Peter hadn't really considered this question. His mind had been consumed with trying to identify the cause of the outbreak at Warm Springs, then the emotional shock of nearly being shot on the drive home, and finally the late-night questioning by Detective MacRostie about the murder of Darren Block right in front of his eyes.

"It's pretty clear that Block was trying to kill me. The motive remains unknown. Fortunately, someone intervened and killed Block before he murdered me. If you ask me, I'd say the mystery shooter is a good Samaritan."

Colson allowed a slight grin to crack her normally terse expression. "Bullshit. You know as well as I do that 'good Samaritans' do not skulk around at night with a suppressed rifle looking for a bad guy to take out. No, we are looking for a murder suspect. The only question is, why? Obviously, the shooter could have just as easily shot you. But they didn't. So why would a skilled shooter just happen to be at the right place and time, with the right weapon, to save your life?"

Peter looked at Colson, dumbfounded. "I don't know."

"You're sure?"

Peter nodded.

"Well, if you think of anything, call me." She placed her business card on the counter and walked to the door. She grasped the handle, then turned back to face Peter. "Oh, one more thing. It's probably a good idea to be extra careful until we figure out exactly what's going on."

"Whoa, check this out." Travis was sitting at a card table in what would have normally passed for the dining area of the double-wide trailer. He had been scrolling through a chat room when he came across a five million dollar contract. Tommy read the details over his shoulder and let out a whistle.

"Shit. This dude must have really pissed off someone. Five million. Man, I could retire on that."

"Yeah, no shit. Hey, look." Travis pointed with his finger. "It says the guy lives in Bend. His name is Peter Savage."

Travis and Tommy developed a friendship attending high school in the small city of Prineville, a community northeast of Bend. With a population of less than ten thousand and an economy based largely in ranching and timber, most residents struggled to earn a decent living. For many adults, the allure of illicit means of making money was strong. The temptation and promise of riches proved too much for Travis and Tommy—both dropping out of high school to sell methamphetamine.

Travis and Tommy had a steady clientel. With a reliable supplier, the cash earnings were good, enough to pay for food, plenty of alcohol, two used cars, and a run-down doublewide trailer on an acre of land just outside of Warm Springs, yet still within the boundary of the reservation. It was a good location, not under the county or state jurisdiction. The tribal police had plenty to keep busy, so chasing after one of many small-time drug dealers never seemed to rise high enough on their priority list to cause problems for Travis and Tommy.

All things considered, life seemed okay. But both men knew there was no future. They were each in their mid twenties, with no high school diploma, no special tradecraft, and selling meth. Even these two could see that unless they changed their lives dramatically, they would be unlikely to live past the age of thirty as free men. If the law didn't catch up with them, a rival dealer or pissed off addict would bring a violent end to their lives.

Candice, Tommy's live-in girlfriend, had joined them, leaning her head on Tommy's shoulder as she also read the text.

Travis read out loud. "Payable by wire transfer upon proof of death." He pointed again with his finger. "Here's his address, and it says he drives a Rolls Royce!"

"The dude must be wealthy," Tommy said.

Candice perked up. "Hey, do you suppose that whoever takes him out can also keep his car? It would be, you know, like a bonus or something."

"Is this for real?" Tommy asked.

Travis shrugged. "Well, sure. This chat group has postings like this all the time. But I've never seen a contract this large. Usually it's only ten grand or so."

"What are you saying Travis?" Candice said. "I mean, you're not out doing murder-for-hire at night or something, are you? You're beginning to freak me out."

Travis laughed. He liked to tease her… it was so easy.

She slapped him on the shoulder.

"Hey, listen," Tommy said. "I've got an idea. Why don't we do it."

"Do what?" Travis turned toward his partner. "You mean

kill this dude?"

"Yeah, why not?" Tommy looked at Candice. "It's our chance to really score."

"You don't know how to kill someone," Travis said scornfully.

"Bullshit. I've shot plenty of deer and elk. More than you have. What's the difference?"

"Duh." Travis touched his index finger to the side of his head and looked squarely at Tommy. "I'll tell you what the difference is, genius. It's not against the law to shoot deer. You kill someone, and the police won't stop looking for you."

Tommy shrugged. "So, we don't leave any evidence. Hey, it's not like we're running a legit business now, you know."

Travis shook his head and turned away from his friend. "You can count me out."

"Fine, that means you don't get any of the money."

"Yeah, I do. Call it a finder's fee."

"A finder's fee?"

"That's right. You wouldn't know anything about this if I didn't find this information and share it with you."

Tommy thought for a moment. It sort of made sense. He'd heard of finder's fees before, usually when one dealer shared the name of a supplier to another dealer. "And how much is your finder's fee?"

"One million. That leaves four million for you."

"One million!" Tommy exclaimed. "That's almost a third. You're not doing nothin!"

Candice wrapped her arm around Tommy. "It's 20 percent baby, and that leaves 80 percent for us."

"You're pretty sharp with the math, Candy," Travis said.

The comment earned him another slap on the shoulder. "Stop calling me that! You make it sound like I'm a cheap hooker."

"I never said you were cheap."

She slapped him again, this time harder.

CHAPTER 13

SHORTLY AFTER DETECTIVE COLSON left, Peter slipped on a jacket and drove across Bend to St. Charles Hospital. He approached the visitor information desk and asked for the office of Dr. Scott Hale.

"Please have a seat in the lobby, and I'll page him," the receptionist said.

The lobby was a large, open room with a wall of glass that allowed ample natural light to flood the space. A wide staircase led to the second floor and cafeteria. The furnishings of supple chairs and sofas were grouped in cozy clusters, separated from each other to provide for private conversations. As Peter meandered toward a chair, he saw a white-jacketed physician speaking in hushed tones with a middle-aged couple. Judging by the smile on both faces, he concluded the news was good.

Peter eased his frame into the chair and mentally reviewed what he knew about orchitis, prioritizing his questions. After a few minutes, a bespectacled man with dark brown hair, graying at the temples, approached. He was wearing a white coat and had a stethoscope draped around his neck.

"Mr. Savage?" he said.

Peter rose and extended his hand. "Yes, Peter Savage."

"Pleased to meet you. I'm Scott Hale. I understand you have some questions about inflammations of the lymphatic system, in particular the testes?"

"Thank you for taking time to meet with me. When I called the hospital yesterday, they said you might be the best person to talk to. I'm helping a friend trying to identify the cause of a number of cases reported recently in Warm Springs. Have you heard about it?"

Hale shook his head.

"Fifteen cases as of yesterday. The director of the health clinic there has not been getting any help from the CDC, and the Oregon Health Authority says the reservation is out of their jurisdiction."

"I see," Hale said, a look of impatience beginning to show.

"I understand that orchitis may be a side effect of the mumps," Peter said, picking up the pace. "But these patients have been vaccinated, so it would seem that mumps is an unlikely cause. What other causes should we be looking for?"

Hale rubbed his chin before replying. "Well, generally speaking, any inflammation of the lymphatic system could result in localized infection of the testicles. But it is rather rare. I'd have to do some research to give you a better answer."

"I understand. Let me rephrase the question. Are we looking for bacterial and viral agents, or just viruses?"

"Standard practice is to run cultures for both."

"My understanding is that the clinic is doing just that, but the results are not available yet."

"It can take a couple days. But my hunch is that you're dealing with a virus."

"What about a reaction to chemicals or foods? Could that result in the reported symptoms?"

"No, not likely," Hale said, and he shook his head. "I'm sorry I can't offer more specific help." He stood, and Peter did, too.

"One more question," Peter said. "Other than the immediate symptoms, are there any lingering effects?"

"Yes. Sterility is the most severe. In cases involving postpubescent men and adults, the rate may be alarming."

"How high would you think?" Peter pressed.

"Difficult to say, since the contagion has yet to be isolated and identified."

"Just a rough estimate—would you think 10 to 20 percent?"

"Oh no, not at all. I wouldn't be surprised if it's 50 percent or more. Good luck with your investigation," Hale said, and he turned and walked away.

As his words sunk in, a terrifying thought entered Peter's mind. Most of the patients were adults.

As he made his way back to the Wraith, Peter dialed Lee Moses. "I think we need to talk in person. This may be more serious than I had initially thought. I need to make a quick stop at my home and then I'm on my way to the clinic. Should be there in a little over an hour."

"Okay, Peter. I'll be waiting for you."

Peter parked in front of his condo and put Diesel on a leash. The pit bull loved to ride, and he readily jumped into the sedan. He preferred to ride shotgun—sitting upright and watching the scenery pass by.

The traffic was light, and Peter made good time, arriving at the Warm Springs clinic right on schedule. "Sorry buddy. I have to leave you here, but I won't be long." He rolled the windows down an inch to allow for some fresh air. Fortunately, the temperature was still cool, and overheating was not a concern.

Lee met Peter just inside the door. "You sounded concerned over the phone. What did you learn from the doctor?"

"Not as much as I'd hoped. But this is more than just a painful, short-term infection. It's potentially much more serious."

"Oh? What did the doctor say?"

"He explained that once a male has gone through puberty, orchitis often results in sterility."

Lee's eyes widened. "That's bad. Most of our patients are young men."

"I know," Peter replied. "I may have an idea to help get the resources here that you need. But first, tell me, how are your patients doing?"

"As well as can be expected," Lee said. "We got ten more last night and this morning."

"Ten? That's not good."

"I agree. At this rate, we could have a big problem on our hands. I called the CDC again this morning."

"What did they say?"

"Same as before. Wait a few weeks. They think it is a minor bump in the statistics, not a true outbreak. They think it is the mumps, and there is no reason to be concerned because of mass-scale vaccinations."

"I hope they're right," Peter said.

"No, I don't think so. All but one of the afflicted patients was vaccinated for the mumps as a child. When I told this to the person at the CDC, they said it was probably a weak vaccine. It's happened before, they said. They do not want to help."

"And by the time they change their minds, there will be a lot more who have contracted the disease. How are the interviews of the patients and their close family members progressing?"

"We have a lot more data. Thought you'd be interested in seeing it."

"Yes, of course."

Lee led Peter to the small office they shared the previous day. Lucy was sitting at one of the desks, inputting data into the spreadsheet. The number of columns had grown considerably over what it was the previous day. Peter looked over her shoulder, reading the pertinent information.

"I don't see any correlation with the food that was eaten, or the places the victims visited during the days leading up to signs of infection." Peter leaned in closer. "There has to be something we're not seeing. Maybe the pathogen is carried in the air or water?"

Lee shrugged. "If that was the case, I would expect to see many more cases as the entire population would have been exposed."

Peter worked his jaw. "I don't know what more help I can offer with interpreting this data. I think it's time we get help from the experts."

"You mean the CDC? I already explained that they have refused my requests. They don't see this as a significant occurrence, or a dangerous illness."

"Then it's time we change their perception."

"You have a plan?"

Peter nodded. "I do. Politicians and government bureaucrats hate bad press. So, we're going to the media. We're going to tell the press how you have a growing outbreak here on the Warm Springs Reservation, that you've asked for help, and have been denied. It wouldn't hurt to insinuate that Native Americans are once again being discriminated against by the federal government. Hell, call it racist—that could draw headline coverage. With a little bit of luck, the story will be picked up nationally."

A grin spread across Lee's face. "I like your suggestion. I will need your help though to elevate the importance of our problem so the Bend newspaper and TV channel will come out here. We are a long way from Bend."

"Leave that to me. And I'll also call my congressman and senator. I'll point out that this is an easy task—all they need to do is say a word or two to the director at the CDC. Won't cost any political capital, and they can come out looking like a hero to the underdog. It's all about image. Plus, I'll remind them I've donated to their campaigns."

"You will do that?"

Peter placed his hand on Lee's shoulder. "I told you I would help."

Lee's eyes glistened. "My people could have benefitted from a few friends like you 150 years ago."

CHAPTER 14

AFTER WALKING DIESEL AROUND the clinic parking lot, Peter started the return drive to Bend. He was already thinking about how to pitch the story to the *Bend Bulletin* newspaper and local TV news editor. He planned to portray the people of Warm Springs as a disadvantaged population being ignored by the government in time of genuine need. He would suggest that if the population of Bend or Portland was suffering from this mysterious illness, the state and federal governments would be racing to find the cause and deploy a cure. While avoiding raising allegations of outright racism, the insinuation would be impossible to miss.

He eased the brakes as he approached a stop sign in a residential area only a quarter mile from the clinic. As usual, Diesel was sitting upright in the passenger seat. Suddenly, the Rolls Royce lurched forward and there was a loud bang and crunch of folding sheet metal. Peter and Diesel were both pushed against the seat back. The canine stumbled to regain his balance.

Peter recognized the sound and feel of a collision. His eyes immediately went to the rearview mirror. A full-sized maroon-red sedan filled the view.

Knowing the drill, he opened the glove box and removed the registration and proof of insurance. Diesel was agitated, his head turning in every direction, his pupils dilated, his muscles taut. "Easy boy. Just a fender bender."

Peter turned to his left to open the door. He was startled to see a young man standing there. He was leaning over, seeming to peer inside the Wraith. Then his face split into a grin. He moved his right hand, which had been behind his back, forward. In his grip was a large revolver.

Before the gun was raised level with the window, Peter shoved his weight forcefully into the car door. It flew open, smashing into the man's arm and body, forcing the gun down. The weapon discharged into the pavement. Peter continued his assault, launching out of the car and tackling the man to the ground. Diesel was right behind him.

"Tommy!" Candice shouted, running to help her boyfriend. She grabbed hold of Peter by the shoulders, tugging to pull him off Tommy. She managed to pull him off balance just enough that Tommy was able to move the gun toward his target.

Diesel was snarling and growling. He lunged and latched his jaws onto Tommy's gun hand. He bit down hard, drawing blood from several deep punctures.

"Ahhh! Get him off me!"

Candice was still pulling on Peter. Seeing that Diesel had restrained the shooter's ability to aim and fire, Peter relented his resistance. The sudden elimination of opposing force placed Candice off balance, and she tumbled back into the open car door. Peter followed her and pivoted on his left foot. He clenched his fingers into a hard fist and swung, connecting with her mouth and nose. Her head snapped backwards and she drooped to the pavement, blood oozing from her lips and nose.

With a firm grip on the shooter's wrist and hand, Diesel was shaking his head and tugging backward with all his considerable strength. Tommy was no match. His right arm was fully extended above his head while his left hand was held close to his chest for fear of it also being mauled. He continued to scream in agony.

With the woman incapacitated, Peter placed his shoe on the barrel of the revolver, pinning it and Tommy's clenched hand to the tarmac. "Diesel, enough!"

Hesitatingly, the canine released his bite, but stared at the hand and arm as if daring it to move.

"I give up," Tommy said. "Just keep your dog away from me." He opened his grip, allowing Peter to pick up the gun.

"Turn over. On your stomach. Hands stretched out to either side," Peter ordered. Candice moaned and started to stand. "You too. Over here next to your boyfriend. Face down, arms out to the side."

Still groggy, she complied without uttering a word.

Peter eased back to the open door without taking his eyes off the pair. For his part, Diesel remained on guard only inches from the bleeding bite wound. Peter picked up his phone from a center console tray and dialed.

"Lee, I need you to do something for me."

"Sure. What can I do?"

"Do you know someone in the Tribal Police Department?"

Lee hesitated. "Are you in trouble?"

"Not anymore. But I have a situation. And I think it will go better if you call someone you know."

"I'll call Captain Meadows right now. What should I tell him?"

"A couple of punks tried to kill me."

"Are you okay? Where are you?"

Peter repeated the names on the street signs to Lee. "I've apprehended both of them—a young man and woman. But better tell the Captain to get over here quickly, before my dog decides to start chewing on them again."

After he ended the call, Peter addressed his two prisoners. "Why did you try to kill me?"

"Piss off. I'm not talking to you," Tommy said.

"Suit yourself." Peter examined the revolver, a Smith & Wesson model 66, .357 magnum. "Nice gun you have here. High end. You earn enough to afford this?"

No answer.

"Yep, I thought so. Okay, so you stole it. You know, this doesn't look good for either of you."

"Like Tommy says, got nothing to say to you mister. Tommy was just defending himself after your dog attacked him." Candice said smugly. She figured if she and Tommy told the same story, there would be enough doubt that charges wouldn't stick. Of course, there was the stolen gun, but that could be explained away as a private purchase at a yard sale. After all, Tommy had no way of knowing if the gun was stolen when he bought it.

"Yeah, that's right," Tommy said, catching on.

"Diesel." The pit bull locked eyes with Peter. "Protect." Diesel emitted a low rumbling growl that built in intensity until his lips parted, showing glistening ivory canines.

"Keep your dog away!" Tommy said in terror.

"Don't so much as move your pinky, or he'll chew your arm to the bone."

"I'm not moving! Just call him off!"

"Tell me what I want to know, and I'll put the dog in the car," Peter said calmly.

Diesel was growling loudly, saliva dripping from his lips.

With his face sideways on the ground, Tommy was looking right at the dog, his face only two feet away.

"Okay! I'll answer your questions! Just put the dog away."

"Diesel. Come." Peter patted his thigh and his canine companion bounded into the Rolls Royce. As soon as Peter shut the door, Tommy let out a sigh of relief.

"Now, why did you try to kill me?"

"The contract. Travis found it."

Peter thought for a moment, trying to make sense of the cryptic reply.

"There's a contract on my life?"

Candice chuckled. "Surpri-ise."

"Five million dollars, man. Travis wants one million as a finder's fee because he showed me the chat room message."

In the distance, sirens blared. The police were getting close, probably less than a minute away.

"Travis is a friend?"

"He's my business partner."

"Shut up, you idiot," Candice said.

"How did you find me? You two don't strike me as super sleuths."

"We just waited outside your condominium until you drove off. Your car is pretty distinctive, wasn't hard to follow. I figured we'd take you down somewhere in Bend. If I'd known you were planning to drive all this way, I'd have put more gas in my car. I nearly ran out."

"So, you and your partner, Travis, run a business. You carry a stolen pistol that you tried to shoot me with so you can collect on a contract listed in a chat room." Peter smirked. "I'm not a detective, but my educated guess is that your business is selling drugs."

"So what?"

"Keep your mouth shut, Tommy!"

The sirens were very loud, and Peter saw two patrol cars turn the corner a block away. "Doesn't matter. You can talk to the police."

A rugged-looking man in police uniform but wearing a black Stetson closed the distance to Peter, completely ignoring the man and woman lying on the roadway. "You Peter Savage?" he said.

"Yes." Peter handed over the revolver, the cylinder flipped open, holding it by a looped index finger under the top strap so there would no misunderstanding.

"Lee Moses called me. He said you have a habit of getting into trouble." Captain Meadows took in the scene. "I'd say he's right."

CHAPTER 15

AFTER DRIVING SOUTH BACK to his condo in Bend, Peter took Diesel on a long walk along the Deschutes River. He needed to clear his head, plus he owed Diesel—again. The sun was low on the horizon, and the air temperature was rather cool, but it didn't bother Diesel. He was in his element, sticking his nose into clumps of grass and under bushes, drawing in the earthy scents.

The fresh air and exercise were helping Peter to shake off the adrenaline hangover from the attack only hours earlier. The revelation that there was a contract out on his life was still sinking in. He found himself looking a bit more closely at everyone he passed. *This is nuts*, he thought. *I won't live my life in constant fear.*

He turned Diesel around and walked back to his condo. Still lacking an appetite, he decided to forgo cooking a meal and opted for a glass of Oban single malt Scotch instead.

He settled into an oversized leather chair in front of the

large stone fireplace in the great room. The room was rustic and yet refined, with polished wood flooring, a floor-to-ceiling bookcase on the wall opposite the fireplace, and French doors opening onto a deck overlooking the retail shops of the Old Mill District. Peter cradled the shot glass in his hand, warming the whiskey and occasionally drawing in the aroma.

He sat quietly in contemplation, Diesel lying at his feet. He finished the Scotch and poured a second. The alcohol took the edge off his nerves, and he found his thoughts to be clearer. Or maybe his judgment was just impaired? Whatever the reason, he came to the conclusion that the cause of his current predicament was rooted in the electronic posting of the contract. And for any computer-related problems, he knew exactly who to call.

"Hey Gary, how are you?" It was Gary Porter, Peter's best friend. They had first met during high school in Sacramento, California, and soon developed a brotherly bond. Matching Peter's height, and with an athletic physique and wavy blond hair, Gary looked like the stereotypical surfer dude. But looks were deceiving, and beneath that carefree appearance was a software genius. Despite Gary's Bohemian attitude, which often provided unanticipated entertainment, Peter knew he could trust Gary with his life. And indeed, he had.

"Oka-ay... You're not going to tell me something to change that, are you?"

"Buddy, why are you so suspicious?"

"Let me see... because whenever I get involved in some misadventure with you, there are always complications. You nearly got me killed in the Sudan!"

"Yeah, but I didn't. In fact, I saved your life."

"That's not the version I remember. Anyway, what's up?"

"I need your help. A problem that requires your considerable computer skills." Gary ran a successful computer security firm out of the gold country in northern California. His list of customers included many Fortune 500 companies as well as a long list of international clients.

"You're flattering me. That's not a good sign. Anyway, go ahead. Tell me more."

"It appears there may be a contract out on me," Peter explained.

"You mean someone like a Mafia boss has put the word out that he'll pay whoever shoots you? I've never been involved in anything like this before. Sounds kinda cool."

"Not from my perspective. Not even remotely cool."

"Oh, yeah. I guess not. So, what can I do?"

"For starters, I hope you can help dig up some clues on who issued the contract, assuming that part is true." Peter proceeded to update his friend on the two amateur assassins in Warm Springs and what the man, Tommy, had said. He also told Gary about Darren Block and his timely demise at the hands of a mysterious guardian angel.

"Wow," Gary said after Peter finished. "I guess you're living that ancient Chinese curse."

"And which one is that?"

"I think it goes something like, 'may you live an interesting life.'"

"Well, it's not my choice. Do you think you can you help me?"

Gary started rattling off a plan of action. "Most likely the chat room those two mentioned is accessible only through the dark web. I can start there, using a targeted search bot and the few leads you've provided to narrow down the possibilities. I'd be surprised if there are many hits. From there, I can access the IP address of the message originator. If we're lucky, they'll not have bounced the message through too many hubs. Assuming that's the case, I can work back to the source. And that's where

I get off the bus."

"If you can do all that, I'll be indebted to you."

"Yeah sure, I'll put it on your tab. So, tell me, assuming I can get the address of the originator, what are you going to do?"

Peter hesitated, and when he spoke his voice was steady, with a hard edge. "Exactly what I have to do."

"Ehhh. Wrong answer. Listen buddy. I know what you're planning by the tone of your voice. The right answer is 'call the police'. Now, repeat after me and say 'I will call the police'. Don't go Rambo on me. That doesn't work out well."

"It's always worked out fine for me, just not so well for the bad guys."

"Peter, listen to me. I'm serious. If there really is a contract on your life, then we're talking about professional killers. You'll be in way over your head."

"You're not keeping score Gary. The way I see it, I'm ahead in this game, two to nothing."

"Maybe, but the game isn't over. And let's not even think about what might happen in sudden-death overtime."

Peter didn't take comfort in the ominous meaning of his friend's observation. But before he could offer a comeback, Gary continued. "Have you told Kate?"

She and Peter had been dating on and off for the past eighteen months. He didn't like the term 'girlfriend', since Kate was a vibrant and intelligent woman, not a girl. Many years his junior, they'd met under difficult conditions when Kate's roommate was murdered. There were times when Peter wondered if the only bond they truly shared was the grief over the loss of a loved one—for Peter it was his wife, for Kate it was a dear friend.

"And exactly what am I supposed to tell her?"

"Oh… I don't know… maybe just that there are guys running around trying to kill you?"

"No, that would only cause her to needlessly worry. I'm not going to put her through that."

"*Needlessly!* Are you listening to yourself? You just told me that you have reason, good reason, to believe there is a contract out on your life!"

"What could she do if I did tell her?"

The line went silent for several seconds. "I suppose you're right," Gary conceded.

"Look, that's why I need your help. Until we find out who issued the contract and stop him, I'll keep some distance from Kate. For her own safety."

"I still think you should tell her. And it could be a 'her'."

"What?"

"You said 'him'. That the contract was issued by a man. It could be a woman, you know. If my memory serves me correctly, when you go Rambo, you pretty much piss off everyone in your way."

Despite the morbid subject of their conversation, Peter couldn't hold back a slight smile. He had been through a lot of pain and suffering with Gary, and some really bad people had been killed. Yet Gary was still always there for him. Peter knew that if he was on his deathbed, and his friend could trade places, he would do so in a heartbeat.

And the feeling was mutual.

CHAPTER 16

DARNELL PRICE SAT AT HIS DESK at Cascade Aqua Company, scrolling through the local news. He started with the Oregon Public Radio news feed, then checked the *Bend Bulletin* and Bend TV news channel. "Bingo!" he said, although there was no one in his office to hear.

As he read, his mind quickly cataloged the pertinent facts. *Twenty-five patients as of two days ago. All showing symptoms of orchitis, a painful inflammation of the testes. No response from the CDC or the Oregon Health Authority. Experts are viewing the outbreak as a weak form of the mumps, most likely very localized. Bend resident and businessman, Peter Savage, condemns the lack of action by the CDC as yet another example of the federal government discriminating against Native Americans through neglect. A similar outbreak in Bend or Portland, he asserted, would bring an immediate response from state and federal Agencies.*

Price leaned back in his chair. *Peter Savage. This man*

could cause problems. He dialed his phone. "Corbett," the voice replied.

"Did you see the news?"

"Yes. Our plan worked. The contagion has performed exactly as expected."

"We may have a problem. Someone is advocating for the people of Warm Springs."

"We discussed this possibility," Corbett said. "The reservation offered both benefits and risks as a test population. You'll recall that you made the decision to proceed over my warnings."

"You wanted to target a homeless population. We'd never have captured the results if we'd done that. Homeless people don't go to the doctor. And if they sought emergency care, it would have never captured any media attention."

"I thought you wanted to run the test at Warm Springs exactly because few would care, being predominantly a Native American population," Corbett countered.

"I stand by my reasoning. And I was right. The virus has raged unchecked for two weeks. Because the patients sought medical care, we have access to the data, albeit a limited data set. We'd never have had this opportunity anywhere else. If we'd selected a mainstream test population, the Oregon Health Authority and CDC would have descended upon the outbreak within forty-eight hours. The reservation, on the other hand, is a sovereign nation, outside state jurisdiction and too far away from Atlanta, or Washington D.C., for anyone to care. If it wasn't for this Peter Savage drawing attention, I doubt the media would have even picked up the story."

Corbett couldn't care less about the politics. As the Director of Security at Utopian-Bio, his concerns were more immediate. He decided to move on. "What are you suggesting I do?"

"Nothing, specifically. What is the status of the culture?"

"Utopian-Bio has designated it an experimental contagion. As a result, access is restricted. My authorization is required before anyone can withdraw samples."

"And you will deny such authorization."

"Of course. We can replicate the virus in 2-kilogram batches within seventy-two hours of notice. It can be stored indefinitely as a dry powder under refrigeration between 5 and 15 degrees Celsius."

"Have your scientists determined the virus's lifetime in water?"

"Not exactly, but we know it's at least several weeks," Corbett replied.

"All we need is a month. That's plenty of time to expose a large population center."

"My understanding is that the experiments are in progress and will continue as long as the results remain encouraging. So far, the virus appears to be very stable in water at temperatures less than 20 degrees Celsius."

"Excellent. It sounds like Dr. Ming's scientists have achieved a remarkable breakthrough. I will let you know when to provide a dosing sample again, although that may not be necessary." Price ended the call.

The pieces were falling into place. And soon, he would implement the final phase to save humankind from itself.

Peter recognized the voice right away as Lee Moses. "Well, my friend, you really know how to poke a stick into a hornet's nest."

"Oh?"

"I just had a long conversation with the CDC—a Ms. Julia Zhong. She made it clear she was reaching out based on recommendations from higher up. She didn't sound at all regretful that my prior phone calls had been disregarded."

"That's all well and good, but what really matters is the action they take going forward. What did she commit to do?"

"She'll be on a flight today to Portland, then by car to Warm Springs. I gave her the names of a couple hotels. She's bringing along an investigation team. I don't know how many. Guess we'll find out when she arrives. She said she would call me tonight when she gets to the hotel."

"That's great news. Are you ready?"

"Yes. Lucy has compiled all the data, including the latest results from the interviews my team has conducted of the patients and their close family and friends. It's everything we have. I hope it's a good starting point."

"Look. You've done everything you can do to protect your people. Every investigation starts with the facts. Where it goes from there—well, who knows? But you should feel good. You did the right thing."

"Peter Savage, you are a true friend to my people. We are indebted to you."

"Ah, forget it. When someone asks for help, you do what you can. But I am curious. Have you heard anything from Captain Meadows about the two people who attacked me?"

"Oh, yes. I spoke with the captain this morning. He said that the young man, Tommy, is a suspected drug dealer. He and his friend Travis have been 'persons of interest' with the Tribal Police for close to a year. They are searching their home and hope to gain useful evidence for the prosecution."

"Did Captain Meadows share anything about a contract on my life?"

"No," Lee said. After a pause he added, "Is that what prompted those two to try to kill you?"

"That's what Tommy said. Supposedly something they read in a chat room. Look, if there is anything suggestive of this from their computer, please let me know. I understand it may be a

breach of procedure, and I'll be discrete with any information you can share. But if there is any truth to this…"

"Then you must know," Lee said. "I pledge this to you."

"Thank you, Lee."

"In the meantime, may I make a suggestion?"

"Of course."

"Carry a gun. I've read about you. And I know you can use one."

"You know too much about my history, but that's not me. I'm not looking for a fight. I don't want to hurt others."

"Sometimes, it's not our choice. Throughout our history, my people only wanted to live in harmony with Nature. Harvest only what we needed to survive, no more. Then, the White Man came to our land. He always wanted more. Whatever we freely gave or surrendered, it was never enough. Eventually, we resisted and fought back. Not because we wanted to, but because we were forced to do so."

"This is not a life I choose. I never forget the faces."

"You mean of those you have killed?"

"They're burned into my memory." Peter paused. "At night, I see them."

"You do what you must, just as my ancestors did. Choice is a luxury reserved for only a few. And that short list does not include you and me."

CHAPTER 17

THE THREE-PERSON TEAM from the Centers for Disease Control arrived at Portland International Airport right on schedule. It was mid-afternoon, and once they collected their bags and loaded them in the rental car, they drove southeast over Highway 26. The views as they passed snow-covered Mt. Hood were spectacular.

"Nothing like this anywhere in the south," Dr. Julia Zhong said. She was the team leader. A veteran of the CDC, Julia had a medical doctor degree, specializing in internal medicine and communicable diseases. She was considered an expert in viral infections, and had spent two months in Africa the previous year working to contain and study a localized outbreak of hemorrhagic fever. Her in-field studies revealed that the particular strain of virus responsible for this sudden rash of illnesses was a new strain of Ebola, likely the product of a spontaneous mutation. Under her leadership, her team acquired sufficient fluid samples to isolate the virus for future studies back in Atlanta.

Julia preferred to ride in the back seat with her tablet already fired up and on her lap, papers spread out to her side. She was accompanied by two colleagues with whom she'd worked before: Dr. Adrian Stone and Dr. Lindsey Weber.

Dr. Zhong was tall and thin with high cheek bones and a somewhat petite nose. With hair the color of roasted cinnamon that just touched her shoulders, she presented a striking appearance. However, her male peers at the CDC had long ago stopped asking her out on dates, keeping the socialization to group events. As the cliché goes, Julia was married to her job. The challenge of her profession provided ample reward, and although she accepted that she had long since passed her optimal child-bearing years, she had no regrets about the choices she'd made.

Other than stopping for fast food, which they ate in the car, they drove straight through to Warm Springs. It was dark when the rental car pulled into the motel parking lot. After they checked into their rooms, Julia phoned Lee Moses.

"I understand the number of patients is growing," she said. "Although it's been a long day for my team, if you don't mind, I'd like to get started tonight."

After the stubborn refusal to help, Lee was pleased with the sudden change in attitude. "Thank you. I can meet you at the health clinic."

Lee gave her the address and they agreed to meet in thirty minutes.

The clinic was still open when the CDC team arrived. Lee opened the door and welcomed the medical experts. All three were wearing brightly colored quilted down jackets, reminding Lee of colored gumballs. Following introductions, Lee brought them into the back office. Two additional folding tables had been set up and chairs added for the CDC team. They wasted no time booting up their laptops and settling in. Clearly, this was something they'd done before.

Lucy joined the group and proceeded to walk the team through the data, including the digital map. All the electronic files had been emailed to the team members prior to their departure from Atlanta, so they were already somewhat familiar with the information. Then Lucy provided printed copies of notes from the many interviews of patients, immediate family, and close friends.

After brief discussion and cursory review of the interview notes, Julia addressed Lee. "Would it be possible to examine a few of the patients? Even one would be helpful."

"Yes, I think so. A young man came to the clinic about an hour ago complaining of symptoms. Our doctor is seeing him now."

"Excellent," she replied. Then she turned to Dr. Stone. "Adrian, would you mind? It will be easier on the patient if you assist with the examination."

Adrian nodded and followed Lee to an examination room. After knocking, Lee and Adrian entered. The clinic doctor accepted the introductions and provided a succinct summary loaded with medical terminology. The patient sat on an examination table with a towel draped over his lap, his pants folded on a chair in the corner.

Adrian spoke to the young man. "I'm Dr. Stone. I work with the Centers for Disease Control, in Atlanta. We're investigating this illness that you contracted. Would you mind answering a few questions for me?"

He shrugged. "Sure."

"When did you first begin to feel pain in your groin?"

"Yesterday morning. When I woke up, it hurt. And then when I took a shower, I saw that my private parts were red and swollen."

Adrian pulled on latex gloves and then launched a series of questions about sexual activity, unprotected sex, what food and drinks the young man had consumed, had he been vaccinated for childhood diseases, and whether he had been in contact over the previous two weeks with anyone he knew to also have the same illness. None of the replies suggested any risky behavior or contact with an infected person.

"I just want to check your lymph glands. Would you mind unbuttoning your shirt?" He reached forward and pressed his fingers under the patient's jaw, and then moved to the glands under his arms. The glands were slightly swollen and with an elevated degree of tenderness, especially under the jaw.

"I do have one more question—a request, actually— and I will apologize in advance. It would be helpful to our investigation if I can take one or two photos, to document the visible presentation of the infection. The photos will not show your face, and if you have any unique birthmarks those may be covered. I understand this is awkward, and I would not ask if it wasn't important."

The young man thought about the request for a moment, then relented. "Okay, I guess."

Adrian gently removed the towel and took two photos, then showed them to the patient. He again asked for his permission, which was quickly given.

"Thank you," Adrian said as he extended his hand. "I assure you my team will be doing all we can to identify the pathogen and devise a treatment." Then he left the examination room.

Upon returning to the office, Adrian updated his colleagues. His summary was filled with medical jargon, and he shared the digital images on his phone. The pictures earned a frown from Julia. "I've seen this degree of inflammation and swelling only a few times. Always with young adults, who were not vaccinated, and after passing through puberty they contracted a severe case of the mumps."

"Except this patient insists he was vaccinated against mumps, measles, diphtheria, and chicken pox. He said his mother insisted on all the normal vaccines. And the standard vaccinations are required by the school district."

"That's consistent with the statements in the interview reports," Lindsey observed.

"So, the simplest conclusion is that we are dealing with a variation of the mumps virus that is resistant to standard immunization," Julia said. She rubbed her chin, a sign of deep thought. Both Lindsey and Adrian waited for her to continue. "Could we be dealing with a natural mutation?"

Lindsey answered. "Certainly possible. But is there a precedent?"

"Regardless, what I saw with this patient certainly presents as the mumps, although I would have expected more severe swelling in the lymph glands, especially on the throat. Practically speaking, it doesn't matter if the virus—assuming it is a viral infection—is the result of a natural mutation or otherwise."

That caught Julia off-guard. She tilted her head. "What do you mean by 'otherwise'?"

"Just a figure of speech. Scientifically speaking, the possibilities are many."

"Agreed." She paused before adding, "And we need to keep an open mind."

"What are you insinuating?" Lindsey asked.

Julia raised her eyebrows. "Well, we could be looking at a naturally occurring pathogen. Maybe something we have previously identified, maybe a new strain. Or, it could be a natural mutation of a known strain. We've seen this many times with Ebola, and it's an annual occurrence with influenza." She raised her index finger to emphasize the final point. "But…

what if this is not a naturally occurring pathogen?"

"Are you suggesting this could be a human-engineered virus or bacteria?" Adrian looked skeptical.

"I'm simply echoing your statement. Scientifically speaking, it's a plausible possibility, isn't it?"

Lindsey spread her hands, not willing to jump to conclusions. "Plausible possibility is a far cry from proof."

"No argument from me," Julia said. "And it's our job to sort through the possibilities and eliminate those that are unfounded, until we do have the proof of the pathogen that is responsible for this outbreak. So, let's get to it. We have more than thirty patients that are suffering, and God knows how many more if we cannot crack this puzzle."

Adrian jumped in. "We need to get samples analyzed. I suggest we start with the obvious commonality—water. There is no correlation amongst the patients on canned or bottled beverages, but maybe there is a general contamination in the water supply."

"You do know that well water supplies the majority of the affected residences and businesses," Lindsey said.

"I do. But we can't rule out a widespread contamination of the aquifer. Therefore, we need samples and laboratory analyses."

"I agree," Julia said. "Let's do it. Lee, can you mobilize your people to collect water samples first thing in the morning?"

Lee Moses had been standing off to the side, watching the interaction. "Of course. Let me know how you want the samples to be collected and what volume of water you need. I'll get my team working on it."

"Nothing fancy. Do you have clean glass bottles? Two hundred milliliters volume should be fine."

"I'm sure we do, let me check. Anything else?"

"No, that's all. Once we've collected the samples, Adrian

will send them off to one of our labs for analysis."

"Are there any other beverages or food samples that you want?" Lee asked. "It will be easier if we collect everything at the same time."

Julia smiled. "Thank you. I think that will do." She glanced to Adrian and Lindsey, who both nodded agreement. "We don't see any correlation among the other variables."

Lee excused himself to seek out the sample bottles. Lucy was one step behind him.

After they cleared the room, Adrian addressed his superior. "You're concerned, aren't you."

She nodded. "The inflammation shown in those photographs is severe. I could understand it if the patients had not been immunized. But all except one state they had been vaccinated. Even if we assume a few are not speaking truthfully, or just don't know with certainty, that still doesn't explain why we have this number of patients."

"Do you think it's a new pathogen?" Lindsey asked.

"I think it is a pathogen that is not affected by the standard mumps vaccination. That much seems patently obvious." Julia clasped her hands. She was the lead investigator in part because of her years of experience with viral infections.

"There's something more," Adrian observed. "What are you not saying?"

She hesitated, then drew in a deep breath and exhaled. "How familiar are you with orchitis?"

Adrian and Lindsey both shrugged.

"It's not that common in developed countries, especially if standard childhood vaccinations have been established for at least a generation. There's the part you know—painful inflammation of the testes. But there is more to the disease, a dark side, if you will."

"Go on," Adrian said.

Julia shifted her gaze from Adrian to Lindsey. "Because the disease is rare, the side effects are little known. And the most severe side effect is… sterility."

"Are you saying—" Lindsey lowered her voice. "Are you saying these thirty or so patients are likely to be sterile?"

Julia looked hard at her colleague. "Yes, that's exactly what I'm saying. If all the patients experienced as severe an infection as the young man Adrian examined, then yes. The chances are very high they suffered permanent and irreversible damage to their testicles. They will not produce viable sperm and will not be able to father children."

Adrian collapsed into a chair. "My God. If this is the beginning of a true hot spot and the contagion is communicable…"

Julia finished his thought. "Then we are looking at an epidemic that could bring an end to humanity within a handful of generations."

CHAPTER 18

WITH THE ARRIVAL OF THE CDC team, Peter felt a weight lifted from his shoulders. He was far outside his comfort zone, and yet he couldn't refuse the honest and humble request for help. Despite the generally heightened public awareness of racial and gender inequities, he felt that the Native American population had been left out of the national dialogue. And whether or not the initial refusal of the CDC to investigate had anything to do with the ethnicity of the Warm Springs population, he could not shake the perception that this *was* a considered factor.

Whatever the cause of the initial hesitation, the CDC seemed to be working hard now for the people of Warm Springs. Lee Moses had phoned Peter already and given an encouraging update. The medical investigators had begun their inquiry last night, and today they were collecting water samples for analysis. Peter would have done the same, except that he didn't know what to analyze for. *Bacteria or virus? And which ones? Do you even have to specify?* In the case of chemical analyses, Peter knew that you did have to specify what you wanted to analyze for, and the approximate range of concentration expected. Failure to provide these two key directions could result in the analytical results being negative.

Peter was surprised when Lee asked him to meet with the CDC doctors later that day. It seemed that Julia Zhong had been told by her superiors to assuage Peter's concerns that the CDC was playing politics. A simple directive, but political in its nature and, therefore, validating Peter's initial suspicions. But before he drove to Warm Springs, he had one important phone call to make.

"Hi Gary. I got your message. Sorry I missed you earlier."

"Hey, no worries," Gary replied. "I've been working on your problem."

"Did you find the source? The party who issued the contract on my life?"

"You know, the dark web is really interesting, but there's a lot of sick and disturbing content there. Have you ever checked it out?"

"No. And I really don't have any interest, either."

"Yeah, probably for the better. Anyway, I found the posting. It's definitely a contract on your life. And it matches what you shared with me, the information spilled by the pair of amateurs who tried to kill you."

"Did you delete it?" Peter said.

"It doesn't work that way."

"Why not?"

"Let's say you want to sell something on Craigslist or eBay. You set up an account with your contact information and then upload your post. You'll include a picture and description of the item you're selling, and how a buyer can contact you. Well, this chat-room post offering to pay whomever kills you works basically the same way, except there's no photo. Now that I think about it, that would be kinda gruesome."

"I'm not following you."

"What do you mean? It should be obvious."

"Sorry Gary, but we aren't discussing an ad on Craigslist to sell my old lawnmower."

"Of course not. But the principles are the same."

"Meaning?" Peter prodded.

"Meaning that when you sell your junk and want to remove the ad—you know, so people don't keep calling you and asking if you'll take twenty dollars instead of the asking price of fifty—you cancel the ad from your computer."

"So far you haven't told me anything I don't know, and nothing that you've shared helps me figure out how to cancel the contract so hitmen will stop trying to kill me."

"Yes, I did. Canceling the contract should be as easy as deleting the posting in the chat room. You just need to use the same computer that was used when the ad was posted. That way the IP address will match the account and... voila!"

"That will work? It sounds too easy."

"Of course it's easy," Gary said. "That's e-commerce and that's what the Internet is all about—making complex tasks easy."

"So how do I find the computer that was used to post the contract?"

"Right now, I can't answer that. I've traced it back through multiple hubs, and then I got stuck in France."

"Stuck?"

"Yeah. The trace just stops. But I know that's not the origin. Whoever set this up knew how to do it right. It's gonna take more time."

"Thank you. I really do appreciate your help."

"Don't mention it, buddy. It's what friends do. As soon as I have something more specific, I'll give you a call."

Peter parked at the Warm Springs clinic, leaving Diesel in the car again with the windows partly open. Lee chided Peter, "I can recommend a good body shop if you'd like," referring to the dented rear fender and trunk lid. Then he patted Peter on the back. "Happy you and Diesel weren't hurt."

"Me too." He followed Lee into the office where the three CDC doctors were cross-referencing labeled jars with a data file. An Asian woman stepped forward.

"Hello. I'm Dr. Julia Zhong."

Peter introduced himself and extended his hand. Her grip was surprisingly firm.

"I understand you believe we should have acted sooner," Julia said, "and that we delayed our investigation because of racial bias."

Peter was taken aback by her directness. "Yes, the thought certainly crossed my mind."

"More than that, I'd say. Both Oregon senators and your congressman placed phone calls to my boss a couple days ago. They all said they were phoning on your behalf."

"I'm glad to hear that," Peter replied. "It's nice to know our represented leaders are willing to fight for the benefit of their constituents."

"Right. Well, I want to assure you that the CDC does not play politics. Our only job is to ensure the health security of America."

"It's unfortunate that it took political pressure to cause your team to start the investigation. However, I am grateful you did."

"Mr. Savage, you need to understand that we do not have the resources, nor is it necessary, to hop on the first flight and travel to every location where a few patients become ill."

"We both know that is not what we are talking about

here. As of last night, there were thirty-one patients with this disease—thirty-one out of a population of about three thousand. That's a pretty high percentage."

"And it could be just a natural aberration, or the result of weak immunity—perhaps due to a bad vaccine. We won't know until we check the vaccination records, assuming there still are sufficient records."

"Dr. Zhong," Peter said, trying to moderate his growing irritation, "I suspect you know as well as I do that this is not about a batch of weak or defective virus. Given the range in age of the patients, it would be impossible that all were vaccinated from the same production lot of vaccine."

"I agree it is improbable, but until we check the vaccination records, we will not know with certainty."

"Which is why it's important that the CDC investigate."

Julia sighed. "I don't intend to debate with you. I merely wanted to assure you that your implications of racial overtones are unwarranted and unfounded."

"Okay. That's good news. Let's call it a draw."

"And I have more good news," she said. "Overnight, the number of new patients declined rapidly, only two. If this trend continues through today and tomorrow, I think we can safely conclude that the outbreak has burned itself out."

"I would be very happy with that conclusion," Peter agreed. He motioned with his chin toward the small brown bottles. "I see you're collecting samples—water?"

Julia nodded. "That is the only commonality among all the patients. We have samples of tap water from all the patients' homes, schools, and businesses."

"That was my suspicion, too. Is there anything I may do to help?"

"Thank you, but we are just about done here. We should be packed before noon and on an evening flight back to Atlanta.

The samples will be sealed and packaged in padded boxes, specially designed to protect the contents, and sent directly to our labs."

Peter started to turn when a thought entered his mind. "Water," he said. He faced Julia. "Bottled water."

Julia returned a quizzical expression. "Good point. We haven't sampled the bottled water, although most of the interviews indicated they had consumed bottled water."

Peter nodded to Lee. "I saw some bottled water in the lobby yesterday."

"That's right," Lee answered. "It's all gone now. We received a large donation of water recently from a company in Eugene named Cascade Aqua. So we were providing it free of charge here at the community center and the clinic. Folks around here can use all the help they can get."

Peter strode into the lobby.

The small table where the bottles had been resting was now empty. But the recycle bin next to the table held a few empty plastic beverage containers. He picked it up and read the label. "Cascade Aqua Natural Pure Water." He turned the label and continued reading. "Bottled in Eugene, Oregon by Cascade Aqua Company." He handed it to Julia.

"It's empty," she said. "The few remaining drops would not provide an adequate sample size. The interviews don't indicate a particular brand of bottled water. There must be a half dozen different brands sold in Warm Springs."

Lee said, "I know for a fact that the market carries three different brands."

"Is Cascade Aqua Natural one of them?" Peter asked.

Lee nodded his head.

Julia said, "We'll collect samples from the grocery store as well as the market at the Deschutes River crossing, and any other major retail outlets that Mr. Moses suggests."

"You'll also stop by the community center?" Peter asked of Julia.

"Yes. We'll stop by the community center. If they still have some bottles, we'll take one for analysis."

"Shouldn't the bottling process ensure the water is not contaminated?" Lee asked.

"That's the idea," Julia responded, cutting Peter off. "And state regulators should be inspecting the lines regularly to ensure adequate cleanliness. But sometimes inspections are skipped, or contamination is inadvertently introduced."

"I agree it's a long shot," Peter said. "But worthwhile looking into. Something has to be the cause of this illness."

Julia faced Lee. "We will be thorough, I assure you. And as soon as we have results from the lab, I'll let you know. It will be a few days. But you need to understand that we cannot always determine with certainty the cause of outbreaks, even major ones, let alone a minor one such as this. Complicating the investigation is the reduction in number of new cases."

"But that's beneficial, right?" Lee said.

"Of course. I'm just saying that if there was a contagion that all the patients consumed or otherwise came in contact with, the reduction in infections suggests that the contagion may no longer be present. And if that's the case, we may never know the cause."

CHAPTER 19

TUMALO STATE PARK, NORTH OF BEND, OREGON
MARCH 17

ALTHOUGH DANYA HAD BECOME ACCUSTOMED to living in a trailer, she still occasionally missed a traditional apartment. She also missed living in a cosmopolitan city. She closed her eyes and imagined a high-rise modern apartment in Manhattan, or a brick open-floor loft in Boston. It was nothing more than a dream, as she couldn't imagine any scenario where she would put down roots and shed her anonymity. It seemed she was cursed to live her life on the run, which meant moving from one RV park or campground to another, always paying with cash and using false identities.

Just beyond the window of her small trailer was the Deschutes River. There were four other RVs to her right, and a collection of nearly a dozen tents pitched in spaces stretching to the left. During the day, families with children splashed in the fast-flowing, frigid water and played games on the expansive lawn filling the space between the river and the camping sites.

It was peaceful, idyllic. It was also temporary. Maybe she

would stay here another week, but soon she would have to move on again. For now, she had business to attend to. She needed answers, and the place to get them was through Carlos.

She powered up her laptop, and then enabled the custom communication software. The program functioned like email, except that every message she sent and received resided only in RAM—nothing was written to the main drive. As long as she was sending or receiving text, the information was placed in temporary memory, and when that was full, it would write over the oldest information. If there was a pause in messaging for more than five minutes, the communication program would close and all the information in RAM would be deleted.

She entered the address for Carlos, and typed a short message: "It's Mara." She always used her alias. "Is that contract you mentioned still open?"

About half a minute later he replied. "I don't know. I can check, but I thought you said you weren't interested."

"I wasn't, but things changed. Now I am."

"Let me check."

She used the microwave to prepare a cup of tea while she waited. Carlos's reply popped up just as she sat down. "The posting is still there."

"Good. Send me everything you can find on the contract as well as the party who issued it."

"Why? What are you up to?"

"Five million dollars is a lot of money. I want to make sure the issuer is legit and can pay."

There was a pause of several minutes, and Danya was beginning to wonder if the session would time out. Then he sent his reply. "I'll dig around, see what I can find. It may take a few hours. I'll check in later."

It was nearly midnight when Danya's computer chimed,

indicating a new email message had been received. It was from Carlos.

"Hit a dead end. After getting bounced through four countries and seven internet service providers, the trace ends."

Danya typed eagerly. "What do you mean it ends?"

"Can't continue the trace. It seems to end in France."

"So that's where the posting originated?"

"No, I don't think so. The trace just ends. I should have a specific location, but it just ends at an internet service provider."

"I don't understand."

"The ISP is like a hub. It routes information received from specific locations, or origins, on to the next receiver. In some cases, that's another ISP."

"Keep digging. Anything you find, forward to me. I owe you."

"Damn right you do."

The email exchange ended, leaving Danya with many unanswered questions. The fact that tracing the source of the message was complicated told her that this was a serious and professional operation. Maybe a state actor or organized crime. What enemies did Peter Savage have and who would want him dead?

She knew at least part of the answer to her question, a party that had reason to want him dead: her former employer.

Mossad.

CHAPTER 20

SIMON MING WAS VERY PLEASED. The experiment had unfolded exactly as planned. The outbreak at Warm Springs was significant, but quite minor in terms of the total number of patients. And just as quickly as it started, it subsided, providing ample reason for the CDC investigators to close their files. It was very likely, he reasoned, they would attribute the disease to a natural mutation that quickly burned itself out.

With no further spread of the ailment, there was no reason for the government health officials to even consider developing a vaccine, not that they would be able to anytime soon. And by the time they realized the true magnitude of the event, it would be too late.

He reflected on the years of research that had been invested in this project, a project he knew his father would be proud of. A brilliant scientist in his own right, Ming's father had pioneered many of the gene-editing tools used in this work. If only his father was still alive... the breakthroughs they could have achieved. Working together, father and son, pushing the boundaries of genetics to new limits—limits that others could only dream of, the work of science fiction.

But it wasn't fiction at all. His genius in using gene editing to create new viruses was only the beginning. Once he released his creations, he would proceed to the next phase and resume his father's work with more advanced organisms.

If God created life, Simon Ming would reshape that life to his liking.

Roger Corbett had been summoned to Simon Ming's office. Like a complex ballet, there were many details to attend to. The choreography had to be executed flawlessly—even a minor departure from plan could result in failure. Too much time and money had been invested to falter now. In very short order, Ming would realize his goals. Revenge was just beyond his fingertips—so close, he could almost feel it.

"Are the drones ready?" Ming asked.

"The entire fleet has been prepared and delivered to your properties, along with the flight teams."

"And I assume you've maintained secrecy?"

"That's what you pay me for."

"And I pay you well. If you want to continue getting your paycheck, a direct answer will suffice."

Corbett pulled his shoulders back, dipped his chin and folded his hands at his waist. "Yes, sir. All crews believe they are operating a training exercise to test the vulnerability of municipal water supplies. Each crew thinks they are working alone—they don't know about the other drones and flight teams."

"Very good. Continue with the training regimen, and keep the teams isolated. We are too close to risk someone talking."

"The pilots and engineers have been ordered to stay onsite.

Compliance hasn't been a problem since the accommodations are comfortable and each man is getting about a year's pay for this short job. But just to be sure, I have a number of guards at each site."

Ming nodded his approval. "Now all we need is the virus. Are we still on schedule?"

"We're ready to transfer production. Just give me the order. The field lab should be equipped, and the operators say they are almost ready."

"Have you confirmed their claim?"

"No, sir."

Ming paused in thought, mentally reviewing the timetable and logistics. It was essential to seed the virus at a great many locations in as short a time as possible. If he could overwhelm the ability of national and regional public health organizations to deal with the sick, the disease would spread relatively unchecked before any antidote or vaccine could be developed. It would be a biological blitzkrieg, and the result would be devastating.

"Perhaps it would be wise to pay a visit," Ming said. "This operation is more sophisticated than a run-of-the-mill meth lab. Let's not make the mistake of assuming our meth chemist is as prepared as he claims to be. A wise man once said, Trust but verify."

"No worries, sir. I have an important staff meeting scheduled for tomorrow. It might raise unnecessary questions if I'm absent. However, if you agree, I can leave the following morning. The lab is located on a remote parcel of land, east of Bend. I can make the trip there and back in a day. Should I let the chemist know when I'll be there?"

"Let's do this without advance notice. That way, you'll get the real picture and not a staged show."

"Understood."

Darnell Price leaned back in his chair. His office at Cascade Aqua Company was modest. The furnishings were limited to a typical business desk with chairs for two visitors. Although functional and clean, it could have been purchased from a thrift store. The walls as well as his desktop were devoid of personal photos, framed diplomas, or certificates of achievement. Instead, there were three large prints showing various stages of the bottling line. A single row of books was arranged on a shelf behind his desk. The titles indicated that the tomes taught manufacturing excellence, quality control, lean manufacturing, water chemistry, and bottling processes.

A private man, Darnell did not socialize much, and he was rarely seen at public events. He was known to be a wealthy man, but his precise net worth was the subject of conjecture, not fact. He drove a late model Cadillac, but so did a lot of people. He lived in an apartment in downtown Eugene. From his balcony, he had a direct view of Spencer Butte.

Darnell Price had a knack for business. Following his BS degree in biomedical engineering from the University of California, Davis, he earned an MBA from Brown University prior to beginning a five-year apprenticeship at his father's company. The senior Price built a successful business manufacturing and selling medical devices. It was a natural fit for Darnell, and he assumed the leadership position when his father died. The company flourished under Darnell's direction, exhibiting double-digit growth year after year. He was at the top of his game when he sold the company for an undisclosed amount.

That same year he married the love of his life. Head-over-heels in love, highly successful, rich, a respected member of society… Darnell was the envy of everyone who knew him. Life was perfect.

But it soon began to unravel.

A week before their first anniversary, his wife died only three days following childbirth due to an infection she acquired while in labor. Seven months later, tragedy struck again as his twin children died within days of each other from influenza. His money and success offered no protection from the illnesses that ripped away his family.

His grief was inconsolable. With no siblings and both parents deceased, he suffered alone, soon sinking into a deep depression. Every day he thought about ending the pain, and twice he came very close to carrying through and ending his life.

It took months, but eventually he began to rise from his self-pity and despair. Even so, the death of his wife and daughters left deep scars on his psyche. He stopped seeing his friends and withdrew into a dark and empty shell.

Darnell became obsessed with the notion that humankind was being besieged by Nature. He found groups on social media with similar beliefs, watched documentaries and read books espousing that people had overpopulated the Earth. He even fleshed out half-baked theories that natural events—such as disease, extreme weather, conflict, and famine—would cause massive loss of human life.

He needed something more immediate and uplifting to occupy his mind, and eventually he bought Cascade Aqua. Running the business provided the needed distraction from thoughts of natural disasters. It was a remarkably simple operation, far beneath his business acumen. But it provided a mental tonic, although he never gave up his new-found passion.

Despite his frequent blogging on the topic and the growing number of followers, he'd been unsuccessful in lobbying congress to enact laws that would limit the number of children a couple could have. Then he met Simon Ming, and everything changed.

He'd passed the point of no return when he left Ming's office at Utopian-Bio that fateful day thirteen months ago. So much had transpired since that first meeting.

The experiment in Warm Springs was successful beyond his most generous imagination. The virus worked exactly as Simon Ming had promised, and the CDC would be closing their investigation now that the outbreak had subsided. He doubted the investigators would ever learn the truth that the contagion was in the bottled water his company had generously donated.

Very soon, he would complete the final act—an act that would be hailed as the salvation of the human race.

CHAPTER 21

EAST OF BEND, OREGON
MARCH 19

THE CLOUD OF DUST ROSE from behind the rented SUV, a large Suburban, as it sped along the unpaved road. Corbett figured it was technically a driveway, not that it mattered. A mile back he'd turned off Highway 20 and drove south until he passed a row of mailboxes. At the next left, he turned onto this gravel and dirt road that, if his GPS was directing him accurately, would end at his intended destination.

The meth chemist came well recommended. When Corbett was tasked by Simon Ming to set up a manufacturing lab, his first thought was to tap into the overlooked talents of the illegal drug community. He reasoned that there should be several well-equipped laboratories manufacturing methamphetamine, fentanyl, and other opioids. Even better, those working the labs would already be trained well enough to carry out his assignment.

He began his search by discretely contacting several dealers in Eugene. Slowly, his search expanded, and Corbett soon learned that the isolated and remote lands of central Oregon offered what he sought.

He slowed the black SUV as he approached a doublewide trailer, easing to a stop near the front door. Even before Corbett exited the vehicle, a man appeared at the front door brandishing a pump-action shotgun.

"This is private property," the man said. "So unless you have a warrant, I suggest you turn around and leave."

Corbett raised his hands. "I'm not the police."

"Then you have no business here. Best you leave, now." To emphasize his point, he racked a shell into the chamber of the shotgun.

"Name's Corbett. Roger Corbett. If you're who I think you are, we have a business deal."

Slowly he lowered the muzzle of the shotgun. "Okay, come on in."

Corbett followed him inside. The man leaned the gun against the sofa within easy reach and motioned to a chair. "Have a seat."

Corbett declined. "I don't want to keep you long. Besides, I drove a long way and would like to get on my way back to Eugene."

"Roger Corbett. Yeah, I know the name. Talked with him on the phone. You sound like him, but I'd rather you showed me some ID—just to be sure."

"You're a cautious man."

"I learned early on that caution helps me stay healthy and alive. Not to mention out of prison."

"Fair enough." Corbett removed his wallet and produced his Oregon driver's license as well as his Utopian-Bio ID badge.

The man nodded. "Okay. Looks real enough. So what brings you out here, Mr. Corbett?"

"I understand you're close to being ready to manufacture

our product. I'd like to see your facility."

The chemist smiled. "Oh, I get it. A site inspection."

Corbett nodded. "Yeah. That pretty much sums it up."

"Follow me. The lab is in the trailer next door."

It was a short walk to the next trailer. It also appeared old and unkempt. The paint was oxidized and faded, and all the windows were completely covered on the inside with aluminum foil.

The chemist knocked on the door and said, "It's me. Coming inside with a guest."

They opened the door and entered. He closed the door behind Corbett without delay on the off chance that someone was surveilling them from a distance. With no ambient light entering through the windows, the only illumination was from a row of fluorescent bulbs running the length of the room. Three men were busy stacking cardboard boxes. All the interior partitioning walls had been removed, resulting in one large rectangular space. Along one long wall were six laboratory ventilation hoods. Several tables supporting a collection of laboratory equipment filled the remainder of the space.

The chemist began his tour. "My men are nearly finished. They had to pack up equipment we don't need and set up new work stations. Those hoods draft downward and vent out the bottom of the trailer. That way, anyone snooping around won't see the typical stacks on top of the roof that indicate we have lab hoods in here. Most of my competitors never figured that out. Dumb asses. Anyway, we got plenty of capacity here to work up the cultures and isolate the agent on absorbent media."

"Sounds like you know what you're doing."

"A scientist from Utopian-Bio taught me, and I'm a quick learner. Not that this virus is that much different from our usual product. Know what I mean? You can't go around being sloppy, or the chemicals will kill you. Same with this virus. Get careless, and you get infected."

"Just make sure you don't get careless." Corbett said. "Do you have room for the tissue cultures?"

"We have more folding tables. We'll set them up in here, enough to hold three hundred and fifty culture flasks. By keeping the trailer at a constant warm temperature, the cultures will grow quickly. As they mature, the flasks will be processed in the hoods, and the cycle repeated. Product will be kept in three large refrigerators that will be installed just inside by the front door."

Corbett looked at the empty space.

"Don't worry, they're getting the refrigerators tomorrow."

"You don't think that buying three refrigerators at one time might seem a bit odd? What if the sales guy calls the police?"

The chemist rolled his eyes. "We don't shop at stores unless we have to. The refrigerators will be bought at garage sales and from listings in the newspaper."

"You can trust these guys? Trust your team?"

"I'm standing here and not in prison. That's because my team is loyal. I take care of them, and they keep their mouths shut." The chemist grinned. "They'd all prefer to have a good paycheck over a bullet in the head. Wouldn't you?"

"I see your point."

"I provide my workers with good personal protection equipment like rubber gloves and full-face masks fitted with air bottles."

"You can find professional equipment like that at garage sales?"

"You can buy almost anything on eBay. And Amazon."

"Good. Expect to start soon, within a few days. How fast can you make the product?"

"It'll take two days for cultures to mature. Processing will take another twelve hours, but we can do that while another culture is started. So, about every two days we can cycle maybe fifty kilograms of product."

Corbett nodded his approval.

"How much are you going to want? I need to plan my staffing and supplies."

"Five hundred kilograms to start." He took one more look around, satisfied the illicit lab was very close to being ready. He had just one more question. "You have the seed culture that was provided earlier?"

"Sure do. It's in the refrigerator."

Corbett made a show of looking for the appliance that he already knew was absent.

"Not here, in my trailer," the chemist said.

Corbett wrinkled his nose. "You put that stuff next to your food? Are you crazy?"

He shrugged. "No harm. The package is sealed, right?"

CHAPTER 22

WARM SPRINGS, OREGON
MARCH 19

TWO DAYS HAD PASSED since Julia Zhong and her team from the CDC had collected samples and returned to Atlanta. Lee Moses was growing impatient, even though he'd been warned it would be a few days before the lab results were in. It was mid-afternoon when his phone rang.

"Hello, Lee. It's Julia Zhong from the Centers for Disease Control. We have the lab results and I wanted to call you right away as promised."

"Thank you," Lee replied. "What did you find?"

"Good news and bad news."

"What's the good news?"

"We believe we've identified the pathogen," Julia explained. "Cultures from blood samples show a common pathogen, a virus very similar to common mumps."

"But if these young men were vaccinated for the mumps and other childhood diseases, why did they get sick?"

"That's the bad news. I said the pathogen is *similar* to

144

common mumps, but not identical. That's most likely why the vaccine had no, or only a negligible, effect at halting the infection. However, this virus shows no indication of being deadly. I think the worst case is that anyone who contracts this rare strain will be very uncomfortable until the virus runs its course. Although it's too early to tell, we do have concerns that in post-pubescent males, permanent sterility may be a side effect."

"That's a pretty severe side effect," Lee observed.

"I agree, but without more studies spanning months to years, we can only speculate. However, given the similarity to mumps, it would not be unexpected. I'd like to recommend follow-up studies of the patients, if they are willing to participate. I'm sure I can secure funding. If you agree, I'll talk to my boss."

"Yes, I'll speak to all the patients myself. This will be a difficult message. My people are proud, and they distrust the American government. But I will do my best."

"I know you will, Lee. Thank you."

"What about the water samples?"

"A complete bust. We didn't find the pathogen in even a single sample."

"Nothing?"

"I'm afraid so. At this time, we don't know the source of the outbreak, what we call ground zero. For all we know, it could be a natural mutation of the common form of the virus. That happens with most viruses. The influenza virus is perhaps the best-known example. It mutates, sometimes dramatically, every year and keeps us guessing as to how to formulate the flu vaccine."

"Did you test any Cascade Aqua Natural bottled water? Peter Savage seemed concerned that could be the source."

"Yes, we did. Fortunately, that brand of water was on

the shelf of several stores in Warm Springs, so they were acquired and tested. All came back negative. However, and this is important, none of the bottles we found match the lot number of what was donated to the tribal council. At least, none matched the lot number on the empty bottles found at the clinic."

"Wouldn't it make sense to initiate a recall?"

"A recall on what? We couldn't find any bottles matching the suspect lot number, and the bottles we did test all came back negative. We can't recommend a product recall just because someone says they suspect contamination. The monetary damage can be significant."

"I see," Lee said. But clearly, he didn't.

"I understand your concern, Lee. My advice—and this is strictly off the record—mobilize volunteers and canvass every store or other outlet that might have Cascade Aqua bottled water. Check their stock, and if you find any bottles with lot numbers matching what was donated to the council, buy them and don't let anyone drink the water. Send what you have to my attention, and we'll take it from there."

Although Julia couldn't see it, Lee was nodding. "I like your idea. Warm Springs is a small community, and the people are close. We will do this."

"Good luck, and please keep me in the loop. But if you want to know my gut feeling, this is a freak mutation, nothing more."

"If that is true, then this could happen again."

CHAPTER 23

THERE SEEMED TO BE A STEADY STREAM of employees to and from the break room during the first hour of the day at Cascade Aqua. And today was no different. It seemed that everyone wanted to be adequately caffeinated—whether from coffee or tea.

Darnell rounded the entry to the break room, empty coffee mug in hand, and nearly collided with Ben Jarvis.

"Oh, sorry," Darnell said.

"Good morning," Ben replied with a smile.

"I didn't expect to see you here today. Thought you were taking the week off to go gambling over on the coast?"

"Just have a couple things to take care of, then I'm outta here. Still have to pack. I'm going to Florence tomorrow, to the casino to try my hand at blackjack. I was going to knock on your door. Do you have a minute?"

"Yes, literally. I've got a meeting in three minutes."

"I won't keep you," Ben said. "Just that I've been thinking

about those cases of water you donated."

Darnell glanced at his watch. "Look, Ben. I told you I wouldn't hold it against your sales numbers. It will have no effect on your bonus."

"Yes, sir. I know you said that. It's just… well, you know… I think it would be best if you would put that in writing. You know how memories can be. I might recall the conversation one way, and you another way."

Darnell resisted the urge to roll his eyes. Instead, he maintained a neutral expression. "Okay, I'll send an email later this morning that documents our conversation. If you don't think it's accurate, come see me when you get back from your vacation. Now, if you'll excuse me, I need a cup of coffee and then have to get back to my office."

No sooner had Darnell entered his office and closed the door when his phone rang. It was the receptionist announcing that Roger Corbett had just signed in and was on his way to Darnell's office.

"You said you wanted to speak with me," Corbett said as he closed the door. He took a seat in front of the chrome and wood-veneer desk.

"Yes. Now that we've successfully completed the test and it appears the CDC will be backing down, I wanted to ask about the progression of our plan. What is the timetable for moving forward?"

"I'm certain Dr. Ming will bring you into his confidence at the appropriate time."

Darnell frowned. Until this meeting, he'd felt part of the team; that he and Simon Ming shared a common goal. Now, it sounded like he was being pushed aside.

"Are you saying now is not the appropriate time? We're all in this together."

"Let me discuss your request with Dr. Ming later today."

"Okay. And once you do please get back to me right away."

Corbett paused, taken aback by Darnell's directness and sense of urgency. "Is there anything wrong? Any problem I should know about?"

"Problem? Like what?" Dapples of perspiration appeared on Darnell's forehead as he fidgeted with a pen.

"That's what I'm asking you, Mr. Price."

"No. Everything is fine."

"Are you sure? None of your employees are acting oddly or asking questions?"

"No. Everyone is fine. Well, almost everyone. Ben, my VP of sales, is not happy with me donating all those cases to the Native Americans in Warm Springs. And he definitely disapproves of my planned donation to Nigeria," Darnell explained. "He's complaining that I'm cutting into his potential annual profit sharing. I've told him not to worry, that I'll take care of him, but he doesn't trust me. He stopped me only ten minutes ago and asked me to put it in writing."

"You need to keep him under control," Corbett said. "We've come too far to have any snags now. We don't need the media running a spotlight on your charitable habits, know what I mean?"

"Relax. I told Ben to take the week off and gave him a nice bonus check."

"How did he respond?"

"Are you kidding? He was thrilled! Said something about going to the coast tomorrow."

Corbett drew his lips into a tight line. "Did he say where he was going on the coast?"

"He mentioned Three Rivers Casino in Florence. He wants to try his luck at blackjack."

"Good. Anything else I should know about?"

"No," Darnell said. "And Ben's taken care of, just relax."

"You better be right," Corbett said, as he stood to leave. "You don't want me to have to take care of the problem."

Darnell walked from behind his desk to meet Corbett. He jabbed his index finger into Corbett's shoulder. "This isn't your concern."

Corbett's reaction was a blur as he latched onto Darnell's hand. His grip was unyielding, and he twisted the man's hand, threatening to break his wrist. "Do that again, and I'll snap your arm."

"Okay! Okay! Relax."

"Just do your job, got it?"

After leaving Cascade Aqua, Roger Corbett phoned his boss. "The meeting was short, sir. I have concerns."

"Does Mr. Price suspect anything?"

"No sir. But we may have a problem."

"I'm listening."

"The VP of sales, a guy named Ben. I've never met him, but Price says he's been asking a lot of questions about the charitable donation Cascade Aqua made to the reservation. He's been complaining that it will hurt the year-end profit-sharing bonus."

"Maybe you should give this Ben person something else to worry about."

"Understood."

"I want daily reports. Use this number; it's not traceable. Stay on this. It's too important to delegate. In a few weeks, we'll have enough product to make a statement."

"And after that?"

"We watch and assess; tie up loose ends."

"What about the operation east of Bend?" Corbett asked.

"Everyone knows that running an illegal meth factory is a hazardous business. Those labs burn up all the time."

CHAPTER 24

WITH A BACKGROUND IN PRIVATE SECURITY, including a short stint as a private detective, Roger Corbett knew how to find missing persons. The treasure trove of information readily available over the Internet made the job of locating a person relatively easy, unless that person went to extraordinary lengths to hide. Only a tiny fraction of the population had any clue how to really remain hidden, so a few routine methods nearly always proved successful. With a phone number, address, photos— even DMV records—locating a person of interest was seldom challenging.

Corbett had parked a few houses down the street from where Ben Jarvis lived. It was supposed to be the first day of his vacation, so Corbett didn't expect him to be up too early. And he wasn't.

Just before noon, Jarvis placed an overnight suitcase on the back seat of his car and pulled away, presumably heading toward Florence.

Corbett had close to a full tank of gas and followed at a discrete distance. Nearly an hour later, he followed Jarvis into the expansive parking lot at Three Rivers Casino. Being the middle of the day, the lot wasn't even close to being full, and he parked only a couple slots away from Jarvis.

He left the engine running, as he pulled on a ski mask and quickly exited his car. He swiftly approached Jarvis from behind. The sound of footsteps alerted Jarvis, who turned. A rock-hard fist slammed into his face, dropping him to the pavement. Corbett kicked him viciously in the head, again and again.

Jarvis tried to protect his head and face with his arms, but that caused the blows to be directed at his midsection. He was overcome with pain and found it impossible to catch his breath from the kicks to his stomach and the repeated blows to his face and head. Blood ran freely from his nose and mouth, and both eyes were already swelling closed.

The beating was over in less than a minute, leaving the battered man lying unconscious only feet away from his car. His face was smeared with blood and mucous. Both cheeks and his nose were turning lurid shades of yellow and purple.

Corbett didn't waste time. He ran back to his car, hopped in, and drove away. Just before he left the parking lot he slowed and looked back over his shoulder. He didn't see anyone lending assistance, and no one at all in the parking lot.

That evening, the local news briefly mentioned that a Eugene resident had been found severely beaten in the parking lot at Three Rivers Casino. The news anchor identified him as Ben Jarvis and went on to say he was in critical but stable condition with head and internal injuries. He was under a medically-induced coma to help manage and reduce the swelling of his brain. Security cameras covering the parking lot showed a masked man approaching Jarvis from behind and then viciously beating him. The man drove away, but the license plate was obscured to the camera view. The Tribal Police Department was investigating but so far had no suspects.

Corbett dialed the number he'd memorized.

"Did you see the evening news?" he said.

"Yes. Was that our problem? The sales executive you mentioned?"

"Yes. He won't be talking to anyone for some time. And when he does regain consciousness, I suspect he'll have many more important concerns other than what his year-end bonus will be."

"I trust you were careful?"

"I was careful. There were no witnesses, not even Jarvis saw my face or license plate. Nothing for the security cameras to pick up either, and no evidence was left behind."

"Excellent. Then we can return our focus to the business at hand."

"May I suggest that you send flowers to Mr. Jarvis tomorrow—anonymously, of course—and a note to Darnell Price expressing your sorrow and best wishes for his employee's full recovery?"

"Good idea. We should act suitably…" the voice paused, searching for the proper words, "sad, and supportive, I suppose. That is the proper behavior, is it not?" He didn't wait for a reply. "What about the schedule? No delays, I hope."

"No, sir," Corbett replied. "The lab is producing concentrated contagion at the expected pace. There hasn't been any slip in the schedule."

"Good. Soon we will be ready for the next phase."

"Price is going to be asking more questions about the schedule. He may be suspicious that we are not having him produce more contaminated water."

"Let him think what he will. In due time I will inform him what the true plan is."

"What if he doesn't go along?" Corbett asked. This had been a concern of his from the beginning.

There was another pause, and then Ming answered. "Then, I'm afraid, Mr. Price will have a most unfortunate accident."

CHAPTER 25

IT HAD BEEN A FULL WEEK since Lee Moses had last spoken with Peter to share the results from the preliminary analysis by the CDC investigation team. They were both equally discouraged that a source of the pathogen had not been identified even though they'd both been warned of that possibility.

Stubbornly, Peter refused to accept that it was a natural mutation of the mumps virus. Although he was no expert on virology, based on his research, it didn't seem plausible that the virus would burn out so quickly. But even if that was the case, there would still be a source. The virus had to come from somewhere; something that was either ingested, inhaled, or in some way allowed into the body of each patient.

Another concern nagging at Peter was that mumps infected the lymphatic system in general and was therefore contracted by both male and female. Yet the mysterious viral outbreak at Warm Springs resulted in severe infection of males only, since the disease seemed to infect predominantly the testes. During the outbreak, the Warm Springs clinic had only a handful of cases involving female patients with symptoms of infected lymph nodes, and those cases were very mild.

He kept coming back to water as the common link between all the patients. And yet mumps was not a water-borne virus. In fact, the few water-borne viruses known to infect humans primarily caused infections of the gastrointestinal tract and liver. These viruses were mostly associated with sewage, or water supplies contaminated by feces—whether from human or animal—and their occurrence was far more common in developing countries.

So how could water be the source if the virus was a mutated form of mumps? He decided to call Julia Zhong and ask her opinion.

"Hello Julia. It's Peter Savage. Do you have a minute?"

"Oh, hello Mr. Savage. Sure. I was just wrapping up before lunch."

"Lee Moses shared with me the essence of your conversation last week, and I understand that your team has not been able to identify the source of the virus."

"Yes. None of the samples we collected tested positive."

"That's what bothers me the most. There has to be a source. Unless the virus somehow mutated once it was within the host body."

"We don't think that's the case at all. There would be absolutely no precedent for that occurring."

"But you agree that there has to be a source, right? If the virus is naturally occurring, and spontaneously mutated to this new form that is resistant to vaccination, it still has to be present in the environment. So why have all the lab tests turned up negative?"

"I don't fault your logic," Julia said, "but that doesn't change the results. Let's face it. There are thousands of potential ways the patients could have come in contact with the virus. We collected samples for only two days, narrowing our search to those items that appeared to share commonality across the patient population. But there's no guarantee we sampled everything we should have. In fact, given our negative findings, I'd say we missed something in our collection."

"Like the bottled water?" Peter asked.

"I understand that's your pet theory, but we did sample water from Cascade Aqua and all results were negative for any pathogens, bacterial or virus."

"We both know that's inconclusive. We need to test all of the production lots that were delivered to Warm Springs over the past several weeks."

"Which appears to be impossible. Unless you know of some stash of bottles from the prior lots."

"Have you made that request of the management at Cascade Aqua?"

"No. There is no scientific basis to believe a strain of mumps virus could remain viable in water. The source must be something else. In all likelihood, it was spread from one person to the next through sneezing or coughing, or from contaminated drinking glasses or cups."

"It still had to originate with someone."

"You're referring to patient zero?" Julia said. "Yes. Answer that question and you've solved the puzzle."

"But if the virus has mutated, couldn't the means of transmission also change? And the new strain is now stable in water? You keep referring to this as a strain of mumps virus, but why does it seem to infect males disproportionately to females?"

"These all are good questions, but I'm afraid that without further study, they'll remain unanswerable."

"What about a vaccine? I understand that the infected patients had all been previously vaccinated for mumps."

"Not all, but close to it," she said. "Best guess is that they received a weak vaccine, or, more likely, simply outgrew their immunity. It happens—fairly often, actually. However, and this is important, it is premature to know how effective the standard mumps vaccine is against this new, mutated strain of virus."

"Can a specific vaccine be made to protect against this new disease?"

"Maybe. But devising a vaccine against a virus is not as straightforward as it may seem, and sometimes efforts are unsuccessful. HIV in particular, but also Ebola and hepatitis C, have proven especially difficult. There is also the complication of conducting clinical trials on human patients."

"I don't understand." Peter said.

"Well, think about it. To run clinical trials, real people must be vaccinated and then subjected to the live virus. At the outset, there is a very real chance that the patients may become infected, either from the vaccine or as a result of exposure to the virus. The ethical question of such trials cannot be ignored."

The call ended with no relief for Peter's frustration. He wanted answers, and he wasn't getting any. Even worse, he didn't see a pathway to getting there. Like it or not, the bureaucracy at the CDC seemed to be getting the better of him. Just then, an idea came to mind.

He opened the browser on his phone and found the webpage for Cascade Aqua. The phone number was displayed, and he dialed, asking for the manager. After a short wait he was placed in contact with the president, Darnell Price.

Peter explained his involvement with the investigation into the cause of the illness at Warm Springs and asked if any bottles from prior product lots shipped to Warm Springs were still available for analysis.

"This seems like an odd request," Darnell said, "coming from a private citizen. Shouldn't the Oregon Health Authority or CDC be making the request?"

Peter explained the situation, that the CDC thought it was a naturally occurring virus that mutated, and that they had collected many samples already. "But they couldn't find any bottles from prior production lots," he said.

"Probably all consumed by now. Store managers keep a close eye on inventory. They'd rather I keep it in my warehouse than have pallets of water sitting unsold for weeks in their own warehouses. It's all about cash flow."

"Would it be possible to visit your bottling line and warehouse? I'd like to check for myself, and it seems like an imposition to ask you to conduct a thorough search for a few stray bottles."

"If this was an official request, I'd have to comply. But under the circumstances—"

Peter cut him off before he said no. "If I appeal to the CDC, FDA, and Oregon Health Authority, it's likely to be picked up by the media. That would be bad publicity, and totally unnecessary if, as you say, there's no issue with your product."

"Your appeal sounds more like extortion."

"I'm sorry if that's what you're hearing. I assure you, I'm simply trying to help solve this mystery."

"Okay, Mr. Savage. It's your time and gas. I can see you tomorrow, if that works for you."

CHAPTER 26

PETER ARRIVED FIVE MINUTES ahead of schedule. He parked in a spot reserved for visitors and entered Cascade Aqua. There were many poster-sized photos of the production line hanging on the walls. A large metal and glass plaque with gold engraving caught his attention, and he moved closer.

"That's the Environmental Stewardship Award from the International Bottled Water Association. We are the first bottled water company to use plastic bottles made from 100 percent recycled PET," Darnell Price said. He was standing behind Peter, his hands clasped behind his back.

"That's very impressive, and commendable," Peter said as he shook Darnell's hand. "Thank you for meeting with me, Mr. Price."

"Please, call me Darnell. As I told you over the phone, I don't know how much help I can offer. I'm afraid your drive over the mountains may be wasted effort."

"I have to try. This is important. Besides, it's a beautiful

160

drive."

"So, what can I do to help you?" Darnell asked.

"Actually, I was hoping we could check your warehouse stock one more time, just in case you still have a few bottles from the lot number I mentioned."

"Ahh. And you really believe there is some sort of contamination, limited to that single lot of bottled water?"

"It's a very real possibility."

"I assure you, Mr. Savage, my company takes the safety of our product very seriously. We have exceeded Oregon state regulations by installing high-efficiency filtration a year before it will be required. Plus, we distribute throughout the Pacific Northwest and Northern California. There have not been any complaints associated with our water. And, as far as I know, this mysterious illness in Warm Springs that you mentioned, there have not been any other cases reported. Anywhere."

"That's true. It's not my intention to malign your product. However, I think we would both be satisfied if we could sample even one bottle from that production lot. If it looks clean, then we can eliminate your product as the source."

"I don't see why that matters," Price said, his tone somewhat defiant. "Let's assume that somehow a pathogen or something contaminated that single production lot. So what? That lot is gone, either consumed or discarded. And the fact that there are no cases outside of Warm Springs, and no complaints of any kind that my bottled water is making people sick… well, I just don't see how this question is anything more than an intellectual curiosity."

"You can't say with certainty that bottles from the lot in question were all consumed. What if there is still product out there? People need to be warned."

Price sighed. He wasn't going to assuage Peter with logical reasoning. "Very well. Let me show you the production line on the way to our warehouse. If any of the lot in question is left, that's where it will be."

Peter walked beside Darnell through the bottling plant. It was a large, open space filled with lines moving rows of bottles past machinery that applied the label, filled the bottle, twisted on and sealed the cap, and then packaged the product. Pointing to a large stainless-steel pipe, glistening like chrome, Darnell explained that clean water entered the plant through that pipe. It was then filtered multiple times before being bottled.

"And those are the filters?" Peter asked, pointing at the three large cylindrical housings with pipe entering and leaving the top of each. Like all of the process machinery and piping, the filter housing sparkled in cleanliness.

"Yes. Three successively tighter filters. The last one, with the smallest particle retention size, will remove single cell microbes—protozoa and the like. It functions just like a backpacker's water purification filter."

"You don't irradiate the water with ultraviolet light to kill viruses that are too small to be retained by the filtration steps?"

"UV irradiation is very expensive, and not required by the state."

"But you said this degree of filtration was not required either. And yet you have chosen to implement it."

"Next year this will be required. I simply opted to start a year ahead of schedule. My brand is all about purity and the highest quality. This gives me a marketing edge on my competitors."

Darnell led Peter through the bottling plant into another large room with stacks of pallets containing cases of bottled water. "We can store up to three weeks of production in our warehouse, although that would be tight. Typically, we have shipments going out several times each week."

Peter swiveled his head, taking it all in. Across the floor

were many squares outlined with yellow tape. Pallets holding cases of water were stacked high within each taped-off area. Plastic stretch wrap held the cases in place. On each palleted stack of cases was a simple lettered card. Peter approached the closest. It listed the name of a retail store and the location. "I gather these are the customer names?" he said.

"That's right. The delivery location."

Darnell flipped the card over. "On the reverse of each card is a barcode that has relevant information about the shipment, such as the lot number or numbers included in the delivery. This information would allow us to track specific customers and production lots if there was ever a reason to do so."

"How is a production lot defined?" Peter asked.

"That's a good question. Other companies may do it differently, but I've insisted on a unique production lot for each shift and each day."

"In other words, if you run two shifts a day, then you have two unique production lot numbers for that day."

"Yes. It's important that we are able to trace any quality control issues to the source."

A new thought popped into Peter's mind. "Is it possible that the production lot I'm interested in went to customers other than Warm Springs?"

Darnell shook his head. "No, I already checked our records. Understand that a production lot is fairly small, since it is the output of only one shift."

"I see. Well, what about the lots immediately prior to and after the one in question? Where were they shipped? Maybe I can acquire samples."

"I'm sorry, Mr. Savage." Darnell's tone had lost all measure of informality. "I have indulged your curiosity and agreed to this meeting. It is not my policy to open our records to just anyone who raises questions."

Peter realized he'd pushed hard and hit a wall, so he changed tactics. He spied a large mountain of cases across the warehouse. He walked over to it and read the destination on the card.

"All of this water is going to Kano, Nigeria? That's a long way from Oregon."

Darnell smiled. "It is indeed. My company tries to help out. Sadly, there are far too many needy people in the world."

Peter nodded. "You're certain you don't have any more cases of water from the production lot that you donated to the people at Warm Springs?"

"Positive. I checked after you called."

"Do you mind if I poke around the wall over there?" he pointed beyond the stacked cases. "Maybe some bottles fell off a pallet when loading."

"Be my guest." He motioned forward.

With Darnell in tow, Peter searched around the perimeter of the warehouse, but to no avail. No loose bottles or stray cases of any production lot were found. There were only the ready-to-ship cases in the designated staging areas. "Well," Peter said. "I guess I owe you an apology."

"No apology is necessary. I hope you understand now that my company takes safety and quality very seriously."

"I do. I've taken up enough of your time." Peter shook Darnell's hand and then followed him to the lobby. He hesitated at the door, and turned back toward Darnell.

"Just one more question, if I might. Why Nigeria?"

"For the moment I've decided to focus all of my company's charitable giving to needy people in Africa."

"Africa is so far away, shipping must exceed the value of the bottled water. Why not just make a monetary contribution?"

"Like I said, there is no shortage of people who are in desperate need of help—food, water, medicines."

"And you've made other donations this year—to Warm Springs, for instance?"

"I fail to see your point, Mr. Savage. Surely you aren't faulting my charitable donations?"

"Not at all. It's just that I don't see how you can make any money. I'd have thought the margins on bottled water were pretty slim."

Darnell's lips drew tight, and when he spoke, there was no pleasantness in his tone. "You may run your business anyway you wish, and I will do the same with mine. Good day."

After driving a short distance from Cascade Aqua, Peter pulled onto a side street and parked. He phoned Lee Moses.

"How did your meeting go?" Lee asked.

"Fine, I guess. Strange is probably a better description."

"Oh? Why is that?"

"Turns out we couldn't find any leftover bottles."

"You knew it was a long shot. Why do you find that strange?"

"In the warehouse there was a pile of cases staged for shipment to Nigeria."

"So?" Lee said.

"Well, why Africa? This is a small-time water bottling company, and they're shipping water to Africa?"

"Maybe they're getting a good price for it? If I were in charge of sales, I'd be reaching out to expand my market, especially if I could make more money. Maybe the people in Nigeria think bottled water from Oregon is... I don't know... exotic?"

"Well, that's the strange thing. Darnell Price, the owner of the company, told me he was *donating* it to Nigeria. And not just what I saw, but he said he planned to make more donations to people in Africa."

"I'm not surprised. The council is grateful for the many

pallets of water he donated to the tribe."

"So, how does he make money?"

"Maybe he doesn't care?"

Peter exhaled a sardonic snicker. "Yeah, right. A businessman who doesn't care about making money? Anyway, as I was leaving, I asked him."

"And what did he say?"

"He as much as told me to mind my own business."

CHAPTER 27

FROM HIS OFFICE WINDOW, Darnell Price watched as Peter Savage drove away. He phoned Simon Ming, and they agreed to meet at Utopian-Bio.

"I gather that this person who visited you has caused you some concern," Ming said. He spoke slowly, appraising his guest.

Darnell shrugged, but he couldn't hold Ming's penetrating gaze. "No. Well, a little, maybe. I just thought you should know."

"I see. Under the circumstances, I felt it prudent to have my associate, Roger Corbett, present." All three men sat around the conference table in Ming's office.

Corbett cast a steely glare toward Darnell, who fidgeted with his hands on the edge of the table.

Ming's eyes bore into the CEO sitting across from him. "Mr. Corbett may have an important take on your meeting this morning."

"Why don't you start from the beginning," Corbett said,

since he was not a party to the brief phone call Darnell had placed to his boss.

"Sure. As I told Simon, this businessman from Bend contacted me a couple days ago. He'd been helping a friend—who happens to be a member of the Warm Springs Tribal Council—to investigate the outbreak of the viral infections. He thinks bottled water produced by my company may be the cause. But, of course, he has no proof. So, he was looking for a sample."

"Which you don't have, so you couldn't give it to him even if you wanted to," Corbett said. Then facing Ming, he added, "I fail to see the problem."

"He's the person who got the CDC to investigate," Darnell said.

"Does this person have a name?" Corbett asked, trying to hide his growing irritation.

"Peter Savage."

Ming's eyes widened, and Corbett noticed. "That name mean something to you?" he asked.

Ming nodded. "Another matter. But Mr. Price, please continue."

"Well, I took him to the warehouse. He wanted to see if there were any bottles lying around from the donated production lot shipped to Warm Springs. I knew he wouldn't find anything, so I thought, why not? So, I was showing him the pallets loaded with cases of bottled water, staged for shipping. All fairly normal."

"If it was all normal," Corbett said, "you wouldn't be spooked and we wouldn't be having this conversation. You're holding something back."

Darnell squirmed in his chair. "There was a shipment slated to go overseas, and he noticed it."

Corbett pressed the issue. "Go where overseas?"

"Kano, Nigeria."

"You surprise me," Ming said. "I didn't know Cascade Aqua had international sales."

"No, of course not. This shipment is a donation to a local aid group." Darnell twisted up the corners of his mouth in a forced smile. "All part of the plan. That water is doped with your virus, just like the bottles my company shipped to the tribal council."

Simon Ming's expression hardened. "We should have discussed this before you acted."

"Oh, come on!" Darnell leaned back in his chair and folded his arms, trying to steady his nerves. "The test was an unqualified success. There's no reason to delay any longer. You just keep sending the powdered agent to me and I'll keep bottling it up and sending it out. First Africa, then the Indian subcontinent."

"I only gave you the one sample," Corbett said.

"That's right. I used it to make the product that went to Warm Springs. But rather than cleaning out the line right away, I had the next shift produce a full production run before they sterilized everything. It only took one phone call to find an eager recipient in Kano. I thought the shipment had gone out already. I didn't realize it was still in the warehouse."

Ming had a menacing edge to his voice when he spoke. "You were only authorized to produce the specific number of cases of doped water that you shipped to Warm Springs. Yes?"

"Dr. Ming—"

"Yes or no!" Ming shouted, cutting off Darnell.

"Yes, I suppose you're right. It's just… Well, I mean this is what we agreed to do. The population is growing exponentially in Africa and the Indian subcontinent. So why not ship water there?"

Ming eased back in his chair. He steepled his fingers, considering Darnell's argument. "Perhaps you are right."

Darnell visibly relaxed with the approving reply, his body molding to the contours of the chair.

"Now tell me, Mr. Price," Ming continued. "And I want you to be completely honest, do you understand?"

He nodded. "Yes, of course."

"Do you have any more samples of my virus? Perhaps locked away in your office, or hidden in storage somewhere?"

"No, no," he stammered. "No, sir."

"You're certain?"

Darnell nodded.

"Good. So there will not be any more *miscommunications*." Ming pointed a finger at Darnell. "From now on, you will follow our plan to the letter. No more improvisations."

"Yes, of course. And I apologize. It's just that…"

Ming waved a hand, ending the matter. He'd heard enough and allowed his head of security to pick up the questioning.

"You're certain all the bottles laced with the virus are staged for shipment?" Corbett asked.

"Positive. I double-checked myself. Anyway, he—"

Corbett interrupted. "You mean Savage?"

Darnell nodded. "Yes. Mr. Savage took special interest in the pallets waiting for shipment to Nigeria. Asked a lot of questions about that."

"What questions?" Ming said.

"Like, why would my company ship bottled water all the way to Africa. And how could I afford to donate so much of my product. Maybe he knows something?"

"Give me a break," Corbett said. "If he knew anything of our operation it would be the state or CDC investigators at your door, and not some nosey guy from the other side of the mountains."

Chastised, Darnell sat silently, glaring at Corbett.

Ming steepled his fingers again, strategizing the next steps.

The pause was beginning to become uncomfortable when he spoke. "Perhaps you are right to be concerned. This is something I must give more thought to. Unfortunately, I have an important business meeting and dinner to attend shortly. But this should not be put off any longer than absolutely necessary. Can you meet me here this evening at ten o'clock?"

"Uh, sure."

"Good. Mr. Corbett will be in the lobby. When you arrive, he'll unlock the door and let you in."

Ming rose, followed by the other two. He patted Darnell on the back and ushered him to the door. "Thank you. You did the right thing by sharing your concerns."

Corbett remained standing at the table as the door closed behind Darnell Price. "Something is bothering you," he said to his boss.

Ming stood at the window, his back to Corbett. "Peter Savage is a name I know. He was responsible for the death of my father. It happened in Sudan, and Savage was working with American Special Forces."

"How do you know this?" Corbett asked.

"Because… I was there." He turned to face Corbett. "My father built and operated a secret biomedical facility. His specialty was genetic modification. Insertion of altered genes into refugees, using viruses. I was a young man, having recently received my doctoral diploma in biochemistry, and was learning first hand in his laboratories. The most brilliant minds worked under my father's direction. And I was there, an eager student soaking up their collective genius."

Corbett was speechless. For the first time he understood how Simon Ming had advanced the genetic engineering of the mumps virus so quickly.

"My father acquired a fortune doing research no one else could do, or was allowed to do. And now, I am humbly following in his footsteps."

"You must have known that Peter Savage lived in Bend. If he's a business owner as claimed by Price, it wouldn't be hard to find him."

"True, I knew where to find him. But I had preferred to enable others to deal with that situation, allowing me to focus on the task at hand. Unfortunately, it appears delegating that task was an error in judgement."

"And now?"

Ming cast a steely glare at his head of security. "I think a meeting is appropriate, don't you?"

"Do you want me to bring him here?"

"No, that would be too conspicuous. Mr. Price is a sufficient liability, and we don't want to add further loose ends. We cannot allow ourselves to be distracted. Soon, when the time is right, I will deal with Peter Savage."

The building was empty except for Simon Ming, Roger Corbett, and three hired enforcers that Corbett knew from his days working private security. These men had no scruples so long as the pay was good. And Ming always paid very well.

Alone in the lobby with only the normal security lights on, Corbett opened the door just as Darnell Price approached. He then locked the door again.

"This way. Dr. Ming is waiting."

He followed Darnell into the executive's office. "Have a seat," Ming said. "I have been thinking about our meeting earlier today."

Darnell turned his palms up and shrugged. "I told you what happened. Mr. Savage is asking questions, but I didn't give him anything."

"I believe you." Ming paused, pressing an index finger to his lips as if he was deep in thought. "But still, I think you are losing control. Maybe your confidence in our mission is shaken?"

"Not at all. I've supported this program without any reservations. I've done my job flawlessly. As soon as you give the order and deliver more powdered agent, we can resume the operation. I can have a quarter million bottles of Cascade Aqua Natural palletized and shipped to Africa within six weeks. We'll keep the runs short—maybe a week or so—and sterilize the line so we can mix in standard production runs to keep up with local sales. After six, maybe nine months, we can begin targeting Bangladesh, or Pakistan, or India, or wherever."

Ming was shaking his head. "No."

Confused, Darnell looked over his shoulder at Corbett, who was standing behind him, and then back to Ming. "What do you mean, no? That's been the plan from the day we first met."

"I'm afraid you misunderstood. That was never the plan. You see, I don't care about ballooning populations in third-world countries. That problem will take care of itself. Disease, famine, war—the rich countries will never expend their resources to save those poor, retched people. Which means there will not be any reprieve for them. Nature will self-correct, just as you wished."

"No, that's not what we agreed to at all. We need to—"

Ming interrupted and rose from his chair, leaning over the table toward Darnell. "We need to do what? Enforce mass sterilization of populations against their will? Does that give you a clean conscious? Allow you to sleep at night?"

"We agreed to this," Darnell said.

"You're pathetic. And weak. That was never *my* plan. I only told you that so you would cooperate."

Darnell started to worry. "I'll destroy the product. Everything that is packaged and ready to ship to Nigeria. All of it."

"Really? Do you think I care? And I suppose you'll also threaten to go to the authorities. How will you explain that you willfully placed a human pathogen in your bottled water? You deliberately supplied that water to the Warm Springs tribe— you'll be labeled a racist. I wouldn't be surprised if you were convicted and sentenced to twenty years in prison."

"If I go down, so do you." He started to rise, and suddenly felt a needle jab into his shoulder. He rounded on Corbett, who was still holding the syringe.

He began to feel light-headed and his legs wobbled, but he still took a wild and ineffective swing at the security chief. Corbett easily ducked out of the way.

"You've got some spunk," he said with a chuckle. Then Darnell Price collapsed onto the floor. "He should be out for a couple hours at least."

"Take him to the warehouse. When he wakes up, have him sign the letter naming you as interim general manager."

Corbett had rolled Darnell onto his stomach and was clasping handcuffs on his wrists. "And if he refuses?"

Ming shrugged. "Then your job will be to convince him. I need that document tomorrow morning."

CHAPTER 28

IN A RUNDOWN WAREHOUSE on the southwest side of Eugene, Darnell Price sat on a rickety cot in a dark room. At one time, the room was a large supply closet, with a floor drain and faucet that still worked. But only cold water came out of the tap, and it was a disgusting shade of brown. The bucket in the corner served as the toilet, and the plywood cap did little to hold back the stench. Darnell figured conditions would get revolting in short order if he was kept here very long.

There were no windows, and an overhead fluorescent light was always on. The door creaked open, and Roger Corbett entered. A pistol was holstered on his hip.

Corbett noticed Darnell's eyes dart to the weapon. "Don't even think about it. No one will hear a gunshot inside here. If you cooperate, you can still live a long and happy life. If you don't… well, use your imagination."

"What do you want?"

"Good question." Corbett produced a folder with a pen

clipped to the outside and laid it on the man's lap. "It's a letter. I want you to sign it."

Darnell read the letter. "I won't appoint you as GM!"

"Acting general manager. It's only temporary, until you are able to return to work."

"I'm able to work now."

Corbett shrugged. "That could change quickly. I'm trying to be reasonable. But the choice is yours."

"What do you want with my company?"

"Dr. Ming has made this request. I'm just following orders."

He tossed the folder onto the cot. "I won't sign it."

Corbett drew the pistol. Darnell knew little about guns, and all that mattered now was that this gun, pointed at his legs, looked very big and very dangerous.

"This is a SIG Sauer 9mm. A very reliable and deadly weapon. A favorite of armed forces and the police," Corbett explained. "I will start at your ankle, and then go to your knee. The pain will be unimaginably excruciating. I've seen really tough men curl up and cry like a baby when shot in the knee. It won't kill you, but you'll probably never walk again."

Darnell knew he had no choice. "Okay. You win." Reluctantly, he signed the document and closed the folder. Corbett snatched it away.

"Now, tell me the password for your phone."

"Why do you want my phone?"

Corbett rasied his brows in an exaggerated expression. "Because I need to check your messages and call log to be certain you are not withholding any important information."

A beaten man, Darnell complied.

"Very good, Mr. Price. You have been most helpful."

"How long are you going to keep me here?"

"That question is above my pay grade. Now, if you'll excuse me, I have to see a certain notary and have your signature authenticated."

"You can't do that."

"I have your driver's license, and you'd be surprised what some people will do for a modest amount of money."

Peter awoke in his room at the Hilton in downtown Eugene. After a quick shower, he dressed and checked out. He had phoned Kate the previous afternoon and asked if she would stay at his place and take care of Diesel for the night. She seemed to accept his excuse that the business meeting had taken longer than expected, and that he thought it better to spend the night and be fully rested before driving over the mountains back to Bend in the morning.

He planned to have breakfast and then, around mid-morning, pay a visit again to Cascade Aqua. He'd come to the conclusion that any samples he could obtain from current or prior production lots would be better than going home empty handed. And if all the samples he could obtain came back from the lab negative with respect to pathogens, then he'd simply have to accept that his theory was bogus.

He parked his car in the same visitor spot he'd used previously and walked inside to greet the receptionist. "Good morning," he said. "I was here yesterday for a meeting with Mr. Price. I have some additional business matters to discuss. Is he available?"

"I'm sorry," she replied. "He's not in. Is there someone else who can help you?"

Peter hadn't expected that Price may not be at work yet. Thinking fast, he recognized an opportunity. "Uh, yes. Is the shift manager available? I just need to pick up some samples that Mr. Price promised to gather yesterday."

It didn't take long for a short, portly, middle-aged woman to enter the lobby. "My name is Wendy. May I help you?" she said to Peter.

After brief introductions, Peter relayed his request. Wendy frowned and said, "I'm sorry, but I didn't get the message. You'll have to come back when Mr. Price is in."

"Well, that's a problem. I live in Bend, and it's a long drive just to come back here for the samples. Mr. Price assured me yesterday that I could pick them up this morning. I only need a bottle or two from each production lot in the warehouse. I'm happy to pay you for them."

She rolled her eyes. "Oh God no. I'll be buried in paperwork all day long if you pay for it. What ever happened to going paperless, anyway?"

Peter stared back in silence.

"Come on," she said with a sigh. "Let's see what I can put together for you."

Peter followed Wendy into the warehouse. She handed an empty cardboard box to him and then went from staging area to staging area, checking the placard and then extracting a couple sample bottles of each production lot. She'd come back later and replace the bottles with fresh product to eliminate any shortages. "Are you sure two of each lot is sufficient?" she asked.

"Yeah, that will be fine."

The last samples came from the cases earmarked for shipment to Nigeria. "You must be proud, your product is going all the way to Africa," Peter said as the last bottles were placed inside his now-heavy box.

"Yeah, I suppose. I don't know why we have to go halfway around the world to give away our water. If you ask me, plenty of good people right here in this community who could benefit from free bottled water."

Grateful for the help, Peter thanked Wendy and went on his way. He exited through the warehouse entrance so as not to attract any inconvenient attention if he traced his pathway back through the manufacturing line and lobby.

While he was carrying the case of bottled water to his car, Roger Corbett entered the lobby. He had visited the company several times, and the receptionist easily recognized him. He extracted an official document from a large envelope and handed it to the receptionist. "This document says I am the acting general manager until such time as Darnell Price returns to work."

"Is Mr. Price going to be okay?" she asked.

Corbett flashed a smile. "Yes. It's a personal matter, and I'm not at liberty to go into any details. This is just a temporary situation. If anyone is looking for Mr. Price, or has business with the company, send them to me."

"Well," she said, "a man was just here asking for Mr. Price. He said he was to gather samples from the recent production runs."

"What did you tell him?"

"He was rather persistent, so I called up the shift manager."

"Where is he now?"

"They went out back, I think to the warehouse."

Corbett dialed his phone, and just started to speak when the receptionist said, "There he is, in the parking lot." She was pointing to the Rolls Royce Wraith. A man had the trunk lid open.

"Yes! Now!" Corbett shouted into the phone and then he ran out of the lobby. The sleek sedan was not parked far from the door, and Corbett had a pistol aimed at the man.

"Stop what you're doing! Raise your hands!"

Startled, Peter looked around the trunk lid straight into the barrel of the gun.

"Who are you?" Corbett demanded. "And what are you doing?"

"Relax. My name is Peter Savage. I'm just placing a case of

water in the trunk."

"We don't sell direct to the public. You must have stolen that."

"No, I didn't steal anything. The shift manager gave me these samples. Her name is Wendy. You can ask her yourself if you don't believe me."

"The shift manager doesn't have authority to give away company property."

"Fine. Just call the police. This can be resolved easily enough."

Corbett smirked. "The police work for me."

"Just put the gun down. It's only a case of bottled water."

"Why do you want that water anyway?"

"For analysis. I have concerns one or more production lots may be contaminated and making people sick."

Two SUVs entered the parking lot and screeched to a stop, drawing Peter's attention. Four men jumped out and surrounded him. One pulled his arms behind his back and cuffed his hands.

"Hey! What are you doing?" Peter exclaimed. "Just call the police!" An unmarked police car with flashing lights in the rear window skidded to a stop behind the SUVs. Dressed in slacks and a blazer, the driver strode forward and flashed his badge. He placed his hands on his hips and faced Corbett. "Problem here? I got a call from one of your men."

Peter exhaled a sigh of relief. "Thank God you're here, officer."

The man swung his head toward Peter. He didn't look to be more than thirty-five years old, with black hair and narrow, beady eyes. He was thin and had a sickly pallor with visible acne scarring. With the exception of a mustache that curled down just beyond the edge of his lips, he was clean shaven. "It's *Detective* Jackson to you, mister."

Peter took a breath and slowed down, surprised by the hostility from the police office. "Of course, sorry. Detective, as you can see, we have a problem here."

Jackson ran his eyes up and down Peter for an uncomfortably long moment, then he faced Corbett. "What's the story?"

"We caught this man stealing company property. When I approached him, he became very belligerent and threatening."

Jackson nodded. "Looks like you have the situation under control. Just be discrete, okay?"

"Wait a minute! Peter took a step forward before being restrained by one of Corbett's men. "It's just a case of water and I didn't steal it! The shift manager, Wendy, gave it to me. It's samples for analysis."

Jackson pinched his eyebrows together. "You'd be wise to cooperate." Then he strode back to his car and drove away, leaving Peter confused and shocked. *What the hell is going on?*

Corbett holstered his pistol. "Take him to the warehouse. One of you drive his car over there and park it inside. I don't want it to be visible from the street. I'll be right behind you. And make sure you take his phone."

The receptionist had seen everything and was agitated. Corbett told her that he was with the FBI and he flashed a fake badge and ID. He went on to say that Darnell Price was under investigation, and that his men had taken Peter Savage into custody. She was not to say anything of the matter, especially to other workers or to the local police. Until the investigation was concluded, there was no telling how many others might be involved.

She didn't ask what crimes Mr. Price and other workers were suspected of, and Corbett judged his threat to have had the desired effect. Hopefully, for her sake, she would be quiet. Otherwise, he would deal with her, too.

CHAPTER 29

THE LARGE WAREHOUSE DOOR opened automatically and the SUV containing Peter and two of Corbett's men entered, followed by the Rolls Royce, the second SUV, and finally Corbett driving a sporty sedan. The slab floor was amply large for all four vehicles to spread out. Diffuse daylight filtered in through dingy skylights in the sloped ceiling.

All four men plus Corbett were brandishing pistols. "Get out," one of the men ordered Peter.

He slid off the seat and stood, slowly moving his head and taking in his new surroundings. "I would have been happy to pay for the water," he said.

"You shouldn't go sticking your nose into affairs which are of no concern to you," Corbett said. He closed the distance, stopping three feet in front of Peter.

"Yeah. I've been told that before."

Corbett raised his eyebrows. "You should have listened."

"In hindsight, I'm inclined to agree with you."

"Bring him." Corbett turned and walked away. Peter, flanked by two guards, followed.

He opened a door that led into an area finished as office space, except that it was dirty, water-stained, and looked like it hadn't been used for at least a decade. A utilitarian desk was to the right of the doorway. "Put his wallet, keys, and phone in the drawer," Corbett ordered.

They passed a large room that, at one time, may have functioned as a breakroom, and two smaller rooms that had most likely been used as offices. They stopped in front of a closed door. It looked industrial, fabricated of metal with a standard latch and a heavy-duty deadbolt.

Corbett inserted a key and unlocked the deadbolt, then he opened the door. The fetid odor of stale urine assaulted his senses. He motioned to one of the guards. "Empty that bucket."

The guard held a deep breath as he entered, grabbed the pail by the handle, and then disappeared, presumably to a washroom. Less than a minute later he returned with the empty bucket and slid it into the cell.

Looking in, Peter saw Darnell Price standing near the far wall. "Are you releasing me?" Darnell asked. But his voice was devoid of hope.

"All in due time," Corbett said. "You have a new roommate. I understand you two know each other?"

"We've met," Peter said. A guard shoved him in and then slammed the door. The deadbolt locked closed with a distinctive metallic click.

Darnell approached Peter. "Why did they lock you in here with me?"

"Can't say for sure, but if I had to venture a guess, I suspect it has something to do with the bottles of water your shift manager gave me."

Darnell hesitated as he considered how much he should

share. "What are you talking about?" he said cautiously.

"I planned to have them analyzed. All of the production lots in your warehouse."

"But you told me that the lab had already analyzed bottles of my water that the CDC people bought from stores in Warm Springs. You said nothing harmful was found."

"That's right."

"So what's the deal? Why can't you just let this go?"

Peter shrugged. "Call it a personality flaw. You see, when innocent people are being hurt or taken advantage of, I want to do all I can to help them. I suppose I favor the underdog. So yesterday, after we met, I got to thinking about all that water you plan to donate to Nigeria."

"And?"

"At first, I thought you were being a genuinely nice guy. After all, the average person in Africa has a pretty tough life by our standards. But then I thought about all those cases of bottled water you gave to the Warm Springs Tribal Council."

"So what?"

Peter shrugged. "Maybe nothing, maybe a lot. I guess I just have a suspicious mind. And I began to wonder why you would ship water all the way to Nigeria when there are so many needy people right here."

"There are needy people everywhere," Darnell said. Even though the room was cool, perspiration dappled his forehead.

"True. But I believe that most of the time people act for a reason. And I just couldn't get over the fact that you had previously found worthy groups nearby to support with your charitable donations. Certainly you're aware of local groups here in Eugene to help the homeless and working poor. No doubt there are similar groups in Salem and Portland as well. So, it just kept nagging at me—why go to considerable expense to ship water to Nigeria? Surely there are many regional suppliers that would be logistically advantaged over Cascade Aqua, and perfectly capable of satisfying the need. I'd imagine you could negotiate a purchase contract with those regional suppliers to have their water delivered—at your expense, of course—and still come out ahead."

"You're being ridiculous. Making charitable contributions is not a crime."

"No, and it's something more people should do. But I'm still left with this quandary. And now—now you've provided the clue I so desperately needed."

Darnell stared back in silence, his face lacking expression.

"Why are you here, Mr. Price?" Peter asked.

"I don't know. Those men are crazy."

"I think you do know. They have kidnapped me because I have samples of water from your recent production lots— samples that could not be acquired in Warm Springs. That, by itself, is hardly of any significance. So I'm betting that those samples are the missing piece of this puzzle, the proverbial smoking gun. And when they are analyzed, the pathogen that infected those young men in Warm Springs will be found."

Darnell shook his head. "Those bottles of water will never be analyzed. They've probably already been destroyed."

"Time to come clean, Mr. Price. What are you not telling me?"

He sighed and sat on the edge of the cot, then lowered his face to his hands.

"You're going to need my help to get out of here," Peter said.

"You know how to get us out of here?" For a moment, a measure of hope crept into his voice.

"There's always a way out of any prison. *How* just depends on the circumstances, as well as the available tools. So, what's it going to be Mr. Price? Are you going to stay here, and take your chances, or answer my questions and leave with me? The choice is yours."

Darnell looked up. "Oh, alright. It's over anyway."

"What's over? What did you do?"

"What had to be done. What weaker men could never do. Don't you see? The global ecosystem cannot sustain unregulated population growth." Darnell told Peter about his first meeting with Simon Ming a year earlier, and the plan they hatched. "Ming said he could develop the pathogen—a genetically engineered virus. My role was to ensure it got into the bottled water."

"You were going to infect men with this virus so it would lead to sterility?"

"It's the only humane way."

"You think forced sterilization is humane? What is wrong with you?"

Darnell sprang to his feet, his voice rising in defiance. "I watched helplessly as my wife and then my twin daughters died of incurable diseases. Mankind is on the verge of global catastrophes unlike anything we've ever witnessed. All because people lack the will power to voluntarily regulate reproduction. Competition for resources, famine, disease, climate change— that's just the beginning. It's the natural course to thin the herd… only we're the herd."

"Is that supposed to be an excuse? Justification for forced sterilization on a massive scale?"

"There are more than seven billion people. And the population keeps growing. You know as well as I do—that's unsustainable."

"We've managed so far. Science and technology have made it possible to grow sufficient food, to make water safe to drink, and to cure major diseases."

Darnell sagged back to the cot, the rusted springs squeaking as it accepted his mass. His expression also sagged into a frown.

"So far. Those are the operative two words. We've cheated the natural order for too long, and our luck will soon run out." He closed his eyes and lowered his voice, the anger spent. "When you turn on the evening news and hear that tens of millions have died from starvation in North Africa, or a hundred million have died from a global pandemic—that war between Pakistan, India, and China has claimed fifty million lives—how will you feel?"

"This is not the way. You have no right—"

"It *is* my right!" The fire returned to his spirit. "It is my duty!"

Peter shook his head, repulsed by what he was hearing. "You're mad. You won't get away with this. I won't let you."

"I don't want millions of families to feel the grief—the pain—that I did when they lose their loved ones, as they surely will. Don't you understand? Do you even know what it is like?"

Peter checked his surging anger. "Yes, I do know. My wife died from an automobile accident several years ago, and I'll always feel the pain. But you aren't God, no one is. As laudable as your goal may be, your method is monstrous."

Darnell cast his eyes downward. "What are we to do?" his voice barely more than a whisper.

"To begin with, we're going to get out. And then we're going to quarantine all the product your company has in the warehouse and halt production while the CDC and Oregon Health Authority investigate. I'm quite certain they'll issue an immediate and urgent recall of all product your company has shipped."

"That won't be necessary."

"Why not?"

"Because, I only added the virus to select production lots. Those cases were shipped to Warm Springs, and then there is the product scheduled to be shipped to Nigeria."

"Why?"

Darnell didn't respond.

"Why only those populations?" Peter said, his voice louder. "Why not also distribute your poison here in your own home town? Share it with your friends and neighbors?"

"It only makes sense to target areas where overpopulation is severe. Those regions tend to correlate with poverty."

"You mean people of color, you son of a bitch. That's always the answer for men like you, isn't it?" It took all of Peter's will to refrain from smashing his fist into the man's face. Instead, he shook his head in disgust. "Move," he said brusquely.

With Darnell out of the way, Peter raised a leg of the cot and unscrewed a leveling foot. It came out easily—a threaded stud about two inches long with a one-inch circular foot that normally made contact with the floor.

"What are you going to do with that?" Darnell asked from the farthest corner of the room.

"I'm going to use it to open the door."

Since the door swung inward, the hinges were located inside their makeshift cell. There were three standard hinges. Peter placed the stud against the bottom of one of the pins and rammed his hand against the circular foot driving the stud upwards against the hinge pin. At first, there was no movement, and he hit the circular foot a second time. The pin edged upward. Again and again he struck the foot until the pin was pushed up sufficiently that he could grasp it and pull it out.

He repeated the process for the remaining two pins while Darnell watched. When he was done, the heal of his hand ached from the repeated blows.

"Now what?" Darnell asked.

Peter struggled to grip the hinge and pull inward. It would have been easy to accomplish if he had even rudimentary tools. He conducted a quick search of the room—nothing. No screwdriver, no pliers, nothing. The bottom of the door had a heavy-duty weather strip that contributed to the sound-proof qualities of the room. It also made it impossible to get a grip on the bottom of the door and lift upwards in order to take the weight off the hinges so the door would fall inward.

"We're one yard from the goal line," Peter said in frustration. "Now we wait."

"Wait for what?"

"For one of the guards to open the door."

CHAPTER 30

IT HAD BEEN NEARLY TWO HOURS since Peter had removed all three hinge pins. With the patience of a hunter, he stood ready, leaning his shoulder against the wall where the hinges were fastened to the steel doorframe.

"I'm hungry," Darnell said. "Think they'll give us something to eat?"

Peter glanced at his watch. "I doubt they intend to starve us to death."

A couple minutes later a metallic clicking emanated from the door. A key was turning the deadbolt. Peter readied, tensing his body. The bolt was thrown back and the guard pushed open the door. As the door swung inward, the hinges separated and at that instant Peter thrust his shoulder forward. The heavy door crashed to the side into the guard, knocking him to the floor, the door pinning his legs.

"Let's go!"

Peter planted a foot on the door, eliciting a grunt from the pinned guard, and dashed out the opening with Darnell fast on his heels. The guard was struggling to slide out from under the weight and gain his feet. Peter paused only long enough to retrieve his personal items from the desk drawer—thankful they'd not been moved. Darnell fell a step behind to grab his wallet; his phone was missing.

They emerged into the cavernous warehouse, and Peter slid to a stop, Darnell nearly colliding into his back.

"That's far enough," the guard said. His pistol was held steady with both hands. "On the floor. Now!"

Before Peter could react, a black streak crossed his field of vision.

Thunk!

The guard's arms fell limp to his side, the pistol clanking on the concrete floor. A bloody, razor-edged steel broadhead protruded from the center of his chest. He stood there for two seconds, then fell sideways.

Peter rushed forward and squatted to retrieve the SIG Sauer 9mm pistol. "Drop it!" The voice came from behind. The other guard had managed to extricate himself from under the heavy door.

Thunk!

Peter turned, trying to follow the sound, but it was incredibly fast. The bolt had just impaled the center of the guard's chest. Eyes wide in shock, mouth agape, the guard fell lifeless to the floor.

Spinning around again and raising the pistol, Peter searched for the assailant. His car and one SUV were parked in the center of the warehouse. In vain, his eyes scanned the shadows along the edges.

"You're safe," a new voice, vaguely familiar, called out. Then Peter saw her step out from behind the SUV. She was holding a crossbow fitted with an optical scope. Very deadly at close range, as evidenced by the two one-shot kills. The weapon was loaded. The four-blade bolt appeared sinister as it rested on the rail, while the taut string was in a state of readiness to propel the bolt at four hundred feet per second.

She was clad in black coveralls. Not exactly form-fitting, but not baggy either. Hanging from her hip was a wicked-looking weapon that reminded Peter of a hatchet or tomahawk. Her head was covered in a black knitted cap, and a black scarf covered the lower portion of her face. Only her eyes were visible.

She strode forward, the crossbow held at the ready, her finger resting against the trigger guard. As she approached, Peter recognized… what? Her stride? Or maybe her eyes?

No, it was that and more. The way she held herself with a weapon. The confidence she exuded as she strode forward. He'd met this woman before.

He narrowed his gaze. "Nadya?" he said.

She closed the distance, stopping in front of Peter. Then she pulled down the scarf. He knew this woman as Nadya Wheeler—but he also knew that wasn't her birth name. She was an assassin, trained by Mossad.

"That is not an alias I use anymore. My name is Danya Biton."

"What are you doing here?"

"I've been following you for almost three weeks."

Peter's hand tightened around the pistol grip, his arm muscles tensed, ready to raise the weapon in a flash.

"Relax," Danya said. "I wasn't trying to kill you. That should be obvious, as you'd already be dead."

Peter cocked his head. "That was you," he said as understanding dawned. "You were the shooter at the river."

"That's right. The guy was a professional hitman. He was about half a second away from putting a smoking hole in you."

She shrugged. "I fired first."

"But why?"

"You mean the contract?" Danya said.

Peter nodded.

"I don't know. I caught wind of it from one of my sources. That's when I became your shadow. I tried unsuccessfully to identify the issuer. Hit a dead end on tracing the posting back to the source."

"I haven't fared any better."

Danya shrugged. "My first thought was Mossad. But the killer I eliminated was too sloppy to be Mossad. I checked with a contact I still have on the inside, and she says the agency has not issued a contract on your life... not yet. Whoever it is that issued the contract, they're professional. We can talk more later. Right now, it's time to go."

"Hold on." Peter reach out and grabbed her arm. "When we met up in the Cascade Mountains close to two years ago, you and your team were trying to kill me. So why have you become my protector now?"

"I told you at the time—I had a change of heart. I'm not a soulless killing machine anymore."

"Just like that?"

"Yeah, I guess so." She turned and walked away.

"Wait a minute!" Peter called before she exited the warehouse. She stopped and turned.

"I could use your help."

She glanced at the SUV and Rolls Royce. "You want me to make an appointment at an auto body shop? You look like white trash driving around in a beat-up Rolls Royce."

Peter smiled. "I'll get it fixed. Kinda busy right now."

"So I noticed. Where are you staying?"

"I was at the Hilton. I checked out this morning."

"Check back in again, and keep him with you," she pointed

at Darnell. "I'll look you up tonight."

After Peter checked into the Hilton, he drove to an electronics store. Figuring that a second phone might come in handy, he purchased one with a pre-paid service plan. Depending on the strategy they eventually settled on, having a phone to communicate with Darnell could be a benefit if they were to become separated. He insisted Darnell tag along to the store. Fearing police involvement, or worse, another encounter with Roger Corbett and his men, Darnell agreed.

Peter phoned Kate and explained that he was delayed. He'd need another day in Eugene. She agreed to spend the night at Peter's condo, taking care of Diesel, and Peter assured her he would be home the following day. It was a cordial conversation, but Kate made her position clear: "We need to talk when you come home."

Darnell was quiet while Peter ordered room service—a selection of appetizers and sandwiches, with two pots of black coffee. He didn't know what Danya had in mind, but he was certain she wasn't planning on a social call.

Shortly after ten p.m. there was a knock on the door. Peter looked through the security viewing sight and immediately recognized the woman.

He opened the door and Danya entered. She didn't waste any time. "Do you know who those men are who kidnapped you?"

"They seem to be associates of my friend." Peter motioned with his chin at Darnell.

"You know them?" She addressed her question to Darnell.

He nodded. "They work security for Utopian-Bio. I don't know the two you killed. But I've met their boss. A man named Roger Corbett."

"Tell her everything," Peter said, his patience already worn thin. It took about ten minutes for Darnell to explain the plan he'd agreed to, and the role his company played in bottling the contaminated water. "Corbett has been my principal point of contact."

"But you haven't explained," Peter said, "why they turned on you."

"Simon Ming double-crossed me. He said he never planned on allowing me to ship that water to Nigeria."

"If not to Africa, then where?" Danya asked.

"I don't know."

"Bull shit!" Peter shouted and grabbed Darnell by the collar.

"It's the truth!" Darnell raised a blocking hand in anticipation of a strike, but that wasn't Peter's style.

Peter released his grip, and he sat on the edge of one of the beds. He faced Danya. "We have to get the water before someone ships it out. We can't allow it to get into circulation."

"Why not just phone in a tip to the local police?"

"No," Peter said, shaking his head. "When Corbett grabbed me, he boasted that he owned the Eugene police. And then a detective showed up—a guy named Jackson. He's definitely on Corbett's payroll."

"Okay. So we snatch the cases of bottled water. How much inventory is there?"

"A lot. At least a dozen pallets, each loaded with 20 cases."

"That's too much for one load in my pickup. And I don't think it's wise for us to attempt multiple trips. We'll be lucky to get in and out of the warehouse once without getting caught."

"We have a company delivery truck," Darnell offered. "Actually, several."

"Is it large enough to carry all the inventory?" Peter asked.

He nodded. "It will easily fit."

"Okay. After we confiscate the cases, I'll phone my contact at the CDC and we turn it all over to them. Agreed?"

"Yes," Darnell replied sheepishly.

"Do you have a key to the warehouse?" Danya asked.

"I do," he said. "They took my driver license and keycard, but nothing else. What Corbett and his men don't know is that I can deactivate the lock using a six-digit code. A perk of being the owner. Anyway, the building has an alarm system, but I can turn it off."

"Unless someone has changed the code," Danya said.

"I don't think so," Peter said. "Why would they? They have no reason to suspect we're planning anything."

"Maybe," she said. "But by now they'll know you've both escaped. To be safe, we approach cautiously." She faced Darnell. "Is anyone working in the warehouse at night?"

"We normally run only two shifts, unless we're behind schedule. There shouldn't be anyone there between midnight and eight a.m."

"Then it should be easy," Peter said with a raised eyebrow. "We watch from a distance and make sure everyone is gone. Mr. Price will open the door and turn off the alarm. Who's going to drive the truck?"

"I will," Darnell said, earning a look of disbelief from Peter. "When you run a small company, you do a little of everything."

"All right. We load the truck and convoy to Bend."

"Why Bend?" Danya asked. "Why not just wait here and turn it over to the authorities?"

"What authorities? I already told you the Eugene police are on Corbett's payroll. We don't know who to trust."

"What about the FBI or state police?" she pressed.

"It's too risky. If word leaked and got back to Detective Jackson or someone else in the department who's on the take, it would compromise everything. Besides, who would believe us? This story is pretty crazy, and we've got no proof."

Danya pinched her eyebrows into a scowl as she glared at

Darnell. "We've got him. We can make him tell his story."

"Trust me, we will," Peter said. "But we need more. We have to have physical evidence. I don't trust the people behind this. They have money and we know they've bought off the local police. Who's to say they haven't done the same with agents out of the local FBI office? They were pretty brazen when they snatched me from the parking lot in broad daylight."

"Then we're on our own."

"For now, anyway. I can hide the cases of water at my company in Bend. No one will think to look for it there, and it will give me time to speak with Dr. Julia Zhong at the CDC."

"And you believe she can be trusted?" Danya asked.

Peter nodded. "I do. The CDC became involved only recently, after I pulled in some favors and applied a little political pressure. She and her team conducted the field investigation at Warm Springs."

"I hope you're right. It's your head."

"What does that mean? I thought you were helping?"

Danya cast a mischievous grin in Peter's direction. "I am. But just to be clear, I have a thing about avoiding contact with law enforcement and government agencies. Do we have an understanding?"

Reluctantly, Peter replied, "Yeah."

CHAPTER 31

THE OVERCAST NIGHT SKY held in the humidity, making the early morning feel even chillier than the temperature indicated. Darnell sat with Peter in his Wraith while Danya was parked a short distance away in her pickup. From their vantage point, they watched as the last of the swing-shift workers drove away from Cascade Aqua Company. It was approaching one a.m., and other than the last worker to leave, they hadn't seen any foot or vehicle traffic at the business for the last forty-five minutes.

Peter phoned Danya. "Darnell says they've all gone home. Looks clear. We're going in."

"Okay. Keep your phone handy. If anything looks odd, I'll call immediately."

The plan was simple. Darnell would enter the code to open the door and turn off the alarm. Then they would load the cases designated for shipment to Nigeria. If police or any visitors showed, Danya would report immediately to Peter so they could exit before being caught in an embarrassing situation. After getting all the water loaded and just before leaving, they planned to sabotage the filter housing that was used to dispense the viral agent so that production would not be restarted, if anyone was so inclined.

Although not expecting trouble, Peter carried the pistol and a spare magazine he'd taken from the guard during their escape from the warehouse.

He and Darnell jogged across the street. There was almost no traffic. At the entrance door, Darnell punched in the code from memory, and a moment later a click indicated the door had unlocked. "It's on a timer, so the door will automatically lock after it closes."

Darnell walked directly to a control panel the same shade of off-white as the paint on the wall. He entered a different six-digit code to turn off the alarm system. Rather than turn on the lobby lights and run the risk of attracting attention from a passing patrol car, Peter used the flashlight app on his phone to illuminate the way as he followed Darnell.

They took the same path to the bottling line as they had on Peter's previous two visits. "Where are the cleaning supplies?" Peter asked.

"Over here." Darnell opened a door leading into a large janitor closet, complete with sink and floor drain. The walls were lined with industrial metal shelving piled with cleaning supplies, cases of paper products, a few cans of paint, and spare light bulbs. Still using his flashlight, Peter quickly found what he was searching for—bleach. He grabbed a jug in each hand.

"Show me the filter housing where the viral agent was added to the water."

Darnell led the way past rows of machinery. Then he stopped and pointed. "It's the last of these three housings. What are you going to do? It was cleaned and sterilized already."

"That's what you say. But you've given me plenty of reason to doubt your moral character. So I'm going to do it again, to be certain."

While Peter studied the machinery, determining how to remove the cap to the filter canister, Darnell slipped a dozen feet away. In the dim glow from the flashlight, his finger found an illuminated button on a control panel. Without a second thought, he pushed the button.

Peter startled at the sound of pumps whirring. Instinctively he pulled his hands away from the filter canisters. Only then did he realize Darnell was not at his side. "What did you do?" he asked.

"You said you wanted to sterilize the line. This system is built with a circulation pump and holding tank so we can periodically clean the system using industrial sanitizing agents. I just started it up. The process is automated. After two minutes, it will shut down. We'll need to let the day shift know they need to flush the line before bottling commences."

Pressing a hand against the piping, Peter felt a slight vibration. "I was going to pour this bleach into the filters," he said.

"That would have only sterilized that portion of the line. This process flushes all of the plumbing, the entire system."

Before they moved on, Peter opened both jugs of bleach and splashed the noxious liquid liberally over the three filter housings, setting the empty jugs on the floor where they would be easily seen when the day shift arrived to work. The smell of bleach combined with the empty containers would alert the workers that something was amiss. But to be certain the line wasn't put into operation, Peter would place an anonymous call to Cascade Aqua first thing in the morning.

The two men continued past the bottling line and to the back of the building where the warehouse was located. Since the warehouse had no windows, and it did not front the street, they turned on the overhead lights.

"We park our trucks over there," Darnell pointed to the far side of the warehouse, close to the overhead doors. "Used to have trouble with vandalism when they were left outside overnight."

Peter turned his attention to the stack of pallets that had previously captured his attention. He approached and checked the tag—Nigeria. Many of the other pallets slated for local delivery were gone. "Looks like your warehouse crew has been busy."

"Shipments go out several days each week. I expect these pallets for Nigeria will go out soon, probably tomorrow."

"Not anymore. You're sure none of your employees know about your plan?"

"Certain. I introduced the virus myself—at night, after everyone left. It's a granular material designed for slow release. After a certain number of days, it completely dissolves along with the plastic bag it's kept in. There's no physical trace left to be found. After producing enough contaminated product, I instructed the day shift to clean and sterilize the piping, filter housings, and all the machinery."

"Naturally. You wouldn't want to sacrifice quality, would you?"

Darnell stared back in silence.

"Come on," Peter said. "Let's get these cases loaded so we can get out of here."

"Why don't we simply destroy the stockpile? Why do you want to confiscate it instead?"

"We've been over this already. I want to have evidence for the CDC. Not to mention that I have no idea what would happen if we dumped all this contaminated water into the sewer system. Do you?"

"No, I guess not. We never discussed that."

"Of course not. Until we know what the agent is, it's best that we don't release it into the environment. Enough talk. I need you to get on that forklift and get these pallets—"

Peter's phone vibrated in his pocket. He answered, knowing it was Danya. "Something wrong?"

"Yeah. Two vehicles approaching. The lead one just turned into the parking lot and the second one is following. You need to get out of there."

"Are they police?"

"No. Civilian. A sedan and an SUV like the one at the warehouse where you were being held."

Just then Peter heard the muffled sound of car engines outside the warehouse doors.

He disconnected the call. "Come on Darnell," his voice barely louder than a whisper. "I think your friends are here. We have to go."

Suddenly, an exterior door into the warehouse opened. Peter heard voices talking as he and Darnell scampered away using the stacks of palletized bottled water to shield their exit from the large, open room.

"Someone forgot to turn the lights off," a voice said. From just on the other side of the door adjoining the bottling line to the warehouse, Peter could not see the newcomers.

"Maybe." The voice was that of Roger Corbett. "Just to be sure, you search the warehouse while the rest of you find the Nigerian shipment."

Crouched in silence, Peter held the door from the warehouse to the bottling line open just a crack while he continued to listen. He glimpsed a man moving among the stacked cases, searching the shadows. It didn't take long to find what they were looking for.

"Here it is," a deep male voice said.

"Good," Corbett acknowledged. "Get it loaded into one of the trucks. Dr. Ming can decide what he wants to do with it."

"Right away, sir."

Peter didn't hear any machinery operating, and he assumed men were loading the cases of bottled water by hand into the same truck he'd planned to use to drive away with the product. Then he heard a familiar voice. "Nothing, Mr. Corbett. There's no one here other than us."

"Good. Now give us a hand. I want to get this loaded and out of here. Still a long night ahead for me."

"Aren't you going back with us?"

"No," Corbett replied. "I have to check in on our chemist and make sure he's still on schedule. One of you can drive this truck over to Utopian-Bio. Put it in the parking garage and keep an eye on it. Once I'm on the highway, I'll phone Dr. Ming and give him my report."

Peter silently closed the door and nudged Darnell, pointing to the front entrance. Together they used Peter's flashlight to make their way around machinery as they ran for the lobby and out the door.

"Get back to Danya, I'll be right behind you," Peter said.

"What are you doing?"

"Never mind. Just go!"

As Darnell dashed across the street, Peter hugged the building and worked his way toward the warehouse entrance in back. As soon as he rounded the corner of the building, he saw the vehicles Danya had mentioned. He easily recognized the sporty sedan, a white Dodge Charger, he'd seen Roger Corbett drive earlier. *The man likes fast cars.*

Peter silenced his phone and hurried to the side of the car. He gently opened the door. The dome light came on, and he hoped no one was watching. He'd know soon enough. He slipped his phone as far as he could reach under the passenger seat. As he closed the door, the click sounded as loud as gunfire in the quiet of night, but it failed to draw any attention. Without lingering for even a second, he dashed back to the front of the building, then crossed the street to the where he knew Danya would be waiting.

CHAPTER 32

Eugene, Oregon
March 29

THE TRIO CROUCHED BESIDE Danya's pickup, watching the driveway to Cascade Aqua from about a hundred yard's distance. There were few street lights in this industrial district of Eugene, and with the overcast night sky, it was unlikely anyone would see the three faces watching intently.

They didn't wait long before they saw Corbett drive away. He was headed east. Less than a minute later the delivery truck slowly exited onto the street. It was followed by the SUV, and both were headed in the opposite direction as Corbett.

"So what do we do?" Danya asked. "Follow the truck or the sports car?"

"Neither," Peter replied. "They're driving the bottled water to Utopian-Bio."

Danya started to rise but was halted by Peter's hand on her shoulder. "They're not going to welcome us with open arms," he said.

"I can fight. You can, too."

He ignored her statement. "Darnell, where is the parking garage located?"

"It's underground, beneath the building. I've parked there on previous visits."

"Does it have security?"

"There's a gate and a metal door that rolls up. I wasn't looking for cameras."

"You can bet they have cameras," Danya said, "at least at the entrance, but probably throughout the garage."

"We can't get the truck," Peter said. "We won't be able to enter the parking garage without being detected, and if we try to break into the building we won't get far. They'll have plenty of armed guards—most likely mercenaries. And once a firefight starts, it won't be long until the police show up. Remember, that building is private property. If the mercenaries don't shoot us, the police probably will."

"We don't have to go there," Darnell said. "Now that we know where the cases of water are, why don't you call your friend at the CDC and have them confiscate it."

"And how long do you think that will take?" Peter said. "They might already be flushing the evidence down the sewer. It'll take days for the government to respond, assuming they take me seriously."

"That leaves us with the car," Danya said. "But with the lead he has, who knows where he is now, or where he's going."

"I overheard Corbett say he needed to check on his chemist concerning the schedule. I think it's safe to conclude he's planning to visit the laboratory where the virus is being produced."

"Darnell, do you know the location of the lab?" Danya asked.

He shook his head.

"We're wasting time. We have to follow that car," she said.

"We will, but let's give him a little space."

"But—"

"I planted my phone in Corbett's car. We can track it." Peter produced the second phone he'd bought earlier.

"Brilliant!" Danya exclaimed.

"If I'm right," Peter said as he downloaded an app, "Corbett will lead us right to the manufacturing site."

A minute later the cell phone screen displayed a red dot overlaid on a map of the Eugene area. The dot was moving east.

After driving for a little over two hours, the mini-caravan, comprised of Peter's luxury sedan followed by Danya's pickup truck, passed through Bend. They had no idea where they were going but assumed their fuel range would be about the same as Corbett's car they were tracking. He'd been on the move throughout the night, and Peter was glad they decided to fill up at an all-night service station before leaving Eugene.

At the eastern city boundary, Peter pulled over to the side of the road and exited his car. Danya stopped behind him and rolled her window down, the engine idling smoothly. Peter leaned over, bracing his hand against the door. "I've been thinking about my plan once we know where Corbett is going. I suspect the lab is out there," he motioned to the east. "A hell of a lot of open and desolate land. Plenty of space to hide a clandestine lab."

"So, let's get going," Danya replied.

Peter glanced at the phone in his hand. The red dot was still moving east on Highway 20. "No. You stay here with Darnell. If this goes badly, you and Darnell must contact Julia Zhong at the CDC and tell her the whole story." Peter shared the phone number. "At first, she may be skeptical, but tell her everything. You must convince her to open an investigation of Utopian-Bio. Insist that her team also investigates Cascade Aqua—maybe they can find traces of the virus or other supporting evidence."

"But they could shut down my business indefinitely," Darnell said from the passenger side of the cab.

"Too bad, Mr. Price," Peter said. "You should have thought of that before you got tangled up in this mess. Considering the pain and long-term harm you inflicted on those young men at Warm Springs, you'd be getting off easy if the only penalty you suffered was to see your business closed down."

"Okay," Danya said. "It shouldn't be too hard to convince Ms. Zhong, if that's what we need to do."

"Under no circumstances can you call my old number. Even though I set the ringer to silent mode, we can't run the risk that the setting changed from the phone being bumped or something. If you must reach me, dial this number." He gave the new phone number to Danya.

"What are you going to do when you get to the manufacturing site?"

"Burn it to the ground. They can't be allowed to continue making the virus."

Danya looked directly into Peter's eyes. He held her gaze, reading the concern she tried to bury. But it was there in her pinched lips and wrinkled brow. Peter straightened to return to his car, but Danya's words stopped him. "It won't be that easy."

He considered her words, knowing she was right. "Should be back to Bend by early afternoon, maybe sooner. I'll call you to arrange a meeting location." Peter paused for a moment. "If I don't, contact Detective Ruth Colson at the Bend Police Department. She can be trusted, and she'll do the right thing."

"I thought we had an understanding. I've made it a priority to avoid the authorities. It's one reason I'm not locked up somewhere far away."

Peter shrugged. "You'll figure it out." Then he twisted his mouth in a lopsided grin. "You know, for a professional assassin, you turned out alright."

After parting ways with Danya and Darnell, Peter drove fast to close the distance with the car he was tracking. Sunrise wouldn't be for another couple of hours, and it would be a mistake to lose Corbett because he turned off the highway and Peter was too far back to identify the exit.

Contrary to the overcast sky in Eugene, on this side of the Cascade Mountains the night sky was clear, offering spectacular views once he left the city lights behind. Before long, the Rolls Royce closed the distance and then paced Corbett's car, staying a few miles behind so Corbett wouldn't notice the trailing headlight.

Although Peter had no idea where they were going, he did know that along this stretch of road the cities, and fuel stops, were few and far between. About thirty-five miles outside of Bend, he slowed. The red dot he was following on the phone had turned off the highway. Peter enlarged the map and spotted the secondary road Corbett had taken.

The pavement quickly gave way to packed gravel, and Peter further reduced his speed and turned off the headlights, carefully navigating by the dim light of a crescent moon.

Against the starlit sky, Peter saw a ridgeline ahead, climbing to a butte off to the right. Unless the gravel road turned, it would climb the ridge. Corbett's car was nowhere in sight.

Peter kept a steady pace as he gained elevation. He stopped at the crest next to a gate and turned off the dome light before exiting the car. The barbed-wire fencing was well maintained and stretched as far as he could see. From his vantage point, looking south, he could see into and across a wide valley. A spot of white and red light was bouncing and weaving across an unseen trail.

Unlike western Oregon, the land on the east side of the

Cascade Mountains was semi-arid, and the range of natural vegetation was limited and sparse. Bunch grass and a few varieties of scraggly bushes dotted the sandy soil. In the dim illumination of moonlight, the scattered juniper trees looked like black blobs dabbed on a light landscape. The terrain was marked by low hills—many ancient cinder cones—and dry washes that temporarily filled with water following infrequent downpours. With vast open range land and only a scattering of towns all the way to the California border, there was no shortage of good locations to hide an illegal drug lab—or a biofactory manufacturing contagious virus.

Peter silenced his phone and tucked it securely in the front of his jeans, then reached behind the seat, retrieving a pair of binoculars. He focused on the moving car. It was the white sedan he'd seen leaving the Cascade Aqua plant in Eugene.

As he watched, Corbett's car came to a stop in the distance beneath an overhead lamp at the top of a tall post. Two pickup trucks and an SUV were parked nearby. A figure met him as he stepped out of his vehicle, escorting him to the door. After a brief discussion, Corbett entered the trailer leaving the guard outside.

To the side and only a few dozen yards away was a second building, but no light emerged from windows or doorways. Peter figured the lab would be located in that building.

The eastern horizon was turning from black to a shade of violet, and he knew the sun would rise soon. For now, at least, the odds were still in his favor.

He continued to glass the buildings, spotting another roving guard. That made two. It looked like they had long guns slung over their shoulders, and both were milling about casually, occasionally stopping to chat or maybe smoke a cigarette—Peter couldn't be certain from the distance even with magnification.

He estimated that inside the trailer there might be as many as four or five additional guards—probably asleep. *But why did Corbett drive out here at this early hour?*

As Peter watched intently, his question was answered. Corbett and another man left the trailer—what he considered to be the living quarters—for the adjacent building, leaving the two roving guards on post outside.

Peter realized he needed to move fast. If Corbett concluded his business and left via a different road in one of the parked trucks—a very likely outcome in order to avoid being trapped if law enforcement should come in from the same direction Peter had taken—he could lose him for good. There was no way the Rolls Royce would be able to traverse rough terrain like a four-wheel drive pickup. But if he was going to survive the inevitable hail of bullets as he approached the buildings, he'd first have to complete certain preparations.

CHAPTER 33

PETER REPLACED THE BINOCULARS behind the seat and quickly got to work up-armoring his two-door sedan. He considered the vulnerabilities of the luxury vehicle. The large V12 engine in the front would serve as a good bullet shield, and he figured he could cover several hundred yards, maybe more, even with the radiator shot through. It was the sides and back of the vehicle that were susceptible to gunfire and needed protection.

Peter had taken stock of his immediate surroundings after glassing Corbett's car across the valley. Range fencing in this part central Oregon was often barbed wire stapled to wood posts fashioned from small trees or split rails. However, because the ground was very rocky, the posts were frequently fixed in place using piles of stone, an abundant and free building material. It was common for gate posts to be reinforced with a large pile of stone held in place with hog wire, or with stacked sandbags.

Perhaps because of the nature of the business being conducted on this parcel of rangeland, the fence near the road was in very good condition, and this supply of materials had given Peter an outlandish idea, but one that just might work.

"It better work," Peter mumbled, "or this fight will be over as fast as it starts."

With the passenger door open, Peter pressed a lever which allowed him to push the seatback forward and gain access to the rear bench seat. Next, he selected the flattest rocks that were used to brace the fence posts. Most of the dense, igneous stones weighed in excess of fifteen pounds, and it took some effort to lean in the open door and heave them onto the leather seats. The top-quality, dyed bull hide didn't stand a chance against the rough rocks, and the upholstery was scuffed and scratched in short order. Still, Peter continued to pile in the stones. They stacked well, and eventually the entire rear seat was filled from side to side and to the top of the seat back.

Feeling confident that he was protected from bullets penetrating through the rear of the car, Peter turned his attention to the front passenger seat. This was more challenging, as he didn't want to risk having a stack of stones become unstable and fall on his lap as the car jostled over the rutted and bumpy road.

He decided the solution was the sandbags used to anchor both gate posts. Starting at the wheel well, Peter stacked in sandbags, one after another, building up layer upon layer, two sandbags deep, that expanded to cover the passenger seat halfway up the side window. He even stuffed the last of the sand bags onto the dash, leaving a small gap in front of the steering wheel for forward visibility.

Closing the door, Peter took stock of his handiwork. "When this is over, I'm gonna need another car. Assuming I survive." He wiped his dusty hands on his pant legs. "Of course, if the Rolls

Royce sales staff ever hears about this sacrilege, they'll probably never let me set foot again in the factory in Goodwood."

He ducked his head and sat in the driver's seat, placing the SIG Sauer pistol on his lap. He looked to the eastern sky. It was turning from violet to ever-lighter shades of gray. It was time to go. He started the engine, the motor rumbling to life with a confident, throaty purr.

He nudged the Wraith off the ridge and down into the valley below. Leaving the head lamps off and navigating by the dim glow of the eastern horizon, Peter kept steady pressure on the throttle, guiding his improvised armored vehicle forward, likely to its doom.

The suspension absorbed nearly all the bumps and ruts, only the most serve causing a soft chatter of the stacked stones. Fortunately, the sandbags and rocks remained in place. As Peter crossed the shallow draw, he rolled down the windows. The depression was deeper than it had appeared from atop the ridge, and it completely swallowed the car.

As he emerged from the gully, the two buildings were ahead in the distance. The approach was straight and level. Expecting to receive gunfire at any moment, he depressed the gas pedal and added speed. With a throaty growl, the twelve-cylinder engine did not disappoint.

Although it was still a half hour to sunrise, the horizon had lightened considerably, and it was not difficult at all to follow the gravel road. He slunk down in the seat to an uncomfortable position with his legs bunched up under the dash and steering wheel, and his eyes just barely able to see above the row of sand bags and out the windshield.

About three hundred yards out, the gunfire started. Peter shifted his eyes to locate the guards. Shadows, one on each side of the road. They were wasting ammunition shooting their submachine guns in full auto. Thankfully, most of the rounds failed to hit the car, but he knew that would change as he quickly closed the distance.

He kept his foot on the gas pedal, and the car roared forward.

The guards reloaded and resumed firing, sending a volley of bullets into the grill and radiator. Steam swept back over the windshield. Peter held his course. With one hand firmly gripped on the steering wheel, he flicked off the safety on his pistol.

Corbett and another man exited the second building. Both raised handguns and added their fire to that of the two guards. Rounds were penetrating the bodywork with regularity now, beginning to drain sand from the bags piled on the passenger seat. The windshield was pock-marked with a couple dozen bullet holes, making it difficult for Peter to see where he was going.

Another fusillade of lead struck the front of the car, impacting the engine. The ominous sound of metal-on-metal grinding filled the cabin. It was soon followed by a tug on the steering wheel as first one tire, and then the other, was shot out. He moved the shift lever to neutral, allowing the full benefit of momentum to keep the once-beautiful automobile rolling forward. Every yard he advanced got him that much closer, all from within the relative safety of his crudely armored vehicle. On foot, he didn't stand a chance.

He swung his door open—a suicide door that was hinged at the rear rather than the leading edge as is the case with most automobiles. This styling quirk offered an advantage that, in all probability, had never been considered by the designers.

Still rolling forward, the open door scooped air inside the passenger compartment, swirling dust and sand like a mini vortex. Keeping a firm hand on the wheel, he leaned to the side and extended the SIG Sauer pistol into the opening. With an unobstructed view forward along the front quarter panel, he brought the sights to bear on the nearest gunman and opened fire. Two shots were sufficient to drop the surprised guard. He shifted his weapon and fired on a second guard just emerging from the house, sending him sprawling face-first into the dirt.

Bullets continued to rip into the right side of the car as it coasted toward the living quarters. Two more guards stumbled out the door, their attention immediately drawn to the shot-up car barreling toward them.

Peter had his sights on them and fired several times, mortally wounding both gunmen. A jarring impact and the sound of crunching metal overwhelmed his senses, causing him to momentarily forget about the gunfight. His brain soon processed the information, and Peter peeked over the dashboard. He'd rammed into the side of Corbett's sedan. The impact was the death blow to the once magnificent V12 engine, and it ground to a halt.

At a dead stop, Peter rolled out the open driver's-side door. There were still armed men on the opposite side of the car trying their best to kill him.

Using the shot-up body of the Rolls Royce has cover, Peter stole a glance and counted four shooters, including Corbett. They were moving apart, working their way around the car. Soon, they would flank him, and that would be game over.

Peter popped up and fired twice through the open passenger window. Shots were returned. Most were absorbed by the sandbags occupying the passenger side of the car—several sent chips flying from the stacked stones on the rear seat. Peter fired again and clipped one of the men in the shoulder.

Another volley of fire from submachine guns forced Peter down again. He figured that if he fired a third time from the same location, they'd nail him. He edged his way to the rear of the car. Peeking around the tail, he got a good alignment on the wounded guard and fired, striking him squarely in the chest.

The man collapsed and lay motionless.

The boom of a shotgun drew Peter's attention to a gunman firing from the corner of the house. He looked young, probably just a teenager. The scattergun roared again, sending a load of buckshot high into the windshield. The recoil sent the kid stumbling backwards.

A barrage of submachine gun bullets ripped into the side of the Rolls Royce. Peter leaned forward and snapped two shots at the kid, enough to send him running behind the house.

He hazarded another glance, pistol ready. But there was only one shooter—Corbett was not there.

A wave of dread washed over Peter, but he couldn't dwell on where Corbett might be, not yet. He leveled the SIG Sauer and squeezed the trigger.

The shot missed!

He fired again and this time the bullet slammed into the guard's thigh. He collapsed to the side as if he'd been hit with a baseball bat.

"Enough! Drop it!"

The words came from Peter's left. He recognized the voice and knew who had given the order.

He hesitated.

"I said drop it! Hands up."

Peter tossed the gun a few feet to the side. He placed his hands on his head and rose to his feet, turning to face Corbett.

CHAPTER 34

WITH HIS BACK TO THE LIGHT POLE and his hands cuffed around the pole, there was little Peter could do. The young gunman with the shotgun was guarding Peter while Corbett and one other guard were loading sealed plastic bags containing a brownish powder into the back of the SUV, a large Suburban. The bags were uniform in shape and about the size of a small briefcase. The two men went back and forth between the lab trailer and the SUV until there was no more product to move. As Peter watched them work, he noticed for the first time that the windows were blacked out using aluminum foil taped in place from the inside.

"That's all of it, Mr. Corbett," the guard said. The back of the Suburban was packed full, the bags piling half way up the windows.

"Good. Take the license plates off my car and clean out the glove box. Wipe it down for fingerprints, too. When you're done, follow the gravel road south until you get to the pit. Turn the engine off and push the car into the hole. Got it?"

"Yes sir. But what about Louie?" he said, indicating the guard Peter had shot in the thigh. He was leaning against the SUV, his hand pressed against the bullet wound. Blood was seeping out, soaking into the sandy dirt. No one had bothered to place even a rudimentary bandage around the wound. He appeared to be on the verge of consciousness, no doubt shock setting in.

"Don't worry about him. Just do your job." The guard took the keys from Corbett and set to work while his boss disappeared inside the lab trailer. The sound of breaking glass soon followed as the windows were systematically shattered, leaving gaping holes in the walls. Peter heard the sloshing of liquid being spilled on the floor and soon after, a flicker of light appeared through the open window frames that quickly grew into a raging conflagration.

Corbett jumped through the doorway just ahead of the flames which shot out the opening and danced wildly above the roof of the trailer. The heat was intense, and even from a distance Peter had to avert his gaze.

The guard tossed the license plates and a few pieces of paper from the glove box into the SUV, then drove off in the white sedan. There would be no evidence to recover from the lab; the fire would consume everything. That left the dead bodies, as well as Peter and the wounded guard named Louie.

The kid addressed Corbett without relaxing his attention on his prisoner, the shotgun aimed in Peter's direction. "You'll help my uncle, right Mr. Corbett?"

"Just do your job kid."

"Yes, sir, Mr. Corbett. This guy isn't going anywhere. I've got my eye on him, and if he tries to escape, I'll blow him away."

"Just relax, kid. I don't want you to accidentally shoot our guest. You with me?"

The kid nodded but kept the barrel of his weapon pointed menacingly toward Peter.

Corbett walked up to the Suburban and extended his hand down to the guard. "Come on Louie. We have to get you into the truck," he said as he helped the man to his feet. With a groan, he hobbled a step, still leaning over to put pressure on the bleeding wound.

Louie winced and said, "How about if my nephew gets the medical kit in the trailer?"

"The kid?" Corbett replied. "He's got a job to do keeping an eye on our prisoner."

"I need a bandage for this," Louie said through gritted teeth.

"Nah, not really." Corbett placed his pistol to Louie's head and pulled the trigger. The lifeless body fell into a crumpled heap, the face no longer recognizable.

The kid jumped at the gunshot, his eyes wide in disbelief and fear. "Mr. Corbett? What happened?"

The kid was facing Corbett's back, so he hadn't seen the murderous deed. Corbett straightened and spun, extending his arm with fluid grace. He pulled the trigger once, twice. Two bullets tore through the kid's chest, ravaging his lungs, heart, and aorta. Blood and gore spouted out the exit holes in his back. His limp body folded forward at the waist before falling to the side.

Still tied to the post, Peter was powerless to intervene. Looking at the body only feet in front of him, he shouted, "You didn't have to do that!" He locked eyes with Corbett. "He was just a kid."

"Shut up. You've caused me enough problems. If it were up to me, I'd put a bullet in your head, too."

Peter closed his eyes and dropped his chin, wishing that would make the horror go away. But he knew otherwise. He was no stranger to senseless killing. He raised his head, his lips drawn in a hard line, his jaw set like stone. "You shouldn't have done that."

Corbett met his stare. "You're in no position to tell me what to do."

"That fire's going to attract attention. Pretty stupid move on your part."

Corbett scoffed. "This is private land for as far as you can see, and no one within five miles in any direction. So tell me, who's going to see the smoke? And who's going to care?"

"You can't destroy all the evidence," Peter said. "When the state police arrive to investigate, they'll figure it out, and they'll find you."

"Here's what they'll figure out. This was a meth lab, and bad things happen to drug dealers all the time. These men," he motioned with his hand, "all have records for prior arrests and convictions. This case will be opened and closed within twenty-four hours."

"What about your car, the weapons?"

Corbett glanced at his watch. "My car is at the bottom of a hole thirty feet deep formed ages ago when the roof of a lava tube collapsed. It'll be years before anyone finds it, and so what if they do? There's nothing to connect the car to this crime scene. And the guns were all purchased on the black market. You see, that's what drug dealers do."

Holding the pistol against Peter's head, Corbett unlocked one side of the handcuffs. "Now, we're going to take a ride." He prodded Peter forward with the barrel of the gun pressed against his spine.

They stopped at the SUV and Corbett ran a hand over Peter's pockets and sides. He confiscated the extra SIG Sauer magazine. "Won't be needing that anymore," Corbett said. "Where's your phone?"

Peter shrugged. "Somewhere inside my car probably, unless

it fell out the door when your men were shooting at me."

Corbett pressed the pistol barrel into Peter's back. "Open the door. Nice and easy."

Peter complied and started to get in, but was stopped by a firm grip on his shoulder. "Not so fast. First we have to put that handcuff back on."

Peter extended his arms, expecting Corbett to fasten the cuff in place. "That's not the way we're going to do this. Bend over."

Uncertain what was coming, Peter hesitated, receiving another poke from the gun barrel. "Bend over! Put one hand between your legs and clasp your hands together."

He did as instructed, and the handcuffs were clamped onto both wrists, leaving Peter in a very uncomfortable position. "Now you can get in."

Corbett got behind the wheel with Peter in the passenger seat, his hands locked together underneath his right thigh. "This is rather uncomfortable. I hope we don't have to travel far?"

"Your comfort is not at all my concern."

Corbett depressed the accelerator, leaving behind a cloud of dust. After a short drive, he found the last guard standing beside the gravel road, having disposed of the white sedan. Corbett got out and took the back seat, behind Peter, while the guard took the wheel.

"I rolled your car into that sink hole just as you said. A shame to waste a nice car like that."

"Never mind. Did you see anyone along the way?"

"Hell, no. There ain't nobody out here. Hey, where's Louie?"

"He couldn't make it."

The guard seemed to understand. He also came to the conclusion that asking questions may result in a significantly shortened life expectancy. He gripped the steering wheel, staring ahead. "Where to, Mr. Corbett?"

"Eugene. The ranch."

CHAPTER 35

THE RANCH WAS EXPANSIVE, just shy of a thousand acres. Bordered by forested land, the property of a large timber company, this additional buffer added to the privacy. The nearest neighbor was three miles away. Seclusion was the highest priority and the reason why Simon Ming had purchased this property.

Over the preceding two years, he'd paid handsomely to renovate the run-down ranch house, where the security detail was based, adding a large barn that included a well-equipped machine shop plus plenty of refrigerated storage. The ground floor of the barn was the high-tech nerve center of the operation, fitted with multiple computer terminals, several high-capacity servers, communications equipment, and a break room. But there was also a second floor that housed the security center and the pilot control rooms. To ensure an uninterrupted supply of electricity to power the equipment, two back-up generators had been installed beside the barn.

Spreading the work among many contractors, and never using the same contractor twice, Ming managed to maintain a low profile and not attract unwanted attention from his rural neighbors or the nearby city of Eugene. The unimproved gravel road leading up to the ranch helped. Intruders were discouraged by the barbed-wire fence surrounding the perimeter which was backed up by state-of-the-art wireless security cameras which numbered more than a hundred.

The flat, open space between the barn and the house was covered by a large lawn about the size of two soccer fields placed side by side. Evergreen trees stretched skyward beyond the manicured grass. The undergrowth—a wide range of shrubs including native rhododendron and azalea, blackberry vines, raspberry, salmonberry, plus young evergreen trees—was meticulously cut to the ground at Roger Corbett's insistence, leaving only mature trees over the twenty-acre buffer surrounding the house and barn. Ever cautious, he wanted a defensible perimeter with limited cover for any intruders. A small tribe of goats maintained the area free of shrubs and vines.

The overnight fog had lifted early, a rarity during spring in the southern Willamette Valley. Simon Ming was enjoying a latte from the comfort of a bent-willow rocking chair on the wide veranda surrounding the house. With a scattering of white, puffy clouds, the temperature was near perfect, and he preferred the crisp and clean air to the mildew aromas still locked within the house from the winter season. Scattered rays of sunlight glistened off dewdrops clinging to every surface like so many gem stones. His phone was pressed to his ear as his eyes surveyed the natural beauty of the forest.

"Seventy bags. That's all our chemist was able to manufacture?" Ming said.

Corbett had phoned from the back seat of the Suburban.

He spoke in a low voice—preferring not to broadcast his conversation to the other occupants of the vehicle. "That's all there is. I checked personally."

"Most likely he overestimated the quantity he could produce based on his experience synthesizing meth. My product is a different beast."

"It's something to keep in mind with the other manufacturers. Simple enough to reduce their projections by ten to fifteen percent."

"Very true," Ming replied. "And the lab?"

"Just as you said. Cooking meth is a dangerous pastime. Sadly, the lab burned to the ground. I'm sure it's a total loss, the fire was very intense." The corners of his mouth turned up in a cruel grin.

"Hmm. Bad luck. And the workers?"

"Let's just say they won't be filing any claims for worker's comp."

"Where are you now?"

"About an hour from your ranch. Everything is proceeding on schedule. We can prep the drone with the inventory I have with me."

"Excellent. I want to strike immediately."

"Sir, you're suggesting we accelerate the schedule by several days. Are you certain that's wise?"

"Do not worry, Mr. Corbett. My pilots and technicians have successfully completed every training mission. And with this unnecessary *distraction* that we are dealing with, I think to wait introduces even greater risk."

"Of course," Corbett replied. He did not agree with his boss, and thought it foolish, maybe borderline reckless, to accelerate the schedule this late in the plan. But he knew the consequences of further argument would not be favorable. "And the target?"

"The Hayden Bridge water intake, just as my men have

trained." Ming ended the call and thought through the plan for the hundredth time. He ran all the detailed steps through his mind as if rehearsing for a Broadway performance. Very soon, he would disperse his genetically engineered product into the water supply for the cities of Eugene and Springfield. Within a day, the combined population of a quarter million people would begin to be exposed to his virus.

And that is only the beginning. His lips formed a thin smile.

Inside the barn, a crew of four technicians clothed in sky-blue coveralls was readying the rotating-wing drone. The craft consisted of a central body surrounded by six ducted fans, each fifteen inches in diameter. The body of the aircraft had no need for windows. But it was fitted with a hatch on the bottom that could be opened to varying degrees. Using construction inspired by much larger aircraft that drop fire retardant powder on wildfires, the hatch was remotely controlled to dispense its load at a specific rate that was indexed to the forward speed of the drone, thus ensuring uniform dispersion once it was over the drop zone.

Electric power for driving the six motors came from an advanced hydrogen fuel cell molded to the desired aerodynamic shape. To save weight, the fuel cell also functioned as the housing for the dry, powdered virus. High-pressure hydrogen was stored in three ultra-light-weight carbon-fiber canisters. Fueling was accomplished from a supply of twenty-four large cylinders of compressed hydrogen located in a bay next to the machine shop.

Carrying a payload of twenty-five kilograms, the drone could complete a round trip flight distance of thirty-seven miles in calm winds—twice that, if it was a one-way trip. And given the mission plan, there was little reason to have the drone return.

The avionics suite was rather simple to operate and based on a very sophisticated navigational system using

GPS. Groundspeed was determined by a small radar system. Positional sensors in each of the ducted fans transmitted the angle of attack of each fan to the operator's control computer. This information was combined with the ground speed and fed to the computers in the flight control center to calculate the wind direction and velocity, essential information to ensure accuracy when the payload was dispensed.

Most of the ground floor of the barn was occupied by the control room—a complex collection of computers, large monitors, and servers. Twelve engineering work stations, arranged in three clusters of four, were located at the center of the floor. Every computational, navigational, and aircraft flight function was duplicated and staffed during a sortie, providing total redundancy. A walkway was suspended over the control room, accessible by a stairway at each end. Corbett's security team was stationed in a room at the middle of the walkway, surrounded on all four sides by glass walls.

The drone was a custom design, fabricated at the machine shop, also located within the barn. In order to prevent abrasive dust, metal chips, cutting oil, and other debris from damaging the delicate electronics, a wall of tempered glass panels separated the machine shop from the control room.

A pilot and copilot comprised the flight team that flew the drone at all times. There were three such teams. Although the backup wasn't essential, it allowed the flight teams to closely monitor all incoming data and provided greater assurance of mission success.

Ming's attention was drawn to the drone as it was rolled out the open barn doors. The aircraft was sleek and painted sky-blue with anti-reflective, matte-finish paint. Against the bright spring sky, it would be very difficult for ground observers to see its approach.

Presently, cornmeal was being loaded into the payload

cavity. Ming watched with fascination. Following extensive work that spanned nearly three years, he was in the final stretch. What he would witness today would be just a small piece of the machination, a prelude of what was to come.

The hatch door was closed, securing twenty-five kilograms of cornmeal inside the drone. The lead ground-support technician spoke into a hand-held radio. "Payload is secured. All clear. Ready to start motors."

"Roger," the pilot radioed back. "Energizing motors, 20 percent."

Immediately, the six fans started whirring. The craft buffeted lightly, but the skids remained fixed to the lawn.

"Looking good," the ground technician said. "You are clear to lift off."

"Roger. Increasing power. Stand clear." The ducted fans steadily increased in speed at the same time the sound intensity climbed until it sounded like a dozen angry, swarming hives of hornets.

With pride, Simon Ming watched the drone climb straight up—twenty feet, forty feet, seventy feet. It was just a small object now, nearly invisible in the morning sunlight. As he stared, the drone zipped forward and out of sight.

The plan for this final test flight was very simple; validate that the aircraft and navigational electronics all worked flawlessly. The pilots were to pass through five coordinates at the specified elevation, all marked by GPS, before returning fifteen minutes later to the ranch and dropping the cornmeal in a controlled release that would blanket the entire grassy area between the barn and house. The pilot team had practiced this before, completing similar maneuvers dozens of times.

Today was different.

This was the final trial flight, and if all went according to plan, the next mission would carry the viral agent.

CHAPTER 36

DANYA WAS PACING BACK AND FORTH inside the small travel trailer. The digital clock on the electric stove indicated the time, 8:05 a.m. From the outset, she'd never liked the plan Peter had proposed. Based on her training and experience, she knew the odds of success were extremely slim, close to zero.

She studied the red icon on her phone again. Copying Peter's idea for tracking Roger Corbett, once she returned to her trailer she'd set up the app to track Peter's new phone. She frowned—the symbol indicated he was considerably west of Bend. Something was wrong.

For his part, Darnell was slouched on the padded dinette, his back against the wall and head drooped so his chin nearly rested on his chest. His eyes were closed as he sat motionless. Danya let him sleep, one less concern to worry about, although he'd offered no resistance or made any attempt to escape.

She called Peter's number. It rang five times and then went to voice mail, not that she really expected he would answer. She turned her gaze to Darnell.

"Okay, sleeping beauty," she said to Darnell. "Rise and shine. You've got a job to do." She held out a pair of chrome handcuffs. "Hands before you. Wrists together. Come on, we don't have time to waste."

"You can't turn me in," Darnell said.

"The hell I can't. You have valuable information that you *are* going to share with the authorities. Most especially, Dr. Julia Zhong and her team at the CDC."

He rose and squared off, facing Danya.

"You're making a big mistake," she said.

"I'm not going to just walk into the hands of the police. I did what had to be done—for the greater good of all humanity. I'm not going to prison."

"You think you'll fair better with Ming's security force? They'll find you within a week. And when they do, you're dead."

He was shaking his head. "I've got money and resources. Without a family, I can run. They'll never find me."

"Don't be stupid, Darnell. You don't know anything about running or going off the grid."

"Maybe, but I'm a fast learner. Now, let me pass. I don't want to hurt you."

Although Darnell was considerably bigger than Danya, he was approaching middle age with a burgeoning layer of belly fat. Plus, he had no training in martial arts. "I'm not letting you go," she said. "If you really think you can make me move, go ahead. Give it your best shot. But don't say I didn't warn you."

He threw a punch at her face. It was sluggish, as she expected. She responded with lightning reflexes, easily blocking the strike, and immediately following through with a solid blow to his nose. Darnell was stunned. He took a half step backwards, then bellowed like a bull and lunged forward, arms out. He planned to wrap Danya in a bear hug and wrestle her down.

She raised a knee sharply into his groin. He doubled over in agony and she clasped her hands together into one large fist and slammed down with the force of a sledgehammer onto the base of his neck.

Finished, Darnell fell to his knees. Danya stepped behind him and pulled both hands behind his back. She ratcheted the cuffs snug around his wrists. She allowed him half a minute to catch his breath. "I could use you as a punching bag all day, but I've got work to do. Let's go. Into the truck."

"What's gonna happen?" he asked meekly.

"In about thirty minutes the Bend PD is going to rescue you."

During the short five-minute drive to Sawyer Park at the north end of the city, she dialed the Bend Police Department.

"Detective Colson, please."

"She's not scheduled to be on duty until eight thirty a.m.," the receptionist said. "I can put you through to her voicemail."

"That's fine."

After the second ring, Danya was greeted by a voice she recognized from memory. "You've reached the desk of Detective Colson. I can't take your call right now, but leave a message and I'll get back to as soon as I can."

"There's a person you want to pick up. His name is Darnell Price and he's handcuffed to a park bench at Sawyer Park. He has a very interesting story to share with you about bioterrorism." She punched the red button, disconnecting the call just as she made the turn into the wooded park along the Deschutes River.

Fortunately, it was still too early for visitors to the park. She stopped at a picnic table and seated Darnell on the ground. She pulled his hands forward and unlocked one side of the cuffs, then secured his hands again, passing the chain around the table support bracing. Darnell would have to carry the table if he planned on making an escape.

"Don't worry, the key is universal, so the police will uncuff you when they arrive."

"And when will that be? I could freeze out here," Darnell complained.

"It's thirty-five degrees and the police will be here in…" she checked her watch, "twenty minutes, maybe thirty. You won't freeze."

Danya hustled back to the idling truck and sped off. She had to be away from the park before law enforcement showed up. Still wanted by the FBI and the Oregon State Police as a person of interest, she knew that if she was anywhere near Darnell when the police arrived, she'd be arrested. And if that happened, she'd likely be sentenced to prison for the rest of her life.

As she left Sawyer Park, she should have turned west. That was the direction across the Cascade Mountains, and the tracking app indicated Peter had already crossed the mountains into the Willamette Valley, approaching Eugene. She stopped and bit her lip, a habit of hers when she was torn with indecision. Then she yanked the wheel to the right, toward downtown Bend. *I hope I don't regret this.*

She still remembered the directions to Peter's condo in the Old Mill District, and it wasn't long before she pulled her truck to a stop in front of his residence. Recalling that his girlfriend, Kate, was house-sitting and taking care of Diesel, she decided to take a big chance.

Danya took the steps up to the entry door two at a time, then rapped her knuckles on the solid wood door. She was just about to knock a second time when the door creaked open and a woman's face peered around the edge.

"Good morning," Danya said. "You don't know me, and this is going to sound like a strange request, but I really need your help."

"Oh?" the woman answered.

"You're Kate, right?"

She cocked her head to the side. "Yes. How do you know that?"

"I'm a friend of Peter's, and he needs our help." Danya spent a full two minutes—time she couldn't afford to waste—sharing the highlights with Kate.

"Have you called the police?" she asked.

"They can't be trusted. We think they're involved."

Kate shook her head. "You're being silly. Look, if you won't call them, I will." She moved away from the door for the kitchen. Her cell phone was resting on the counter next to a steaming cup of tea.

Danya followed her through the door and was stopped by Diesel. His feet were planted evenly, his head lowered. It looked like he could charge in a heartbeat—but he didn't.

Danya froze. "It's alright boy. I'm not going to hurt you or Kate."

"Diesel, sit," Kate called.

Danya walked into the kitchen. "I can't let you make that call. If the police are involved, and we're pretty sure they are, it will only make things worse. They don't know I'm tracking Peter."

"What?" Surprise was evident in Kate's voice.

"We're wasting time. Please! I need your help. We only have one chance to get Peter back alive. You have to trust me."

Kate locked eyes with Danya and after several long seconds decided she needed to trust her. "Okay. What do you want from me?"

Diesel had settled for watching the intruder from the entry hall. He wasn't displaying aggression, but he was wary. Danya was certain that if she made any threatening or aggressive moves toward Kate, the red pit bull would be on her in a flash.

"I need him," she nodded her head toward the canine. "As backup."

"You know Peter's dog?"

Danya nodded. "We've met." She decided not to elaborate.

Kate clapped her hands and Diesel jogged up to her, tail wagging. She rubbed her fingers over his thick neck and blocky head. "It's up to Diesel to choose."

"But, he's a—" Danya's objection was cutoff.

"Peter tells me that Diesel is a good judge of character. And from what I've seen, I have to agree. So, if he agrees to go with you, I'm good with it. But if he refuses, I'm not going to force him. You'd be wise not to try, either."

Danya quickly realized this wasn't a negotiation. "Okay." She knew that canines were very perceptive at understanding body language, scenting and interpreting pheromones that were indicative of stress and fear, and reading the emotional state of people. She hoped that her sincerity and urgency would be correctly interpreted by Diesel. She had one chance, and if it didn't work, her odds of success would be greatly diminished.

She squatted, facing the red pit bull, holding her hands outstretched with the palms up. "I need your help," she said. "Peter... he's in trouble. At least I think he is." She paused for a moment of reflection. *This is ridiculous. I'm actually trying to have a conversation with a dog.*

Diesel cocked his head in response, and his eyes brightened. "Do you understand what I'm saying?"

Danya raised her eyes to Kate, who simply shrugged.

She decided it was a make or break moment. "Okay, buddy. Ready for a car ride?" His tail wagged vigorously with anticipation. She breathed a silent sigh of relief.

Kate wrote her phone number on a slip of paper and handed it to Danya. Then she said, "His leash is hanging by the door."

"Thank you."

While she was clipping the leash to Diesel's collar, Kate added, "You'd better bring him back safe, or there will be Peter and me to answer to."

"I'll try," and she slipped out the door.

⊕

Danya drove west as fast as she dared. She stole a frequent glance at her phone. The object she was tracking had just entered Eugene—she was still half an hour away.

She picked up the phone and redialed the Bend Police number again. "Detective Colson, please."

"I'm sorry. She's away from her desk—"

Danya cutoff the receptionist. "Put me through to her cell. It's important. Has to do with the case she's investigating right now, the man at Sawyer Park."

After several seconds, Colson came on the line. "Hello? May I help you?"

"Did you find him?"

"You mean Darnell Price? Are you the person who left him handcuffed to the bench?"

"Did he tell you my name?"

Colson was taken aback by the unexpected question that implied a deeper meaning. "He said a woman named Danya did this to him. Is that who I'm talking to?"

She remained silent. All of her training told her to avoid law enforcement at all costs. But that bridge had been crossed and she had to continue. The events she was embroiled in were far bigger than she could manage on her own. She needed help. "Yes. My name is Danya Biton."

"Where are you now, Danya? We have a lot of questions. Did he harm you? Did he attack you?"

"You have no idea!" Danya shouted into the phone, before calming herself. "Mr. Price has been engaged in a plot to poison bottled water, produced by his company, with a virus. He tested it not far from you, on the reservation. The CDC has already begun an investigation, but they failed to find the source."

"Are you referring to the outbreak in Warm Springs?"

"Precisely. Mr. Price will be happy to explain how he laced his water with the virus and then donated that water to the Warm Springs Tribal Council. He will also tell you how he came into possession of such a dangerous contagion."

"Why are you telling me this over the phone? I need you to come into the police station and make an official statement."

Danya let out a short, mocking laugh. "That will never happen."

"Why not?"

"You don't know who I am, do you?"

The line was silent while the detective collected her thoughts. "Should I?"

"Oh, I think so. You see, we met at the United Armaments test facility in eastern Oregon. I was the woman who phoned to report the kidnapping."

Colson paused, searching her memory. "You were involved in the shootout on Broken Top." She couldn't mask her incredulity. "But at that time, you went by the name of Nadya Wheeler."

"Yes, that's right."

"Why are you telling me this? Please, come into the station. Whatever happened before, you can help me clear it up. You don't have to keep running."

"I said I'm not coming in," Danya replied, her voice sharp.

Colson's mind was racing, recalling her conversation a few weeks ago with the Deschutes County District Attorney, and his revelation that fingerprints from one of the Broken Top shooters were found on a weapon at a homicide crime scene near La Pine.

"Were you in La Pine a while ago?" she asked. "Were you

involved in that dog-fighting ring? We have your fingerprints on one of the weapons."

"I don't have time to waste. Are you interested in learning what I know about this bioterrorism or not?"

Colson's experience told her not to push, but play along. The longer she could keep Danya talking, the better. "Sure. But there's something more, right?"

Her question was answered with silence.

"You didn't need to speak with me. You could have simply left a note on the bench, or an anonymous tip. But you didn't. Why?"

"I need your help. There are lives at stake. I was told I can trust you."

"Told? By who?"

Danya spent the next thirty minutes bringing Detective Colson up to speed, stopping many times while the detective caught up with her note taking. When she finished Colson said, "That's an interesting story. But sounds like the Eugene PD has jurisdiction; certainly not Bend PD. Perhaps if you knew where this lab was located, I could help get the sheriff engaged. Do you have anything more to go on?"

"No, I've shared all I know."

"Well, I know a couple detectives in the Eugene PD. I'll make a call and see what they know about Utopian-Bio and Simon Ming."

"I don't think that's a good idea. Ming has hired a security force that operates more like a paramilitary team. They seem to show little concern for attracting attention from the law, and I have reason to believe they have police officers on their payroll. If Ming is as wealthy as he's rumored to be, paying large bribes would easily be within his means."

"Okay, Danya. You called me. What do you think I can do

to help you?"

"Keep Mr. Price in protective custody. They've already tried to kill him once. Since he knows about their organization, he represents an unacceptable liability."

"You sound like someone who is speaking from experience."

Danya bristled at the thinly veiled accusation, but she also knew it to be true. "And phone Dr. Julia Zhong at the CDC in Atlanta. You need to convince her to interview Price and shut down his bottling company while an investigation is conducted. She led the investigation at Warm Springs and knows Peter Savage." She repeated the phone number Peter had shared.

"Wait. Don't tell me he's involved, too."

"Yes. He's been working with the tribal council to find the cause of the illness, and he's the one who got the CDC to investigate."

"The two of you, working together. Just like old times. That can't be good."

"Listen, Detective. Forget about what happened before. That's history, done and over."

"I have your fingerprints linking you to a triple homicide and a dog-fighting ring. This isn't over until I have you in custody."

"You aren't listening! What part of bioterrorism don't you understand? These people are serious! So if you want to do something positive to help avert a disaster, I suggest you focus and forget about the little shit."

CHAPTER 37

IT WAS SHAPING UP to be a very busy day, and Detective Colson didn't have time to waste. Back at her desk, she dialed the phone number at the Centers for Disease Control and Prevention in Atlanta. She was greeted by a pleasant, feminine voice. "This is Dr. Zhong."

The detective introduced herself. "I'm calling with information that may be relevant to a case you were investigating at Warm Springs, Oregon."

"Still am," Julia replied. "We've not officially closed the case, but I am skeptical we will find the source of the outbreak."

"Well, that's the thing. I have a suspect in custody who may be responsible for contaminating bottled water that was donated to the tribal council."

"Let me guess—the bottled water was produced by Cascade Aqua?"

"Yes. You seem to be familiar with the company."

"The case was brought to my attention by Peter Savage. I

believe he lives in Bend."

"He does," Colson said. "We've met."

"An interesting character, I'd say. Rather persistent. Wouldn't you agree?"

"Interesting is an understatement when describing Mr. Savage. Anyway, please go on."

"He was advocating a theory that the virus was introduced through bottled water from Cascade Aqua. Trouble is, we couldn't recover any samples of the manufacturing lot representing the donated water. All the bottles we were able to find in grocery stores were from different lots, and they all tested negative for any harmful pathogens."

"I have the CEO of Cascade Aqua in custody. His name is Darnell Price. Ever heard of him?"

"No, not that I recall."

"He's shared some interesting information under questioning."

"Really?" The surprise was evident in Julia's voice.

"I'll come back to him in a minute. First, I'd be interested to hear what you think. You're the expert."

"Let me tell you what I know. It was definitely a virus that infected the people at Warm Springs. But my team has been unable to find the source of the virus, and the cases of new infections ceased as abruptly as they started. This would be consistent with a transient source of the virus, rather than a persistent cause."

"So you think it could be a specific lot of bottled water that introduced the virus?"

"That would be consistent with these facts, yes. However, few viruses that infect humans are transmitted through contaminated water. Those that are, such as hepatitis, result in much different symptoms. The cases we examined involved symptoms similar to mumps, but not identical."

"I'm not sure I understand," Colson said. "Are you saying that this is a new virus? Something that you haven't seen before?"

"Yes. We've isolated the virus from blood samples taken from the patients and have been studying it in detail. Preliminary results from the gene sequencing are fascinating and suggest a new virus that has traits found in mumps, HIV, and hepatitis. That's why this case is still open. I suspect we will be studying this for years to come."

"Is the virus fatal?"

"No, we don't think so. But it does target the human lymphatic system, with a proclivity to target the testes. The infection is severe, and based on similarity to the mumps, we believe sterilization of infected males is highly probable."

"Why only for males who are infected?"

"Well, that's one of the fascinating aspects of this virus. By blending select base sequences from three unrelated viruses—mumps, HIV, and hepatitis C—this new pathogen has acquired a measure of stability in water and it selectively targets the male reproductive system."

"Where do you think this virus came from? Could it be from a natural source, you know, a mutation or something?"

"Doubtful," Julia said. "The fact that this virus is a combination of genetic sequences known from other viruses suggests that it was engineered in the laboratory. What has your suspect shared about his source of the agent?"

"He says it was manufactured at a biolab in Eugene named Utopian-Bio. Cascade Aqua is also located in Eugene. According to Mr. Price, the lab specifically engineered the characteristics you described into the virus."

"Have you contacted the Eugene police yet?"

"No. I wanted to speak with you first." She decided not to offer the theory of crooked officers on the Eugene police force.

"I'm going to elevate this to the FBI and Homeland Security as a possible terrorist threat. Sometimes they jump on these threats right away, other times the agents require more evidence before they take it seriously. Just depends on who you talk to. So, I suggest you call local law enforcement immediately and see if they can get a warrant and search both the lab and the bottling line. If there is any physical evidence, it needs to be secured."

"We're still questioning Mr. Price, and I'm not sure I want to contact the Eugene PD, not yet. I'd have to transfer Mr. Price into their custody. My boss may not agree that is the right move just yet."

"If this is an interjurisdictional squabble, I suggest you and your boss get over it. There's a lot at stake, and time is of the essence."

"Relax, Dr. Zhong. This isn't the CDC and we have our own way of doing things. I'm just glad we caught this in time."

"Don't let your guard down. Mr. Price may control one piece of the overall plot, but there is still the question of who manufactured the virus, and can they move that operation to another, unknown facility. The threat still exists until the source of the virus is removed."

"You're working on a vaccine, right? Just to be safe?"

"I wish it were that simple, detective. Vaccines usually require years to develop, and even then, in some cases, we aren't successful. That's one of the reasons we're concerned about this particular virus."

"I don't understand," Colson replied.

"Well, one of the component gene sequences in this new virus was copied from HIV. This is concerning because there is no effective vaccine for HIV because of the way vaccines work. You see, a vaccine is a cocktail of dead or weakened virus that stimulates the human immune system to produce antibodies.

These antibodies attack the live virus and stave off infection. However, HIV attacks the very part of the immune system that would ordinarily produce these antibodies."

"I'm no science expert, far from it. But it sounds to me that whoever engineered this virus knew exactly what they were doing."

"They successfully designed a viable virus that infects males, likely causing sterility, and for which we have no precedent to develop an effective vaccine. Fortunately, it appears to be spread through water, at least if what Mr. Price has shared is truthful. It would be worse, much worse, if it was an airborne contagion."

Detective Colson was silent in thought for a moment. "That's an interesting point. Let's assume that a person, or group of people, deliberately developed this virus with the goal of infecting a civilian population center. It stands to reason, they would want to be able to limit the spread so as not to inadvertently be infected themselves."

"They could simply vaccinate themselves and those they want to be immune to the disease."

"You're assuming that whoever engineered the virus also developed a vaccine. You tell me, is that a safe bet?"

"Well," Julia hesitated, "for the reasons I've already shared, it's a long shot."

"What you're saying is there's no guarantee a vaccine was also developed along with the viral agent."

"I see your point," Julia said. "In that case, a water-based virus makes perfect sense. I have a bad feeling this is only the beginning. I've been warning about a global pandemic and no one in congress wants to do anything to prepare."

"Whoa. You think this could spread around the world?"

"If the virus is introduced into a major water supply, hundreds of millions could be infected. Once a localized population is exposed, it's possible the disease would spread through the exchange of body fluids—possibly even through coughing and sneezing which introduce tiny aerosol droplets in the air and others then breathe in those droplets. We've modeled these scenarios, and the results are frightening. In dense population centers, the virus spreads at a phenomenal pace."

"But what you've just described about the spread of the disease, that would also place the developers at risk, wouldn't it?"

"Not necessarily. Not if they isolated themselves from any local outbreaks until it burned itself out. This could be the perfect bioweapon."

Detective Ruth Colson debated calling over to the Eugene PD for several minutes. Finally, she decided that paranoid suspicions did not carry equal weight with professional relationships she'd developed. She knew a detective there from a conference both had attended a year earlier.

"Hey, Hector. It's Ruth Colson from over in Bend."

"Hello, detective. It's been a long time. What's up? My skills at deductive reasoning tell me this isn't a social call."

She shared the information gleaned from Darnell Price and relayed a summary of her conversation with Dr. Julia Zhong.

"And you think this guy's for real?" Hector Lopez said.

"Yes, I do. I'm going to send a file over to you later today. It'll have everything we've got on Price. Let me know how you want to coordinate the transfer, as we have no jurisdiction here. It will be up to your captain and the DA to decide if they want to charge Price or not."

After the call ended, Detective Lopez looked at the stack of files on his desk. It leaned to the side, threatening to fall over. He grabbed the top half of the stack with both hands and plopped it onto another portion of his desk. With a sigh, he rose and walked to a colleague. "Hey, Jackson," he said.

"What's up?" Jackson was younger than Lopez by ten years. He'd just made detective and seemed to get along well with everyone.

"I just had an interesting call with a detective I know over in Bend. I'm slammed with cases and wanted to see if you could help me out." He shared only the most essential portions of his prior conversation with Colson.

Jackson raised an eyebrow. "Sounds interesting. When the file comes in, forward it over to me. I'll fit this in with my workload."

"Thanks, man. I owe you."

"Damn right you do," Jackson said with a smile. "Now, if you'll excuse me, I've got a potential witness to interview."

When he was several blocks away from the police station, Jackson pulled to the side of Franklin Avenue and placed a phone call using a cheap burner phone he'd bought using cash.

"Yes," the voice said.

"Something just came across my desk. I thought you should know."

"Go on, I'm listening."

"The Bend police are holding a suspect, name is Darnell Price. Know him?"

"Yes. The owner and former president of Cascade Aqua."

"He's told them a story about virus-tainted bottled water. Said the virus came from Utopian-Bio."

"Is that so? Anything else?"

"I'm expecting a file from a Detective Ruth Colson later today. We are being asked to seek a search warrant on Utopian-Bio and Cascade Aqua. They're calling it bioterrorism."

"Have you been contacted by the FBI or Homeland Security?"

"Not yet," Jackson replied. "But I expect we will."

"When you get that file, get me a copy of everything it contains. And bring it personally. I'll be at the ranch."

"You can count on it."

Roger Corbett ended the call. Local and federal law enforcement could search all they wanted. There was nothing to find.

CHAPTER 38

AFTER TRAVELING THROUGH EUGENE, Corbett ordered the car to stop on a deserted stretch of road. He placed a canvas hood over Peter's head, then instructed the driver to continue. They drove on, passing heavy timber and old clear cuts that had been replanted with fir and hemlock. The young trees were only as tall as a man. The last house they'd passed was miles ago.

"Where we going?" Peter asked. His question was answered with silence. "These handcuffs are digging into my wrists."

"Just relax. It's not much farther," Corbett said.

No sooner had he spoken the words when the SUV slowed. The driver steered the Suburban onto a one-lane, gravel road. He covered about fifty yards, then stopped at a gate just long enough to enter a code on a control panel to allow passage. The gravel drive cut left and right as it meandered through the forest. Finally, the trees ahead thinned, and they entered a large clearing, pulling to a stop.

The driver helped Peter out of the SUV and removed the

hood, while Corbett maintained a safe distance to the side, his pistol drawn. Peter was forced to bend over at the waist, his hands still bound behind his right leg. "Remove the hand cuffs," Corbett ordered the driver.

Free of his restraints, Peter stood straight and stretched his back. He rubbed the marks on his wrists where the metal cuffs had bit into flesh during the long drive.

"This way," Corbett said, motioning with the gun. Far to the left was a large barn, and Peter saw men dressed in light-blue coveralls scurrying about on the lawn. They seemed to be working on some contraption, but he couldn't make out what it was. Ahead and closer was a large ranch-style house painted robin's-egg blue with white trim, and a large wrap-around porch. He noticed a man sitting on the porch, although from the distance, he wasn't certain he recognized him.

"Keep moving," Corbett prodded him with the pistol barrel against his spine.

Peter trudged onward along the flagstone path. To either side, daffodils and tulips had erupted in bloom, a vibrant pallet of yellow, orange, purple, and red showing bright against a carpet of green. The bucolic landscape stood in stark contrast to his dire situation.

Peter climbed the steps to the porch, his eyes on the man in the chair. Corbett was three steps behind Peter. Two other guards joined them.

"Do you know who I am?" asked the sitting man.

Peter studied the face, then shook his head. "No. Should I?"

A thin smile crept across the man's face. "My name is Dr. Ming—Dr. Simon Ming."

Peter eyes widened. "So you're the one."

Ming smiled in amusement. "The one what?"

"The psychopathic mad scientist behind this operation. There's always one, right?"

The smile quickly vanished from Ming's face. "You have no idea the sheer genius behind my work, do you?"

"I see modesty is not your strong suit."

"I've often wondered what it would be like to meet you. I never imagined you'd be so brash."

Peter raised an eyebrow. "You know me?"

"In a manner of speaking. Yes, you could say so. But, I digress. I trust my men have treated you well?"

Peter glanced over his shoulder. As expected, guards were still blocking his escape. "Let's just say I won't be posting a five-star review for the car ride."

Ming's lips curled into a grin. "Mr. Corbett," he motioned toward his head of security, "tells me you have met Darnell Price and are aware of his work on my behalf."

"I know Price. He told me about your plans to introduce your engineered virus into the bottled water so you could infect large populations, rendering the men sterile. You won't succeed."

Ming chuckled. "Why is that?"

"Because my partner has turned Price over to the police, so he can tell his story."

"I own the police."

"In Eugene, I've no doubt you do. But Darnell Price was surrendered to the Bend police—to a particular detective I know to be untouchable."

"Everyone has a price. Even you, Mr. Savage."

"Don't be so sure."

Ming locked eyes with Peter. He expected to see uncertainty and fear. Instead, he saw fierce determination and unwavering conviction. "It doesn't matter," he said after a moment. "Darnell Price can talk until he goes hoarse, and it won't change anything. There is no physical evidence to support his outrageous claims."

"There's the bottled water he earmarked for shipment to

Nigeria," Peter said.

"That water has already been disposed of, flushed into the sewer system after Mr. Corbett and his very capable team removed all of it from the warehouse at Cascade Aqua. And the manufacturing facility in eastern Oregon—well, you know that it no longer exists, burned to the ground. But not to worry, I have other facilities."

Peter shrugged, hoping his charade of indifference would fool Ming. "The CDC will reopen their investigation based on the testimony of Mr. Price. My guess is they'll receive support from the FBI, maybe even Homeland Security. The government doesn't take kindly to threatened acts of terrorism."

"Of course they will. In fact, my sources tell me they are already making plans to investigate Cascade Aqua as well as Utopian-Bio. Alas, it will be futile. There is nothing to find."

Peter's air of confidence cracked as the realization dawned on him. "You removed the virus from your labs."

Ming nodded. "Naturally. As soon as manufacturing was shifted to our remote facility, there was no reason to maintain supplies at my research laboratories. In fact, to continue to do so would have represented an unacceptable liability."

"And I had Darnell Price sterilize the bottling line." Peter felt like he'd been punched in the gut.

"How considerate of you!" Ming's mouth curled into a reptilian smile. "Believe me when I say I am sincerely grateful."

"So why bring me here? Sounds like you figured everything out."

"Indeed, I have." He rose and paced a circle around Peter, who stood motionless. After he completed his circuit, he stopped and faced his captive, appraising him. Then he said, "You don't fully comprehend the gravity of your situation, do you?"

"I think I have the general idea."

"Do you? This is much more than my simple science experiment and exercise in genetic engineering."

Ming stood in front of Peter, staring into his eyes with smug satisfaction. "Think," he said. "My name should have much deeper meaning to you than merely the recent events."

Peter pinched his eyebrows in thought. He had met thousands of people over the years, many Asian, and Ming was a fairly common surname in China. But still…

Could it be? He recalled only one person named Ming. Someone he had crossed paths with years ago.

"No. It can't be you," Peter said, shaking his head slowly for emphasis.

"The Sudan. You do remember, don't you?"

"No. It's not possible."

"Can you be certain?"

"Colonel Ming was killed. The entire complex was destroyed, along with everyone within it."

"Hmm." Ming motioned his chin toward a chair and one of the guards moved it closer. "Have a seat, Mr. Savage." Ming eased again into the bent-willow rocker. Peter resisted, remaining on his feet. "Sit down!" Ming commanded.

Peter lowered himself into the chair, uncertain where the theatrics were going.

"Colonel Ming was my father."

Peter's eyes widened. "You are his son?"

A discrete nod was sufficient reply.

"Do you know what your father was doing?" Peter said. "The research he was directing?"

Ming's hands gripped the rocker arms, his fingers attempting to dig into the bent willow twigs. His eyes appeared to be bottomless pits, black and foreboding. They bore into Peter with electric intensity, his lips pursed.

Peter continued. "Homothals—that's what he called them.

He infected men and turned them into animals."

"He was my father!" Ming launched himself from the rocker, sending the chair flying in the opposite direction. He slid to a stop in front of Peter, dropping to one knee so he was face to face.

"I'm sorry," Peter replied in an even voice.

"Sorry about what? That I am his offspring or that you murdered him?"

The events of that ordeal in the desert came flooding back. Memories Peter had tried to lock away, denied from conscious thought. His son, Ethan, had been beaten nearly to death. It was a miracle they got him out alive. As much as he wanted to forget those horrible events, he knew he never would.

"I never met your father." Peter paused for a heartbeat, and then added, "And I didn't kill him."

Ming slowly rose and returned to his chair, which a guard had righted and put in place. "No, perhaps not directly. But you are responsible nonetheless. I was fortunate to survive the bombs. Only a handful of us escaped. It took many surgical procedures," Ming absently brushed his fingers along the side of his face, "to hide the scars."

Peter's mouth fell agape. "You were there?"

"Of course," Ming snorted a laugh. "I studied under the brilliant leadership of my father. I knew the day would come when it would be my duty to carry forward his work."

"You're mad."

"You should be more polite. You must have figured out that I plan to kill you, yes?"

"The thought crossed my mind."

"And did you know that I placed a contract on your life?"

"You? Why?"

"Really? I thought you were smarter than that. Why? Because I want you to pay. You, and everyone else who is responsible for murdering my father! For destroying his life's work. It took time, but eventually I learned who you are, where you work and live… everything about you."

"How?"

"Ah. Always the inquisitive mind. It was old-fashioned detective work. I started with sources I have inside the Department of Defense. You know, if your government paid their analyst better, it would be much more expensive to buy them off. Anyway, for mere pocket change I got my first lead—the name of the team that infiltrated my father's compound."

"SGIT," Peter said.

"That's right. The Strategic Global Intervention Team. And it is under the direction of Commander James Nicolaou. Some more research eventually connected his name with you. Fascinating history—best friends in high school and all. And that brings me to you. Seems like you are a veritable legend in your insignificant, little hometown. Rumors of your exploits are repeated in certain circles, and, well, people do like to talk."

Peter's eyes were drawn beyond Ming, to activity in the grassy open area between the house and the barn. Several men were pouring a tan powder from bags into the cargo hold of a large drone.

"Are your men loading the virus into that drone?" Peter said.

Ming glanced over his shoulder, following Peter's gaze. "Very observant. The viral agent was engineered under my direction."

"So that's it. You never did plan to use bottled water as the means to spread the virus. You plan to contaminate the municipal water supply."

"Bravo. I see you do possess an above-average intelligence. The bottled water was merely a convenient test vehicle."

"Not to mention that it would misdirect any investigation

that might ensue."

Ming nodded. "Indeed. You see, the virus was designed with certain characteristics."

"And?" Peter prodded.

"The protein shell, or capsid, that surrounds the genetic material had to be specifically engineered to meet certain criteria. Namely, stability in water and the ability to selectively target certain organs in the host. Of course, we also employed gene editing techniques to appropriately modify the virus genome."

Peter was repulsed by the notion, but by virtue of his training in science and engineering he also understood the academic perspective. He said, "You had to test the virus, to be certain."

"Yes! As a scientist, I see you appreciate the challenge I faced. I had to put theory to experimental test to know how it actually functioned. I needed a live population to test the virus and infection method. At first, my team suggested testing it on homeless people. But we eventually abandoned that plan. Many of those infected might not seek medical attention. Instead, after considering several alternatives, I decided to conduct our experiment on the people of Warm Springs. It was Darnell Price's idea, actually."

"Of course. They have a clinic and the patients would be inclined to seek treatment. But being a native American reservation, jurisdiction would be complicated and likely to slow any coordinated response from government agencies."

"Not to mention the fact that American politicians really don't care much about what happens on the reservations, as long as it stays on the reservations."

Peter shook his head. "Like father, like son. You don't value life at all. Unless it's yours, of course."

Ming's mouth drew back in a smirk that, paired with his

black, beady eyes, reminded Peter of a serpent. All that was lacking was a thin, forked tongue flicking in and out. "Come now," he said. "Can you honestly claim to be any different? After all, you were instrumental in the murder of my father, as well as the destruction of his life's work."

"You can't succeed. I know your plan. And others will figure it out pretty fast. It just isn't that sophisticated."

"You flatter yourself. But, there is one more thing I want to show you before my men—*dispose* of you."

Peter swallowed the lump in his throat.

Ming rose and faced Roger Corbett. "Bring him to my office."

With Ming leading the way and well out of reach, Corbett prodded Peter into the house, his pistol pressed firmly into Peter's spine.

His office was immaculate and decorated in a decidedly masculine tone. A large bay window on one wall overlooked the open grassy space all the way to the barn. The walls were painted a deep burgundy red, with white-oak trim and polished oak planks covering the floor. Occupying the exact center of the space was a massive desk constructed of ebony and carved in an intricate pattern with dragons scaling posts at each corner.

Ming was already seated as Peter entered. He swiveled his head, taking in the beautiful surroundings. "You have good taste," Peter said. "Perhaps that's the only thing we can agree on."

"I couldn't care less about your approval."

"Spoken like a true psychopath."

Corbett rammed the gun barrel painfully into the lower vertebrae of Peter's back. "For a man whose life expectancy is measured in minutes, you might want to show more respect."

Peter glanced over his shoulder at Corbett. "Would it matter?"

"How you die is my choice. So yeah, I'd say it matters."

"Enough," Ming said, and he flicked the fingers of a raised hand dismissively. "Do you believe in an afterlife, Mr. Savage?"

Peter's eyes narrowed, uncertain where the question was leading. "I believe in God, if that's what you mean. Good and evil—and that good will always prevail."

"Hmm. I thought as much, and very soon your beliefs will be tested. So, I want to give your spirit or soul, whatever you would call it, something to contemplate after death."

In a gesture of defiance, Peter raised his chin and pulled his shoulders back.

"Step closer. I have something to show you."

He turned an open laptop so Peter could see the screen. It was logged onto a page that appeared to list items and services for sale. "So?" Peter said.

Ming's reptilian smirk returned. "This is where I posted the contract on your life. Only after Mr. Corbett assured me he had you—alive and well—did I cancel the contract."

"How thoughtful. Am I supposed to say thank you?"

Ming chortled. "Well, I don't think you'll want to thank me after you take a closer look." His index finger moved to a particular line at the middle of the monitor.

Peter took a half step forward and leaned closer, reading the post. He raised upright and attempted to lunge toward Ming but Corbett's hand clamped hard on his neck. At the same time, he thrust the SIG Sauer pistol deeper into his flesh. "You son of a bitch." He spat the words out.

"Oh really, Mr. Savage. You must have known that I had no choice but to issue contracts on the lives of *all* the men responsible for my father's murder. Let's see. I have Todd Steed, Gary Porter, Jim Nicolaou and the entire SGIT team—oh, and last but far from least, your son. Ethan Savage."

Peter struggled against the vise-like grip on his neck. "Do

me a favor and go up against Jim first."

"Maybe, but probably not. All these contracts have been issued. Just a few minutes ago. Before long, hired killers will be rushing to get to each mark first. The exceptionally large monetary bounty on each man assures these contracts will get an enormous amount of attention—and from the most skillful assassins."

Peter glared at Ming. What could he say? As much as he wanted to, he couldn't attack Ming, not with a gun in his back. But he couldn't ride it out either. Time wasn't on his side.

"Oh, don't fret, Mr. Savage. There really is nothing you can do to stop me. I suspect your friends and son will be murdered first. Then, one by one, the SGIT team will be eliminated. They have no idea this is coming, and every man has his moments of vulnerability."

CHAPTER 39

PETER WAS ESCORTED FROM THE HOUSE just as the drone helicopter lifted off from the lawn. He watched it rise slowly straight up until it blended seamlessly with the cerulean sky. Then the buzzing sound of the six fans slowly faded away, and Peter knew the aircraft was flying toward the target. What that was, he could only guess, but he had a pretty good idea.

On the large porch, Corbett turned him over to the two guards, who each trained their handguns on the prisoner. "Heinrich," Corbett said, "take Mr. Savage to the pit. Logan, you go with him. When you get there, shoot him and kick his dead body in with the other garbage."

As the name implied, the pit was simply a deep hole in the fertile valley soil. Having been dug with a backhoe, it was located a hundred yards beyond the barn and out of sight of the ranch house. Peter approached with his hands raised. He smelled the rancid odor of rotting garbage. Since the property was well outside the boundary of any incorporated city, there

259

were no municipal services. Water was pumped from a well, sewage flowed into a septic tank and drain field, and trash was buried in a deep hole.

Now, Peter was about to be added to the refuse.

"Step up to the edge," the guard named Logan said, his voice cracked with uncertainty. He was thin and sported a thick mane of wavy blond hair. His face was pock-marked from a bad case of acne, and he didn't appear to be a day older than twenty. In the brief moment when Peter had looked into his blue eyes, he saw a rebel, but not a killer.

Heinrich stood ten paces to the side, his SIG Sauer pistol aimed at Peter with a solid, two-handed hold. Logan held his ground as Peter stepped forward several paces until he was at the edge of the deep hole. He peered down. The cavity appeared to be ten feet deep, and across the bottom was strewn all manner of refuse. It reminded Peter of a city landfill, only on a tiny scale. Motion caught his eye, and he saw a rat dart under a folded sheet of cardboard, only to emerge a short distance away and feast on spoiled salad greens.

"You don't have to do this," Peter said, his hands still held above his head. "You can let me go and no one will know. But if you kill me, there's no going back. The police will eventually find you, and you'll get the needle."

"What's he talking about?" Logan said, his head twisting toward Heinrich.

"Never mind. Just do your job."

"Don't listen to him kid. They have the death penalty in this state, or didn't your boss tell you that? Lethal injection. You know that isn't always quick and painless. They say it can be pretty bad, with the convicted screaming for ten or fifteen minutes until they die. I've heard it feels like your whole body is burning from the inside."

"Mr. Heinrich? Is that true?"

"Shut up."

"Heinrich is setting you up kid. Can't you see it? You kill me, and he shoots you. No witnesses."

"Don't listen to him, Logan. Just do your job. It's as simple as pointing and pulling the trigger. We get this done and go back for a cold beer. What do ya say?"

"There's no walking back, kid. He's using you. You kill me, and you die about two seconds later."

"That's enough lip from you, Savage. There's two guns trained on you. And from this distance, there's no missing." Heinrich shifted his eyes to Logan. He read uncertainty in the face of the young man as his gun arm sagged a little. "Logan, we've discussed this already. You know what you have to do, right?"

Peter couldn't see Logan's face, but he sensed what the young man was feeling—uncertainty, fear, trepidation. All emotions Peter had felt before he'd killed for the first time.

"Listen to me, Logan," Peter said.

Heinrich interrupted. "Logan, you have three seconds to either shoot Mr. Savage and throw him in with the garbage, or I shoot both of you."

"Logan, you have a choice."

"Shut up!" Logan said. "I'm not listening to you."

"One," Heinrich said, his voice even and confident.

"Have you ever killed a man before?" Peter continued. "It doesn't just end with the bullet. It will haunt you for the rest of your life."

"Two."

"Talking is over," Logan said. Then he raised the pistol in one hand, extended his arm, and cocked the hammer.

Peter recognized the distinctive metallic click, and knew that in a second, two at most, his life would abruptly end. He glanced down at the rotting, fetid garbage, knowing that would be the last thing he would see.

Danya had tracked Peter's cell phone ever since leaving Bend a couple hours earlier. When the icon slowed and remained in a small area not any larger than a football field, she concluded he was no longer traveling by car. Trouble was, the icon did not appear on any mapped road on the phone app. She navigated secondary country roads that should bring her in close proximity, and then she would have to wing it.

The road she was following had skirted just south of the icon, and she slowed, looking for an unimproved road or driveway that might head off in the right direction. Ahead and to the right she saw a gated driveway that looked promising. She slowed her red pickup, noticed the camera on the gate post, and made a snap decision to keep driving onward. A half mile beyond the gate she pulled off the road.

A barbed wire fence with "No Trespassing" signs paralleled the shoulder of the road. A quick examination indicated the wire wasn't electrified. She parted the lower strands and Diesel slipped through. She followed right behind him.

"Diesel," she called, and the canine stopped. He looked back at her, waiting.

Danya entered the woods outfitted for combat. The FN shotgun was slung from her shoulder. A bandoleer of shells was draped diagonally across her chest. The combat tomahawk was sheathed at the small of her back, and a SIG Sauer pistol was secured in a tactical holster on her right thigh. She quickly left the road for the deep shadows in the timber, picking a direct route toward the beacon on her phone that should indicate Peter's location.

Initially, the understory was thick—a combination of dense brush, blackberry vines, rhododendron bushes, and evergreen trees. But as she closed the distance to the icon, the brush gave way to clearings. That made movement easier, faster, but it also left her vulnerable. Clothed in blue jeans and a drab green hoody, without the thick brush she could be easily spotted by stationary or roaming guards.

Staying at the edge of the clearing, and using the brush for cover, she unlimbered the shotgun, deriving confidence from its close-range stopping power. Ahead Danya spotted several goats at the edge of the clearing happily munching away on everything green, even the blackberry vines. She slowed her pace, hoping not to spook the goats for fear it might give away her presence. Diesel stayed close by her side, ignoring the temptation to chase the four-legged herbivores. As she passed, two goats looked at her momentarily and bleated, then lowered their heads and continued grazing.

Soon a barn came into sight, and beyond it, a ranch house. Both structures appeared to be in very good condition, a rarity for farm buildings in the wet climate of western Oregon. She spotted two satellite dishes mounted atop the gabled roof of the barn. There were no windows in the barn visible from Danya's position. But she saw a row of four air conditioning units against the nearest wall. *Odd*, she thought.

Stretching before the front of the barn was a large open space. As she watched, several men dressed in light blue coveralls were servicing a sizable drone. Then the drone took to the air. After it flew out of sight, the men entered the barn.

Danya paused again to study the phone and judged that the icon indicating the location of Peter's cell phone was close, probably just beyond the barn. Preparing to move, she glanced to her side—Diesel was gone. "Diesel!" she said as loud as she dared, and then waited several moments, expecting the brush to move and the red dog to rejoin her. But he didn't. He had simply vanished.

It was a setback, but she'd come too far to give up. Besides, quitting wasn't in her playbook. She crouched and resumed her stalk. Her pace became more deliberate with care going into every footstep, the foliage breaking up her silhouette.

She swung a wide circle around the barn, checking the tracking app on the phone frequently. The distance to the blip was decreasing with every step she took, but it was also taking her away from the two buildings. Then she scented a pungent odor and halted. It was not the normal musty smell characteristic of the woods. Rather, it was the strong, fetid odor of rot. She resumed her advance, even more cautious than before. After another dozen steps she came across a road that had been cut through the forest using heavy machines.

She followed it to the left, and soon she heard voices. Danya cocked her head to capture the soft sounds. The voices were masculine but too distant to understand.

Wishing Diesel were still with her, she slowly but steadily advanced another forty yards, following a sweeping bend, before halting again. The talk was louder, and she was certain she recognized one voice as that of Peter. The other two were unfamiliar.

But the message was clear. One of the men was going to kill Peter.

With a renewed sense of urgency that bordered on desperation, she moved deftly through the brush toward the voices. Her footing needed to be certain as she angled and threaded her body between evergreen branches and dense shrubs. To become reckless and noisy now would mean disaster. After covering a dozen yards, she caught a glimpse of Peter and a second man with an unkempt mass of blond hair. Danya slowly parted rhododendron branches to get a better view.

Only ten yards away, a guard stood with his back toward Danya. He was facing Peter and very close. He appeared to have a weapon trained on Peter, but his body obscured any details.

Judging from the conversation, she concluded his name was Logan.

Farther to the side was a second guard, bearing a semi-automatic pistol in his hand, pointed in Peter's direction. She knew he would not have the weapon in his hand if he did not anticipate using it very soon. He was definitely the one in charge, and there was no doubt about their intentions.

About ten paces separated the two gunmen, making it difficult for Danya to take them both out before one of them fired. Even worse was Peter's location. He was on the other side of Logan, the man who was moments away from executing him. Clearly, Logan was the highest priority threat, and she could shoot him easily with either the tactical shotgun or the SIG Sauer pistol holstered to her thigh. But the human body seldom stops modern ammunition, and at this close range she knew that to shoot the gunman would also mean striking, and likely killing, Peter.

Danya was mentally running through her options, considering and discarding plans, when the gunman to the side said, "Logan, you have three seconds to either shoot Mr. Savage and throw him in with the garbage, or I shoot both of you."

She judged the distance again—*yes, it could work*. Silently laying the shotgun on the ground, she shifted her weight and tensed her muscles.

"Talking is over," Logan said.

With a feeling of foreboding, Danya watched Logan raise his arm, point the gun at the back of Peter's head, and cock the hammer.

Inside the barn, two guards were watching remote camera feeds on a bank of color monitors. Several feeds showed the two-lane road approaching the property as well as the driveway leading up to the ranch house.

One of the guards leaned closer to the monitors, looking for something that wasn't there. "Hey, did you see a red pickup on camera 14?"

The other guard shook his head. "No. Should I?"

"Yeah. I picked it up approaching the driveway. But it didn't turn off the main road. It's not coming to the house or barn."

"So?"

"Well, camera 14 is what—two hundred yards past the entrance gate? If it didn't turn onto the driveway, and you didn't pick it up on 14, then what happened to the pickup?"

CHAPTER 40

AS PETER GAZED INTO THE PIT, the silence was cut by a swoosh, the whisper of a combat tomahawk slicing through the air. The spiked end planted deeply at the base of Logan's neck. He collapsed immediately, his muscles unable to respond once the hardened steel severed his spine at the base of his skull. The kid was dead even before his knees buckled and his body fell to the ground.

Heinrich had seen it all—the shiny blade tumbling toward its target, sunlight glinting off the razor-sharp edge. And then Logan falling dead.

He spun in the direction the edged weapon had come from and caught a glimpse of a human form running between cover. He swung his handgun and snapped off a shot before Peter's shoulder rammed into his abdomen, knocking the wind from him.

With a grunt, Heinrich hit the dirt, Peter on top of him, fists pummeling Heinrich's face. He tried to raise his pistol, and Peter clasped the man's gun hand while simultaneously ramming an open palm into Heinrich's nose. Cartilage and bone broke at the same time his head whiplashed into the hard ground.

His strength ebbed, and Peter struck again, driving bone into the man's brain. His struggles stopped, replaced by ineffective and random muscles spasms as life ebbed from his body.

Peter grabbed the SIG Sauer pistol and quickly searched the corpse for spare magazines, radio, and phone. He scored on all three. He also removed a key card that had been hanging around Heinrich's neck before pushing the body into the hole. Then he returned to Logan's body. "I tried to tell you this would end badly," Peter whispered. He pulled the tomahawk from Logan's neck and ran the handle underneath his belt at his side. He rolled the body into the pit, just in case someone came looking. *Such a waste.* Peter wondered what the kid might have accomplished if his life had taken a different path.

Staying in the forested perimeter to avoid observation, Peter plotted a course back to the ranch house. He moved in a crouch with care to avoid making sounds. Fortunately, the fog, which had only lifted with sunrise, had dampened the detritus on the forest floor aiding with his stealthy approach.

Although he suspected Danya had thrown the tomahawk, he didn't know with certainty. *If it was Danya, how did she track him to this location? And what had prompted her to deviate from the agreed-upon plan? She should still be in Bend, awaiting contact from him.*

With so much uncertainty, Peter decided to be conservative and work solo.

As if he were stalking a bull elk, Peter approached the house from the forest with slow and deliberate motion. He angled toward a back door that exited onto a wooden deck. From fifty feet away, he clung to a mature fir tree, just edging his head around the side, watching for activity. After several minutes of observation, no guards were visible, and Peter concluded that they were all occupied with getting the drone in the air. Still, he calculated that when Logan and Heinrich didn't report in, it would draw attention. And probably sooner than later.

In a crouch, he dashed across the deck for the door. With his back to the wall, he tested the door latch. It was unlocked. He eased the door open and entered a large, open space. It was furnished like a living room with two sofas facing toward a TV mounted on the wall.

To the right was a short hallway that was familiar—it led to Ming's study. Leading with the pistol he'd taken from Heinrich, Peter quietly crossed the room and worked his way to the study. It was empty. He ducked in and closed the door, taking care not to make any noise.

Through the bay window he saw Ming and Corbett conversing by the barn. They were far enough away that he didn't think they'd notice him as he did his work. Motion was his enemy—if he was moving about in the room, the chances of being noticed were many times greater than if he was sitting mostly stationary.

Ming's laptop was still on the desk with the monitor open, just as he'd hoped. He covered the distance in three strides and squatted with the desk shielding his body from the large window. Slowly, he slid the laptop around until it was facing him. Only then did he exhale the breath he'd been subconsciously holding.

He lowered the computer down to his lap. It was still powered up and on the page Ming had shown him. Peter reached into the front of his pants and removed the cell phone he'd stashed there, correctly betting the guards would not get too personal when they patted him down at the manufacturing facility. He dialed a number from memory.

After three rings, the other party answered. "Gary Porter speaking."

"Gary, it's Peter," his voice barely above a whisper.

"Hi buddy. I didn't recognize your number. Get a new wireless account?"

"Listen, I don't have time to talk and I need your help."

"Of course you do. Why else would you call?"

Ignoring the sarcasm, Peter said, "It's a long story, and it's related to that contract on my head that we discussed."

"Oh yeah. Like I explained, unless you have the computer IP address, not much I can do."

"How about the laptop? I have it powered up and the owner still logged in. Can you access it remotely?"

"Really? That question doesn't merit an answer. Okay. Type this URL into the browser." Gary rattled off the address and Peter repeated the characters back as he typed, cognizant of the fact that every second he spent there put him at ever greater risk. Moments later he received a prompt to accept external control. Without hesitation, he clicked the mouse on the box and watched as the laptop seemingly took on a life of its own.

They were still connected by phone, but Gary had gone silent while he was accessing Ming's laptop. Abruptly, Gary's voice blurted from the phone. "Whoa. This site has issued a contract on me! Oh, and Todd and—"

"I know," Peter cut him off. "I need you to cancel the contracts. All of them. You can do it, right?"

"Just another day in the office." While Peter watched the monitor, the text changed and one by one the postings offering to pay for the murders were deleted.

"Is that it?" Peter asked after the last contract was deleted.

"Hold on. Just one more thing to do."

After another minute Gary said, "Done. I'm assuming

it's not practical to deliver the laptop to me, so I constructed a virtual copy of it on my machine. I'll monitor this web page for a few days and make sure there's no activity related to the contracts. If there is, I can spoof the laptop and shut it down."

"Good thinking. Thanks, I have to go."

"Have you called the police?" Gary asked, but his question remained unanswered. The line was disconnected.

Wasting no time, Peter swung the tomahawk down and smashed the spike into the laptop where he thought critical components were located. He repeated the movement over and over, aiming to destroy the hard drive and memory chips in the computer. After inflicting a dozen thumb-sized holes in the case, the screen remained dark, and he stopped.

He really wanted to phone law enforcement, but who could he trust? It was a short list, only one name—Detective Ruth Colson—and even that carried some risk. He needed something substantial, concrete information, not just speculation.

Pushing the mutilated laptop aside, Peter rolled to a crouch and discretely exited Ming's office. He surmised that the center of action was within the barn since that's where personnel seemed to be congregated. That became his destination. Ming's plan to infect water supplies with his virus required people and equipment. So, he reasoned, it could be easily disrupted by either disabling the equipment or the personnel.

Peter had initially believed that the grand plan was to inoculate bottled water with the virus and then ship that water to various locations around the world, as in third-world countries with impoverished populations. But after listening to Simon Ming, he knew that was simply a diversion. Could Ming's plans extend beyond the immediate vicinity of western Oregon? And if so, how did he plan to execute his scheme? The drone Peter saw had only limited payload and range.

He kept coming back to the idea of seeding viral agent

into city water supplies. But that only worked for nearby water reservoirs and treatment plants. To be effective on a grand scale—and Peter reasoned that Ming would only plan on a grand scale—the virus had to be widely distributed, and in a short period of time. *How can Ming do that from this isolated location?*

There would be time later to ponder that question. Right now, he had to intervene. And that meant he had to infiltrate the barn, learn what the hell was going on there, and cripple the operations.

CHAPTER 41

AS SOON AS DANYA LET LOOSE the tomahawk, she was in motion. Leaving the shotgun, she dashed for cover just as a single shot rang out. That was enough encouragement for her to keep moving. Still crouched, she plowed a path through the foliage, seeking distance and cover. After running for ten heart-pounding seconds, she slid to a stop and squirmed behind a large, two-foot-tall tree stump. The bark had long since fallen away, leaving gray timber exposed. The wood appeared solid, not that she was in a position to be choosy—it certainly was a better shield against bullets than the leafy understory.

With her side pressed against the stump, she waited, catching her breath, expecting bullets to gouge into the old timber. But the shots never came. Cautiously, Danya eased her head to the side until she could just glimpse the area near the pit where Peter had stood, awaiting execution.

No one was there. No bodies, either.

Although she doubted Peter had seen her—how could

he, since his back was turned in her direction when she threw the tomahawk—she judged they had a better chance of spoiling what Ming was up to if they worked separately. The disadvantage was that she and Peter would not be able to coordinate their efforts. But on the plus side, the two working independently would likely confuse the guards and force them to split their defenses. At least, she hoped it would work that way.

Failing to see any guards, she backtracked and retrieved the FN shotgun. In close-quarters combat—which is what she expected—it would offer superior firepower over handguns. Plus, the intimidation factor was not to be underestimated. A large man may be easily tempted to challenge a woman holding a pistol, but he would think differently when staring into the business end of a 12-gauge scattergun.

Danya gathered her thoughts and considered her first target—would it be the ranch house or the barn?

Her decision came quickly, drawn from years of training and field experience in many of the most dangerous areas of the world. Gaza. Syria. The West Bank. Iran. Lebanon. Her resume read like a travel guide to the hotspots of the Middle East. As an agent of Mossad, she'd been challenged with many dangerous and important assignments. Until…

Her thoughts instantly rolled back in time to a mission not far from her current location, in the Cascade Mountains of Oregon. Her government had sent her and four other Mossad agents to track down and kill an American. A man named Peter Savage. The reason why seemed inconsequential, something about a political embarrassment to the Israeli Prime Minister.

On all of her previous missions, she had been tasked with matters of national security—politically correct language for assassinating terrorists and their financiers. The public liked the term "national security" as it made them feel safe while masking the true nature of her violent profession.

But this mission was different. It was on American soil, thousands of miles from the anarchy of the Middle East, and Peter Savage was no terrorist. In no way did he threaten the national security of her country.

Danya would never forget looking down the barrel of her gun at this man whose only fault was being in the wrong place at the wrong time. At that moment, she was reborn and began living off the grid, in near-complete anonymity. No longer a tool of political demigods and paranoid bureaucrats.

Returning her focus to the problem at hand, the answer was easy. The barn was topped with satellite dishes and had enough air conditioning for four houses. Plus, the activity she'd seen was centered around this structure, not the ranch house. Her priority target was the barn.

With his back pressed flat against the rear wall of the barn, Peter debated his options. He wanted to believe it was Danya who'd saved him from certain death minutes ago, but he couldn't be sure. *Who else could it be?* he asked himself rhetorically. He had to assume she had a good reason for not joining up with him, that she preferred to press the initiative against Ming independently. By default, that meant he, too, had to work solo.

Based on his brief observations when he arrived at the ranch, he was betting the drone operational control was conducted from the barn. The fact that he encountered no one within the ranch house simply reinforced his conclusion.

He paused in contemplation, trying to visualize what defenses he would encounter within the structure. Trouble was, he had no way of knowing or even making an educated guess. He did not know the layout of the barn. Nor did he know the number of guards, where they were located, or what weapons they possessed.

His face twisted into a frown. He grasped the tomahawk in his left hand, 9mm pistol in his right. Although the bladed weapon would have felt reassuring in his grip if he was going up against a hoard of zombies, Peter didn't see himself using it in combat. At least not as long as he had a gun and bullets. He was about to slide the handle beneath his belt when an idea suddenly came to him.

Only a few feet away, a thick conduit snaked from the ground, traveled three feet up the outside wall, and then disappeared inside. *Electrical power*, he thought.

Peter holstered the pistol and transferred the tomahawk to his dominant hand. He hefted the weapon, visualizing the devastating blow it would deliver. *This could work, if I don't kill myself in the process.* Taking a step forward, he clenched the handle, rotated his arm back, and then swung forward with all his strength. The razor-sharp blade did not disappoint, performing as it was designed to.

A blindingly bright bolt of blue-white light erupted from the slashed electrical feed as 480 volts of power shorted at the severed end of the cable. Too late, Peter raised his left arm as a shield from the brilliance. He closed his eyes to regain his vision while his body relaxed. *Okay. That ought to introduce some confusion. And if I'm lucky, it will screw with their remote piloting of that drone.*

After waiting ten seconds to regain most of his visual acuity, Peter advanced around the side of the barn looking for the nearest entrance.

He stopped beside the door and tested the latch. It was locked. Next to the door latch was a magnetic strip device. Wasting no time, Peter swiped the card he'd taken from Heinrich. With a barely audible click, the lock opened.

He took three deep breaths, readied the 9mm pistol, and eased the door open. Taking a glimpse inside, the room was filled with frenetic activity. People were running to and fro. Peter quickly recognized it as a state-of-the-art control room. A voice rose above the rest: "Get that power back on!"

In the chaotic confusion, no one noticed the stranger slipping through the open door.

He plunged inside, hugging the wall and closing the door again. The room before him had been plunged into total darkness when he severed the main power cable. A moment later the battery-powered emergency lighting came on, providing limited illumination. The beams were adjusted to cast ample light into the control room to allow the technicians to carry out their tasks as well as to navigate around the consoles and other furnishings. But this came at the expense of lighting the perimeter, which was smothered under a Stygian black veil.

Mounted on the wall above Peter's head was one of the emergency lights, the beams adjusted toward the workstations in the central portion of the room. Anyone looking his direction would be blinded by the bright lamps. As long as his motion was slow and limited in range, he calculated he would not draw any attention. He held the pistol with both hands, close to his chest, ready for action.

Whereas the outside of the barn looked like a stereotypical farm building, a throwback to simpler times, replete with red-painted rustic wood boards and white trim, the interior was the polar opposite. His eyes moved left and right, trying to take it all in. A dozen workstations were clustered in three groups of four, each manned by a frantic technician. Beyond the control room was a glass wall that separated a machine shop, equipped with computer-controlled milling machines and lathes, an electronics shop, and an assembly room. A mold was laid open revealing a fiberglass body of a drone similar to what Peter had seen earlier, staged for flight on the expansive lawn.

A constant electronic hum was punctuated by excited

orders and terse replies.

"We only have about five minutes of battery backup," someone shouted. "Then we lose flight control."

"Why aren't the generators online?" another technician asked.

"The diesel engine on generator number one is running," came the reply. "The engine just reached operating temperature and the generator is engaged. Transfer switch is… Wait a minute… Transfer switch is not activating."

"Say again?"

"The transfer switch has not engaged. The generator is online, but the power is not connected to our main."

"Must be a faulty indicator."

"Negative. Instrumentation checks out. I repeat, we have no generator power to the control room."

A steel staircase led to a second-floor catwalk that extended in front of a wall of glass. Subdued lighting within revealed what appeared to be an office space—*probably security*, Peter thought. As he looked upward, a man wearing the now-familiar sky-blue coveralls and a pistol holstered in a black tactical rig strapped to his thigh stood on the cat walk. It wasn't until he walked into the beam of a flood lamp that Peter recognized him—*Corbett!* He pointed toward the floor and shouted an order. "Beckman! Check the generators. Activate the transfer switch manually if you have too. If we don't get power restored in four minutes, I'll have no choice but to abort the flight!"

A technician rose from his console and urgently strode for the door. He lowered his head, squinting his eyes against the bright battery-powered flood lights. He cleared the beam only a few yards in front of Peter, who was standing motionless, a shadow on the periphery of chaos.

The man extended his arms to open the door, and abruptly pulled up short. "Can't let you do that," Peter said.

"Who the hell are you?" the technician asked.

"What's going on down there?" Corbett asked from the catwalk, straining to see into the deep shadows. "What's the problem?"

In a low voice, Peter said, "Step back, away from the door." He pointed the handgun at the technician. "I don't want to hurt you. But I will if necessary."

"Beckman!" Corbett yelled. "I gave you an order. Get that transfer switch engaged. Now!"

Beckman raised his hands and spoke in a loud voice, "Intruder, sir!"

"I wish you hadn't done that," Peter said.

Corbett leaned over the railing on the catwalk. He squinted his eyes as he stared past Beckman into the shadows. Then he saw it; a glimmer of light off the muzzle of a pistol. The rest of the gun, and the hand holding it, were obscured from view. *How long had the intruder been standing there?*

"Guards!" Corbett shouted.

Immediately, four armed men appeared on the catwalk aiming MP5 submachine guns in the direction of Beckman and the intruder. Bright beams of illumination lanced out from the lights fastened beneath the gun barrels. Others took up defensive positions behind computer consoles and desks across the control room, pointing weapons in the direction of light beams from the catwalk.

Outgunned and outnumbered, the only thing Peter had going for him was the shadows, and the gun-mounted flashlights were eroding that advantage. Even so, he knew the guards would have a very difficult time aiming within the bright flood lights that were shining in their eyes. He reached forward and grabbed Beckman's shirt, yanking him forward. Then he pressed the SIG pistol against Beckman's forehead and ordered, "Turn around. And keep your hands up."

The technician did as he was told. Peter clamped his left hand onto Beckman's collar and pulled him in close. It would be just about impossible for the guards to shoot Peter without hitting their own man. Still, that gave Peter little comfort. Honor among psychopaths was very rare.

"Don't do anything stupid, Corbett," Peter yelled. "I've got your man in front of me."

The light beams danced back and forth, attempting to zero in on the voice. Seconds later, they settled on Beckman's head and the intruder right behind him.

Corbett recognized the man immediately, even though his face was partially shielded by the technician. "Well, Mr. Savage, I see we meet again. I'd thought the gunshot I heard earlier signaled the end of your meddling in the affairs of Dr. Ming."

"Sorry to disappoint you. What can I say? I'm a survivor."

Corbett shrugged. "No matter." He made a show of motioning to the guards to either side lining the railing, weapons steady and aimed in Peter's direction. "Your luck has run out."

Eyes squinting from the bright beams on his face, Peter was not aware of guards closing in from the sides. But his instinct told him that to remain in one position was a losing proposition. He had to move, and there was only one direction to go—back out the door.

Maintaining a firm grip on Beckman's collar, Peter started to edge to his left, to the door he'd entered.

"Stop him!" Corbett shouted.

"But we don't have a clear shot," the nearest guard objected.

"Shoot!"

"Sir…" another guard started to speak. In exasperation Corbett drew his sidearm. He leveled the sights on Beckman's chest and squeezed off two shots in quick succession—a double tap—and then gazed down over the gun sights, expecting to see

Beckman and Peter slumped to the floor. Instead, Beckman's face grimaced in pain, but he remained standing. Peter was still pulling him to the door.

As if the two pistol shots were understood better than the verbal order, the guards on the railing opened up, delivering a storm of copper-clad 9mm bullets into Beckman's torso. With each strike, the technician jerked in pain, and a continual agonizing cry could be heard over the gunfire.

With shotgun in hand, Danya broke cover and dashed for the barn just as Peter entered a side door. She cut the most direct path to the building, which happened to land her very close to the severed electrical cable, still sparking vigorously from the live feed. She cast an approving glance at Peter's handiwork.

A torrent of gunfire exploded from within the building. As long as the gunfire continued, she had to assume Peter was still alive. Should she follow his path, and enter through the same door? She could provide crucial backup and superior firepower with the tactical semi-automatic shotgun. On the other hand, she could also run into an ambush.

Where in hell was that damn dog? Danya knew from experience that Diesel possessed very effective skills when it came to defending his master. When she first met Diesel, she was the opposition force. Now, she wished the canine was here to be her ally.

She opted to trust Peter's survival skills and go the other direction around the barn, find a second entry door, and hope to catch the guards in a murderous cross fire. In theory, it sounded like a winning plan.

Trouble was, she knew that combat rarely unfolded according to theory.

Even worse, whatever could go wrong, usually did.

As quickly as it started, the shooting stopped. Beckman's body was prone on the floor. But the searchlights failed to show Peter. The door was cracked open, sunlight spilling through the thin opening between door and jamb.

"Did anyone see where he went?" Corbett said.

"Must've gone out the door," a voice replied.

"Three minutes!" a technician announced from the control center on the main floor, refocusing Corbett on the priority to restore power before they had to abort the mission. "Gedde, get outside and manually close the transfer switch."

The technician rose from his console and ran for the door. He paused a second to look at Beckman—he was lying motionless, but there was no blood.

Then, he grabbed the door latch and pulled it open. He was already thinking through the task. The transfer switch was mounted next to the two backup generators. In the event of a power outage, it was supposed to automatically disconnect the grid power lines and connect the generator electrical output to the control center. So why had it failed? He knew from the gauge readings that the generator was running normally.

Gedde took two strides out the door. Even before the door latched closed, he was beginning to turn toward the generator housing when a blur of motion from across the lawn drew his attention. He froze in absolute terror.

The red pit bull reached full speed of thirty miles per hour in three long strides. His mouth was open wide, drawing in copious amounts of air, expanding his already large chest even more. The inch-long canines gleamed white in the sunlight; his eyes were dilated so large they appear to be black marbles. The huge, blocky head was low, a streamlined missile aimed directly at Gedde.

The technician managed to make one step backwards,

hoping to return through the entry door for the safety of the control center. Diesel leaped, his full forward momentum smashing into Gedde's torso. The canine dug his rear claws into the technician's thighs and kicked, propelling his open mouth higher. He clamped down on the man's throat, choking off his scream and turning it into a pained gurgle as he tumbled backwards. His head and shoulders pushed the door open again, blocking it in place.

Diesel was thrashing his head wildly has he bit down with enough force to break bone, easily crushing the man's trachea. Every twist and pull ripped skin and muscle. In seconds, the carotid artery was lacerated, and blood spurted from the hideous wound. But even then, the pit bull pressed the attack. Only when Gedde was still and silent did Diesel release his bite.

"What the hell?" a guard exclaimed upon witnessing the mauling from just inside the doorway. He was only feet away from Beckman, planning to check for signs of life and then continue the search for Peter Savage, who had seemingly vanished.

Stunned by the unexpected and ferocious attack, the guard hesitated before raising his pistol. He aimed the weapon toward Diesel… and fired.

CHAPTER 42

THE WEIGHT OF BECKMAN'S BODY on top of him made it hard for Peter to breathe. He didn't know how many bullets had struck the guard. Probably well north of a dozen. Fortunately, Beckman was wearing a level II ballistic vest, designed to stop most handgun ammunition. It was a relatively thin garment, not as bulky as standard bullet-proof vests worn by law enforcement personnel. Which is why Peter had failed to recognize that Beckman was wrapped in one. Although the 9mm rounds had not penetrated the vest, they did cause blunt-force trauma, akin to being hit in the chest with a hammer. And in sufficient number, blunt-force trauma could prove fatal. At the moment, Peter had no idea if the body he was hiding under was dead or alive.

He glimpsed another guard approaching cautiously. He appeared to be attempting to see into the dark shadows, his eyes still affected by the bright illumination he'd just left. He stopped only a few feet away—had he seen Peter's arms or legs beneath

Beckman?

Suddenly, the exterior door burst open and a furious commotion spilled into the doorway. Diesel was on top of another man, the one named Gedde, his jaws clamped down on the man's throat.

"What the hell?" the guard closest to Peter said. Then he raised his SIG, aiming to fire. Swiftly, Peter pulled his gun arm from beneath Beckman and snapped off a shot just as the guard fired.

The guard jerked as the bullet slammed into his chest. His shot went wide, gouging a hole in the door frame and missing Diesel.

Peter shoved aside the motionless body on top of him and pulled the trigger again, sending another bullet into the man's chest. The guard turned toward Peter, his eyes wide. Already, he was backpedaling, attempting to put distance between himself and Peter.

Not seeing blood on the man's chest, Peter surmised that the guards and technicians were all wearing ballistic armor. He raised his sights and fired a third time, and the 9mm round ripped through his throat. The guard threw a hand over the wound, blood seeping between his fingers. In a panic, he stumbled, falling onto his back. Unable to speak, his mouth moved like a fish out of water. A raspy, gurgling sound emanated from his throat as he quickly bled out.

The four guards on the catwalk, two on either side of Corbett, were stunned by the mauling of Gedde, which they were able to glimpse as sunlight washed through the open door. Their surprise turned to shock when Peter erupted from beneath the prone body of Beckman, and to disbelief as they saw him gun down one of their comrades.

"Get him!" Corbett shouted. In unison, four MP5 machine guns were snapped to the guard's shoulders. But just as they took aim, a new sound exploded through the cacophony of shouted orders and gunshots in the control room. It was the sound of gunfire, but deeper and louder than the crack of pistol ammunition.

BOOM! BOOM! BOOM! BOOM!

Four rapid, successive reports, and three of the four guards on the catwalk were hit. Corbett dropped to the decking. The fourth guard spun around and immediately opened fire in the direction opposite from Peter. The deep report reverberated again and the chatter from the MP5 ceased.

It was the break Peter needed, and he didn't hesitate.

While Corbett and his guards had been preoccupied with trying to take down Peter, Danya had approached an entry door on the far side of the structure. Without a key card, she wasn't going to gain access unless she used the shotgun to breach the door, shooting out the latch mechanism with buckshot. Crude, but effective. Also, very noisy. Anyone nearby would hear the shot and she'd lose the element of surprise.

As she was contemplating an alternative plan, a technician exited the door. He halted abruptly, startled to see Danya. With both hands she raised the shotgun and rammed the receiver across the bridge of his nose. He took a half step back, blood and mucous flowing from his nostrils even as his nose turned unnatural shades of yellow and purple.

Danya raised her leg and viciously kicked him in the groin. As he bent over, she slammed the butt of her weapon into the back of his head. He collapsed forward, unconscious but still alive.

Without wasting more time, she grabbed his key card and opened the door. Once inside, motion on the overhead catwalk caught her attention. And then there was gunfire. She couldn't see who it was they were shooting at on the far side of the control center, but she had to assume it was Peter. Sliding through the shadows, working her way to a defensible position, she spotted a large barrel and rolls of fabric next to a molded drone airframe resting on a large table. Adjacent to the table, a sturdy steel bin appeared to contain scrap of some type; she couldn't be sure in the dim light. She moved closer. It was a workstation for fabricating fiberglass and carbon fiber panels, parts for the helicopter drone.

She checked the barrel. A label indicated it was epoxy resin. She grabbed the lip of the barrel and tried to move it. No joy, it wouldn't budge. And the top was clean, with no spilled resin, so she judged it to be full. *This will make a good barrier*, she thought.

From behind the barrel, she shouldered the FN tactical shotgun and fired round after round, the semi-automatic action functioning smoothly, flawlessly. Four gunmen on the catwalk, all dressed in sky-blue jumpsuits, went down. A fifth spun around and returned fire. Bullets punched into the barrel but the thick, viscous resin worked exactly as Danya had hoped, trapping the 9mm bullets.

She sharpened her aim and fired again. The cluster of 00 buckshot spread to a pattern a foot in diameter and then hammered the gunman. He dropped his MP5 submachine gun and stumbled backwards. His hand felt for the grip of his holstered pistol, but Danya fired again. The shot was slightly higher, and lead pellets found the man's head, killing him.

The other four guards had started to rise, and Danya saw that some had wounds to their legs, but none displayed blood on their torsos. The sudden realization they were wearing body armor forced her to change her tactics. Still loaded with buckshot, and unable to take time to reload, she emptied the last shells into their legs. Agonizing screams and falling bodies were ample evidence her aim was true.

The shotgun magazine was empty now.

The pause in gunfire was the signal Corbett had been waiting for. Not suffering any wounds, he raised himself and dashed off the catwalk and into the security room, where he disappeared from sight.

Rolling out from under Beckman, Peter dived for the partially open door. He grunted as his shoulder clipped the doorframe, and then rolled to a stop on the grass. Quickly, he grabbed Gedde's feet and yanked him out of the opening, allowing the door to close, muting the sound of gunfire from within. Unable to secure the door, he knew others would follow. But at least they couldn't look through the opening and see which direction he'd gone.

Diesel padded over and began licking his face. "Yes, I'm happy to see you too," Peter said as he rubbed the dog's head and neck.

Expecting more guards to come pouring out at any moment, Peter rose to his feet, aiming the SIG Sauer at the door. "Time to go, boy," he said, glancing at Diesel.

CHAPTER 43

DANYA LOWERED HERSELF BEHIND the resin-filled barrel and reached to the bandoleer hanging across her chest. She'd stuffed both buckshot rounds and slugs in the shell loops. But rather than ordinary lead slugs, she'd packed armor-piercing slugs. And this was just what she needed to overcome the ballistic armor all the bad guys seemed to be wearing.

With the tubular magazine full, she placed a shell into the chamber and released the bolt. She peaked her head around the side of the drum and glimpsed four guards moving around the side of the control center. They were trying to flank her, while others to the front fired their pistols to keep her down.

She lay down underneath the table and alongside the rolls of woven-glass cloth and carbon-fiber cloth used to mold the shell of the drones. She steadied the shotgun, knowing she'd have to shoot fast and accurately to take down all four.

With a momentary lull in the shooting, the cavernous room sounded eerily quiet, and all Danya heard was the ringing in her ears. Then she saw them—boot-clad feet coming around from behind a collection of tall file drawers and bookcases. Pistol fire resumed to the front of her position. The thudding sound of 9mm bullets punching into the barrel sounded odd against the sharp crack of gunfire.

As the first guard stepped into view, Danya fired. The FN shotgun barked and shoved firmly into her shoulder. But she easily absorbed the recoil, and from her prone position, she was rock steady. She fired again and again as the trailing three guards rushed toward her, perhaps putting too much trust in their body armor. The shotgun slugs, designed to penetrate mild steel, blasted large ragged holes in the ballistic vests the men wore. Tissue, organs, and bone fared even worse.

Danya nudged her head above the stacked rolls of cloth, trying to spot the remaining guards and technicians. Her curiosity was rewarded with a renewed volley of gunfire, although it seemed to be diminishing in intensity. Their numbers had to be dwindling; she'd already eliminated at least eight. The pistol rounds buried in the carbon-fiber and glass-fiber rolls, not able to penetrate through the thick layers of tough fabric.

She rolled out from under the table, pushed to her feet, and sprinted for the bookcase and file cabinet where she'd stopped the flanking team. Gunfire chased her, but she made it, sliding to a stop.

Peeking through a gap between the bookcase and file cabinet, she could see much of the control center. She assumed technicians would normally be manning the work consoles, though now the chairs were vacant. Across the room she saw several men clustered near a door. She couldn't make out what they were saying, but the hand gestures and waving arms suggested they were planning some action, maybe outside the building.

From above, she heard a frantic voice. "One minute! That's all we have. One minute to get the backup generator on line or we risk losing the flight!"

"Get that goddamn generator online!" a commanding voice echoed.

The team across the room dashed out the door, leaving Danya alone on the floor of the control center.

Since Peter hadn't passed the backup generators on his way into the control center, he continued on a path around the barn, expecting the machines were on the far side of the structure. As he rounded the corner, he saw them. Two large steel boxes sited on concrete pads about ten feet from the wall of the barn. A large conduit extended from each machine and travelled to the wall, passing through a couple feet above the ground.

Peter watched and listened for several seconds—but there was no indication any technician had reached the generators. At least, not yet. He knew from the overheard conversations that they needed to activate the transfer switch and restore power to the computer and other electronic equipment inside the control room.

"Diesel," Peter said. The two amber eyes looked up at him with anticipation. Extending his arm to the side, he said, "Go. Hide." The pit bull cocked his head, maybe expressing confusion, or was it reluctance? The dog remained at Peter's side. "Go! Hide!" This time, the canine jogged away into the trees and bushes beyond the generators, looking back over his shoulder just before he disappeared into the thick vegetation.

Even from a distance the rumble of a diesel engine obscured all other background sounds. Peter dashed forward to the nearest of the two machines. He laid a hand on the sheet metal and felt the vibration of moving machinery and warmth radiating from the running engine. Diesel exhaust was ejected from a pipe on the top of the metal enclosure. A thick, black cable extended from the generator to a metal box on the wall of the barn. He concluded it was the transfer switch. For a moment, he considered using the tomahawk to sever the cable as he'd done to the main power supply along the back wall of the barn. Quickly, he discarded the idea reasoning that a cable splice could be applied with relative ease by an industrious technician. *No, better to disable the generator itself*, he thought.

He grasped a latch on an access panel when a voice boomed from behind him and commanded, "Stop whatever you're doing! Raise your hands!"

Slowly, Peter turned, hands above his head. Another guard or technician dressed in the same sky-blue coveralls stood before him. He was tantalizingly close, but out of reach nonetheless. His pistol was aimed squarely at Peter. "Before you shoot me," Peter said, "you might want to think about that bullet passing through me and doing some serious damage to this machine. I don't imagine Dr. Ming and Mr. Corbett will be pleased if that happens."

The man's eyes looked Peter over and then he moved his head just barely to the side, trying to see what might be in the line of fire. After another couple seconds of deliberation he said, "Move to the side."

Peter shook his head. "No, I don't think so."

"I said move!"

Just then a blur of red fur launched from the tree line behind the guard. He never saw the charge and didn't have time to prepare for the seventy-pound pit bull slamming into his legs.

As soon as contact was made, Diesel clamped down on the man's thigh. He was trying to recover his balance following the collision, extending his left leg forward to stay upright. Burning pain fired through his leg as four canines pierced a full inch into the muscle. Through some ancient instinct, a knowledge coded into human DNA, he knew he had to remain on his feet—if he fell, the dog would be at his neck and face.

Diesel began shaking his head furiously, and the guard struggled to stay afoot while also trying to get his weapon aimed at the creature shredding his leg. He didn't have time to work out the problem. Peter was in motion as soon as Diesel connected, covering the distance to the guard in two seconds. He lowered his shoulder and extended his arms, driving him over backwards.

They tumbled to the ground, Peter on top and slamming his fist into the man's face. He started to maneuver his pistol toward Peter, but Diesel released his grip on the leg and bit down hard on the gunman's wrist. Peter was certain he heard bone snapping, and the man cried out in pain. The SIG Sauer pistol fell harmlessly from his hand, but Diesel wouldn't release. The guard's agonized wail continued as the canine tossed his muscular head from side to side causing the broken bones to separate and lacerate the surrounding tissue inside his wrist.

Peter rammed his fist forward once more, mercifully knocking him out. "Diesel. Release," Peter commanded.

Quickly, Peter stuffed the guard's pistol between the small of his back and his belt. Then he grabbed an extra magazine before hastily stripping off his ballistic vest.

Knowing he had little time, Peter fitted the vest around Diesel by slipping a front leg through one of the arm holes and then pulling the garment around the animal's deep chest. Although large for a dog, Diesel's chest was not as big as a man's and so a couple hasty field modifications were in order.

Peter marked the location where the second leg hole should be. Then he removed the vest and used the pointed end of the tomahawk to pierce a hole in the fabric. He widened the hole with the razor-sharp cutting blade. Diesel stood obediently while Peter fit the ballistic vest around him. Not exactly tailor-quality, but it would do. Lastly, Peter pulled the belt from the guard's trousers and cinched it snug to hold the vest in place.

Diesel gazed into his master's eyes. Peter didn't know what to read in them. His best friend was panting but not excessively. The vest would certainly make it more difficult to shed heat, but that was a trade-off Peter would accept any day if it meant stopping a bullet.

He rubbed Diesel's head. "It's okay, boy. Time to get back to work."

CHAPTER 44

WITHOUT WARNING, THE COMPUTER monitors throughout the control room flickered, and then went black. Upstairs in the flight control center, the lead pilot said, "Oh crap. That's it. Power's gone."

"Can you recover the flight?" Corbett asked, already knowing the answer.

"It's possible, but only if power is restored quickly. As in minutes. The drone is programmed to return to the launch point in the event of a failed communication link. If power can be restored, we'll have to reboot the entire system and upload new programming to the drone. No guarantee it will work."

"Be ready to reload the flight program, Mr. Corbett," a new voice said. It was Dr. Ming, watching from the back of the flight control center. His body was straight and rigid, like a statue. When he spoke, only his lips moved.

"Yes, sir."

"Have the second drone prepared. As soon as it's ready

and we have power again, I want you to launch it. Same target. Understood?"

Corbett nodded and descended an elevator on dedicated backup power, along with three technicians. The doors opened onto an assembly bay that housed the store of virus and a second helicopter drone. A wide sliding door opened onto the expansive lawn. "Fill the tanks with hydrogen," Corbett ordered one of the techs.

As the man busied himself with connecting a steel-braided, high-pressure line to the composite tanks on the drone, Corbett and the remaining techs went to work loading the virus into the cargo bay.

Peter turned his attention back to the generator, trying to quickly decide the best way to sabotage the machine. He had the access panel open. There were several circuit breakers and gauges indicating oil pressure, engine temperature, current, and voltage. Although he was very comfortable with machines and technology, he also recognized the complexity they represented. And in this case, it was a matter of deciding how and where to deliver a crippling blow, and quickly. *If only the internal working components were visible instead of being shielded behind metal panels*, he thought. *Oh, what the hell*. He gripped the SIG Sauer pistol, aiming into the control panel.

"Stop! Freeze right there!"

Several guards aimed their guns at Peter from behind. Then three more rounded the corner of the barn, weapons drawn. Peter was caught in a crossfire, with no cover.

"Diesel, ready?" he said in a low but firm voice. The dog stared at Peter's eyes, eager for the next command.

"Drop the gun, or we drop you."

"Just take it easy."

"Last warning. Drop the gun!"

"Okay, okay!" Peter turned slowly to attract the attention of the guards. He extended his arm, holding the pistol away from his body in a non-threatening fashion. He tossed the gun a few feet away. It landed on the grass with a thump. The guards seemed to relax, if only a bit. But that was what Peter had expected. He looked at Diesel again. His plan was risky, but it was all he had. "Go. Hide!"

Diesel took off at a run. The sudden motion surprised the guards who all turned their guns toward the fleeing dog, many firing.

With their attention on Diesel, Peter yanked the tomahawk from his belt. He readied to strike when he heard a sickening sound—a yelp of pain and then a crashing sound, as if a heavy mass had tumbled through the brush at the tree line. And then… silence. Diesel wasn't running into the vegetation any longer. He was motionless.

"I think we got him," one of the guards said.

All their eyes were back on Peter. Anger welled inside him, like a geyser ready to blow. The lines on his face were deep and his eyes narrowed, filled with rage. Fueled by adrenaline, Peter swung down with the tomahawk, driving his torso forward in concert with the motion of the blade. With strength born of desperation and amplified several fold by fury, he propelled the steel downward.

It all happened in a heartbeat, too fast for anyone to react.

Peter closed his eyes the instant before the hardened-steel blade severed the power cable running along the ground from the generator to the transfer switch. The electrically energized cable shorted against the blade in a brilliant arc that momentarily blinded the onlookers. Peter heaved on the handle, extracting the blade which had buried deep into the earth. He turned in the direction Diesel had gone and sprinted for the trees before the guards recovered their vision.

It took several seconds for their sight to return. There was little point in searching for Peter. Where exactly he had fled was unclear, only that he'd dashed away from the barn for the surrounding forest. Once he disappeared into the thick brush, finding him would take hours of searching, maybe longer. And their only priority was to restore power.

The electrical short when Peter severed the power cable caused all the circuit breakers to open. The techs merely shut down the first generator and started up the second one. In less than two minutes it was running at full power. Then they manually activated the transfer switch, sending power into the control center.

It required only a couple minutes to fully charge the high-pressure composite gas cylinders on the drone with hydrogen, and then check the setting on the pressure regulator. The advanced fuel-cell power system provided the helicopter drone with unprecedented range and payload capability.

"We have power again!" one of the technicians said as preparations of the second drone neared completion. The overhead lights came on and simultaneously the emergency illumination turned off.

A temporary electrical cord was connected to the drone to power up the onboard microprocessor and navigational computer, rather than waste hydrogen to run the fuel cell while the flight program was uploaded and diagnostics completed. Next, a technician plugged a communication cable from his laptop into a port on the drone and typed a series of commands on the keyboard. Code scrolled by on the monitor, too fast to read.

"How long?" Corbett asked.

"Five minutes," came the reply. "Have to complete the internal checks, purge the fuel cell, and ensure the program uploaded correctly."

"Stay on it. I want this drone ready to fly."

"Program upload progressing," one of the techs said. "At 30 percent. All indicators read normal."

Corbett rode the elevator up to the flight control room. He strode directly to Dr. Ming who was still standing at the rear of the room. "The second drone is being prepped. It will be ready in a few minutes."

"Good," Ming said. He appeared to be in a trance. His hands were clasped behind his back, his eyes staring forward at the lead flight team.

Corbett moved to the lead pilot. "What's the status of the first drone?" he said.

Without taking her eyes off her monitor, the pilot replied, "We just re-established the communication link. Looks like our bird is…" she glanced at the co-pilot and information displayed on his monitor. The co-pilot pointed at the screen. "There," the pilot said. "Over Eugene and on course back to base."

"I want you to turn it around. I want that payload dropped on the Hayden Bridge water intake."

The pilot rolled her shoulders. "I hear you boss. As I said before, we have to first reconnect the communication link and then upload the flight profile. Step one is done. Working on step two."

"Fuel status?" Ming asked.

The co-pilot was monitoring fuel and other flight data. "Forty-three percent."

"Is that sufficient to turn it around and reach the target?"

A quick calculation yielded the answer. "Yes," the co-pilot said. "Provided we get the drone back on course soon. It'll be close."

Corbett's frustration was mounting. There was nothing he could do to help the flight team, but he also didn't take well to just standing around and watching as events unfolded. He decided to descend again to the assembly bay, where at least he could participate in getting the second machine ready to fly. Then his attention was captured by a voice in the control center below the catwalk.

"Hello? Anybody home?" It sounded like a female voice. "Come out. I'm just trying to be friendly."

"Mr. Corbett," Ming said without shifting his gaze from the pilots furiously at work at the flight control station. "I want him… alive."

He left Dr. Ming and the pilots and looked out the window of the security room. Below he saw that the room was fully illuminated again and the computer terminals were rebooting. The monitors flashed new images as the boot routines were completed.

"Hello? You're not being very nice." Danya aimed her pistol at the nearest computer console and fired twice. The monitor blacked out.

"What? No one's home?" She fired two more shots into the next computer.

Corbett burst out of the security room onto the catwalk. He aimed his SIG Sauer and fired.

Danya heard the door slam open and heavy footsteps from above. She looked up just as the head of security fired his weapon. She dove to the side, but not fast enough. The bullet pierced the front of her thigh, fortunately missing bone and major blood vessels, but it still hurt like hell.

She raised the pistol, the shotgun still slung on her shoulder. Firing three rapid shots, she rolled to the side using the computer console as cover.

Corbett dropped to the deck when she fired, narrowly

avoiding the brief volley of bullets. He raised his head over the edge just in time to see Danya glancing over the console. He pointed his pistol and fired two shots in her direction, not expecting to hit but intending to keep her in place until his men arrived.

She dropped to the floor as pieces of the computer monitor were shot off above her head. Slowly she crawled forward, aiming to relocate without being observed from above. She knew the electronic circuit boards and cabinet would offer little resistance to bullets; she needed more substantial cover.

Random gunshots continued to rain down from above. It was clear the gunman had not pinpointed her location. But it was also a stalemate. She couldn't flee, and the gunman couldn't pursue her, without each exposing themselves to hostile fire. Danya knew that stalemates seldom last for very long. Unfortunately, she was about to be proven correct.

CHAPTER 45

SATISFIED THEY'D SUCCESSFULLY RESTORED POWER, the team of technicians and guards re-entered the barn only to find a new gun battle underway. They drew their weapons and began searching for threats. From the overhead catwalk, Corbett was firing his pistol at an unseen adversary who seemed to be in the middle of the control room.

"Spread out and encircle the work stations!" Corbett ordered upon seeing the men enter. Quickly the guards spread in both directions, the five men drawing a tight circle around the computer consoles while methodically shooting at any perceived hiding point.

"There!" one of the men shouted, pointing his gun at Danya, lying prone against an electronics cabinet. He fired a single shot that pierced the sheet metal right above Danya's head. "Stop! Hands up!" he ordered.

Danya knew her situation was untenable. Her training had taught her that as long as she was alive, there was a chance to escape and survive.

"Okay! Okay!" she said, pushing the FN shotgun and pistol out onto the floor. The weapons slid forward well away from her reach. She rose to her feet, grimacing when she put pressure on her wounded leg.

"Hands above your head!" one of the guards ordered.

Beaten, she had no other option than to comply.

"Bring her up to me," Corbett said. With pistols aimed at her back, two of the technicians escorted her up the stairs. She stopped and faced Roger Corbett.

"Who are you?" he asked.

Danya remained silent.

"Do you have any idea how much trouble you've caused me?"

She smirked despite the pain. "Oh, I think I do."

He lashed out, viciously striking the back of his hand across her mouth. Blood oozed from a split in her lower lip.

Shaking off the blow, she refocused her eyes on Corbett. "It was fun," she said. "You know the way sensitive electronic equipment sparks when you shoot it up? I really like that."

Corbett rammed a meaty fist into her stomach and she doubled over, coughing and gasping for breath.

"Why are you here?" he demanded.

She slowly straightened, still struggling to fill her lungs with air. Her eyes were defiant, her lips pressed tightly together.

"This is all we found on her, sir," one of the technicians said, offering Danya's cell phone.

"Remove the SIM card. Have someone extract the data. I want to know who her contacts are and what information she's shared."

"Good luck with that," Danya said, breaking her silence. "It's a burner. I prefer going low profile."

"Really? You sound like a professional."

She shrugged. "You could say so."

"Is that so? And who do you work for?"

"What difference does it make?"

His eyes narrowed. "Military? Maybe intelligence?"

"Intelligence, if it makes you feel better to know."

"And why are you involved in my business? The CIA and NSA have no jurisdiction in domestic affairs."

"I never claimed to work for those agencies."

"Who, then?"

Despite her split lip, she drew the corners of her mouth into a mocking grin. Corbet backhanded her again. Her head jerked to the side, but she remained fast in place, held firmly by the guards on both sides.

"Which agency do you work for?"

Danya held Corbett's gaze. "You should be thinking internationally."

Corbett considered her statement. "What is your mission? Why are you here?"

With exaggerated eye movements, Danya made a show of looking around the complex. "I'm just passing through. Thought it would be fun to drop in and shoot up your small-time operation."

He struck her cheek again, turning it an angry red as swelling started to set in. "Whatever your mission, you failed. Your employer should have trained you better."

Danya snorted. "If you ask me, I did pretty well against your team of amateurs."

"And yet, you are my prisoner. Seems you didn't do as well as you'd like to think." Corbett's eyes found the nearest guard. "Cuff her hands and bring her." He turned and strode toward the flight operations room and Dr. Ming.

Roger Corbett spoke in private with his boss for several long minutes. They had a growing list of problems: the property surrounding the barn was littered with dead bodies; several more were wounded and would require medical attention; and there were the two outsiders who had caused these problems. But the priority remained completing the mission and dispersing the virus aerosol over the municipal water supply for Eugene and Springfield—twin cities with a combined population of more than 250,000.

And that was only the beginning. Ming had planned meticulously over the preceding several years, buying rural property within drone-flight range of twenty-six major U.S. cities, all with exposed potable water supplies. Although for years experts had warned of this vast and widespread vulnerability in America's infrastructure, none of the local, state, or federal politicians wanted to address the problem in a time of over-taxed budgets and mounting deficits.

Infrastructure was the soft underbelly of America, and Dr. Ming was going to strike hard and fast. Stockpiles of the virus were already being manufactured near each and every remote launch center. Within a few days, drones would disperse the pathogen and contaminate the drinking water for more than fifteen million people.

By the end of the week, hospitals and clinics would be overrun with patients. Local governments would quickly be overwhelmed with the mammoth challenge of cleanup and decontamination. Efforts to provide alternative supplies of water would swamp the logistics networks, adding to the frustration and anger while bringing about more chaos. The cost would be astronomical. Voters would blame their elected officials, and the courts would be mired in lawsuits for years as victims sought to blame someone.

But mostly, America would be demoralized, brought to the brink of anarchy. There would be political turmoil for years, perhaps decades. The government of President Taylor, the man who had sent a military force to destroy his father's work, and take his life, would be brought down.

Ming would have his revenge, and it would be sweet. The thought brought a smile to his face.

"You don't know who she is?" Ming asked.

Corbett shook his head. "She claims she works for an unnamed intelligence agency. But I don't believe her."

"She is skilled at her craft. She bested your team."

Corbett bristled. "It makes sense that she's working in concert with Peter Savage. But how and why? I don't know."

Ming considered the implications. "If that's true, then she is not with the authorities. If that was the case, a paramilitary team would have already stormed my complex."

Ming started to pace, tracing a tight circle around Corbett. "No, I think we are dealing with two people who just happened to have the misfortune of being in the wrong place at the wrong time."

"That would be quite a coincidence," Corbett replied.

"Yes, it would. So we need to be certain. Put her in a chair and have your men keep an eye on her. Then make sure the second drone is prepped for flight."

Corbett turned to descend in the elevator, but was stopped by Ming's booming voice. "And find Peter Savage!"

CHAPTER 46

AS PETER ENTERED THE DENSE evergreen forest, he searched in vain for Diesel. The thick understory obscured whatever tracks may have been left, and all he could do was wander aimlessly. The barn was no longer visible, hidden behind a green curtain, and the generator, although running, was barely audible.

Peter stood still in the waste-high brush, listening. There it was, a rustling sound—faint, but definitely real. He cocked his head trying to locate the source. "Diesel," he said, his voice low so as not to carry far. "Diesel."

Again, he heard the dim sound of leaves brushing against nylon cloth. He moved forward into a small clearing only about eight feet in diameter. The sound grew louder, but only barely. Suddenly, Diesel popped into the clearing, emerging from behind a pitch-covered tree trunk.

Tail wagging side to side, his canine companion trotted up to him. Diesel wasn't limping, and there was no obvious sign of blood. Peter's heart beat with joy. He squatted and made to undo the belt holding the ballistic vest in place. At the tugging on the strap, Diesel yipped once, then silenced.

Peter stopped and examined the vest. Soon he spotted a blemish in the fabric where a bullet had impacted. If not for the protective material, the bullet would have entered the dog's chest and passed through both lungs. Thankfully, the bullet-proof vest had done its job and saved Diesel's life. Now Peter understood the source of the pain his friend felt.

After gently removing the belt and then unwrapping the vest, Peter placed his hands along the canine's rib cage, feeling for injuries while Diesel stood still. All of the ribs felt normal, no indication that any were broken or dislocated. Pulling his hands away, he examined them for blood—none, a very good sign. Undoubtedly there was one nasty bruise hidden under the red fur, a result of the blunt-force trauma from the bullet impact. But otherwise, Diesel appeared to be okay. The dog was still panting from the exertion, but he'd soon cool. The morning air was a very comfortable temperature and it would not warm too much as the day progressed.

Peter turned his face toward the sky. It was pale blue and bright; the white puffy clouds were gone. Briefly resting there in the clearing with his best friend, Peter felt the peace and beauty Nature offered.

He sat down, and Diesel came in close, pressing against his outstretched legs. It was in forests like this one, not too far away in the Cascade Mountains, that Peter had formed some of his happiest memories. His mind filled with visions of past times hiking and camping with his children, Ethan and Joanna: sitting by Todd Lake with Maggie, as the toddlers splashed in the shallow water near the grass-covered shore.

Now, those memories seemed so distant, and with each recall, somehow less vivid and lacking in detail. It had been years since Maggie had passed; the acute pain of her loss now seemed to have softened to a dull ache, fading like his memories. It didn't feel right, as if his failing memory was unfaithful.

He turned his eyes toward Diesel and rubbed both floppy ears with his fingers. It would be so easy to just sit where he was; for a while, anyway. Just enjoying the solitude, being one with Nature while trying to remember happier times.

Peter closed his eyes, recalling hunting in the Cascades with both Ethan and Joanna. When was the last time he'd taken a trip into the mountains with either child? How long had it been— five years, or was it six? The images in his mind seemed more like a collage, a collection of snapshots rather than a complete memory. Would he eventually, with the passing of time, forget his history? He shuddered at the frightening thought.

He pushed the notion aside and tried to relax, but all he felt was fatigue. Not just physically, but mentally as well. He and Diesel could sneak away. It wouldn't be difficult at all, especially with everyone at the barn absorbed by their work. And why not? He'd done all he could do. He stopped them from flying the drone to the city water supply by disrupting the main electrical power as well as the backup generator. He'd heard the technicians say they didn't have sufficient battery backup to power the computers and other equipment long enough to complete the mission. Once he got away, he could call for help. Maybe call Detective Colson.

It was a tempting plan, and one that made sense. Only it wasn't true. The distant mechanical hum of the diesel generator was ample proof that he'd failed to render both backup generators inoperable. He couldn't allow the drone to disperse the virus over the city water supply. And then there was Danya. It had to have been Danya who brought Diesel and who had saved him from execution at the pit. He had her combat tomahawk as proof. And it had to be she who attacked the guards when he was trapped under Beckman near the door.

With a sigh, Peter rose to his feet. "Well Diesel, looks like we have a lady to rescue and a world to save. Well, not the whole world, but a tiny sliver of it just the same."

An unmarked police sedan drove up the gravel driveway from the paved road at a reckless speed, leaving a billowing dust cloud in its wake. Jackson skidded to a stop where the driveway ended at the corner of the ranch house.

"Hey, Corbett? You here?" he called as he stepped out of the car, leaving the door open. He took the steps to the porch two at a time and knocked on the door. No answer. He peered in the windows but didn't see a single person.

Looking around, he spotted four men in powder-blue jumpsuits working near an open bay door at the barn. He headed toward them at a trot, his black windbreaker flapping as he ran.

"Mr. Corbett," he said, panting slightly from the brief exercise. "I have the file you requested." He extended the folder and Corbett stepped forward and snatched it from his grasp.

"Does anyone know you're here?" the head of security asked.

"No, sir."

Corbett nodded approvingly while behind him work continued to prepare the drone for flight. He opened the file folder and scanned the contents. As he read, his eyebrows pinched together. "The FBI and Homeland Security are taking this information seriously?"

"That's right, Mr. Corbett. That's what I wanted to tell you. Apparently, a small group of egghead doctors at the CDC are making this into a big deal."

"Oh?"

"Yeah, it's in the report. Well, sort of. Most of it."

"What are you *not* telling me?" Corbett said, his words clipped from mounting irritation.

"Yeah, sure. Okay. Detective Ruth Colson of the Bend Police Department referenced a conversation she had with Dr. Julia Zhong at the CDC. But the detective didn't go into much detail over what the doctor said, and I knew better than to speak directly with Colson. So, I decided to call the CDC and speak to Dr. Zhong myself."

"Oh? You did that?"

"That's right. I told Dr. Zhong that I was following up, standard police procedure. I told her this report had come across my desk, and I asked her why she felt this was a serious matter and not simply another crackpot trying to get attention."

"I see. And I assume you identified yourself as a police detective?"

Jackson smiled proudly. "Let me tell you, when you've done this as long as I have, you learn pretty fast how to judge a suspect or potential witness. You know, how to approach them to get the results you want. Sometimes, you have to be a real hardass. Other times, the best way is to be very official. Most professionals, white-collar employees, respond to authority figures. Know what I mean? Yeah, I figured out right away to play this one by the book. Impress the doctor with my authority." His smile broadened, and he forced out a short laugh. "Hey, let me tell you, it worked like a charm. I mean, she just started talking and I hardly had to ask any questions."

"And what did she tell you?"

"Mostly that they'd figured out what the virus is. I mean, it's structure, based on fluid samples they'd taken from infected patients on the Warm Springs Reservation. She said it was their opinion that this virus represented a severe risk. Shit, she was talking global pandemic. Really scary stuff. No wonder the FBI and Homeland Security are taking this seriously."

Corbett nodded, listening carefully to every word spoken by Jackson, which served to further inflate his ego. "Are your notes in the file?" he asked.

Jackson shook his head. "That would be sloppy and careless. And I'm not careless. No notes, nothing for a colleague to accidentally find." He placed his index finger on his temple. "It's all here, Mr. Corbett."

Faking a smile, Corbett said, "You did the right thing. Being cautious is very wise."

"Thank you, sir. Say, you're going to share this with Dr. Ming, right? I mean, I hope you do. I hope he is very appreciative about how hard I'm working for him."

"Rest assured. Dr. Ming has instructed me to personally demonstrate his gratitude," Corbett said with a generous smile.

Before Peter broke cover, he decided to place his call. "Detective Colson, it's Peter Savage."

She sighed. "I've been half expecting your call. Had an interesting conversation with a friend of yours. You haven't been completely honest with me."

"Look, detective, you can be angry with me later, if I live that long. Right now, I need your help. I'm trusting you, I hope that's not a mistake."

She paused for a moment, realizing that she had no understanding about what was going on, but that the situation was grave. "Okay, you have my attention."

With an efficiency of words, Peter did his best to bring Colson up to speed. He concluded with the Eugene Police Detective named Jackson.

"I haven't met him," Colson said. "But I did phone Detective Lopez. I trust him, but he could have shared information within the department. If he did, Ming and Corbett could know everything."

"That means the local police are out of the question."

"Let me ask around, maybe I can refer this to the Lane County Sheriff."

"Respectfully, Detective, this is a war zone here. I need help now if you want to prevent Ming from contaminating the Hayden Bridge water intake."

"Understood. I'll speak with the chief right away, and also bring DA Lynch up to speed. Between the two, they can pull strings with the FBI and get some agents from the Eugene office out to your location. Where are you?"

"I don't know. Somewhere near Eugene, but it's a large rural property surrounded by forest."

"That's rather general. I need something more specific."

"Sorry, it's all I've got. You know the bad guys usually don't make a point of advertising the address of their hangout. You'll have to trace the signal from my phone."

"We can do that. It'll take a little more time, though."

"Just don't take too long, okay?"

Peter ended the call and pocketed his phone, making certain the ringer was still silenced. He looked down at Diesel. "The cavalry is coming, buddy. We just have to hang in there a little longer."

The sound of an engine gunning as a vehicle sped along the driveway caught Peter's attention. Once he'd lost sight of the barn after entering the forest he didn't really know where he was. He was paying too much attention to finding Diesel to notice the distance or direction he'd travelled.

He took a dozen tentative steps toward the sound. Then he heard the sound of tires sliding on gravel and the engine was turned off. He reached a break in the foliage just in time to see Jackson jog across the lawn toward the barn.

The non-descript sedan was left unattended. It was an opportunity he couldn't pass up. "Stay," he said to Diesel with the palm of his hand facing the dog. Diesel dropped his hind quarters and sat obediently.

Peter left the brush in a crouch and came up to the back of the car. Fortunately, it was angled such that his movement was screened from view of those working at the barn. He glanced inside the car, hoping to find a shotgun, but the interior looked like an ordinary car. He returned to the trunk and felt for the button to open the hatch. It took a few seconds, but he found it and popped the trunk, only allowing the lid to rise just enough to see inside. There it was, just as he'd hoped. He snaked an arm in, snapped open two latches holding the riot gun in place, and removed his prize.

Pressing his luck, he peeked inside again and spied two boxes of shot shells. He grabbed both. Each box held five rounds of 00 buckshot and he emptied both, stuffing the shells into his pockets.

CHAPTER 47

"THIS WAY, DETECTIVE," Corbett said. "Dr. Ming wishes to express his appreciation for your efforts." He motioned with his hand to a door at the rear of the assembly bay. The door was thick, and it sealed tightly to the frame.

Jackson had stepped through the doorway, when he seemed to realize something was amiss, but it was too late. Corbett shoved the door closed and locked the latch. Inside, Jackson banged his fist against the door, desperately trying to get out. But there was no latch, and the door was solid and unyielding. The walls were filled with sound-absorbing insulation, and outside his pounding and screams for help could not be heard. The detective turned around, taking in his surroundings. The space was small, and the walls were painted steel panels. There were no windows, and only one overhead light. A chair was next to the wall.

It was a decontamination chamber. Electrical heating elements beneath the steel wall panels allowed the chamber to be heated. Heat combined with various gases was used to sterilize the payload chamber of the drones. Until further study was completed, the scientists at Utopian-Bio didn't want to risk an unwelcome interaction of bacterial viruses with their engineered virus.

In the assembly bay, Roger Corbett grasped a valve connected to a large cylinder of liquified carbon dioxide. He opened the valve fully.

Jackson slowed his breathing, trying to calm his mounting anxiety and take stock of his situation. Then he heard a faint hissing sound. His eyes darted over the four walls and ceiling, trying to isolate the source of the sound. A moment later, he found it: a small nozzle directly overhead, next to the light fixture. Jackson raised a hand and felt a gentle flow of gas. His pulse raced. *They're going to poison me!* As the small, sealed room filled with carbon dioxide, Jackson felt his respiration and pulse quickening. An intense headache overcame him, and he struggled to breathe, even though nothing was obstructing his mouth and nose.

He was taking deep breaths and exhaling forcefully, but his body still craved oxygen. Panic began to take hold, growing in strength by the second as his mind screamed for air. The throbbing pain in his head increased, fueling his panic. His respiration was so rapid he should have been hyperventilating, but it was just the opposite—he was suffering acute oxygen deprivation. His last thought before losing consciousness was that somehow they were taking the air out of the room.

"Mr. Corbett," one of the technicians called. Corbett left the open gas valve and returned to his priority. "The flight program is downloaded and confirmed. All diagnostics check out. The payload is secured, and the hydrogen cylinders are at max pressure. We are green to go."

"Very well." Corbett replied. "Move the craft out into the open. Prepare for launch."

The three technicians each grasped one of the arms that the rotors were attached to and carried the machine about fifty yards from the barn, setting it down on the open lawn.

"Fire up the motors. Ready for launch," Corbett ordered. As hydrogen gas entered the fuel cell, the motors began to turn, slowly at first, but within a minute the fuel cell had reached normal operating conditions and the sound intensified as the rotors whipped the air. The sound became a loud buzz, like a massive swarm of bees.

"Final checks are good," a technician said.

Corbett spoke into a hand-held radio. "Turning over flight control."

"Bravo team has flight control," came the tinny reply. "We are green across the board. All systems check. Request permission to launch."

"Launch," Corbett ordered without hesitation.

The drone helicopter started to rise. It wobbled a little as the flight team on the second floor of the barn took control, adjusting the speed and pitch of the rotors. Slowly the aircraft climbed in a straight, vertical trajectory.

Peter squatted, his back against the rear bumper, and checked the magazine of the pump-action shotgun. It was loaded with buckshot. He worked the action, placing a round in the chamber. Safety off, the weapon was ready.

No sooner had he finished when he heard a buzz, slowly growing in intensity. It reached maximum volume and seemed to hold. Peter glanced over the trunk and through the windshield of the car. In the open grass between the house and barn a team had prepared a drone for flight. The copter was hovering stationary about sixty feet above the ground. And then it started to move toward him.

Based on his prior observations and the information from

Ming, Peter was certain this drone was also loaded with the virus. He didn't know where it was going or what the target was, and it didn't matter. He reasoned the craft was likely loaded with a dangerous pathogen, and it had to be stopped.

Staying at a constant altitude, the aircraft closed the distance toward Peter. He rested his elbow on the trunk lid and took aim.

BOOM! But the shot missed, and the drone continued level flight. *BOOM! BOOM!* Still it continued on.

The shots had alerted the men near the barn. En masse they charged toward Peter's position. They were more than a hundred yards away, but that distance would be covered in seconds.

Peter fired again.

Miss. The drone was overhead, forcing Peter into an unnatural firing position. *BOOM!*

The drone was now moving away and gaining speed. Soon it would be out of range. He only had two shots left before he'd have to reload, and there was no time for that.

BOOM! came the thunderous report. The aircraft wobbled just a little and seemed to slow. With one shot left, Peter took aim. Leading the drone just a little… holding steady… *BOOM!*

As Peter recovered from the recoil he saw two of the rotors disintegrate, sending pieces of metal and plastic flying in all directions. The aircraft tilted to the side, unable to maintain proper trim and lift, then it crashed hard into the gravel driveway, shattering into hundreds of pieces.

The gunfire had agitated Diesel to the point that Peter was worried he might break his command and dash for the forest. In a stern voice, Peter said, "Diesel! Stay!" He held the palm of his hand toward the dog, visually reinforcing the command.

Peter slumped behind the trunk. Bullets were raining in on the sedan, smashing through the windshield and exiting the rear window. But the mass of the engine served as a very effective shield, affording Peter precious seconds to reload the riot gun. He rammed shell after shell into the tubular magazine, mentally counting down the seconds until he estimated the assailants would overrun his position.

After only four shells were loaded, Peter stopped and jacked a round into the chamber, safety off. He darted around the passenger side of the car, shotgun shouldered and seeking targets. And they were right in front of him. There were four in total—the men who had just launched the drone.

Peter fired. The space separating him from the gunmen was about thirty yards. He kept moving to the side. They returned fire, pistols spitting out 9mm bullets at a furious pace. One of the technicians stumbled, buckshot striking high on his leg. His gun hand dropped as he fought to stay on his feet, only to lose the struggle and tumble to the ground.

Pumping the action, Peter fired again, still moving, trying to keep distance which worked to his advantage. The 00-buckshot spread into a deadly pattern about a foot in diameter before tearing through a second technician. One of the pellets smashed his forearm and others ravished both thighs. The ballistic vest he wore saved his life, but he fell to the lawn, bleeding profusely.

The remaining two gunmen seemed to hesitate. One of them was reloading, and Peter recognized him as Roger Corbett. The other technician slowed but kept firing his weapon. Both assailants held back, not daring to charge into the business end of the shotgun.

With his SIG Sauer pistol reloaded, Corbett faced Peter and aimed. Looking down the sights of the riot gun, Peter fired first. The shot hit Corbett low in the belly. His vest prevented penetration, but the blow was like six hammers slamming into his gut, all at the same time. Three of the lead pellets hit below the vest, striking him in the groin and hip. He doubled over as if hit by a steel beam. And then he fell in a heap on the lawn.

The remaining technician, realizing he was alone, dropped his gun and raised his hands. "I give up!" he shouted.

Peter approached, but never lowered the shotgun. When he was a few yards away, he said, "Do you have any other weapons?"

The man shook his head.

"Okay. Go to the trunk of the car and get the first aid kit. Make any move that appears threatening, and you're dead. Understand?"

"Yes," he replied nervously.

With Diesel by his side, Peter kept a safe distance as the man retrieved the medical kit spotted earlier in the trunk. "Go to your friends and see what you can do to stop the bleeding."

The technician started toward Corbett but was stopped. "No, not him. He's last."

The first two men to go down were writhing in pain and showed zero interest in any further conflict. Still, Peter kept his weapon pointed at each one as he kicked their guns away and watched diligently as gauze was applied and wrapped around their wounds. They needed serious medical attention, but this was the best he could offer under the circumstances.

That left Corbett. The technician had few supplies left in the first aid kit. He came up to his boss, who appeared to be on the verge of blacking out. He was on his side, legs drawn up. Even so, the amount of blood loss was evident as the pool of crimson grew ever larger on the grass. Corbett was muttering something incomprehensible.

"I don't know what to do," the technician said.

"Roll him onto his back. See if you can get some gauze onto those wounds."

The man leaned over and placed his hands against Corbett, but he resisted. "No," Corbett said. "Need to tell you…"

The technician shook his head. "He's saying something. Says there's something he needs to tell you."

"He's got nothing to say that I'm interested in. Roll him over."

The man tried again, and as soon as his hands touched Corbett he said, "No! You have to listen! There's more..."

The technician removed his hands from his boss, and Peter paused a moment to consider the unexpected turn of events. *What if Corbett had something important to say?*

"On your belly," Peter ordered the technician. He complied readily. "Diesel. Guard." The red pit bull stood only inches away from the man's face, the amber eyes locked onto his, watching, waiting for any sign of aggression.

Peter leaned closer to Corbett, the shotgun still firmly held in his right hand. "Make it quick, you're bleeding out," he said.

Corbett moved his lips, but the words were too soft to make out. Peter lowered his head further, straining to hear. Suddenly Corbett lashed out with a knife he'd held tight against his body. Peter jerked back, the blade narrowly missing his chest, but it slashed across his right forearm.

Reflexively, he squeezed the trigger on the shotgun. The barrel was nearly touching Corbett's chest. With no distance to spread out, the cluster of buckshot behaved more as a single mass, ripping through the ballistic vest. As the shot entered his body, the pellets spread like a fragmentation grenade, shredding his lungs and organs.

Roger Corbett was dead.

CHAPTER 48

BLOOD WAS FLOWING READILY from the gash on Peter's forearm. He sat near the prone technician and opened the medical kit. "You're right, there's not much left in here," Peter said rhetorically. He suspected the man was not going to dare move or speak as long as Diesel was inches away from his face.

He opened four sterile gauze pads and placed them over the laceration, then wrapped an elastic bandage over them to keep everything in place. It would have to do for now.

"Get up," he said to the technician. They walked to the two wounded men. "Strip out their shoelaces and heave their shoes into the brush. Then yours, same thing." After he'd complied, he looked to Peter, expecting further instructions.

"That one." Peter indicated the man who had wounds to his forearm and thighs. "Leave him. If he tries to go anywhere he's likely to win a Darwin Award." Then he looked at the other wounded man. "Him, take his vest off and toss it over here, then tie his hands behind his back." After the man finished the task

Peter told him to sit on the lawn and remove the vest he was wearing. When he finished, Peter secured his hands in the same way as the other wounded technician.

Peter removed his shirt and donned both bullet-proof vests, then tugged his shirt over the flexible armor. It was a snug fit, the fabric tugging at the buttons.

Satisfied, he hefted the riot gun and loaded the magazine with the remaining shotgun shells from his pockets. Then he picked up two pistols from the lawn, stuffing them into his waistband.

"Come on Diesel, let's go." With leaden legs, Peter trudged toward the barn. He didn't want to go there. He didn't know what he would find inside, how much force he would encounter. Was Danya inside the barn? Was she still alive? She had to be.

Peter wanted to sit this one out, let someone else take over. He'd done enough, time for the next string to come in and take on the fight. Trouble was, he had no idea when, or even if, relief would show up. And he owed Danya his life. It was a debt he was determined to pay, even if it was a one-for-one exchange.

He checked his phone. It was still on, somehow surviving all the mayhem. He decided to call Detective Colson again. The number rang, and then the call went to her voice mail.

He pocketed the phone and turned his gaze down to Diesel. "Well buddy, I guess it's just you and me. I'd like to think we've been in tougher scrapes… but I'm not so sure." Diesel cocked his head, a reaction that always left Peter thinking his dog was trying to understand his speech, but falling just short.

Peter entered the assembly bay and spotted the elevator. He recalled his brief survey of the control room on the ground floor and the catwalk overhead that seemed to connect to a security center. He also estimated that flight operations were conducted from the second floor since he saw no indication of that activity within the control center. *The elevator must open onto either security or flight control*, he thought.

He pressed the button, and the polished chrome doors opened. Reaching inside, he pressed the button with the number 2, and quickly withdrew his arm. Ignoring his fatigue and drawing upon energy reserves he didn't know he had, he and Diesel were already running around the outside of the barn toward the entry door as the elevator closed and started to ascend.

Using the key card he had taken earlier, Peter opened the door and ducked inside, Diesel right beside him. He hoped that the elevator opening on the second floor would serve as a distraction of sorts, drawing attention away as he entered the passage to the control center.

His plan worked. There were no guards or technicians on the ground floor, and two guards near the catwalk were facing away as he entered. Peter quickly closed the door.

The center looked much different now that power had been restored and the overhead lights were on, brightly illuminating the computer consoles. He surveyed the scene. The floor was littered with bodies clothed in blue coveralls, evidence of a pitched gunfight.

Some of the monitors were shot up and non-functional, others were showing what appeared to be weather maps and lines of data. And on another monitor he saw what appeared to be a navigational map with a green arrow moving slowly along a lined route. *That must be the first drone. They must have got the power restored in time to resume the mission.* The arrow was over Eugene, still miles away from the municipal water supply along the Mackenzie River in Springfield, but it was closing the distance at a rapid pace. A count-down timer was displayed on the upper corner of the screen. It read 4 minutes 53 seconds.

He didn't have much time.

In the middle of the floor he saw Danya's shotgun and the bandoleer of shells. He still had the riot gun, but wanted the extra firepower of the semi-automatic shotgun.

With the police shotgun at his shoulder and sweeping the room, he moved purposefully and silently to retrieve Danya's weapon and extra ammunition. Not knowing how many, if any, shotshells were in the magazine, Peter plucked shells from the bandoleer and shoved them into the magazine until it would hold no more. He noticed they were slugs, not buckshot, appreciating the added punch of the solid projectile.

The sling on the FN semi-auto shotgun came in handy as Peter draped it over his shoulder. Loaded down with two pistols and two shotguns, not to mention the combat tomahawk tucked under his belt behind his back, he felt slightly more confident.

Peter was not a military veteran, nor did he have law enforcement experience. But he had been on missions with some of the world's most elite soldiers, the SGIT team under the command of his friend Commander James Nicolaou. And through those experiences, he'd learned some basic tactics. Such as you never want to fight uphill, or from the ground floor moving up in a building.

Unfortunately, he had no choice. He was on the ground floor and the pilot team flying the drone was located on the second floor, likely adjacent to the security office. *Could that be where Danya is being held?* he wondered.

Considering the carnage, he knew Danya had put up a strong fight and extracted blood, and plenty of it. *Was she still alive?* If she was, he vowed to find her and bring her to safety.

But first, he had to stop the drone.

In a crouch, Peter climbed the stairs to the catwalk, carefully placing his foot down with each step to avoid noise that would alert the guards on the second floor. Diesel padded beside him matching his master's pace. The riot gun was shouldered, his finger just barely touching the trigger.

He stopped just before the top of the stairway, listening for any sound of motion. There was none.

Sighting down the shotgun barrel and both eyes open, he resumed his methodical pace. As he cleared the top edge of the stairs, the two guards came into view. They appeared to be engaged in conversation, but they must have been speaking very softly because he couldn't hear their words. Peter continued to inch forward, closing the distance. Beyond them Peter noticed a large room. The elevator was centered on the back wall. To the right, two persons were seated at a control station, each focused on the multiple screens before them. To the left were three more guards, but their backs were turned toward Peter.

Just three steps before the top, one of the men caught Peter's movement and turned. His hand dropped to the holstered pistol on his hip. Peter fired, then pumped the action, and fired again. Both guards were hit with a tight cluster of buckshot, knocking them onto their backs. They struggled to draw their weapons, but Peter fired again and again until the men stopped moving. The .33 caliber lead pellets had done serious damage as both men were bleeding from multiple wounds to their legs and lower torsos. Arterial blood was pumping from severed femoral arteries. Within a minute, both guards bled out.

The remaining three guards jumped to action. Peter fired at the first guard to face him. The buckshot hit the man in the chest, but he stayed on his feet. He pumped the action and pulled the trigger again. *Click!* He dropped the empty weapon, his hand going for the FN shotgun hanging from his shoulder. He was swiveling the weapon up when another guard raised his pistol. He had the drop on Peter, and he fired.

Peter was pushed back as if a massive fist had punched him in the chest. At first, he couldn't breathe and was gasping for air, but then his rhythm started to return. He was still bringing up the shotgun when two more rounds hit his chest simultaneously, forcing the air out of his lungs with an audible grunt. He'd never felt such a powerful blow to his body, imagining it was like a 200-pound man jumping on his chest.

Staggering, and trying to stay on his feet, he got the FN to hip level. The three guards seemed to come to the realization at the same time that Peter was wearing body armor. They were adjusting their aim upward when Diesel took off like a rocket. The sudden blur of motion distracted all of the men. One managed to lower his sights and squeeze off a single round at the charging canine, but it missed and then Diesel was on him. Jaws latched onto his gun arm and began lacerating flesh like it was tissue paper.

The momentary distraction was enough time for Peter to level his gun and fire. The first slug blew through the chest of the middle guard. He was still falling backwards when Peter nudged the muzzle and sent another armor-piercing slug into the belly of the guard on the left. He fired a second round into the man's chest, ending his fight.

That left one guard struggling against the powerful pit bull. It was a chaotic fight, intense and vicious. Driven by an instinctive desire to protect one of his pack, Diesel was ablaze with bestial fury. With jaws clamped like a vise, his head thrashed back and forth in a frenzied whiplash. Blood flowed freely from the ever-opening wound. As muscle tore and tendons severed, the guard lost control of his hand and the pistol thudded to the floor. Panic over-rode his sense of pain. He was desperately attempting to pry the dog away, his free hand grasping a fistful of lose skin on the hound's neck. But it was no use.

Peter raised the shotgun, aimed the sights on the struggling guard, and fired. The slug struck the man just above the bridge of his nose. The result was grisly, leaving little of his face that could be recognized as human.

The pilots at the flight control station had ejected from their chairs and hugged the floor as soon as the gunfire started. Although they were both armed, neither wanted to jump into the fight. Perhaps because they'd seen nearly all their comrades be killed or wounded—perhaps because they were here to be pilots, not soldiers. Whatever the reason, it mattered little to Peter.

He aimed the FN shotgun at the two prone figures. "Gently, unholster those sidearms and throw them toward me." They complied without hesitation, taking extra care to be slow, deliberate, and above all, non-threatening.

"Diesel, come!" Peter commanded. Then he pointed to the two pilots on the floor, a man and a woman. "Guard!"

With no other immediate threats, Peter gazed around the space. No one was there other than the pilots on the floor.

"Are you two flying the drone?"

"Yes," the woman replied. "I'm the pilot, responsible for flight control."

"What's your name?" Peter asked.

"Abresch," the pilot replied.

"And your partner, Ms. Abresch—what is his job?"

"He's the co-pilot, and in charge of the dispersion once the drone reaches the designated target."

Peter walked closer to the flight control consoles, looking over the multiple monitors. "How long until the drone reaches the Hayden Bridge water intake?"

"Several minutes; three, maybe four. The count-down timer is located between the two keyboards."

Peter's eyes quickly found the digital display. It read 3:17. "What happens when the drone reaches the target?"

"It's flying on autopilot right now. Once it's over the water supply, I have to take control of the flight, managing altitude and speed, taking into consideration local windspeed and direction. Then the co-pilot will initiate the release of the virus. It's a powder that needs to be dispensed at a calculated rate."

"That's a lot of data to collect and numbers to crunch. Is that why there's enough computing power in this building to send a satellite into orbit?"

Abresch hesitated before answering. "Yeah, sort of."

"Sort of? I want straight answers, Ms. Abresch. It's been a very long day and I'm very tired. I've been kidnapped, shot at, and nearly executed. And it is not even time for lunch yet. Don't test my patience."

"Okay, okay. You're right. There's a lot of meteorological data to collect and that feeds into calculations that determine the altitude, direction, and speed to fly the drone. But…" The pilot paused.

"Go on," Peter urged.

"This center is linked to all the other launch locations. The drones, all of them, will be flown and operated from here."

"There are other locations?"

"Yes, across the country. Drones will be launching against dozens of municipal water systems."

"We'll see about that." Peter checked the timer again—2:14. "What happens if your co-pilot doesn't activate the release of the virus?"

"There's a failsafe. If the dispensing is not activated, or there is a mechanical failure, the aircraft will automatically return to the launch point. But it doesn't have enough fuel—hydrogen—to make it back here."

"When it runs out of fuel, will it crash and spill the powdered agent?"

"No. A second failsafe. When the fuel level reaches critical, the onboard computer will find the nearest landing zone on its programmed course, and touch down. The onboard battery will power a transmitter for three hours, enough time to retrieve the aircraft."

"Good. Thank you for your cooperation, Ms. Abresch. You two are done working for today."

"Are you going to shoot us?" Abresch asked, her voice quivering.

"Not if I don't have to."

Peter rotated his head, taking in the flight control center. There were two other stations. "Where are the other pilots?" he asked.

"They left when the shooting began," Abresch said. "They went down in the elevator."

They could be rounded up later, Peter reasoned. Right now, he had more important concerns. "The woman. Where is she?" he demanded.

Before the pilot could answer, the elevator doors opened. Danya was standing rigidly, Ming was behind her holding a gun to her head. "I think I have someone you care about," Ming said.

CHAPTER 49

PETER SPUN TO FACE the voice, one he knew too well. The muzzle of the shotgun moved with his eyes, and now Ming was staring into the gapping maw. Danya's hands were bound behind her back,

"Drop your weapons," Ming ordered.

"Nope. Not gonna happen," Peter replied.

"Do it, or I will kill her."

Peter starred back in defiance. "She means nothing to me."

"Oh, I think she does. Why else would she risk her life to save yours?"

"She's an assassin, probably here to kill me and collect your bounty."

"If that is true, then shoot her yourself. You'll have a clear shot at me, too."

Several tense seconds passed. Ming had called Peter's bluff. But he wasn't going to drop his weapon either.

"It's a standoff, Ming. I can stay here all day. I've got

nowhere to go."

Ming shrugged. "Me too. Besides, in a few minutes, my drone will be over the Hayden Bridge water intake and it will dispense the virus. We can celebrate together."

"Your flight team is under my custody. They won't be able to activate the release command."

"I see your point. Call your dog off."

"And why would I want to do that?" Diesel was still focused on the pilot and co-pilot lying face down on the floor.

"I see your dog is very obedient. Undoubtedly your partner. Am I correct?" It was a rhetorical question, and Ming didn't wait for a reply. "I have read that the bond between man and dog can be very strong. Maybe I will shoot the animal first and then the woman."

"The last person who shot my dog is dead," Peter replied.

"I could aim for his head. But no, that would be too quick. The bullet proof vest is clever, makes it difficult to find a vulnerability. Oh, I will aim for the dog's unprotected rear quarters. The bullet will do severe damage to muscle and bone, I'd imagine destroy the intestines too. Death will be slow and very painful."

Peter's mind was spinning. He had too many points of vulnerability to cover them all. None of his options were acceptable—he could shoot Ming, and likely kill Danya in the process; he could allow the flight team to resume their job, but that would result in the virus being released over the water supply; he could continue to have Diesel hold Abresch and the co-pilot, but Ming could inflict a horrible and fatal gunshot wound to his best friend.

There was no good answer. It was the Devil's dilemma—being forced to select from three options, knowing that whichever he chose would result in harm to innocents.

"What will it be, Mr. Savage? Or shall I choose for you?"

As seconds ticked by, Peter's pulse pounded in his head. Finally, he relented.

"Diesel," Peter said. "Come. Sit." The canine followed his master's order and sat by his feet.

"Excellent choice," Ming gloated. "Abresch! You two return to your station."

"Don't do it, Abresch," Peter said, but his weapon remained aimed at Ming.

"Seems you have another quandary, Mr. Savage. If you turn your gun to the flight team, you will be open to my aim." He chuckled, like he was sharing an inside joke. "I should warn you, I am a very good shot."

Peter's eyes shifted toward the flight control console. One monitor displayed a track progressively closing on a circle that he presumed was the municipal water supply. The timer read 1:39.

The two-man flight team hadn't moved, frozen in indecision. Ming shouted, "Abresch! Return to your post and complete your mission." The pilot and co-pilot snapped to their feet and occupied their stations.

"Shoot him," Danya said. Ming pressed the pistol barrel tighter into her head. "Don't worry about me. Just kill this bastard."

"She has a point. You could shoot through her into me. Take us both out. If she really is just an assassin, like you claim, then you would be well advised to kill us both. Go on, what are you waiting for?"

Ming read the indecision in Peter's eyes. "Or maybe you were bluffing, and this woman does mean something to you."

Peter's grip on the shotgun tightened, but he knew the illusion of the standoff was merely that. He couldn't kill Danya in order to stop Ming.

"You see," Ming said. "I know you well. As I said, I did my

homework. You are a man of honor, and as such you will not sacrifice an innocent to kill me. That is your weakness."

Peter recognized the truth in Ming's words. With no other rational choice, he lay the shotgun down.

"Now the pistols."

He drew each slowly and tossed it aside.

Ming's chuckle grew into full laughter, mocking Peter. He was defeated, at Simon Ming's mercy. But he didn't expect mercy—he expected a bullet. Death didn't concern him; he didn't fear dying. He'd faced death before, and somehow luck had always intervened on his behalf. But now, he felt sadness and regret.

Sad that he could not save Danya, who had risked so much to save his life. Sad that Diesel would also likely be killed. Two friends who had come through on his behalf, asking nothing in return–and yet they were going to pay with their lives.

Regret that their sacrifices would be in vain. Both his friends would surely be shot dead moments after Ming put a bullet in Peter's head. And no good would have come from their loss; nothing would have changed. The outcome would still be a poisoned water supply, the psychopath's plan still in motion.

"You win, Ming. Let her go. You have me."

"Yes, I do have you. And her, and your dog. And I—"

Danya rammed her head back into Ming's face, bloodying his nose and launching a bolt of pain that caused him to release his grip on her and lower the pistol. His hand reflexively rose to his broken nose.

She turned and dropped onto her back. Demonstrating the flexibility of an Olympic gymnast, she bent at the waist until her knees were almost touching her nose, stifling a cry as the thigh muscles around the bullet wound were stretched. Refusing to yield to the pain, she swiftly worked her cuffed hands around her legs.

Ming's eyes were watering profusely, blurring his vision, but he'd recovered from the blow and was raising his weapon, searching for a target.

"Danya!" Peter shouted as he whipped the tomahawk from his belt behind his back and tossed it to her. She grabbed it with both hands and swung. The steel spike pierced Ming's shoulder.

He screamed in pain, but Danya wasn't done. She yanked the metal away and rotated the handle so that the cutting blade was facing her enemy.

His eyes were filled with loathing and pain-fueled rage. Hatred drove him on despite his wounds. His gun hand swung toward Danya.

She drove the blade forward, slashing through his sternum. The steel sliced into his heart. A new wave of burning pain wracked his body, seizing his chest. The intensity was unlike anything he'd ever felt. All his muscles cramped. He couldn't even breathe.

Danya rotated the handle like it was a lever, tearing Ming's heart open and splitting his chest. His eyes, wide and filled with shock and disbelief, locked onto hers. She extracted the tomahawk and allowed his dead body to fall backwards with a satisfying thump.

CHAPTER 50

AS DANYA STEADIED THE BLOOD-COATED blade between her feet and cut the plastic ties binding her hands, Peter retrieved the FN shotgun. "You two better move out of the way," he said as he swung the muzzle at the flight control console. Abresch and the co-pilot dove for the floor just ahead of the first shot.

The count-down timer read 0:29.

Peter fired the shotgun into the computers and electronic equipment. The next shell loaded even before he recovered from the recoil. He fired again... and again... and again, until the magazine was empty. Then he reloaded from the bandoleer hanging across his chest and continued the onslaught, sending a violent barrage of slugs and buckshot into the equipment. Sparks emanated from some of the many ragged holes. The monitors were all smashed, and the timer was frozen at 0:02.

Diesel eyed the pilots suspiciously. A deep, guttural growl was sufficient to send Abresch and her partner to their knees

336

with their hands on their heads.

"Easy, Diesel," Peter said. He faced Danya. "You okay?"

She tilted her head to the side. "That was close."

"It's not over. Law enforcement should be on the way."

Danya contemplated the meaning of Peter's warning. "Detective Colson doesn't have jurisdiction here. And the Eugene police can't be trusted."

"If she managed to pull it off, it will be federal agents. You should go. Slip out while you can. I'll cover for you."

"You'd do that? Even with our history?"

Peter cracked a sly grin and handed over the FN shotgun. "Yeah. Exactly because of our history."

She returned the grin. "Thanks for returning my tomahawk and shotgun."

"Thanks for bringing Diesel. How'd you do that? I'm surprised he'd go with you."

"Kate made it clear the choice was up to him. I don't know why he came along, but he did."

Peter rubbed Diesel's head. This was just another example confirming his belief that Diesel was keenly in tune with him, and that he understood people at some basic level, maybe body language or pheromones. He didn't know. But somehow Diesel, more often than not, got the message.

"You know," Danya continued, "you need to let go and move on. Kate won't wait forever."

It was a subject that Peter considered off limits. He rarely discussed his relationship with Kate even with his best friends and children. For Danya, almost a stranger, to bring it up caught Peter off guard. And it stung.

"When did you become an expert on relationships? Seems to me you have plenty of personal baggage of your own."

"I do. That's why I know what I'm talking about. Look, you can't change the past any more than I can, any more than anyone can. We all make choices. Some are good, some aren't. Sometimes life deals us a crappy hand. Regardless, you have to move on. Accept the past. Learn from it. But above all, don't give up on *life*."

"Spoken with conviction."

"In case you haven't figured it out already, I'm really good at killing people. But when it comes to relationships, I get an F. You don't want to make the mistakes I have."

Peter nodded. Her words carried a lot of weight, and he vowed to seriously consider them. "What are you going to do?"

"What I've been doing since we first met on Broken Top. Fly below everyone's radar, stay on the move." She shrugged. "It was the choice I made when I aborted the mission and stopped reporting to my superior."

"And if you'd completed your mission?"

She raised an eyebrow. "You'd be dead, and I'd probably still be working for Mossad. But I *chose* otherwise. No regrets. None."

"Can't your government just accept that you no longer work for them?"

She smiled, but it was a sad smile. "I wish it was that simple. But the truth is that no one quits Mossad. There is a price on my head. Alive is better so I can be interrogated, but dead will suffice."

"I'm sorry, Danya."

"For what? Like I said, it was my choice." She paused, reflecting on her reasoning, what brought her to this point. "I realized that I was a pawn. Sometimes what I did was good. My work saved innocent lives. But that wasn't always the case. And when I woke up to that understanding, I made a decision." She smiled again. "I have no regrets, Peter Savage."

"Godspeed, Danya. Remember, you always have a friend in Bend. Two, I guess, counting Diesel." That drew a polite laugh from Danya. "You better go now. I'll wait outside for the FBI and stall them. Get as far away from here as you can."

Peter extended his hand and Danya accepted it. Her grip was firm and unyielding, like her spirit. In that brief moment they shared an unspoken understanding. Two individuals with a common code of honor, who had found themselves, through a quirk of fate, on similar pathways. Neither could stray from the course they had charted any more than they could willfully change their DNA. Two different individuals, from different cultures, but forged with the same moral fiber.

Outside the barn the air was reverberating with the approaching helicopter. The letters FBI were boldly displayed on the side. It landed on the lawn and three agents dressed in slacks and wearing FBI windbreakers exited. Detective Ruth Colson was the last out. With guns drawn, they spread out, searching for danger.

Peter was standing next to the barn, Diesel by his feet as usual. The dog growled at the approaching agents. "Easy, boy."

"Drop your weapons!" Someone shouted.

"I'm unarmed," Peter announced as he raised his hands.

"On your knees! Hands on your head!"

"My God," a second agent exclaimed. "It looks like a war zone here. I'm calling in backup." He keyed his radio and stepped away as he began his preliminary report.

Diesel was getting anxious, a throaty rumble escaping his clenched teeth. "It's okay, boy," Peter said as he complied with the orders.

"Is that dog safe?" one of the FBI men said.

"He'll follow my commands, if that's what you mean."

"It's okay, agent," Detective Colson said as she stepped forward. "This is Peter Savage. I'll vouch for him. It's his phone we tracked."

Peter nodded. "Never thought I would say it, but it's nice to see you detective."

"You really do have a knack for getting into serious trouble."

"I'm not looking for it, believe me. I'd much prefer a boring, ordinary life."

"Yeah, sure. I guess shit happens, is that right?"

"Yeah, I suppose so."

Colson made a show of looking left and right. "And where, pray tell, is your partner?"

Peter squinted his eyes. "Who?"

"Don't get cute with me, Mr. Savage. You know exactly who I'm talking about. Danya. She called me, and we had a very interesting conversation. She also turned over Darnell Price."

"Sounds to me like she was a valuable asset that helped you and your friends," Peter motioned with his head to the agents surrounding him, "thwart this terrorist attack."

"That's beside the point. She is a potential witness, and we need to question her."

"What you really mean to say, is that she is wanted from the prior affair on Broken Top, right? I'm the person who had first contact with Darnell Price, and I'm the one who was kidnapped by Dr. Ming and involved in the 'incident' here. You've got me, that's all you and the DA need."

"Just to be clear, this will most likely fall under federal jurisdiction."

"Good. Because if I'm not mistaken, that unmarked police car over there," Peter pointed at Jackson's car, "belongs to a crooked Eugene detective."

Colson rolled her eyes. "This just gets better and better."

"It's exactly what I told you on the phone."

"Well, that and the fact that this is being reported as attempted bioterrorism—"

"Which it is," Peter interrupted. "Inside that drone wreckage just beyond the police car is evidence you'll need. The virus they planned to seed over the Hayden Bridge water treatment facility."

"That's why the FBI is likely to take charge of the investigation."

"Fine. I really don't care who runs the investigation. Just make sure they're professional and take this seriously. You've got a lot of dead bodies here, and some who are still alive. You'll find more of the virus agent in refrigerators inside the building, and a massive computer and flight control center. The plan is vast, spanning the country, but the drone control was to have been from here."

"Was? Is there still a credible threat?"

"Have the fed techs check it out, but I don't think so. I shot up the electronic equipment pretty good."

"I see," Colson frowned. "Is there anything left for forensic analysis?"

"Plenty. When you go inside, you'll understand. Now, if you and the feds don't mind, I'm just going to lie down here on the grass and take a nap. It's been a long day. When you're done, I'd like a ride back to Bend."

"It might take some time to process the crime scene."

"I know. But I'm guessing that the FBI won't just park that chopper here. As an asset it's too valuable to leave sitting at a farm south of Eugene."

"You want the helicopter to transport you to Bend?"

"Hey, my car is totaled at a drug lab somewhere out by Burns in eastern Oregon. It's either the helicopter or Uber."

"Okay, okay," she held up her hands in surrender. "I'll see what I can do."

EPILOGUE

LIKE A GHOST, DANYA had simply vanished. There was no further communication between her and Peter following her departure from Ming's ranch south of Eugene. And judging by the questions from the FBI, Detective Colson, and the Eugene police department, no one knew where to find her. Colson, in particular, suspected that Peter was withholding information concerning her whereabouts, but he stuck firmly to his story.

Under the direction of Dr. Julia Zhong, the CDC had a team on the ground in Eugene within twelve hours of the FBI's arrival at the crime scene. Dr. Zhong was emphatic that work was already underway to develop a vaccine for the virus. However, given the unique biochemical and genetic structure of the engineered virus, she could offer no timetable as to when a viable vaccine would be available.

When the flight-control computers were destroyed, the lone drone in the air followed its failsafe programming and set down in a parking lot only a quarter mile from the water treatment facility. It took many hours and the combined efforts of the Springfield police and the FBI to locate it. Fortunately, the payload was still secure when it was recovered, adding to the growing volume of evidence.

With information from the pilot named Abresch, the FBI began a search for the other launch facilities across the country. Enough information was also recovered from the computer hard drives to provide additional leads where the information from Abresch was lacking. Although it would take time, the investigators were confident all the drones and stockpiled virus would be recovered.

Darnell Price had been transferred into federal custody and was awaiting indictment on multiple charges, including conspiracy and terrorism, which was expected within a few days. Peter had sworn a statement implicating Price in poisoning the donated bottled water to the Warm Springs tribe, and Price was cooperating with investigators. He seemed to accept the error of his ways and he expressed remorse for his actions. To his credit, his arrest had raised awareness of overpopulation and catalyzed national debate. Whether or not it would lead to meaningful change was anyone's guess.

Following a brief refueling stop in Eugene, Peter and Diesel were granted helicopter transport back to Bend. By the time he arrived at his condo, he felt like the walking dead.

"Oh my God! You look awful," Kate said when she answered the door to Peter's condo. Diesel sauntered inside like he'd just returned from a short walk.

"You should work on your greeting," Peter answered. He gave Kate a hug and a kiss on the cheek. "I'm exhausted."

"What happened? You haven't called, and a strange woman stopped and wanted to take Diesel with her—"

Peter held up his hands. "Please. I promise to answer all your questions. But first, I need to take a shower and put on clean clothes. Then I'll sit down with you and tell you everything."

Kate forced a smile, but Peter knew it was an act. Twenty minutes later, feeling refreshed and invigorated, he sat down with Kate in the great room. The clean dressing on his arm was covered by his shirt sleeve. Peter turned the two leather chairs in front of the fireplace so they faced each other. Diesel collapsed on the rug near the hearth and was already snoring, fast asleep.

Kate looked at Peter expectantly, waiting for him to start the conversation. He reached out for her hand, which she reluctantly shared. He smiled. "We've been seeing each other for a while now, and I feel that we share something much more than just friendship. When you're with me, I feel something that I thought was lost."

He gazed into Kate's eyes, but he only saw confusion and disappointment. "Is something wrong?" he asked.

She extracted her hand from his. "Oh, I don't know. I mean, what could possibly be wrong? Other than you disappeared again for several days without any explanation. Do I mean anything to you?"

"Of course you do, Kate." He reached for her hand again. "I've been thinking, and there's something I'd like to ask you. Something I should have done a long time ago."

"Oh no you don't, mister." Anger flashed in Kate's eyes and she again released Peter's hand. "You can't do this to me. It's not fair. I'm not hired help that just pops in to house-sit and take care of Diesel whenever you decide it's time to go on a road trip."

Peter dropped his head until his chin touched his chest. "I'm sorry. I got caught up in…" he stumbled to find the words.

"In what?" Kate asked, concern having replaced her anger.

"You heard about the people getting sick in Warm Springs?"

She nodded.

"Well, I stumbled upon a conspiracy between two individuals in Eugene to engineer a virus that only infects males and causes sterility. Together, they hatched a scheme to contaminate bottled water, which they provided to the reservation. But the bigger plan was to infect municipal water supplies across the country."

Kate leaned back in the padded chair, the corners of her mouth turned down. She rolled her eyes, looking at the ceiling before returning her gaze to Peter. "Why is it always you?"

"I... I don't understand?"

"Lord knows the world needs a lot of help. But why *you*? It always seems to be you."

Peter shrugged, surprised by her response. "I don't know. Bad luck I suppose. I can't turn my back when people are threatened and need help."

"I know, Peter. And that's one of the things I really admire in you. You are a decent and honest man. I knew that from the day I met you." She paused. "But..."

"I know. You don't have to say it."

"Always the gentleman, is that it?" Before he could answer, she continued. "But I am going to say it. You need to hear it from me. I... I can't live this life, wondering each day if you will return or not after your latest misadventure."

The words cut deeper into Peter than any wound he'd every suffered. It felt like the air had left his lungs, and the room spun about him. "I... I don't know what you want me to say."

She shook her head. "I'm not asking you to say anything. Don't you get it?" As Kate spoke, her eyes glistened, tears ready to spill down her cheeks. "I don't want you to pretend to be someone you're not."

Peter frowned. "I'm sorry."

"Don't be." She wiped her cheeks and snuffled her nose.

"We can still be friends."

Peter closed his eyes and leaned back in the chair, suddenly feeling very tired again. He knew Kate was right. He'd been shot, kidnapped, slashed, and involved in international incidents. His life seemed to be frequently in peril. It wasn't fair to expect Kate to accept that. She deserved better.

He nodded in agreement, but when he opened his eyes he avoided looking directly at Kate. "I understand. It's just that I thought… well, maybe we could…"

Kate leaning forward and placed a tender finger on Peter's lips. "Shhh," she said, her voice gentle and loving. Peter shifted his eyes and held her gaze. "You will always hold a special place in my heart," she said.

She rose and slowly walked to the door. Peter called after her, "I'd like to see you again, if that's okay?"

She looked back over her shoulder through tear-filled eyes. "Sure. And if I ever need to be rescued, I know you'll be there."

The door closed, immersing the room in silence. Peter shut his eyes as tears welled. "I love you, Kate."

AUTHOR'S POSTSCRIPT

BY NOW, YOU SHOULD HAVE FINISHED *Lethal Savage*. At least, I hope you have. But if you've jumped to this section without reading the preceding chapters, let me warn you that there are spoilers—or semi-spoilers—herein that will reduce the thrills and excitement of the plot. You've been warned.

In the opening pages we learn that Darnell Price is obsessed with correcting what he believes to be out-of-control human population growth. And it's true, as pointed out in the Author's Notes, that the number of people inhabiting the Earth has grown at an alarming and exponential rate since about 1800. However, over the past decades, population growth has slowed in the nations with the highest GDP. Indeed, Japan and many European countries have a negative population growth rate. This trend is broadly attributed to more women choosing a professional career and deferring, or forgoing, child bearing. Whether the trend will continue, and whether the decline in some regions will be sufficient to offset gains in other regions (namely, Africa and South Asia), remains to be seen.

Drones have made minor appearances is previous *Peter Savage* novels, but they are essential to the plot in this book.

I have to admit, remotely controlled unmanned aerial vehicles frighten me (but they do not hold first place, see below). They are small, agile, hard to detect, and damn near impossible to take down. Drones can carry explosives, biologicals (as in this plot), and cameras (visible and infrared) for real time video. We've heard news reports of drones flying near operating commercial runways where the small aircraft could intentionally or accidentally damage passenger aircraft on takeoff or landing. Although it is illegal to fly drones in the vicinity of manned aircraft, the practice still happens too often.

Due to the drone's small size, getting a good radar reflection is difficult. Shooting them down is also very tough for the same reason; not to mention that shooting at aircraft over population centers is virtually guaranteed to lead to collateral damage, perhaps extensive.

The U.S. Department of Defense has experimented with methods to defend against drone attacks. Two promising methods are shooting a net at the drone in flight, and jamming the radio control signal. Obviously, specialized and/or sophisticated equipment is required to carry out either option—more work is needed.

Finally, I was drawn back to viruses and genetic engineering in writing this novel. You may recall that genetic modification was a central theme of *Relentless Savage*, and the smallpox virus figured prominently in *Deadly Savage*. Recently, advances have been coming at a furious pace in the field of specific genetic modification using the CRISPR-Cas9 method, which has attracted widespread publicity. This technique has been reported in scientific journals as a tool for modifying human pathogenic viruses; the goal is to arrive at novel therapeutic treatments.

The potential for the CRSIPR technique to yield robust and high-yield crops, reduce disease, cure cancer, cause pigs to grow human organs, etc., is difficult to overstate. The field of gene editing, and through that, genetic modification, is still embryonic. A host of questions and guidelines concerning ethical practices must still be resolved.

However, there is also a dark side to this technology. Major food crops could be genetically altered to make the plants more susceptible to disease, potentially causing widespread famine. Viruses could be altered to make them more contagious, or transmitted in new ways (as in this story). And yet with all this risk of CRISPR, the technology is not regulated. Anyone can buy the reagents and tools and carryout genetic modifications at will.

Unlike terrorist attacks employing conventional weapons (firearms, explosives), or chemical or radioactive materials—which are localized and cause casualties at or near the time of the attack—once genetically modified organisms are released in the ecosystem, they will continue to reproduce and spread. Eradicating dangerous genetically modified plants or insects or viruses would be challenging to say the least.

Natural viruses such as smallpox, Ebola, and HIV are frightening enough. The prospect of genetically modified viruses is truly terrifying, and this occupies the top position on my most-frightening scale.

As humankind races forward, developing powerful technologies unlike anything we've known before, will we be equally successful as a society in restraining the harmful applications of these miracle discoveries? For the sake of all, I hope so.

Cheers
DE

ABOUT THE AUTHOR

DAVE EDLUND IS THE *USA TODAY* bestselling author of the award-winning *Peter Savage* novels and a graduate of the University of Oregon with a doctoral degree in chemistry. He resides in Bend, Oregon, with his wife, son, and three dogs (Lucy Liu, Murphy, and Tenshi). Raised in the California Central Valley, he completed his undergraduate studies at California State  University, Sacramento. In addition to authoring several technical articles and books on alternative energy, he is an inventor on ninety-seven U.S. patents. An avid outdoorsman and shooter, Edlund has hunted North America for big game ranging from wild boar to moose to bear. He has traveled extensively throughout China, Japan, Europe, and North America.

www.PeterSavageNovels.com

THE PETER SAVAGE SERIES

BY DAVE EDLUND

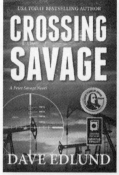

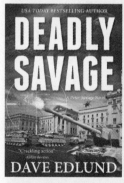

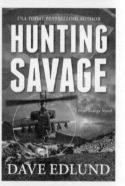

MORE TO COME!

Visit Dave Edlund at PeterSavageNovels.com

Tweet a message to @DaveEdlund

Leave a comment or fascinating link at the author's official Facebook Page: facebook.com/PeterSavageNovels